HIDEKI SMITH AND THE OMUKADE

HIDEKI SMITH AND THE OMUKADE

BEING THE SECOND BOOK OF THE HIDEKI SMITH, DEMON QUELLER SERIES

A.J. HARTLEY   HISAKO OSAKO   KUMA HARTLEY

Charlotte, NC

FALSTAFF
BOOKS
WWW.FALSTAFFBOOKS.COM

To everyone still figuring stuff out. We get you.

My name is Caleb Hideki Smith, and—spoiler alert—I'm still a loser's loser. That's in spite of saving the world or, at least, my corner of it a couple of weeks ago. I'm heir to Raiko Watanabe, an ancient Japanese demon queller, though I didn't know it until recently, and I have some of his speed, strength, and agility, though I'm still learning my way around a katana. I'm mixed race, which makes some of this a bit less straightforward. I should be kind of a superhero, but I have to live incognito and according to the way I was before I got my mystic abilities, and that means that if I don't fall on my face from time to time, people get suspicious.

I should also say that I'm not the only member of the family who is a tad to the other side of weird. My sister Emily (AKA Kazuko) is what's known in Japanese as a *kitsune* or—to use the female form she prefers—a *megitsune*. She's a fox. And I don't mean, like, a cute girl. I mean, she's an actual fox. The animal. Sort of. She's also a high school girl. It's not just that she can change into a fox; she is a fox and a human at the same time and can choose which form to shift into. In theory. She hasn't quite nailed the choosing part down, so shifting into something with a fluffy tail can be stressful, since she's not always sure she can get back. If she gets stuck, we go either to Bachan—my Japanese grandmother—or to Mr. Saito, a tengu (a sort of mountain spirit with a nose like a zucchini) to get her back. My Japanese-American mother knows all this, but my dad—who is originally from England—doesn't.

Oh, and my sister saved my life when I got stabbed by my grandmother's evil sister who was trying to break her massive demon brute of a son out of the mystical prison under one of the mountains around our dull little North Carolina town.

Nuts, right?

Trust me, I know. Unfortunately, almost no one else around here does, hence my continued status as legendary loser. I have a couple of friends at school, though that overstates the case a bit. One is DeMarcus Murphy, who's kind of a jock, but not part of the cool set, and the other is Joey, a non-binary Goth who is cool in the same way that I'm a superhero, which is to say, not really.

Emily and I were raised as if we hadn't noticed we were part Japanese, my mother operating on the assumption that if she pretended we were like everyone around us, they would start believing it. You can imagine how well that worked. I'm glad to say that Mom has relaxed her All Things Japanese Ban over the last few weeks when she realized that in terms of me fitting in, that horse left the barn long ago, probably right around the time I burned it down. That, as my English teacher Mrs. Springer would point out, was a phrase which began as a metaphor and wound up being a statement of historical fact, but I'll spare you that particular recap.

Anyway, Mom still looks faintly alarmed every time my dad asks Emily what she's listening to and she comes up with something wild like Polkadot Stingray or BABYMETAL. Lately she's been bouncing around the house to some powerhouse girl group called Atarashii Gakko. When she does, my mom gets this frozen look on her face and you can almost hear the effort it takes for her not to grab the nearest radio playing Taylor Swift. I think Em kind of enjoys it. Sometimes she gives me this sly grin which reminds me that she's half fox.

So that's the 'Previously in my life' part done.

My parents own a convenience store on the edge of Portersville, North Carolina, a town which was once a hub of the lumber and furniture trade but isn't much of anything anymore. Compared to the area's rival villes, Portersville is not as quaint as Hendersonville or as hip as Asheville and is just far enough from the Blue Ridge Parkway to be off the tourist radar. We get a few hardcore hikers trudging through the mountains, but the closest thing to a real influx of newcomers happened when

Southern Shale set up their fracking shop on Redscar Mountain. Unfortunately (or not, depending on how you feel about such things) they took off after generating an earthquake everyone noticed, and causing the rupture of an ancient mystical prison containing Japanese monsters which most people didn't. Since then, we've been left to get on with our slow economic collapse by ourselves. Parts of the town have been abandoned for years, which is why my parents' store has gotten a whole lot less convenient for the people who still live here.

I actually like the inconvenience store. Working there in my off hours is mostly dull, but it's quiet and familiar, and we live above it, so that's okay. One of my mom's concessions to me and my sister deciding to explore our Japanese heritage, is that the store is now stocked with all kinds of weird and cool new snacks: crisp and salty rice crackers, green tea Kit Kats, those chocolate-covered bread sticky things called Pocky, and a ton of different fruit-flavored candy. My friend DeMarcus—who is generally obsessive about healthy eating—discovered these fizzy peach things and now eats them by the handful.

My dad's latest bright idea for the store, which he pretends is a marketing strategy but is really just him playing, is adding a model railway line running along the back wall and round the register.

"Portersville has a long relationship with the railways," he announced as he assembled the track under my mother's dubious stare. "Hence the name of the town. This will appeal to the locals."

"But you bought a Japanese bullet train," my mother observed skeptically.

"In honor of your heritage," he managed to say with a straight face.

"It's annoying," she replied. "Endlessly zipping around while people are trying to buy gum and cookies. We're a store, Stephen, not a theme park."

"Come on," he said, unable to suppress the gleeful twinkle in his eye every time he looked at the sleek aqua-colored train as it sped round the room. "Right, Caleb?"

"What?" I said, not wanting to be drawn into it.

"Our Shinkansen!" he exclaimed. "Isn't it cool?"

"Kinda," I conceded, giving my parents a noncommittal shrug.

"The kids love it," said Dad. "We've had customers coming in just to show it to their children."

"And they stand there staring, not buying anything," said my mother, as if this proved her point.

"They buy stuff," Dad protested. "Eventually. And it's not just the kids. A lot of the men think it's great."

"And their wives think it's annoying," said Mom with finality. "Just don't buy any more. That stuff is expensive."

"Got a bit more track coming in another shipment," Dad murmured, avoiding Mom's stare.

"No more after that. You hear me, Stephen?"

"Loud and clear," said Dad, shooting me an unabashed grin. "And how are you, Caleb?"

"*Genki*," I said. "That means, I'm fine. I'm good," I said. I had taken to watching a couple of anime series on my laptop; between that and Google translate I had picked up a few words of Japanese.

"Cool," said Dad, beaming as he pushed strips of paper onto the spike driven into the wall behind the register. "It's always good to expand your range of knowledge and experience."

I'm not sure if this kind of wholehearted support was supposed to buy my allegiance in the Great Train Expansion scheme, so I just nodded, feeling Mom's eyes on us.

"We should come up with a new way of storing old receipts," she said, eyeing the spike.

"Get rid of the spike?" Dad exclaimed. "It's tradition."

"It's untidy. Why can't we just put them in a drawer or filing cabinet?"

"After a couple of months, we do! But here, they are easy to get to. Handy."

"You just like putting them on the spike," said Mom knowingly.

I didn't need to look round to know that Dad would be grinning in that way he did when he got busted but thought no one saw. I went to the front window and looked out over the hand-lettered signs advertising bargain prices on kitchen towel and canned goods, the card stock all in suitably autumnal colors. Dad had wanted to go full on Halloween décor, but Mom said the store—and Portersville generally—could use all the class it could get, so we got pumpkins and maple leaves.

"What's going on at the Haversham house?" I asked.

"Sold, apparently, "said Dad who always had his ear to the ground where town chatter was concerned. "Some rich out-of-town business-man. Doing it up."

My mother drifted over to join me.

Though we lived at the unfashionable end of town, we had the best views of the mountains. A few hundred yards down the road, Portersville effectively fizzled out and became the woods, streams and hill paths that were—to me—the best thing about the area. There were a couple of small farms, a few old ranch-style homes with chain link fences, and about as many vacant lots, but that was about it. The exception was the Haversham house, a great tumbledown ruin of a place known to local kids as the Haunted Mansion.

It had been built around the turn of the last century by a logging magnate, but it had been empty since the seventies, derelict like so much of Portersville, and surrounded by a dense screen of trees. As a kid, I could just make out one of its shuttered turrets from my bedroom upstairs, but the trees were taller now, and you couldn't see anything of the house from the road. Frankly, that was a relief. Some of the kids at school went there on a dare, or to drink and smoke, but one of them had broken his leg when he fell through a rotten upstairs floor a couple of years ago, and the place had been pretty much off limits ever since. I figured it would burn one day.

"It's good news," said Dad, "because the word on the street was that Chris Collington wanted to have the land rezoned for industry."

"Chris Collington of…?" I began.

"Southern Shale, the fracking company," said Dad. "Right and correct. When they closed the plant and drove their trucks and equipment out of town, he stayed. Tried to build some good will with the town council, hoping to bring all those trucks back and start over, like we don't remember what happened last time."

Dad hadn't been a fan of Southern Shale even before their involvement in our recent local apocalypse.

"The Collingtons don't trust outsiders," said Mom. "Chris is local. You wouldn't know it to speak to him, but he's from Winston-Salem, and his wife, Maureen, went to school with me. Not that she'd admit it. Wouldn't darken the door of a shop like this if her life depended on it. I see her in the street sometimes or at PTA meetings. Always smiles but never speaks, which says a lot, since she's a terrible gossip. He came from money. Fancy private school and all that. Their daughter seems nice enough. What's her name, Caleb?"

"Sofie?" I said. "Sophia? Something like that. I think Em knows her."

She was part of the cool set, a year older than me, like my sister. Of course I didn't know her.

"Anyway," said my father, redirecting the conversation, "I think we dodged a bullet. I don't know who this new guy is but having him live over the road has to be better than turning the lot into some industrial park while Southern Shale plans its destructive come back."

"He's gonna actually live there?" I said dryly. "Bit of a fixer upper."

"More of a knocker downer," said my mother, dryer still.

"No!" exclaimed Dad, ever the enthusiast. "Great bones, a house like that. Fine Victorian craftsmanship. Just needs a little TLC."

"Needs a bulldozer," said my mother. "But if it helps to revive the area, maybe bring in a little more foot traffic, all power to them."

"Jennie, Jennie, Jennie," sighed my father wistfully. "You have no romance in your soul."

"Says the man playing with toy trains," she replied, shaking her head but giving him an indulgent smile.

"*Model* trains," my father corrected her.

"Ah," she replied. "Because toys are for kids and models are for..."

"Mature and serious hobbyists," my father replied with a wink.

"Is that right?" she said, moving in close and matching his mischievous smile while arching an eyebrow invitingly.

"Gross," Emily observed as she breezed in, shrugging into her school backpack. "Ready?" she asked me.

"Yep." I considered her. She looked exhausted already, pale and bedraggled. "You okay?"

"What?" she snapped. "Yeah, fine. Just...had a lot of homework. Didn't get much sleep."

"What'ya working on?"

"Just computer stuff," she shot back, annoyed.

"Don't be late home," said Dad. "I'm firing up the grill. New recipe to try."

Em shot me a knowing look, and we both rolled our eyes.

"What?" said Dad. "You're gonna love it!"

"Can we go?" said Em.

I held up my hands in mock surrender, but before we could leave, the front door opened and Bachan—my ancient Japanese grandmother—bustled in looking flustered.

"What?" Mom asked.

Mom had barely spoken to her mother for years, but our exploits with the massive ogre thing in the mountains had mostly fixed their relationship. I say 'mostly' because Mom still associated Bachan with those aspects of old Japan she was least comfortable with; I mean the mystic and supernatural stuff. You'd think that Bachan would pick this up and dial all her spooky mess back a bit. No such luck.

"I just saw a dog walking in circles in the middle of the road!" Bachan exclaimed, as if announcing that it was raining toads.

"And?" said Mom, eyes already narrowing.

"It's a terrible omen!" Bachan said with a dramatic gesture, fingers splayed and eyes wide.

"Or the dog was chasing its tail," Mom replied, unmoved.

"Chasing its tail?!" Bachan echoed, appalled that her news wasn't generating sufficient panic and anxiety. "Hideki!" she called, turning to me. "Do your senses tell you nothing?"

I shot dad a wary look—he knew nothing of my status as demon queller—but he seemed unconcerned, as if he was just dealing with old person superstition. I gave Bachan a sympathetic look but shook my head.

"Dogs do chase their tails," I said.

"It's true," said Dad. "Famous for it."

"Kazuko, what about you?" Bachan pressed.

Em—who didn't use her Japanese name but was used to Bachan addressing her with it—did another rapid check on dad, then shook her head quickly. Bachan had been coming with similar accounts of birds and animals being weird—all apparently signs of imminent disaster—all week. We were getting a little sick of it.

"This could be a sign of terrible things coming!" Bachan tried again.

"Or it could be that Ronda Simons still hasn't gotten that invisible fence working," Mom commented, returning to the cash register and running a tally of its contents.

"Also a definite possibility," Dad added. "I saw Ronda the other day and suggested she got a regular fence and an invisible dog, but I don't think she got it."

"Oh, you people!" Bachan muttered, casting her hands up, and then plonking herself down on a stool by the counter. "You have no sensitivity to the way the natural world alerts us to disturbances in the spiritual energies which surround us."

"Also true," said Dad helpfully. He gave her a broad smile, and she relented a little.

"Maybe it was Ronda Simons' dog," she conceded. "But that doesn't mean its behavior is insignificant."

"Let's see how things go, yeah, Bachan?" I said, holding her gaze and nodding significantly at Dad. "If I see anything super weird, you'll be the first to know."

Bachan frowned, smiled that wrinkly smile of hers, then gave a satisfied nod that was almost a bow.

"Have a good day at school," called Mom.

"And keep your cool, Caleb, yeah? If you need me to come get you..." Dad added.

"I'll be fine," I said.

"*Itterasshai!*" called Bachan, a Japanese phrase she used whenever someone left the house. It meant "see you later" or "don't die before you get home." Something like that.

As we pushed through the door, Em gave me a sidelong look.

"What was that about?" she asked.

"Bachan seeing signs and omens everywhere? Just the usual..."

"No," she said, cutting me off, "that *keep your cool* business."

I stared across the road to the Haversham house, but apart from the new chain strung across the driveway with a "Private: Keep Out" sign, I couldn't make out anything through the screen of trees.

"Nothing," I said. "The name thing."

I had decided that while I would still go by Caleb at home, at school I was going to be known as Hideki—my Japanese middle name.

"You're going through with that?" she said, her brows furrowing.

"Sure," I said. "No big deal."

It was a huge deal. A note had been sent around my classes and my day began with Miss Malinski announcing in home room that from now on I would be called Hideki. Except that she didn't pronounce it Hideki. She said something like High-deeky, and I had to correct her. Twice. She had clearly made an effort but had memorized it wrong.

"Hideki," I said. "Hi—as in *his*—decky."

She blushed, and apologized, and I smiled and said it was fine, while the other kids gave each other little sideways glances of bafflement, amusement, or disdain. Suddenly I wasn't so sure changing my name had been a good idea. When I left home room, I noticed that Miss Malinski was murmuring "Hideki" to herself quietly, over and over, like she was saying a prayer.

My friends DeMarcus and Joey got it right, of course, but they had been warned in advance and were keen to show their support.

"Insisting on the correct term by which people address you is an act of political self-empowerment," said Joey, who knew about these things.

"O...K..." I said.

But in English class, Mrs. Springer looked long and hard at the new name on the roll call list and said, "I can't say that. How 'bout we stick with Caleb?"

I caught Joey's fierce head shake and took a breath. "It's Hideki, Ma'am," I said. "It's easy when you get used to it."

The teacher gave me a level look then shrugged.

"If you insist," she said, though she didn't actually say the name, and went through the rest of the class list looking irritated. She looked up only when she reached a name I had never heard before. "Nathan West."

She scanned the room, and all the kids turned to see a blond, blue-eyed boy sitting in the corner. In the stupid anxiety about my name, I hadn't even noticed that there was a new kid. I considered him with the others. This is going to sound weird, but the guy had a kind of shine about him. It wasn't just that he was good looking and athletic. He had an easy, couldn't-care-less charm about him. Even under all those curious stares, he just jutted his chin a little and said, "Hey."

Just that.

A couple of the girls giggled and nudged each other, and I couldn't help but feel a mixture of fascination and envy. With one word, the newcomer had vaulted past me on the coolness meter. Instantly, all my careful strategizing about going by a new name seemed pointless and stupid. You either had it or you didn't, and this West kid had it in spades.

"Perhaps you'd like to introduce yourself, Nathan," said Mrs. Springer, beaming, as if even she was a bit mesmerized.

"Not much to tell," he said with a casual shrug. "Moved here from LA. Dad wanted a break from the rat race, so." Another shrug and the kind of micro smile that was just a wrinkle of knowing amusement.

"My father knows him," said Tyler Miller, the closest thing a high school kid like me could have to a nemesis.

The new kid just looked at him. "Yeah?" he said.

Tyler blushed and hurried to clarify the connection. "My father's the mayor," he said. "He helped clear the way for your dad getting the Haver-sham place."

Another noncommittal chin jut and half smile from the new boy. He didn't care. He certainly wasn't impressed. One of Tyler's buddies—Jason Blakely—gave him an uncertain look, and there was a second of stunned silence.

"The Haversham place?" I blurted to fill it. "That's across the street from me."

Half the class turned to stare in disbelief at this display of uncoolness, but Nathan West nodded.

"The convenience store, right?" he said. "Cool."

I felt myself glowing.

"Less cool when you go in," said Tyler.

"And not exactly convenient," said his buddy, Bobby Davenham. Bobby's family was rich and well connected by Portersville standards, and Bobby—swaggering, sneering Bobby—had blond, curly hair and an athletic build to rival Tyler's.

"Looks cool to me," said Nathan, not so much defiant as correcting an obvious error. Tyler and Bobby looked momentarily paralyzed and then, as if to set the moment in a gold frame and shine a spotlight on it, Nathan added, "Hideki, right? I'll come over and we'll hang."

He said my name right. Everyone stared from him to me in mute disbelief and, in spite of themselves, I felt their sense of me and my place on the great social ladder which is high school, shift up.

Pretty cool.

Of course, this was Portersville, so while my good mood got me through the day, by evening the town had remembered that it was sitting on the edge of a kind of Appalachian Hellmouth whose special gift was the constant possibility of death and destruction.

So there was that.

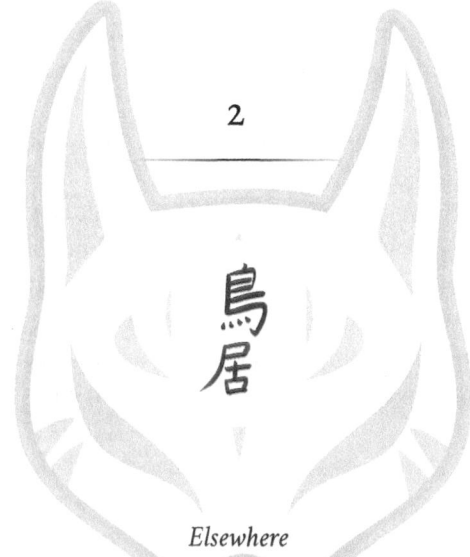

2

鳥
居

Elsewhere

Ron Blakely checked the clock in the Hummer's dashboard and smiled. They were making good time, and the new car ate up the mountain road.

"See?" he observed. "No shortage of power there."

"Yes, dear," said his wife, Amanda, who was half turned to face the backseat. "Don't torment your sister, Jason."

"Mom!" wailed Caroline, on cue.

Ron barely noticed. His head was full of that distinctive new car smell, the deliciously synthetic blend of oiled leather and new plastic. It was intoxicating. If money had a smell, Ron thought vaguely, it would smell like this.

And the truth was he hadn't had to spend a lot to get it. Though the dealership had somehow managed to revive that new car aroma, the car was actually a decade old with a hundred thousand miles on the odometer, and its unblemished Silver Ice metallic exterior looked like it smelled: showroom fresh. His wife had balked at the Hummer's gas consumption, but it wasn't like this was going to be their day-to-day vehicle, and at under fifty grand he'd have been a fool *not* to buy it. Today's little jaunt into the mountains was just to prove the point.

Ron was Portersville born and bred, though most people in town were. Not much attracted transplants these days, though things had looked up when the fracking company came to town. That hadn't lasted, of course. There had been a cave-in at the site and a couple of workers had been lost. By the time they were found, it was too late. Then the tree-huggers and their lawyers got involved, and that was the end of Southern Shale in Portersville.

It was too bad. An influx of engineers and a little more money flowing through the town would have been good for business. Ron was in real estate, and things had been slow for a while. He had started eying the Hummer when Southern Shale first arrived but had finally bought it only when the fracking company bottomed out, as a kind of consolation prize. He had to move some money around to afford it, and some of that money wasn't strictly his, but with a little creative accounting, he'd have it all back in place within a month or two, and no one would be the wiser.

Amanda didn't know that part. She had asked if he was sure they could cover a "luxury item" right now, and he had given her the confident smile, the knowing, swaggering chuckle that he used on his clients and told her not to worry about it. In truth, he had been of two minds about buying the car from Steverson's—the closest thing Portersville had to an upscale car dealer—but Amanda's referring to the boxy, tank-like vehicle as a *luxury item* had actually sealed the deal in his head. It made him feel like he was buying a palatial second home or an island. Maybe a yacht. He wasn't entirely sure what a yacht really was, but he liked the idea of owning one.

So yesterday he had bought the great four-wheeled behemoth and spent the afternoon showing his son, Jason, pictures of the Hummer's military antecedents roaring through the sand and rock of distant places.

"Cool," Jason had said.

And it was. The Hummer was cool, and Ron was cool for owning it.

They had driven east through town, past the old Haversham house which Ron had been annoyed to find had been sold quietly before he even knew it was available, across the street from the weird little store run by that Chinese family whose kids went to school with Jason. Ron had deliberately taken the steeper, less trafficked roads so he could show off what the Hummer could do, savoring those gravelly spots where the wheels churned up a plume of grit and dust.

"Pretty impressive, right?" he said, glancing into the rearview mirror, but the kids were too busy niggling each other, and they ignored him.

"Kids?" he repeated, a note of irritation creeping into his tone, despite his rigid smile. "I said it's pretty impressive. The car. Yeah?"

"It's very nice, dear," said Amanda.

Her pacifying, head-patting manner, like she was dealing with a child no older than the squabbling kids in the back, annoyed him, and he shot her a look.

"What?" she asked, amused. "It's a nice car. That's what you wanted me to say, isn't it?"

"Don't be smug," he said, low and warning.

She looked at him then, startled and confused. "You know me and cars," she said. "If you like it, that's all that matters."

Not good enough, he thought, his mind suddenly as hard as the granite formations which reared up through the tree trunks to their left.

"You know, I work really hard to provide for this family," he snapped. "The least you can do is be supportive."

"I am being supportive!" she replied. "What has gotten in to you?"

"Nothing has *gotten into me*," he shot back, mimicking her phrase and pushing the accelerator so that the wheels spun, spraying chippings. "Y'all have gotten into this fine vehicle which I have paid for, securing it in an excellent deal which none of you seem to appreciate, and you can't even be bothered to say something positive that sounds like you mean it!"

They were going fast now, too fast for the narrow and windy mountain road. Ron felt the family's unease and, enjoying it, sped up.

"Mommy?" whined Caroline. "I don't like this."

"Ron," said Amanda, clutching her arm rest, "slow down."

"Just putting the Hummer through its paces," said Ron through gritted teeth, staring ahead through the trees crowding the road. "Showing you what it can do."

He gave it even more gas, and the engine roared with satisfaction as its hunger was fed. The Hummer surged forward like a galloping grizzly, and as the road swept to the right, suddenly the trees on that side fell away, revealing a long drop down the mountain side shielded only by a slender barrier.

"Ron!" snapped Amanda, sharper now. "You're scaring the kids."

Ron checked the mirror again and saw that she was right. Caroline was crying and Jason was white-faced and stiff. He saw it, and for reasons he couldn't explain, he liked it. He was in control, and they were dependent on him.

As it should be.

He pressed the accelerator a little harder.

And then Caroline's tearful wail became something else entirely. It went up in pitch and volume, become shrill and mad with fear, and before Ron had a chance to process it, Jason joined in. The boy—usually so surly and quiet—was wide eyed and screaming.

"What?" demanded Ron.

"Bug!" yelled Caroline.

"Roach!" added Jason.

"Where?" asked Amanda. But then she saw it.

No. She saw *them*.

They were coming out of the vents, out of the door handles, out of the gaps in the body panels, and from under the floor mats. They were huge and shiny as hard candy, their shells almost black, their long antennae flicking, their legs skittering as they swarmed through the car.

One of the insects ran across the underside of the roof, and Ron swatted at it wildly, trying to keep it out of his hair, but even as he did so he felt the hard little feet on the back of his neck, and he lurched forward with a stifled shout. The movement wrenched the steering wheel, and the car swerved across the road toward the empty plunge into nothingness. He turned it hard the other way, and they rocketed back across the asphalt with a shriek of tires.

The bugs were everywhere. Amanda was shaking two off her arm. Jason had his hands over his mouth to stop them getting in, and Caroline was screaming and flailing wildly as one scurried up her sleeve. They were on the windows, including the windshield, swarming in the dozens. Maybe hundreds.

And then there was something else, similar, but very, very different. It emerged from the AC vent just right of the steering column. It was long and snakelike, but its body was made up of hard, black scorpion-like segments, and it had many jointed, yellow legs with pointed tips. It was a foot and a half long and its head was a fiery red, as were its twitching antennae. If Ron had been in the headspace to give the thing a name, he would have called it a centipede, but that didn't do it justice, and nothing like it had even been seen in the mountains of North Carolina before. It slithered out, its feet clicking audibly on the hard plastic of the dashboard, and then it was moving over the controls and up toward Ron's face.

Ron wasn't aware of it, but he had begun to shout, a long, unbroken cry of outrage and revulsion. He was barely conscious of what he was doing but had the presence of mind to brake hard as the car slid towards the rocky embankment on the left. He wrestled with the heavy vehicle, but he couldn't stop it. He felt it slide, its tires smoking, and then the torque was too much and the Hummer's center-of-gravity shifted upwards. He took his foot off the brake, but it was too late. The wheels on the right side lifted off the road when the car hit the rocky verge and jumped the barrier. But even as it flipped, he couldn't take his eyes off the monstrous centipede.

If there had been space, the Hummer would have rolled, but it came up hard against the tree-lined embankment and stopped so firmly that it was kicked back. For a moment, it teetered on two wheels then crashed back onto all four tires and came to a shuddering halt inches from the edge.

There was no time for relief. Pausing only to make sure that the centipede was not on him, Ron shouldered his dented door open then went round the car yanking the others, dragging his family free, his stomach churning as the Hummer's interior writhed with insect forms like something out of a nightmare.

Once out, they backed away from the car, huddled together but watching it warily, as the roaches popped out and scrambled off into the woods, so that slowly, very slowly, the horror subsided, the madness drained away, and they were themselves again. Or as much themselves as they could be for a while.

Ron stared at the battered, smoking vehicle, but if the centipede emerged from the wreckage, he didn't see it, and privately he resolved to sell the car for whatever he could get for it immediately. He wouldn't be getting in it again. He didn't ask Amanda or the kids if they had seen the thing with the legs. He didn't want to talk about it. It felt like it hadn't just slithered into his car. It had skittered and crawled into his mind. He would dream about it, he was sure, and though he was suddenly exhausted beyond all reason, he found he didn't want to go to sleep for fear of seeing it again.

3

英希

Saito-san, the tengu, ran an improbable Japanese restaurant-cum-dojo in a strip mall on the west side of town where I went to train after school. My sword skills had improved, and I was faster and stronger than he was when I really needed to be, but he could still beat me handily. It got pretty tiresome.

"It is good to be bad at things," he pronounced after another failed attempt to divert his strike.

"Gee, thanks," I said, then thought about what he had said. "Wait. What does that even mean?"

"It is better if you find the answer for yourself," he replied with maddening calm, adjusting the tie which kept his wild hair back.

"How can it be good to be bad at things?" I demanded. "That's a contradiction. Good versus bad. They are, like, opposites. Maybe it's a translation thing," I added, glancing at the far end of the room where the tengu kept his Library of Imposing Japanese Books.

"It is not," said the tengu flatly.

"Okay, man, whatever."

He read my downcast expression, but instead of offering me an explanation for his cryptic remark, he said simply, "Break. Tea."

I put the wooden swords away and swept the tatami while he made green tea in a delicate ceramic pot which—unlike the one I had semi-inherited from my grandmother—did not sprout legs and walk around by itself.

We sat cross-legged at a low wooden table.

"Bachan thinks something is coming," I said out of the blue.

"Something?"

"Monsters. Magic. Something."

"She thinks this why?"

I grinned. "She saw a dog running around in circles," I said.

He did not return my grin but nodded soberly. "Animals sometimes sense things we do not," he said.

"You're as bad as her," I said.

"Thank you," he said, bowing.

This was as close to a joke as Saito-san was ever likely to get, so I smiled. "Could you tell if something weird was happening, or was about to?" I asked.

He frowned and said nothing for a moment, then tipped his head on one side and made a noncommittal noise. "There are ceremonies of purification to protect against ill fortune, defilement, malevolent forces, but detecting their presence is harder. Sometimes we read the natural world."

"Dogs behaving weird," I inserted.

"Perhaps," he said, clearly not liking my use of the word 'weird.' "And there are charms, rituals to analyze unnatural presences or energies, but they need to be attached to a specific place or thing."

"Nothing to just identify a general..."

"Do not say weirdness."

"I wasn't going to," I lied. "A general...mystical presence or energy?"

He shook his head, his massive eyebrows bunching, then got up, and—without a word of explanation—went to the far end of the practice room where a curious stacked cabinet bound with black iron straps stood. I had never seen him open it before but had always been curious about it because it looked old and strange, each drawer and cupboard a different size and shape. He opened a pair of small doors and pulled out a drawer from inside. In it sat a lacquered box bound with faded red cord. He brought it over to the low table and sat down, moving with his usual slowness that made everything he did feel like a ritual.

He sat on his haunches then opened the box. It was lined with ancient, faded fabric, and in the center was a bag made of gold-colored silk with a draw string. He opened it carefully and removed a metal disk with a handle made of bamboo. It looked like a very small frying pan. It was bronze, green with age; its rear side intricately ornamented with swirls and geometrical patterns. But when he turned it over, it flashed bright and clear; its front was coated with some other metal and polished to a shine.

"It's a mirror!" I exclaimed. "Is it old?"

The tengu cocked his head again.

"*Tabun,*" he said. "*Muromachi, to omoimasu.*"

He had a tendency to speak Japanese to me even though he knew I couldn't understand it.

"Yeah, I don't know what that means," I said, irritated.

"Older than your country," he said.

"Cool," I said, because it was. "What does it do?"

"It reflects things," he said.

"Well, yeah, I figured that much."

"Perhaps it reflects things as they are, rather than as they appear."

I liked the sound of that but was hung up on his first word.

"Perhaps?" I asked.

"Perhaps," he replied. "Sometimes when I look into it, I think I see myself. Sometimes, not."

"O...K..." I said. "So what exactly does it show?"

"It is not certain," he said. "Many things are not certain."

"Oh," I said, deflated. "Right. Words to live by."

"But you may take it," he said, slipping it back into the silk bag and handing it to me. "It may be of use."

And that cheered me up.

Back home, I found Mom working the register in the store and, in the backyard, Dad, enveloped in sweet smelling smoke, standing over the charcoal grill.

"Try this," said Dad.

"What is it?" I replied, immediately wary.

"Just try it!"

He worked a knife into the rack of ribs he was smoking and sliced one off the end.

"New sauce?" I said. Dad was always experimenting with barbecue rubs and sauces, not always successfully.

"Just try it," he repeated.

Now, Dad was a master on the grill and the meat would be tender and smoky. The issue would be the flavor which could be anything. He had a thing for hot peppers, curry spices, and exotic fruit. At their best, the results were very tasty, at their worst, downright nasty. I braced myself, then lifted the bone to my lips and took a cautious nibble.

It was good. In fact, it was amazing! I took another bite. It was salty and spicy with a tangy sweetness that came out of nowhere and gave my tastebuds a slap.

"Woah!" I said. "What is that?"

"Soy sauce, honey, mustard, tamarind paste, smoked Japanese chillis, and a little vinegar," he said. "Kind of an ethnic hybrid. The soy sauce and hot pepper are Japanese, the vinegar and tamarind is the core of a good English brown sauce, but the honey and mustard are pure North Carolina. It's us," he said, grinning broadly, "all our favorite ingredients in a perfect blend. Pretty good, right?"

"It's amazing," I said. "You could bottle that and sell it."

"You know," he said, "we just might."

The following morning a curious advert appeared in *The Portersville Chronicle*. It read, "Mr. Kieran West cordially invites the town of Portersville to a housewarming party at 184 Main Street (formerly the Haversham House) on Saturday from 6 p.m. Semiformal dress, no gifts of any kind. Residents only, no phones or cameras. RSVP promptly to avoid disappointment. Dinner and drinks will be served, and an announcement made."

Similar notices arrived on stiff, elegant card in the mail, and by the end of the day it had made Action News Twelve.

"The sleepy mountain town of Portersville is abuzz with speculation and excitement at a mysterious invitation from one of the town's newest and wealthiest inhabitants," gushed Katie Marsden, a well-groomed blond reporter who positively twinkled at the camera. "Little is known of Kieran West, who purchased and rebuilt a dilapidated mansion on the rundown east end of town, and no one this reporter could find has any good leads on what Mr. West's *announcement* will be, but he's bringing a little California pizzaz to the Blue Ridge."

Here the footage cut to a series of locals shrugging and smiling and offering their guesses as to what was going on. "Maybe announcing a new factory," said one, "and a return to the good old days of furniture manufacturing." "A car dealership," said another, less enthusiastically. "That's the kind of thing which gets all the hype." "I'm just going for the party," said another.

The section concluded with a series of kids from the local middle school speculating as to what they would like the town's richest new arrival to bring to Portersville; an ice-skating rink, a theme park like Disneyworld, or—better—Jurassic Park with real dinosaurs, or—somewhat more attainably—a chocolate fountain. All very cute and wholesome.

"Apparently the Haversham house will be open to visitors for the whole evening and guests will be given a specific entrance time to allow as many people in as possible," said the reporter in a tone of impressed amazement. She wrapped things up by saying the station intended to have a representative at Mr. West's generous soiree but they had been told there wouldn't be any exceptions to the "no cameras" rule. "We'll just have to tell you about it," she added with a cheeky wink and a smile as wide as a barn door. "I hope the canapés are worth the report!"

Most of the kids at school weren't too sure what canapés were, but they were indeed abuzz, studying the announcement on their phones as we waited for the field trip bus.

"It's probably just for adults," said a girl.

Her friend shook her head solemnly. "Doesn't say that on the invitation," she said with a defiant little swagger. "Fancy food for free? Let's see them try and turn me away."

We took our seats on the bus, the excited chatter about the brand of Hollywood glitz the Wests were bringing to Portersville getting louder and more gleeful. I glanced over to Nathan who was sitting alone with his eyes closed, wearing the kind of headphones that cover your whole ears, clearly unwilling to discuss his father's latest round of news-making.

I figured I'd seen the end of field trips when I left middle school, but once in a while Portersville high mandated an excursion to a Site of Local Importance, though, they were pretty thin on the ground, especially of late.

"Usually we'd visit the Nye Family Barn," Joey observed as we reached our destination and filed off the school bus.

"Constructed circa 1870," added DeMarcus, grinning at them. "What happened to that again?"

"If I remember rightly it fell victim to an act of senseless vandalism by a local delinquent," Joey supplied.

"Hilarious," I observed. "And, for the record, I was also involved in the barn's reconstruction, and the new version is way better."

"I think that was mostly Mr. Saito's handywork," DeMarcus supplied, enjoying himself, "and lovely though the new structure is, it lacks that special 1870s crapness."

"So we come here instead," said Joey, taking in the sign outside the little ranger station. "The Portersville Forest Refuge and Museum of Natural History which, by the looks of things, will be a cabin containing some charts aimed at kindergarteners and some moldy amateur taxidermy. Be still my heart."

"It'll be at least as entertaining as that old barn was," I said. "Birds and animals beat buildings made out of logs any day."

"Spoken like a true arsonist," Joey returned grinning.

I frowned, but at that moment Nathan West—the new boy—strolled by and nodded in my direction. He was with Tyler, Bobby Davenham, and Jason Blakely, and they all looked caught between confusion and outrage that he acknowledged my existence.

"Hey Hideki," he said flicking me a little salute.

"Hey Nathan," I replied.

Joey and DeMarcus raised their eyebrows.

"See, that's just weird," said DeMarcus.

"You are not wrong," Joey agreed.

"What can I say," I quipped, "unburdened by this town's petty prejudices, he recognizes coolness when he sees it."

They laughed a little longer than was strictly necessary, then DeMarcus's eyes slid past me and his face broke into a goofy smile. I turned to see Emily with Madison and Ayisha—DeMarcus' twin sister—getting down from the other bus. Maddie spotted me but avoided my eyes. She'd been doing a lot of that lately.

"Hey Em," I said. "Didn't know you were coming on this."

"No choice," she replied, clearly not happy about it. "Reveling in Portersville's lameness is apparently mandatory for all students regardless of grade or whether they could have been in the pool getting some extra training in between classes. This town's absence of culture must be celebrated, so here we are."

"*Masaka*," I sighed sympathetically, another word I'd recently learned from bingeing Japanese cartoons. I wasn't entirely sure what it meant, but people said it when bad things happened.

Em gave me a sour look. "That's getting annoying," she snapped and walked on by. Ayisha gave DeMarcus a baffled smile and a shrug, obviously jarred by Emily's bad mood.

"What got into her?" asked Joey.

"No idea," I said. "She was fine this morning. The woods aren't cool enough, I guess."

"Seemed like more than that," said DeMarcus. He looked after her and I gave him a shrewd look. When he caught it, he blushed, smiled, and looked away. When he sensed I was going to say something, he snapped back to the previous conversation as if I hadn't said anything.

"They say that Nathan kid is a decent wide receiver," he said.

"Who says?" I asked. "I don't think we get a lot of scouting reports from California high school football programs."

"He did," said DeMarcus, slightly shame-faced.

"Good source," said Joey. "I can tell you some pretty cool things about me if you'd like to hear them."

"He wasn't bragging," DeMarcus protested. "It was kind of implied. He was talking about coming to practice, maybe trying out, and Bobby asked about his playing experience out west. He was a starter in a big city school. Must be pretty decent."

"Maybe you should join the cheerleading squad," said Joey. "You're obviously smitten."

DeMarcus waved the joke away. "Just saying, it would be nice to have someone who can catch a pass on the team. No offense," he added looking at me.

"None taken," I said, meaning it. Joey and DeMarcus were on a very short list of people who knew that I had deliberately flunked out of the team so that I could keep my recently inherited strength, quickness, and dexterity under the general radar.

"Apparently he can do a forty in 4.6 seconds," said DeMarcus.

I didn't know what that meant but I made a suitably impressed noise and DeMarcus seemed satisfied.

"You know," said Joey, "I wasn't too keen on looking at a bunch of dead animals in cases, but after all this sportsball talk, I'm starting to see the appeal."

DeMarcus and I exchanged a suitably manly eye roll, but I was actually quite looking forward to the museum. I have always been a bit of bird nerd, and not only because—until very recently—I'd generally prefer to be by myself in the woods than doing regular stuff with other kids. Em said I was antisocial, but she had always been one of the popular kids and didn't get it. Even with my newfound composure, other people mostly made me nervous which, in turn, made me awkward. And when people who don't know you well find you awkward, they either get away fast in case they catch your uncoolness like flu, or they look to amuse themselves at your expense. Not always, of course, but, you know, more than I'd like.

So, yeah. Yay birds.

Of course, the taxidermized birds in the cases at Portersville's grandly titled museum were dusty, moth-eaten things which had been stuffed about a century ago and left to molder in front of bored school kids. There was a decent red-tailed hawk and a barred owl, but the smaller birds looked like they had been freeze-dried. Among the mammal specimens, a graying raccoon had comically mismatched eyes and a bobcat looked like it had been hit by a truck before the hopeful taxidermist got to work on it. I would bet good money that whoever produced the half-fossilized result had never seen a live cat of any kind. Meanwhile, the black bear specimen was weirdly shrunken and dog-like; like it had been stitched together not just from two bears but from two different animals entirely.

It was pretty depressing, and the fact that most of my classmates thought they were hilarious made it worse. There were some live animals in a series of dimly lit aquarium tanks: frogs and toads, bugs of various kinds, and a few snakes and lizards. Bobby Davenham went round the room proclaiming every snake a copperhead regardless of what it said on the label, and spouting internet nonsense about how quickly they could kill you. They had a timber rattler, which was pretty cool, and a red rat snake which squirmed constantly across the glass flicking its tongue. Some kids shrieked in horror, and Bobby flicked the glass until he got bored and wandered off looking for a vending machine.

Mr. Watkins, the retired woodshop teacher, was one of the designated chaperones, and he steered the students through the exhibits, periodically telling them to keep the noise down and get off their phones. I moved slowly through the exhibits. Dingy and predictable though they were, I kind of liked them, and it made a nice change from being in school. At each illuminated case, I could get in close and forget that anyone else was there, so that by the time I looked up from studying the skinks and anoles, I found I was alone.

Or nearly so. One other person was huddled up against the glass of a case of spiders. I edged a little closer and he startled, turning quickly and staring at me with wide eyes. I was surprised to find that it was Jason Blakely, one of Tyler's lesser minions and someone who had barely spoken to me in all the years we had attended the same schools. He looked flushed and agitated but also embarrassed.

"Pretty cool," I said, offering what I thought was a lifeline and nodding toward the spider in the case. "What is that, a wolf spider?"

His agitation seemed to increase, but he responded with, "I hate bugs."

"I hear you," I said, smiling excessively. I had always been wary of Jason, not so much because of any particular vibe I got from him, but because I didn't like his friends.

"They can get in your car," he said vaguely. "Come out while you're driving. Roaches."

He had a distant, hunted look, and his eyes were fixed on something only he could see.

"Wait," I exclaimed, "that was you?! There was something in the paper about it."

We always had copies of *The Portersville Chronicle* in the store. Sometimes Mom even ran ads in it. The story in question had appeared in the previous evening's edition and Dad had taken great joy in reading it out over dinner until Mom told him to stop. According to the story, the driver—apparently Jason's father—was threatening to sue the car dealership where the infestation had taken hold.

"How do you not find and fumigate a nest of roaches in a car that has been sitting on your lot for three months?" Dad had asked in delighted amazement.

Jason's thousand-yard stare rather killed the horror-movie comedy of the thing, however.

"There were hundreds of them," he said blankly. "I thought we were going to die. I thought..." He paused, and his eyes narrowed. "You know about wildlife and stuff, right?"

"Some," I said. "Birds, mostly. Why?"

"You ever seen a bug like a snake with legs?" He said it quickly, like the phrase might turn and bite him.

"Like a silverfish or...?"

He shook his head vigorously. "No, man," he almost whined. "Long and with, like, a ton of legs."

"Like a centipede?" I said. "I don't think those are technically insects."

His eyes flashed with triumph. "Yeah!" he said. "Centipede. But, like, a foot long. More. With a red head and yellow legs."

"Woah," I said, shaking my head. "No. I've seen the little house centipedes with the wispy antennae things and the legs like hairs. They can be pretty big, like three or four inches..."

But he was already shaking his head again. "No, this was huge, and its body was hard and black and..."

But he didn't finish the sentence and looked suddenly self-conscious, as if just remembering who he was confiding in. He shook his head again, this time as if to shake something loose, and repeated the first thing he had said. "I hate bugs."

And with that he walked quickly from the room without a backward glance.

I considered his back for a moment then drifted over to the little spider tank. There was a dense spiral in the center which I knew without looking meant that the spider was one of the funnel web species. I studied it, conscious that the hair on the back of my neck was prickling. Jason's odd behavior and dreadful fascination had gotten under my skin. The spider stared back at me with shiny black eyes until I shuddered and moved on to the next, even smaller tanks which featured the dreaded black widow with its distinctive red hourglass, and the nondescript but potentially lethal brown recluse. I may not be at Jason's level of terror where creepy crawlies were concerned, but I am not a fan, and his tale of foot-long centipedes had given me the serious willies. I sauntered through the exhibit a little faster, pausing only when I saw out of the corner of my eye a curious movement from an aquarium of huge stag beetles with antlers like twigs.

They were, for lack of a better word, swarming: seven or eight of them bustling around on the front of the tank like they were urgently, even desperately, trying to find a way out. It made my skin crawl.

Suddenly feeling the emptiness and darkness of the place, I hurried to catch up to the rest of the group. I found them, of course, in the gift shop, browsing animal plushies and candy bars. Jason had rejoined his pals and was laughing loudly at something, unrecognizable from the spooked boy he had been moments before. They were being lectured on the habits of the local woodpeckers by a ranger with the kind of beard you could hide a chicken in, so that probably accounted for the amusement.

Ayisha, Madison, and a couple of other girls from the swim team were giggling and whispering, casting sidelong looks at Nathan West, who was in the middle of the room but talking to no one. He was scanning the crowd coolly, and when his eyes met mine, the corner of his mouth puckered into a tiny smile, and he nodded fractionally. I returned it, wondering whether I should go over and chat, you know, like a regular person, but then I spotted my sister. Emily was sitting by herself staring fixedly into the throng of gabbling kids, sulking. With a sense of doing something very slightly selfless, even heroic, I opted not to join the cool new boy and headed instead to my mopey sister, plonking myself down on the bench beside her.

"What?" she snapped, clearly not appreciating the scale of my sacrifice.

"Just visiting," I said. "You okay?"

"I'm fine. Go away."

"Check this out," I said, ignoring her as I rummaged in my backpack and pulled out the mirror Saito had given me. I thrust it into her hands, and she looked at it like she was doing me an immense favor.

"It's a crappy mirror," she said. "So?"

"It's a very *old* crappy mirror," I corrected her. "And it might be magic."

"Might be?" she answered.

"It's not clear. But look at yourself in it."

She sighed then held it up and looked into it.

"What do you see?" I asked.

"A slightly blurry version of me," she said, pushing the mirror back toward me.

"No glimmer of your inner fox?" I asked, disappointed.

"What?" she demanded, annoyed again. "No! And keep your voice down."

I took the mirror from her and tried the direct approach.

"You don't seem very...*genki*," I said.

Emily glared at me. "You're not Japanese, Caleb," she snapped, "and bingeing *Inu Yasha* on Netflix won't change that."

I was taken aback and if I was honest, a little hurt, but if she saw that in my face, she showed no sign of remorse, and her icy stare didn't thaw.

"Fine," I said stiffly. "I was only trying to help."

"You can't," she said, getting to her feet abruptly. "No one can. So just leave it, okay?"

I opened my mouth to reply with some crushing retort, but she was already walking away.

I glanced back to her friends, to see if they were paying attention to her odd behavior, but they were chattering away as before and seemed not to have noticed. Madison's hair was in a complicated braid. She looked happier than she had for weeks. It pained me a little to think that if I went over now, her good mood wouldn't last. Though I had actually saved her life, she associated me, as the school guidance counselor had observed, with trauma. Trying to reconnect with her would reopen old wounds. If I felt anything for her, the best thing I could do was leave her alone.

So...that was awesome.

I realized that one of the group was Sophia (Sofie?) Collington, daughter of the Southern Shale guy my parents had been talking about. As I watched, a tall, blond woman I didn't know came over to them and touched Sofie/Sophia on her shoulder in a way a teacher would never do.

Her mother? Mom had said she had known her for years but that she thought herself too good to associate with the likes of us. That tracked. Maureen Collington. She looked...polished, somehow. That bit brighter and shinier than the other parents and teachers, as if she had come here on her way to some Charlotte gala, where wealthy bankers had their pictures taken donating money to art galleries. She was dressed in white trousers and gold open-toed shoes with a matching jacket that hovered between high-end style and super trashy kitsch. I didn't know anything about fashion, as my sister would be quick to point out, but it was the kind of outfit that would be super cool for about twenty minutes and would become embarrassingly old-fashioned just as fast. My instinct was that Mrs. Collington would know just when to dump it.

She muttered something to her daughter who was, I was pleased to note, clearly annoyed by her presence, and then inspected the crowd. That was exactly the right word. Her eyes were like search lights, scanning, assessing, not so much to make sure the students weren't writing on the walls or stealing fridge magnets, but to see who did and didn't measure up according to some private ranking. Her face was haughty, head tipped back on her long, elegant neck, so that she literally looked down her nose at everyone. As I watched, her gaze came to rest on Nathan West at precisely the same moment that his, not wholly dissimilar gaze, found her.

There was an odd, thoughtful moment in which they considered each other coolly, strangely given the age difference between them, as if processing the glow which hung around each of them, and then their eyes swept on, like they were checking boxes in their heads, deciding who was worth their attention and who wasn't.

Neither of them looked at me.

But it was kind of amazing. Mrs. Collington was—at least to everyone but her own daughter—something like the pinnacle of Portersville society, and while that might not sound like much, it is if you live here. So the idea of this fifteen-year-old boy staring her down, totally unintimidated, like he was her equal? It was impossible not to be a little impressed.

I rejoined DeMarcus and Joey who were considering questions on the Junior Ranger board, the latter with their customary irony turned up to eleven.

"What factors most influence the habitat loss of the American black bear?" DeMarcus read aloud.

"Well," Joey said with false brightness, "it certainly couldn't have anything to do with strip mining the mountains for lumber, coal, natural gas and anything else that might make someone a ton of cash."

"Correct," said DeMarcus, deadpan. "That would be patriotic American capitalism which can do no wrong."

"Having fun?" I asked.

"Beyond ecstatic," said Joey. "I especially liked the dead birds. Most uplifting."

"I think they are supposed to make us appreciate the living ones," I said.

"Yeah, not sure that's working," Joey replied.

"Woah," said DeMarcus, staring out of the window. "When did it start raining?"

"Pretty much now," said Joey. "But it wasn't in the forecast."

"Microclimate," said DeMarcus wisely. "All part of the joys of living in Portersville, where life is like a box of chocolates: you never know what is going to kill you."

"Still," I said, staring out to where the trees were straining against a wind that hadn't been there minutes before as the windows were lashed with rain, "this is pretty extreme."

It was. The light outside had halved in the last thirty seconds as heavy, slate-gray clouds rolled in, seemingly out of nowhere. There was a flash of lightning followed seconds later by a rumble of thunder. The next flash was considerably brighter, a ragged blue-white flicker which threw shadows around the little museum and caused a stir of wonder among the students. The thunder crack that followed was so unexpectedly loud that I actually ducked a little.

"Everyone move away from the windows!" called the ranger. "Just to be on the safe side. It will pass shortly."

I wasn't so sure. This had blown up fast, as fast as any storm I'd ever seen hit Portersville, but it was also a fierce one. Twisters weren't common in the area, but they were certainly possible, and when they came, they could do a lot of damage.

I was considering this when there was a flat pop in the distance and all the lights went out.

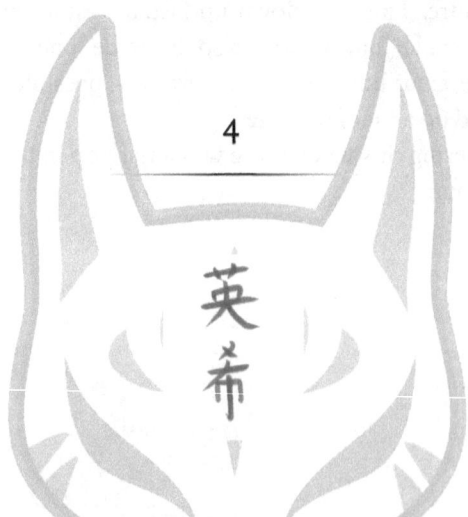

4

There was an immediate collective shout, some of it genuinely scared—mostly at the bang which had accompanied the power cut—but also sort of gleeful, like when someone drops a plate in the cafeteria and everyone claps. Most of the students were bored by the ranger station/museum, and this provided a much-needed shot of drama; it was still light outside, and the building had windows, so even though the storm had made it darker, it wasn't like we'd been plunged into blackness. While the teachers, rangers, and chaperones told everyone that everything was fine and they should stay calm, the kids buzzed excitedly, watching the torrents of water carrying fallen leaves and branches through the parking lot. I had to admit, it was pretty cool, and every time an additional crackle of lightning rippled through the air, the kids oohed and ahhed with excitement. Except for Jason.

"What if the bugs get out?" he asked.

"Because the power's out?" sneered Tyler. "It's not *Jurassic Park*. They are in glass boxes."

"Yeah, Jason," Bobby agreed. "Don't be an idiot."

Jason managed a grin, but he looked rattled, his eyes flashing round the shadowy corners as if he expected a river of roaches to explode from every crack or electrical outlet. There was another long roll of thunder like we were standing directly under the marching band's drum line, and we exchanged nervous smiles, but that was pretty much the end of it. The rain was slackening off and the gap between thunder and lightning got steadily longer as the storm moved away. Within fifteen minutes of the first rain drop falling, it had stopped and—amazingly—the sun was coming out, so that the trees and shrubs outside looked impossibly green and steaming, their leaves laminated in water.

But we weren't done. In fact, the full horror of our situation was only just beginning to register.

"Does anyone have phone signal?" asked Ayisha Murphy to the room in general. "Mine has died."

"The wifi is powered by the building's main electrical supply," said the ranger. "We'll get the generator going, but I'm not sure it's hooked up to the same circuit as the router."

"I wasn't on the wifi," said Ayisha. "I was just using cell data."

"My phone has no signal either!" someone called out, a note of hysteria in his voice.

There was a lot of hasty scrolling, some frantic keyboard tapping, and for a moment it seemed that everyone in the place was bent over in the gloom, their faces lit only by the glow of their phone screens. At last, the stunning awfulness of our predicament fully landed.

"I'm offline!"

"My Insta won't load!"

"My email is down," said one of the teachers.

"TikTok is frozen!"

"What the hell!?"

The sense of disaster crackled like the electricity we had lost. You'd think we'd crash landed in the Arctic with nothing more than a ham sandwich and a small coke between us.

"Okay, okay," Mr. Watkins announced, raising his hands palms down in a calming gesture. "It's not the end of the world."

"How do you know?" someone called. "We can't get online to find out!"

"It's just a power glitch," Watkins went on managing to sound soothing and certain at the same time. "Probably a downed tree somewhere. Those were some strong winds. But we managed without cell phones for thousands of years, I think we can survive until we get back to school."

This was certainly true for the species as a whole, but my generation hadn't actually lived without cell phones at all, so even someone like me who had never been especially invested in the virtual world, felt...*off*. Not sure how else to put it: an unnerving sense of disconnection, maybe. But

31

Watkins sounded sure, and the other adults exchanged knowing smiles, so people calmed down some, filing dutifully out in the late morning light toward the waiting school busses, while the bearded ranger repeated his apologies and said we'd be welcome to come back any time.

Except that our phones didn't find cell signals as we re-boarded the busses, continuing to show grayed out networks all the way back to school. There was a line of stationary cars and trucks at the first real intersection, and Tyler was quick to spot the problem.

"Traffic signals are down," he said, adopting his father's take-charge manner. "Power must be out all over town."

He was, annoyingly, right. There were no lights on in school, and the teachers were called to a hasty huddle in the principal's office.

"Gonna send us home," said Bobby, blue eyes flashing with delight, his fears for the end of the world apparently crushed by the prospect of being excused from algebra. "Bound to."

Right again. Within ten minutes, the building was closed for the day, and we were told to watch local news outlets for updates, though how we were supposed to do that with the town blacked out, no one said.

"Fire department and power company teams are out doing what they can to restore electricity," the principal announced from the front steps, "so y'all should check in with your teachers about how best to use the time off then head home. Anyone who has literally nowhere to go can wait in the library, but lights, computers, wifi—everything really—are all down, and we'll have to lock up at five. If you have nowhere to go by then, you should go to a friend's place. If you don't have anyone you can go with, talk to Mrs. Thompson; she will compile a buddy list."

So we left. I spotted my sister and flagged her down. "Heading home?" I asked.

"Eventually," she said. "Something I have to do first."

"What? Maybe I'll come with…"

"No, Caleb. This is private."

I frowned. "You okay?"

"Why does everyone keep asking that?" she exclaimed, her exasperation boiling suddenly. "Yes, I'm fine. Just let me get on with it, okay?"

"If I can do anything to help…" I tried.

She closed her eyes, pursed her lips, and did this thing where she tipped her head on one side, like she was summoning all the strength she had not to kill me. "Thank you," she managed. "I'll see you at home, Caleb, okay?"

"Okay."

She stomped off. I watched her long enough to see that she wasn't rejoining her friends, then when it started to feel like I was spying, I turned away. Hopefully, whatever she planned to do before going home would improve her mood.

I headed home and set up with my homework at the cash register with a battery-powered lantern. The rest of the store was gloomy, the only real light coming from the front windows. Dad had overridden the power controls on the register, and Mom left me with strict instructions.

"Cash only tonight," she said. "Personal checks only from people on the list. No credit. But politely."

"When am I not polite?" I asked.

"Keep a running tally of sales on the notepad and put them on the spike," Dad added. "We'll update the electronic books later."

"We will, will we?" Mom asked, amused. She always did the books.

"Royal we," said Dad with a quick grin. "I'm English."

"Doesn't the royal we actually mean 'I,' meaning you'll do the books by yourself?" Mom asked.

"This is the Lancashire royal we," Dad improvised, "which means, less me, more you."

Mom shook her head as she headed back into the house, but she had that little private smile on her face, the one she reserved for Dad. The bell over the door rang. I glanced over and stared.

It was Nathan West.

He came in cautiously, gazing around him like he'd entered Aladdin's cave. He gave me a little chin jut.

"Hey Hideki," he said. "'Sup?"

"Nathan," I said, caught between delight that the coolest kid in town should be visiting and horror that he was visiting me here, in the least cool place in town. "Hey, man. Welcome. I mean, can I help you find anything?"

"You work here?" he asked, eyes wide.

"I mean, yeah," I said, embarrassed. "My family owns this place."

"Oh yeah, I know," he said. "I just didn't know you actually worked here."

"Oh, you know," I said, trying to sound casual, "just a bit in the evenings."

"And weekends," Dad inserted, grinning as he appeared from behind a rack of canned soup. "Stephen Smith," he said, extending his hand. "You're Nathan West, I take it?"

Oh no, oh no, oh no...

"Yeah," said Nathan. "How you doin' Mr. Smith?"

"I'm doin' very well, Nathan," said Dad. "Particularly since..." he added, gesturing to the toy train, "I got this little baby running."

This was it, where my coolness came to die.

"Wow," said Nathan, shooting me an unreadable grin. "That's pretty cool, Mr. Smith."

"Isn't it just," said Dad without a trace of irony. "This is the Hayabusa shinkansen. Needs power, of course, but still pretty great just to look at, right? I have one of the original bullet trains in HO scale, but this N gauge beauty is one of the current..."

"Okay, Dad," I cut in, my voice sounding shrill with panic. "I'm sure Nathan was looking for something in particular. Chips, maybe. Candy?"

"Actually, I was just checking the place out," said Nathan. "Thought I'd swing by and say hey if you were around."

"And he is," said Dad helpfully. "Right Caleb? You're around."

"I am indeed," I said, as my social life circled the drain. "I am indeed around."

It was as if the power outage had affected my brain; all higher reasoning and language functions were down, and I was babbling like an idiot while my father brandished toy trains like a madman.

"Power out at your place too?" Dad asked.

"All over town, I hear," said Nathan, who had torn his gaze from the toy—sorry, *model*—train and was now appraising the snack aisle, nodding thoughtfully. "Oh, you have those little rice cracker things! Cool."

"Senbe," I said, shouting like a crazy person.

He started and stared at me.

"That's what they're called in Japan," I explained. "Senbe. Or sembe. Not really sure which is right. I don't speak much Japanese."

"Oh, they are Japanese?" said Nathan. "Nice."

"Take a bag!" Dad prompted. "Housewarming gift."

I stared at him. By all accounts the Wests could buy and sell us a thousand times over and my father was making a gift of a bag of rice crackers like it was the crown jewels.

"That's kind of you, Mr. Smith," said Nathan. "Thanks!"

"You're from California, eh?" said Dad pulling up a chair with the air of a man settling in for an hour or two. "That must be nice."

That must be nice???

"I guess so," said Nathan with a half shrug. "But Portersville is cool too. Different, of course."

"I'll bet," said Dad.

I had to do something. Dad could English-Small-Talk people to within an inch of their lives. He'd be offering tea and biscuits next, then explaining that what we called biscuits were different from what English people called biscuits (*"wouldn't want gravy on my chocolate digestives, would I?"*), listing the different kinds and telling us why jammy dodgers were his favorites…

"So school, huh?" I blurted. "That must be pretty different here. You see yourself trying out for any sports or anything?"

Another shrug. "Kind of did the football thing at my old school," Nathan replied. "Sorta over it."

"Caleb was on the football team for a while," Dad piped up.

"For, like, ten minutes," I cut in, waving it away like I was glad to be rid of it. "Been there, done that, right?"

"Right," said Nathan.

"Caleb got cut for burning the barn down," said Dad. I glared at him, mouth open and he backtracked hastily. "Not that it was his fault. Not really. And the barn is back up now. Not the same barn, obviously. A different one. Better, really. I expect Caleb could get back on the team if he felt like it. He was pretty good for a while there. But I suppose he's over it too."

Nathan was watching him like he was something cute but weird in a zoo. A platypus, maybe. A platypus with a Lancashire accent.

"Why do you call him Caleb?" said Nathan. "I thought he went by Hideki."

"That's new," said Dad. "We always used to call him Caleb. We're all a bit more up front about my wife's Japanese heritage lately. Hence the Shink," he added, beaming at the ridiculous train which was usually shooting round its little loop, at about a hundred miles an hour.

I blushed, feeling stupid, but Nathan just nodded.

"Cool," he said. "Okay, well, I gotta head. See if my father has found something he can eat in town, if anyone has power."

"Drake's Barbecue is good," said Dad, guilelessly. "If you're going to be in North Carolina, you may as well eat what we do best."

Nathan considered him, and something shrewd flashed through his face.

"You're from England, right Mr. Smith?" he said.

"Guilty as charged," Dad replied. "Near Manchester."

"But when you talk about North Carolina, you say 'we', like you belong here."

Dad's amiable grin fractured for a second, then returned. "Been here a long time," he said emphatically, though I thought his eyes looked wary.

"Interesting," Nathan concluded. "Thanks for the rec. I'll check it out. See you in school, Hideki." And he left, holding the bag of rice crackers up with a slightly ironic wave as he opened the door to the street.

Dad watched him go and the flicker of doubt I had glimpsed in his face vanished. "He seemed nice," he pronounced.

I glared at him. "You are unbelievable," I said, slamming my textbook closed and marching out of the store. I'd do the rest of my homework in my room.

"What?" my father called after me, but I didn't wait around to explain that he had just blown my credibility with the first cool kid who had ever tried to make friends with me.

That night I woke a little before three in the morning, which was unlike me. As I lay there, trying to decide if I needed to go to the bathroom, I heard a distinctive squeak on the landing. Someone was moving around. Probably Em getting a glass of water. That was probably what had woken me.

I listened for a moment. Somewhere in the trees over the road a barred owl called its 'Who Cooks For You.' But then there was another creak, thin but sharp and I knew that that one was the second step from the top of the stairs because it was the only bit of the floor that sounded like that anywhere in the house. I noticed things like that more than I used to since I got my ancient Japanese superpowers. They gave me a heightened sensitivity, particularly to unexpected things that might want to kill me.

Whoever was walking around the house was heading not to the bathroom but downstairs. That piqued my curiosity. Quietly I pushed back the sheets and swung my legs round. I made my soundless way to the bedroom door and turned the handle with a safecracker's care. It rotated noiselessly and I felt the moment the door unlatched. I pulled it gingerly toward me, knowing that if I opened it wider than about eighteen inches, that would creak too.

I slipped out, leading with my head, and stepped cautiously out onto the landing. I knew where the noisiest floorboards were and avoided them with one long stride, then another which took me to the top of the stairs. There were no lights on, but my eyes were sharp enough to make out Emily's distinctive long hair and cream-colored robe at the foot of the stairs as she moved silently away.

I considered hissing her name and demanding what she was doing, but my parents' door was close enough that I could hear Dad's heavy almost-snoring breathing and didn't want to wake them. I gripped the handrail and reached with my left foot, bypassing the creaky second step, then moved swiftly and silently down.

I figured Em would have made for the kitchen in quest of a snack, and I planned to catch her in the act, but she moved to the back door. That surprised me enough to make me still and watchful, holding my position on the stairs as I heard the distinctive snap of the latch.

What was she doing heading outside at this time?

I hesitated another second, then decided to ask her, but when I reached the door, she was gone.

Her nightgown was hung neatly over a branch of the dogwood that grew by the shed. I glanced down the path and caught the orange and white streak of a lithe fox, slipping into the undergrowth at the bottom of the garden, and out of sight.

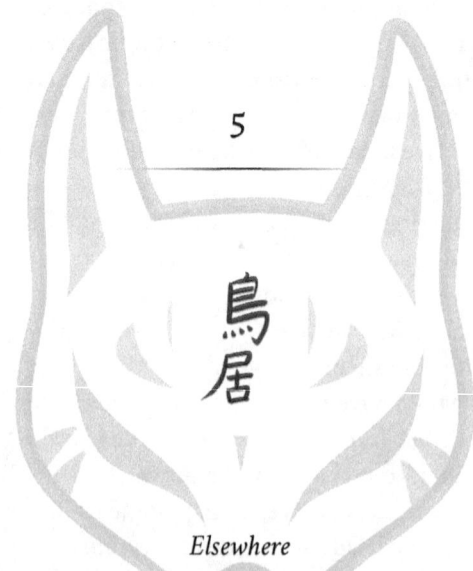

5

Elsewhere

Bernice Sartovski was seriously cheesed off with Marge Williamson, owner and so-called manager of the Tidy Shack diner where Bernice had waited tables, ran the register, set up, cleaned, and closed every day but Monday for the last seven years. Marge had always been inattentive to the needs of the little restaurant, but it hadn't been so bad when old Jake Simpson had been the cook. But Jake had retired and now the kitchen was being run—in a manner of speaking —by his idiot nephew, Hal, a kid Marge had hired as a favor to his uncle.

There was a lot of that in Portersville: little favors and helping hands offered to the people you had known for years, or to their lazy kids. There had been other candidates. Heck, Sally Greenwich's girl had a degree in hospitality from UNCW where she had worked in a Cajun restaurant all through college! Might have been Creole. Bernice wasn't sure of the difference. But either way it was a real restaurant in a proper tourist town.

But no. Marge felt she owed Jake, so she had hired the good-for-nothing, barely-made-it-through-high-school Hal, and Bernice's life had been a misery ever since. The kid could barely flip a burger without causing an international incident. Twice in the last year they had had to call the fire department when Hal's incompetence had left the customers sprinting for the exits in clouds of black smoke. The health department inspector had been summoned when Hal served chicken breasts which were still frozen in the middle! How does that even happen? A cook can't tell that meat is rock hard in the center? He can't look at his watch and figure out how long something has been cooking, or remember to get supplies out of the freezer the night before? It ain't rocket science.

Those were the spectacular failings. Worse were the slow drips of shiftless, bone idleness, and idiocy: the forgotten orders, the confused orders, the orders that got sent out for delivery when the customers were sitting at a table, the fries that took an hour and arrived as the party was finishing desert. This malarky was a daily feature of life at the Tidy Shack. And who suffered for it? Bernice, of course. She was the one who got the impatient remarks, the annoyed looks. She was the one—more to the point—whose tips were down seventy percent since Hal took over the kitchen.

Seventy percent! That was serious money in this economy and Bernice couldn't afford to lose it. She had said so to Marge, laying it all out in no uncertain terms; either Hal was given his notice or Bernice would take her "Best loved waitress in Portersville" award—three years running, thank you very much—and move down the road to Drake's Barbecue.

And what had Marge said?

She'd need to think about it!

Seriously. What was there to think about?

So Bernice had come home fuming and had decided to have a relaxing bath. Nothing calmed her down like a good soak. There was a roach on the kitchen counter, and she had sprayed it as the tub filled but spotted two more on the underside of the table edge.

"Time to get the exterminators in again," she sighed, annoyed rather than revolted. They had treated the house less than two months ago and the noisome little vermin were back already. Maybe she should try a different company. She remembered Bernie Flatbush, the guy who had done the spraying last time, from high school and he had never been much use at anything. After her soak, she'd take a look in the local paper, see if she could find someone who looked remotely competent. If not there, then she'd look online when the power came back on.

Bernie Flatbush, she thought, shaking her head, and Hal Simpson. Sometimes it felt like Portersville's primary export was losers.

She undressed and put her glasses on the counter by the sink, added the good bath bubbles that made the house smell of lavender and pears, and slid gratefully under the suds. The water was piping hot (praise the lord for a gas water heater!), making her gasp, but she knew it was what she needed. If Marge put her on the spot and said she was choosing Hal over her, she wasn't sure what she'd do. She liked her job, and for all the irritations of working with a cook half her age and a quarter of her skills, she was used to it. She didn't know Harry Drake very well, and worried that she wouldn't adjust to being at the barbecue restaurant. There was a bar there, and pool tables in the back, and it always smelled of smoke and vinegar sauce. She had barely been there in years.

She took a deep breath and settled into the foam, leaning back with her head between the taps until her toes peeped through the fragrant froth at the far end. The bathroom light flashed on, stalled, then came back.

Power at last!

But a minute later, it flickered again.

Bulb or another storm? she wondered, but when the light stayed on, she reached for the strawberry soft soap, rubbed it into a lather and massaged it into her face and neck, closing her eyes and bending her knees so that her shoulders slid deeper under the water.

As she did so, something long and black slid unseen across the bathroom floor. Its body was made up of many hard segments, and though there was something serpentine about its movement, it ran on forty amber legs with a couple more trailing behind. Jason Blakely had glimpsed it in his father's new car right before they had crashed, but it had been almost a foot shorter then. Now it scurried and slid across the glossy bathroom tiles, its long antennae flicking, until it reached the side of Bernice's fragrant bath, and began to climb. It tiptoed lightly across the side of the tub, all legs moving in uncanny unison, until it reached the wall and arced upwards, becoming still as Bernice splashed a little water on her face, rubbed the soap away and opened her eyes.

She didn't see it, partly because she was shockingly nearsighted without her glasses, and because the bathroom was steamy from the hot water. Her gaze was fixed on the end of the tub and the shaded window beyond, so she didn't notice the giant centipede until it started to move. It appeared in the corner of her eye as a black, squirming line, wriggling on its nightmare legs as it arced across the wall and down toward the bath.

Bernice screamed, scrambling madly against the slick sides of the tub, trying to get enough purchase to lift herself out. She missed and sank back into the water, her face going under, her shrieking mouth half filling with suds, as her wild eyes focused on the slithering thing inches away. She flailed, splashing water all over the floor in a great wave, then rolled and grabbed the faucet for leverage. She forced herself up and out, banging her knee hard on the rim of the tub and collapsing in a slick, naked heap on the bathroom floor.

But only for a second. The thought of that thing in there with her was all the incentive she needed to scramble out into the hall and slam the door behind her. For a second she stood dripping on the hardwood, then she was off, bare feet slipping on the floor as she hunted for a towel and… what? Bug spray? The thing was enormous. A yard long at least. She'd seen black snakes that big, bigger, but this thing had legs, she was sure of it.

It was impossible. She blundered over to the fireplace, picked up the poker and hefted it thoughtfully, her eyes on the bathroom door. Then, revolted by the idea of going back in there with nothing on her feet, she managed to slip on some old gym shoes and hastily shrugged into the green robe she had retired but not gotten around to throwing away, all without taking her eyes off the door.

There was a sudden brilliance, as every lamp in the room came on, flickered, then popped out with a hum and the electric scent of lightning.

Bernice's heart was racing, but she couldn't delay any longer. She put her left hand on the doorknob, while her right raised the poker to head height, poised to bring it slashing down if she got so much as a glimpse of the monster in the bathroom. When she was ready, she pushed the door open slowly with her foot and leaned in.

There was nothing. She moved the towels and her good robe aside with the tip of the poker, and she flipped open the doors of the cabinets under the sink, but there was no sign of the thing which had spooked her. At last she drained the tub, hating to waste all that hot water after so brief a soak but not about to risk getting back in, and as the suds shrank away, she waited to find the remains of the drowned creature.

It wasn't there. She rinsed the bath, the poker still held in her right hand, then replaced the plug, in case it had gone down the drain, though she didn't really believe that was possible. It had been too big.

When it was clear that the thing was gone, she returned to the living room and poured herself a glass of the brandy she kept—she was fond of saying—strictly for medicinal purposes. Then she went back into the bathroom and propped the window open, just in case, and called the exterminators. She wasn't sure what to call the thing she had seen, but they said they'd be by in the morning to lay down some boric acid and other deterrents.

At last, she put the TV on and watched a game show and the local news which finished with the Powerball drawing, but she didn't win. She never won, and the familiar feeling of annoyance soothed her, until she started to believe that she may have imagined the whole thing. Maybe she had been so tired and stressed from work that she had fallen asleep in the tub and the snaky thing with the legs had been nothing more than a nasty dream.

She said it aloud, because that made it true, then figured she'd get an early night just as soon as she'd had one more nip of the brandy to help her sleep. Even so, she made one last check of the house, poker in hand, before getting ready for bed, and she positioned the industrial-sized can of roach spray in easy reach, setting it alongside the poker. She seriously considered getting out her daddy's old shotgun, but she didn't want to be blowing holes in the walls, and she knew enough about guns to be wary of them.

Bernice took a while to get to sleep, partly because it was still light outside and she was still a little jittery, but she rehearsed the story in her head a few times, imagining how she would hold the Tidy Shack diners spellbound by her adventure (after they had finished eating, of course) and fell asleep smiling.

A little after three in the morning, she rolled over under the feathery duvet and put her hand on something hard. Her sleepy brain fished around in the recesses of memory and came up with...

The poker?

But it was way too wide for that.

And then it moved, a sudden, wriggling horror which snaked across her, its pointed feet scurrying over her bare legs, her stomach, her face.

Which was impossible. It hadn't been that long, had it?

Bernice fought to escape from the duvet and whatever was in there with her, but it writhed and twisted around her, the dread of the thing wiping her mind so that she couldn't think. Its antennaed head reared up in front of her face, mandibles flexing, and then it lunged at her neck. She felt the stab of pain and woke the street with her screaming.

6

S chool was buzzing again, this time with reports from kids whose relatives worked at the hospital in Hendersonville. Apparently, Bernice Sartovski, a waitress down at the Tidy Shack diner, had been rushed there after being attacked by something; by what was unclear.

"My mom said it looked like a snake bite," said Kyle Richards, "but bigger. Like, the fang marks were too deep and too far apart."

"The doctors were talking to the sheriff," added Sofie Collington, carefully, as if trying to recall the exact words. "Said there were deep puncture wounds on the victim's throat which were red and heavily swollen because of the venom."

"Is she gonna die?" asked Bobby, running his hand through his curly blond hair and not bothering to conceal his interest.

"They said the venom wouldn't be fatal in small amounts," said Sofie, expert witness. "But there was so much injected that they didn't know how the victim would react long term, or if her reaction was anaphylactic. She is now in stable but critical condition."

This—clearly rehearsed—speech sounded suitably impressive, and everyone nodded thoughtfully as if they knew what 'anaphylactic' meant.

"Where did you hear this?" asked Bobby.

"Oh, I have my sources," said Sofie.

"But here's the thing," said Kyle, not wanting to be outdone, "whatever tooth injected that venom had to be about three inches long. To be snake fangs—like from a copperhead or a rattler—the snake head would have to be, like, five or six inches across."

"That would make the snake ten, maybe fifteen feet long," said Tyler. "Ain't no poisonous snakes round here anything like that long. Sartovski must be lying."

"I wouldn't put it past her," Bobby agreed. "Last time I was in the Shack my burger was all burned and when I complained she said *she* didn't cook it. Like it wasn't her problem."

"Right," said Nathan with a wry smile. "It's a small step from being a sassy waitress to faking attacks from giant snakes."

There was one of those odd, silent moments when everyone tried to decide how to process what had just been said, before deciding it was a joke and laughing. I stiffened. I hadn't seen him approach and was immediately on my guard to see how he would treat me after my dad had torpedoed any chance of Nathan thinking I was cool. Bobby scowled.

"You think she's telling the truth about a giant snake in her bed?" he sneered. "Sounds to me like she had a nightmare and stuck herself with the poker."

"And the venom?" I asked, trying to look like I had been involved in the conversation from the start.

"How should I know?" Bobby shot back, glad of a more familiar adversary. "I leave the weird stuff to people like you, *Haideeky*."

Considering this a victory, he grinned at his pals and strutted away. Tyler went with him, with a wary backward glance at Nathan, as if he was still figuring out how to deal with the new boy.

"What a delightful person Bobby is," Nathan remarked, smiling, and this time the joke was clearer. "You think he might be capable of sneaking into the home of a waitress he didn't like and jabbing her with a poisoned poker?"

Another joke, greeted by laughter. I glanced at the others, DeMarcus and his sister among them, and you could feel how captivated they all were by him, how much they liked him and wanted him to like them. I couldn't blame them. The kid glowed with more than his California tan. Only Sofie seemed unimpressed, but then Nathan's dad had snagged the real estate her father had wanted to develop, so no wonder she didn't like him. I watched him, braced for how he would deal with me.

"Hey, Hideki," he said casually. "Sorry I couldn't stay. But you can tell your dad, that barbecue place was the real deal."

"Yeah?" I said, relief washing over me even as I saw DeMarcus' eyebrow arch with curious amazement. "Yeah," I repeated with more conviction, "it's pretty great."

"Totally," said Nathan.

And that was it, I was cool again. You could feel it in the group, as if some of Nathan's shine had rubbed off on me and everyone had to take a moment to adjust. That weird little half Japanese kid who burned the barn down was kicking around outside school with Nathan-freaking-West.

In your face, Tyler J. Miller the third!

"If it wasn't a snake," said Jason Blakely, "you think a person did this?"

He looked to Nathan for an answer, as if he might have the inside scoop, but Sofie Collington piped up.

"They only said snake because of the stab wounds. Bernice said it was more like a huge bug, one of those long ones with lots of legs, but the doctors didn't listen."

"Yeah," said Kyle, "we had them under our stairs: those skinny little things with al the legs. They're gross, but they are, like, a couple of inches long, three, tops."

My eyes flashed to Jason who had gone pale. I tried to give him an encouraging nod, but his face had sort of frozen up and he didn't seem to be able to see me.

"There must have been two of them," Sofie concluded. "Bernice said she saw one when she was in the tub, and it was big, but not as big as the one that attacked her in her bed."

"Two impossible bug-things in her house at the same time?" said Ayisha with a theatrical shudder. "I don't like that at all."

Well, who would?

I caught up with Emily in the pool after school where she had been swimming extra laps by herself and raised a disturbing possibility.

"So, not a snake, but too big for a bug," I said, squatting by the edge of the pool.

"What's your point?" she demanded, stripping the swim cap from her head and kicking to stay afloat. She seemed annoyed again. She always seemed annoyed lately: tired and irritable, though if you creep out in your fox form in the small hours, maybe that's to be expected. I didn't say so. I knew what kind of grief I'd get if she thought I was spying on her.

"That perhaps it's not local," I said, lowering my voice.

"Don't start, Caleb," she warned.

"I'm just saying that if we can't find a natural explanation, maybe we should consider some supernatural possibilities."

"This is nothing to do with us."

"But what if it is?"

"Look," she said, glaring at me even as she bobbed up and down in the water with each kick of her legs, "I know you like to feel special and all, and things have been kind of quiet lately, but that doesn't mean you have to start trying to make the town revolve around you again."

"Woah!" I exclaimed, stung, "where did that come from?"

"I'm just saying that you're not getting to do your superhero thing, that you're back to being loser Caleb…"

"Hideki," I corrected.

"Whatever. The point is that, in spite of your secret talents you're still the invisible man, and I get that that's annoying and you want to feel like you're at the center of things again, like when Maddie was taken, but that doesn't mean there's any reason to think that this stuff with Bernice has anything to do with you."

"With us," I said.

"With *you*," she said firmly. "It absolutely has nothing to do with me."

"So long as you can still turn into a fox you are still in this up to your furry neck," I shot back.

"What *this*? A woman got bitten by a snake or stung by a bug. It's not a demon invasion!"

"What if it is?" I replied, checking around the echoing pool to make sure there was no one else there. "What if—and hear me out here—this isn't actually a new invasion, but the end of the last one?"

She had been treading water, but now she got hold of the side and grew still.

"Meaning what?"

"We closed the rift in the cave," I said. "We resealed the mystic prison."

"Yes. Exactly. Job done."

"But it took time," I replied with forced patience. "Things escaped before we got the fissure closed. We defeated the things we knew had gotten out, but what if there were other things, and what if we didn't seal it as completely as we thought we did? Think about it. What could come through cracks that are almost too small to see?"

Emily considered this, frowning.

"Snakes," she said at last. "Bugs."

"Or their *yōkai* equivalent," I agreed. "Like the swarming roaches that came out of the Blakely family car and the improbably large and absolutely not local centipede-thing which attacked Bernice."

Emily blew out a long sigh. "Why do you always make things harder?" she asked.

"Another of my superpowers," I said. "But I'll bet money there are all kinds of slithery Japanese monsters in ancient folklore. We should ask Saito-san and Bachan. If anyone will know about this stuff, it's them."

A door banged open, and the swim team coach's voice boomed out.

"Out you get Smith. Got to lock up in time for the party."

"The West family event!" I exclaimed. "I'd forgotten that was tonight."

Emily's face which had been more like her old self moments before froze again. She took a breath, held it and thrust herself under the water for an unnervingly long moment.

7

The evening of the West's party had arrived with a hum of excitement across the whole of Portersville. Some people had secured their places quickly, keen to see what was going on at the old Haversham house, while others had taken longer to get caught up in the general frenzy of interest, and that had cost them.

"No spaces available!" exclaimed Candace Marks. "Can you believe it?"

"It's a big house," said Ayisha, "but it's still just a house. They had to set a limit on how many people could go. Wouldn't be safe otherwise."

"Why didn't they say that?" Candace wailed. "I told my Mom to get on it, but no: *I might have to work that night* and *I can't have you wandering into a stranger's house by yourself,*" she quoted in a sing-song voice. "Like there wouldn't be dozens of people I knew there. Now I'll be stuck at home watching it on TV."

"You won't," said Ayisha, shaking her head sadly. "No cameras, remember?"

"You can sneak your phone in though, right?" Candace urged. "I have to see that house!"

"We'll see," said Ayisha with a noncommittal shrug.

"You really going to try and sneak your phone in?" I asked as soon as Candace was gone.

"Nope," said Ayisha. "Video your host's place when they've expressly asked you not to? Not cool."

48

"But you said…"

Ayisha cut me off with a hard stare. "Because if I say no to Candace, she'll tell Sofie who will tell everyone else. Easier this way."

"Someone will sneak their phone in," I said.

"Totally," Ayisha agreed. "But it won't be me."

And as it turned out, no one got their phone inside, though several tried. The Wests had a metal detector installed in the front hallway, if you can believe that, and a pair of security guards checking pockets and purses. A couple of the local civil liberties nuts refused to go through a screening and were asked to leave, but for most folk, their curiosity beat out their outrage.

Still, the camera thing was a bit odd, though, as several people observed, these west coast tycoons were all crazy. Too rich. Too Hollywood. Who knew what they had been used to dealing with before coming to live here among "real people?" So we filed in as our numbers came up and all our skeptical cynicism was blown away bit by bit.

I am not kidding. It was a night such as Portersville had never seen before, and it began with the house itself. Like I said, there had never been much to see from the road: just a weedy driveway snaking back through trees toward the gloomy old mansion itself. But before the day of the event, Mr. West had crews working day and night, I guess, because when we woke up there was a pair of impressive brick gateposts topped with stone lions on either side of the drive, and all the overgrown vegetation had been trimmed and tidied up so that it looked symmetrical and imposing. I assume some of that work had been done during school hours, since I didn't notice it until it was done.

Neither did anyone else. We were, as people were fond of pointing out, at the unfashionable and mostly abandoned east end of town, so we didn't get many people coming out except to visit the store, but the speed and totality of the transition were all anyone could talk about as they lined up to go in.

The house had always had, as Dad said, good bones, but even he was amazed at the transformation, the way the architect had preserved everything that worked about the original and given it an elegant contemporary tweak. Based on my childhood memories I was amazed the place was standing at all, so I was completely unprepared for this understatedly swanky palace. It was a monument to comfortable sophistication and good taste inside and out, and—this was even stranger—everyone seemed to think so. No matter whether they thought the peak of domestic living was a log cabin or a high rise with a gold toilet, every single person agreed: this was the most impressive house they had ever seen.

Just so you can see it in your head, let me lay it out a bit. The marble hallway opened into a round room with white stone columns like you were entering an ancient Greek temple, but it was arranged with soft-edged chairs and brightly-colored couches. An elegant wooden staircase coiled up to the second story, the handrail trailing out from the mane of a dramatically carved horse which looked like it was cantering up from the hall. Its richly oiled timbers glowed with warmth, as if the wood was still alive. Display shelves hung improbably on walls without clear means of support, and potted plants of iridescent green laced themselves over surfaces and around architectural features. It felt like the wilderness had come in and made itself at home, but had been tamed in the process, made welcoming and full of a life which nurtured everyone who came inside.

Which is nuts, right? But that was how it felt. I'd never seen anything like it, except maybe in those ridiculous AI images of made-up houses people share online, and neither had anyone else. And everybody was there. I mean, *everybody*! In fact, the only person I knew who had decided not to attend was my sulky sister.

"I'm too busy with schoolwork," she had snapped a couple of hours before the rest of us headed over. "Plus, there's somewhere I have to be, and don't ask where because it's none of your business."

Her loss.

I saw Tyler's family standing by a grand piano, dressed like they were about to go golfing, looking around with wide-eyed envy, while Maureen Collington, wife of the Southern Shale CEO, was on a constant patrol, craning her neck to inspect every detail of every mantlepiece, alcove, and book case as if determined to find something out of place or poorly designed. I watched as her disappointment swelled like a gorged slug, before she rejoined her family with a tight little smile. She muttered something to her daughter, Sophia/Sofie, who stood a little taller but looked annoyed about doing so, and then went back to what she had been doing at the ranger station before the power cut, scanning the crowd with her head cocked slightly, as if directing her ears toward whichever nearby conversation might prove most instructive.

I knew none of the servers. They, like the architects and construction crews, the woodworkers and plumbers and electricians and carpenters, had all been brought in from out of town. No one in Portersville knew any of them, and before tonight's little soiree there had been a lot of resentful mutterings about that, and not just because people felt like they were missing out on a substantial payday.

"He thinks he's too good for the likes of us," Tommy Cricklock, the town's largest concrete and stone supplier, had said to Dad one day when he came into the store for propane. "Like we couldn't do the work to his standards!"

But now that I saw the place, the staff, the food, I suspected that Mr. Cricklock had inadvertently hit on the truth. No one in Portersville could have done this, not because they didn't have the materials or skills. They didn't have the imagination or—the word came to me as I gazed around the place—the vision. Maybe the Wests *were* a little Hollywood. The house, and the party within it, were like something out of a movie. And no, no one in town could have turned out that buffet with its prime rib bar, endless mini quiches, and dozens of other delicious things I could barely name, even as I wolfed them down. The dessert station looked like the final round of one of those TV baking shows, and the more I sampled, the hungrier I got.

I gazed around me, amazed, and for a split second I thought I caught a strange and unwelcome smell, like you get from water that has sat too long in the same place, the sourness of decay.

Probably still working on the septic system, I thought, *or a blocked drain in the grounds.*

But then I saw Mr. West, and I forgot the smell. Maybe I had imagined it.

Kieran West had the angular good looks he had passed on to his son, but what really struck me was that he had a sort of poise, which I realize is an odd thing to notice. But I watched him talking to people and marveled at how still he was most of the time, standing with his shoulders perfectly balanced over his feet like a tree which shifted slightly in high winds but remained firmly grounded, sure of itself. When he moved, it was with an economical efficiency, a lack of fuss or wasted effort, which was mesmerizing. He didn't hesitate or second guess himself. He gestured, picked things up, walked like a man who, in every moment, knew exactly what he wanted and how he was going to get it. By comparison, everyone else looked bumbling and clumsy.

He made easy conversation with his guests in the vast, granite-topped kitchen, the men laughing heartily and slapping each other on the backs in a kind of panicked joy, while their wives smiled and nodded, stopping just this side of curtseying. Mr. West was more than a businessman. He was, in ways I couldn't completely understand, royalty, and the fact that he was actually handing out bottles of beer himself, rather than relying on the army of servers he had employed for the evening, somehow managed to add to that impression rather than detract from it.

"How did he make his money again?" my mother asked without taking her eyes off him.

"Computers, I think," I said, though the house was surprisingly low tech, and I had seen no laptops or tablets anywhere. "Some kind of Silicon Valley tech. Why?"

"No reason," said my mother, still watching him. "He should run for President."

"Maybe he should start by being mayor," I said, eyeing Tyler's dad, pleased to note that the man looked uneasy. He and the Collington family had drifted together, with the Davenhams and the Blakelys: what Dad called Portersville's self-appointed movers and shakers. They were the only people in the place who didn't seem to be having the time of their lives. Brian Davenham, Bobby's dad, stood with his arms folded, nursing a beer bottle, shoulders thrown back and a half sneer on his face, as if waiting to be impressed. His wife, whose name I didn't know, was wearing an outlandish dress of bold colors which made her look like she had survived an explosion at a florist's. She was giving Maureen Collington shrewd looks, as if they were privately taking notes on everything and everybody and finding it all as they had predicted. Maureen had that distinctive focused look that said she was eavesdropping on a neighboring conversation.

"Looks like there's a new sheriff in town," said Dad. "Figuratively speaking. I think the actual sheriff might have had the same idea."

Sheriff Halpern, who I would normally expect to be orbiting the mayor like a minor moon, was gazing at Mr. West with the vacant smile of a fan meeting a rock star. I realized I hadn't seen Nathan and looked around for him, but there was no sign of him. Maybe he was going to make a big entrance. That would figure given the stagey glamor of everything. That increased when the pianist (live, of course) gave a little *chingaling* to attract our attention, and the house lights dimmed except for a single spot by the immense fireplace where Mr. West was picking up a microphone and turning with an easy smile to face the crowd. You could hear the hum of anticipation as surely as you could the static of the sound system. I've heard sports commentators saying "the atmosphere is electric" but I'd never felt it until that evening. Something was coming.

Kieran West waited for absolute stillness, like a conductor in front of a symphony orchestra, looking perfectly calm, unruffled, and in control.

"Thank you," he said finally, as the last of the whispering and giggling died away. "Not just for your attention, or for coming to our home, but for welcoming my family to your town. I have traveled widely and seen much of the world, but I can think of nowhere better or more hospitable than Portersville, North Carolina, to be my home for this next phase of my life."

I thought the wording of that a little odd, but everyone loved it. A spontaneous burst of applause erupted, punctuated by a few whoops and cheers. Whatever the local equivalent of 'patriotic' was, people were feeling it in spades, and that made them like him all the more. As I said, a lot of them had come out of curiosity or the promise of an open bar, but he had them now, and they hung on his every word.

"So it seemed appropriate to express my thanks in some palpable way, something deeper and more enduring than a little housewarming party."

There was a respectful chuckle at that. There was nothing "little" about the party, and I knew for a fact that most of the people there had never experienced anything like it.

"Good food, drink, and the company of friends—however new—well, you can't beat that, can you?" It was a rhetorical question, but people answered it anyway, some of them a little flush from the free booze. Mr. West, nodded, smiling still, and waited, then said, "I'd go so far as to say we don't need much more. Food, drink, and the friendly company of a good and supportive community. That's it, right there. All we need. But the modern world doesn't believe that. The modern world—and I know because I was one of those who built it—wants to distract you from those things, make you feel like you'll be happier, healthier, more secure if you buy whatever they are selling. You know what I mean. Cars, nice clothes, even big houses like this one." He smiled self-deprecatingly. "I'm not immune to those messages, even if I can see them for what they are. I just wish we could turn them off, you know?" he added, chatting, as if he was making this whole speech up as he went, like he was just talking to a friend over dinner.

"And then I had an idea," he said. "What if we could? The things that make us feel inadequate, needy, the things that distract us from what really matters. What if we could take all those things, put them in a little box, and close it forever. That would be good, right?"

There was less response to that. His earnestness was getting to people, and they focused intently on him, so that even the cheerful agreement had gone silent as they waited to see where this was all going.

"It has been like this for a while," he continued, "but lately that sense of distraction, of not being satisfied with what is right in front of us in reality, has gotten a whole lot worse, and I think I know why. You remember the other day when that storm came through and blew out the power? We were all getting on with our lives and suddenly—poof!—no wifi, no internet, no cell phones. And what did we feel then? Panic, right? A sense of disconnection, of being shut out of something. You know that phrase FOMO? Fear of missing out. That's what drives us so much of the time. The kids here know what I'm talking about, right? That sense that if you aren't keeping track of your phone all the time, you might not see the thing that everyone else is talking about, and then you won't be able to participate. You won't be relevant.

"But relevant to what? And missing what? Most of it is nonsense. And if it's real and important, a news story, say, would it not be better if it came to us *not* immediately, when no one knows what's really going on and we can be easily misled by speculation and craziness, but when people we trust have gathered the facts? The older folks will remember sitting down to listen to Walter Cronkite, or reading the news over breakfast in a printed newspaper coming from journalists who have been up all night making sure they got it right. Remember?"

Another murmur of approval from the parents there, cautious bafflement and a whiff of anxiety from the kids. Where was this leading?

"I think we have a crisis in American culture," he said. "We don't know what to believe, so we choose the angle we like and run with that. We can't talk to each other about the great issues of life, society, politics, because we have no shared floor of reference. We don't agree on the facts, so we can't possibly agree on what to do about them. And technology is only making things worse. You've heard about AI—artificial intelligence —right? Very useful in some areas of life, I am sure, but speaking as a software designer and engineer turned Silicon Valley billionaire—also incredibly dangerous. I'm not talking about the robots rising up and fighting us in the streets. I'm talking about our dependence on computers which have been trained to simulate reality so well that we can't tell what's real and what's made up. Is that a real bird in the picture you shared on your Instagram page, or is it a computer-generated mirage of something that doesn't exist? Is that really your favorite politician caught on video saying those appalling things, or is it AI? Who knows? And when we don't know, how do we decide what we believe, and how to act in response? I'll tell you. We don't. We act as if nothing is real. As if there is no such thing as truth or fact. It's all just perspective, right? While we are being distracted from the real, the machines—and the people who make money off them—are stealing your wisdom, your instincts, your souls. I know, because I was one of them."

The silence in the great room was growing restless now. People weren't sure what to think, but they were a lot less content than they had been a couple of minutes earlier.

"But there is a solution," said West, finding his smile again and turning it on like a lamp, "and it's a simple one which might solve some of Portersville's other problems. See, after the panic and anxiety when my cell phone died in the storm, I felt something else, and I'll bet some of you did too. I felt relief. I felt free. I didn't have to check my email because I couldn't. I couldn't check the news or see where I was being tagged on social media. There was a moment of worry, and then there was…peace. I could smell the rain on the tree branches. I could hear the storm overhead and it was just the world reminding me that so much of what I had grown used to caring about didn't matter. It was just a distraction from the real. And then I thought, what if I could live like this all the time?

"I've gone on too long," he said with a kind of shrug and an apologetic grin, "so here's the thing. I want to thank Portersville for accepting me, and I want to offer you something in return. I said before that it would be great to take all those distractions from the real world, put them in a box, and seal it up, but what I didn't say, is that you already have them in a box."

West reached into his pocket, pulled out a cell phone and held it up like it was something rare and strange.

"Your phones," he said. "All we need to do is get rid of them, and not just for tonight. We need to get back to the real, to the things that make a town like this the special place that it is, a place that will attract like-minded residents and businesses."

"In the coming weeks, I intend to draw up a proposal to go before the mayor and the town council proposing a significant influx of my personal capital into the town in return for the abolition of cell phones and the internet inside Portersville's city limits. Simple as that. It will save this town and could change the shape of the nation for the better."

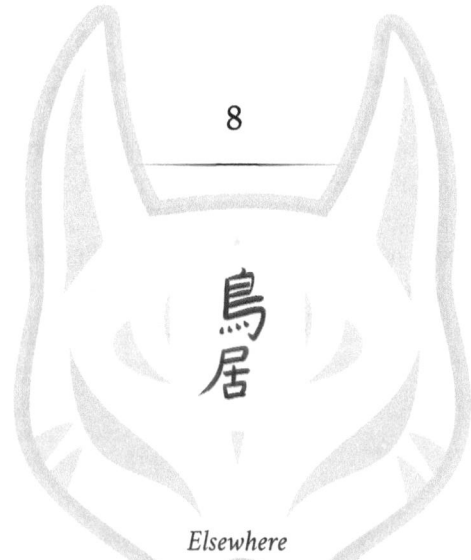

8

Elsewhere

Brian Davenham looked out of his office window at the rain which had blown in after the West's bizarre party, and the even more bizarre idea the California tycoon had raised about cutting the town off from the internet and cell phones. He thought about his son, Bobby, who would be mooching around downstairs, playing video games or texting his friends instead of doing his homework. Apart from playing football, Bobby wouldn't know what to do without his phone and his gadgets. But then Bobby rarely knew what to do…

Bobby was failing algebra. Or he should have been. Everyone knew it. He had, his wife said, a blind spot where numbers were concerned: a form of dyscalculia, a word she had been wheeling out with a manic determination since Bobby nearly failed basic arithmetic in middle school. Brian and his wife were also no good at math, but they didn't need to be because they could afford accountants.

Decades ago, Brian Davenham had sold his daddy's farm the moment he had inherited it and had invested in a local plastics firm which made disposable shopping bags, the kind you get offered at the grocery store checkout. Though there was now a movement to go back to paper bags, Brian had made his money in less environmentally anxious times, and he was keen to use it to ensure that his son's life was as easy as it could be, with or without math.

Family, right? It's what you do.

But it hadn't been easy. They had tried tutors, but Bobby resented being taught by his classmates, or even by recent graduates, and even taking extra classes from his math teacher, Mr. Lewisson, hadn't moved the needle on Bobby's scores. In private, Brian didn't think Lewisson was much of a teacher, but he was the one assigning his son's final grades so Brian couldn't afford to tell him what he really thought.

The solution had appeared six months ago when Brian had met with Lewisson after Bobby had bombed another midterm. He had gone in as close to all guns blazing as he dared, demanding why Bobby haven't improved at all despite the quite costly tutoring sessions, but Lewisson had been unmoved.

"He's not doing any better because he won't do the work," said Lewisson flatly.

"What do you mean he isn't doing the work?" Brian demanded. "He shows up, doesn't he? Sits in your office after school, comes over to your house for extra sessions?"

"Yeah," said Lewisson, taking off those heavy black glasses which Brian thought made him look like a pretentious owl and polishing them on his shirt, "but he just sits there. His brain isn't engaged, either in school or in private sessions, and I can't change that. I walk him through every problem, but he just makes dumb jokes, and the moment I leave him alone to work, he's playing on his phone. I can't make him learn if he doesn't try."

In his heart of hearts, Brian found this all too easy to believe, but he wasn't about to admit that to the teacher. "I'm paying you fifty bucks an hour!" he exclaimed.

"You could pay me a thousand," Lewisson retorted. "It wouldn't change how much of the lesson he absorbed because he just doesn't care."

That little chance phrase of Lewisson's had changed the conversation, though Brian was never sure if the teacher had intended it as a hint. "I guess I could pay you a thousand dollars," said Brian cautiously, watching the other man's eyes.

"I just said, it wouldn't make a difference," said the teacher.

"To what he learned, no," said Brian. "But when it comes right down to it, what he actually learns matters less than how he scores. On tests and such. What matters, especially for college, is his GPA. You are his math teacher. I know what you guys pull down a year, and it can't be easy, even in a place like Portersville. I expect an extra grand or two from time to time could really help smooth things over."

"Won't change his SAT scores," said Lewisson. "I don't grade those."

Brian smiled, knowing the battle was already won. "SATs matter less and less," he said with a dismissive wave. "Half the colleges out there don't take them into account, and I can always get someone to write a letter saying Bobby doesn't test well."

Lewisson had licked his lips, but otherwise did not move, and by the end of the conversation had quietly agreed to a couple of thousand-dollar payments on the eve of Bobby's major exams. That had been six months ago, and though Bobby still needed both hands to figure out how many points his football team needed to win, his grades had been flawless.

Payments were made in cash to avoid any unfortunate cyber trail. Brian Davenham didn't trust computers and had long since determined that used bills were considerably harder to track than secret accounts and digital deposits. They met at Brian's place, away from prying eyes because Brian said the idea of his going to the math teacher's little ranch house on Lower Lane was socially implausible. Lewisson hadn't liked that but had wanted the money too much to debate the point.

So Brian sat in his office on the second floor of his house in the Magnolia Park subdivision over on the west side of town, considering the bright, soulless eyes of the various animal heads he had mounted on the walls. Brian had always been a deer hunter, but a few years ago he had taken the chance to go trophy hunting in South Africa, returning with the heads of a spectacular kudu with long, spiral horns and a black wildebeest. It was amazing what you could do legally if you had a few thousand dollars to burn.

His golfing buddy and local real estate magnate, Ron Blakely, had done the deal for the house, and Brian's wife, Glennis, had overseen the decoration—of every room except the office/ trophy room—personally. Glennis knew about the payments Brian was making to Bobby's math teacher, and though she had made faces and urged her son to make more of an effort, she had eventually gone along with it, though she now pretended it didn't happen.

She was careful not to meet Lewisson when he turned up at their house after dark twice a semester and had actually bought Bobby a cake when he aced his first exam, even though she knew that his efforts had had nothing to do with the grade. Tonight, when the doorbell rang, she stayed pointedly in the living room with the door closed and the TV volume up high, so that even upstairs Brian could hear the news reports about the West party and his lunatic anti-internet ideas over the rumbling of thunder and the drumming of rain on the roof.

Bobby showed Lewisson upstairs, smirking as he opened the door and melting back into the gloom of the hallway outside with a snide "Enjoy," that almost made Brian rethink the whole arrangement. He gazed out of the window, but it was dark and rainy outside, so he could make out nothing beyond the leaves of the sugar maple they had planted too close to the house. He realized in that vague, surprised kind of way, that despite cramming his face with Kieran West's canapes and prime rib buffet, he was ravenous.

Get this over with, he thought, *and I'll see if Glennis can be talked into making a sandwich...*

He scowled, and remembering the teacher's hovering presence, turned to him.

Lewisson looked even shabbier than usual, his jacket dripping from the storm, but there was something stiff about his manner which rang some of Brian's internal alarm bells. When he declined the opportunity to sit, Brian was sure something was up. He reached for the envelope in the wall safe anyway and put it on the desk between them.

"I gotta say," Lewisson began, avoiding his gaze, "that I'm having second thoughts about all this. It doesn't feel right."

Because it isn't, Brian almost said, *but you knew that from the get go.*

Instead, he put on a puzzled look and cocked his head. "How so?" he said.

"I'm a teacher!" said Lewisson, still standing, still performing the idea that—despite all evidence to the contrary—he had some backbone after all. "It's not fair to the kids who do the work. Tests should be an even playing field where everyone has a shot at doing well or doing badly. It's not right."

Brian nodded sympathetically, but the smile didn't reach his eyes, and when he spoke it was in a low, calculated tone, reasonable, and without emotion. "You are right, of course," he said, "but it's rather late for qualms of conscience, wouldn't you say, Harold?"

Lewisson flinched at the sound of his first name, something Brian had never used before, but just shook his head, saying nothing.

"I mean," Brian continued, "you can't, as they say, put the toothpaste back in the tube."

"What do you mean?" said Lewisson, mustering a little defiance. "I can refuse all future payments, and Bobby can take the tests like everyone else."

"Well, he was already taking the tests, wasn't he Harold?" Brian said smoothly. "The issue was how you graded them."

"Well, perhaps, but my point is that going forward..."

"We will continue exactly as we have been doing," Brian cut in. "Because if we don't, I'll be forced to report you for taking bribes, breach of public trust, violation of professional ethics, and a host of other offenses which will cost you rather more than your job."

For a moment, there was only the sound of the storm, drowning out even the TV from downstairs. Lewisson stared at him, and for a moment, his eyes behind those absurd glasses seemed to swim.

"But I am trying to stop, to do the right thing..." he babbled.

"I think you'll find that the school and its overseers will consider that too little too late. But I'll tell you what. To ease your pangs of conscience, how about we raise this month's payment to a nice one thousand five hundred? What do you think? Can't say fairer than that, can you?"

Lewisson, hands clasped in front of him, eyes lowered and brimming, nodded hastily. "That would be... Yes," he managed. "Thank you."

Brian made a show of opening his wallet, removing five crisp hundreds and casually slotting them into the envelope. He offered it to the teacher with an easy smile, holding it just far away from him that he had to reach for it.

It was in the moment that he did so that Brian felt something strange, something wrong. He turned quickly to the window and there, ghastly pale and pressed up against the glass, was a face.

Which was impossible. It was too high up, unless someone was on a ladder...

It was blurry, distorted by being pressed up against the rain-streaked window pane, but even so there was something ghastly about the face. Something not quite human. The mouth lolled hungrily open, and the eyes were focused and malevolent.

Brian recoiled, almost falling out of his chair, and in that instant, the head pulled back from the window, withdrawing into the rainy night in ways no person on a ladder could possibly do.

As Lewisson babbled questions and moaned his terror and panic at being caught in the act, Brian surged toward the window. Frustrated by the glare on the glass, he snapped the catches back and raised the sash.

Rain blew in and stung his face, but by the ornamental lights on either side of the house's front door, he could just make out a figure standing below, its face turned away and facing the street. How it had been up against the window a moment before, he couldn't say, but confusion or fear had never mastered Brian Davenham's defiance, and it spilled out of him now.

"Who's there?!" he bellowed into the storm. "What do you think you are doing on my property? I'm calling the sheriff and charging you with criminal trespass..."

Only then did the figure turn, its head rotating and tilting weirdly so that Brian hesitated. In the next moment, the head leapt up toward him, its neck snaking out behind, its eyes flashing with rage and its mouth shrieking.

Brian leapt back but with the presence of mind to slam the window down. For a second, the monstrous head seemed to worry at the outside of the sill with its teeth, as if trying to tear it open again, but Brian snapped the clasps in place to lock it and backed unsteadily out of the room, the teacher staggering clumsily after him.

Brian slammed the door behind him and stood in the dim hallway aghast, listening to the buffeting of the head against the window.

"Take it," said a wide-eyed Lewisson, thrusting the envelope of cash into Brian's unwilling hand. "I don't want to hear from you ever again."

Then he was bounding down the stairs and into the rain-swept night, an act which—given what they had seen was out there—was more courage than the teacher had shown in his entire life.

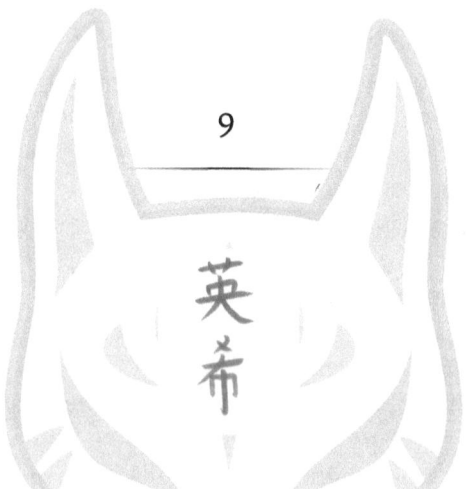

9

T urning our backs on phones, the internet and—effectively—the modern world? It was insane.

So why didn't everyone else seem to think so?

Suddenly, every kid at school was recounting conversations with their parents and older family members in which the horrors of life before TikTok, before Facebook, before even something called Myspace, were being hailed as the good old days when everyone knew who they were, the sun shone, and you always got change from a nickel. It was genuinely bizarre. The kids themselves were mostly confused with a side order of freaked, but it seemed like Kieran West had cast a spell over the town's Boomers and Gen Xers, the upshot of which was that his proposal was actually being taken seriously.

Even my parents were discussing it like it might be a good thing.

"He's pledging support to both local newspapers so they can hire full writing staffs again," said Dad, looking up from the stove and nodding at the open copy of the Chronicle on the counter, "and promising zero editorial oversight."

"And how long will that last?" snarled Em, who had been conspicuously absent from the party and had responded to news of Mr. West's proposal with frank disdain. The new subject of town gossip had done nothing for her mood. "One person funding the only news coverage in the area? That's a conflict of interest waiting to happen."

"There'll still be Action News," said Dad. He had our biggest stock pot on the stove and was sprinkling ingredients in as he stirred intermittently.

Mr. West had also offered "no strings attached" financial support for the local TV and radio stations.

Em snorted in derision. "You know Kieran West has already made a substantial donation to Tyler Miller's mayoral reelection campaign?" she said.

"Where did you hear that?" asked Dad.

"Sofie Collington," said Em. "Got it from her mom."

"We don't listen to gossip," said Mom.

"We do when it's obviously true," Em fired back.

Mom didn't seem to hear her. "Might not be so bad," she mused. "Going back to simpler times."

"What is with you people?" said Emily, real anger flashing through her eyes. "You can't just snap your fingers and make it the sixties."

"Hey, don't be mocking the sixties," said Dad, stirring his pot. "A lot of great stuff came out of that decade, or do I have to make you listen to every Beatles album again?"

"And there was the moon landing," said Mom, looking nostalgic.

"Were you even born then?" Emily demanded. "And what about the assassination of the Kennedys, Martin Luther King, Malcom X...?"

"Okay, so it wasn't perfect," said Dad, "but at least when you turned the TV off the world was silent. We weren't *on* twenty-four hours a day."

"I don't know what that means," said Emily dismissively.

"Well maybe we give it a try and find out," said Mom.

"While the rest of the world moves on and Portersville—a town with no significant industry—falls back into the dark ages?" Emily replied.

"No internet is hardly medieval," said Dad, dipping a spoon into his pot and sampling the dark fluid within approvingly. "Might help us reprioritize. And Mr. West says it will bring a lot of income."

"By disconnecting from the world's basic marketing system. How's that going to work?"

"New kinds of investment into older crafts," said Dad, as he began lining up glass jars and ladling the sweet and aromatic contents of the pot into them. "This was a woodworking hub for decades until the world got caught up in cheap, mass-produced crap. We can offer hand-crafted wood products, fabrics, artisan goods of all kinds. Mr. West says tourists will flock to a place like this to get a break from the rat race: unwind and decompress. Maybe we'll make money selling our family recipe barbecue sauce. Here, try this."

He held out a spoon, but Emily ignored him.

"I assume we'll be growing all the ingredients ourselves?" she said with withering scorn. "What else can we look forward to in our rush to rejoin the past? Will we be allowed to use wheels? Antibiotics?"

"Mr. West says people are craving a step back to old values..."

"Oh, if Mr. West says it, then it must be true," Em snapped.

"I don't think you are giving him a fair shake," Dad said. "Maybe you should go to the next town hall meeting and listen to what he's proposing."

"Think I'll pass," said Emily. "Now, if you don't mind, I have to do my computer science homework, unless Mr. West has decided that school will just teach basket weaving and butter churning."

She stomped out. Dad watched her go, still holding out the spoonful of sauce and looking momentarily deflated. He gave me a look.

"You're quiet, Caleb," he observed. "No thoughts to share?"

I considered the question seriously. "Not yet," I said.

Because the truth was, I didn't know what to think. On the one hand, the idea of trying to turn the clock back like this seemed suicidally risky for a town as economically strapped as Portersville, let alone the strangeness of cutting ourselves off from the constant stream of cyber activity. But I didn't know enough about business to know whether Mr. West's ideas for a remade Portersville tapping into a hunger for a simpler life made sense or not, and of all the kids at school, I'd be one of the ones who missed the web least.

I was mostly quite happy with talking to my friends, with books, with walking in the mountains, looking at birds and all the other stuff that meant I was about as uncool as a borderline superhero could be. I barely used social media, and though I knew there would be things I would miss if we cut the digital cord, it didn't seem as big a deal to me as it did to Em, who was always hooked in and active, and not just because she was a whiz with computers.

I didn't know what to think.

That evening, as Dad packaged the first batch of what he was calling Smiths' Smoking Sauce, I trained with Saito-san, the tengu, and in between sparring sessions I asked him what he thought of Mr. West's odd plans for the town.

"I like it," he said solemnly. "Get back to the old ways. I see no need for all this technology."

"Wouldn't you miss your phone?" I asked.

"Don't have one," he replied, eyeing the edge of his wooden sword blade critically.

Of course he didn't. Saito was old school, and I'm talking about a school that had been bulldozed in the Edo period. He was probably not exactly impartial or representative on the question of jettisoning the internet. He caught the realization in my eye.

"What?" he demanded. "New is not necessarily better."

"Neither is old," I said.

He scowled at that, his massive eyebrows hunching like giant furry caterpillars. "You don't trust him?" he asked.

"I don't know," I said simply. "I mean, I get what he's worried about, tech-wise, echo chambers, AI misinformation and such like, but I don't see us fixing the problem by banning cell phones."

He looked at me blankly, and I knew he had no idea what I was talking about which was, ironically, the best argument he had made so far. I matched his frown, minus the caterpillar eyebrows, of course.

"But don't you think it's weird?" I asked, setting my practice sword down on the tatami floor of the dojo. My eyes slid to the old books he kept shelved at the far end, their spines marked with Japanese characters I couldn't read. A suit of ancient samurai armor with a scary face mask complete with bristling mustache glared at me. "I mean, this guy shows up out of nowhere and wants to completely redefine the town, and everyone seems to go along with it. Don't you think it's strange?"

"As I understand it," said the tengu sitting back on his haunches, "the town council is still in its fact-finding stage, and there will probably be some kind of local referendum before anything actually happens."

"But we're talking about it!" I exclaimed. "Like it's a serious thing. Like it makes enough sense to discuss it and maybe act on it."

"You don't think it makes sense?"

"I think it's weird!" I shot back, feeling confused and stupid, "and I think it's super weird that no one else thinks it's weird!" Not exactly a brilliant argument, I know, but it just spilled out of me as if it had been simmering for days and finally came to a boil.

Saito considered me gravely. "You think something supernatural is going on?" he asked.

It wasn't dismissive or sarcastic. He said it like he was taking the idea seriously not in spite of my irrational passion but because of it.

"No!" I said. "Yes. Maybe. I don't know. Could it be?"

He bowed his head and half closed his eyes. It was always amazing to me that a man with such an absurd nose could command such authority.

"Portersville is not an ordinary town," he observed. "Our presence here demonstrates that. We resealed Raiko's mystical prison, but we knew there was a chance that other *yōkai* had escaped, or that there might be future attempts to reopen it."

"So it's possible," I concluded. "That's what I said to Em!"

"But what would a *yōkai* want with a town cut off from the internet?"

"They are old, like you," I said. "No offense. Maybe they want to rebuild a world closer to what they know."

Saito shook his head doubtfully. "It is too elaborate and complicated a plan for such a slender purpose," he said. "Weeks, maybe months of planning and dealing with human institutions such as local government, for the purpose of nostalgia? No. Cutting Portersville off from the digital world might feel like a big thing to you, but for ancient beings like me, it is nothing. Maybe it makes the town closer to what it was a few decades ago, but that is a mere blink of an eye to *yōkai* and it does not make the place any more Japanese. I would be amazed if a *yōkai* even knew what the internet was. I have lived among humans for generations but I have, as you have been quick to point out, almost no knowledge of or interest in it."

He had a point.

"Now we return to our practice," he announced with finality.

I frowned, annoyed by the way he closed down things he decided weren't interesting or relevant. Privately I decided to get my own back during our sparring, though that would be a first. In spite of all my speed, agility and strength, I still found it almost impossible to beat Saito-san.

Today was no exception. However much I leapt supernaturally high and danced out of his reach, I couldn't get a clear strike on him, and the more frustrated I got, the worse things went. In one pass he parried my cut deftly and finished with a precise lunge of his wooden sword, which caught me square in the throat, leaving me doubled up and gagging. I caught a glimpse of myself in the mirror the tengu sometimes set up for gauging form and posture, and my annoyance blossomed.

"What is the point of me training with a sword if it's no use against yōkai?" I demanded as soon as I could speak again.

The tengu gave me his trademark scowl. "The sword is the best weapon in your arsenal," he said. "You must learn to wield it."

"But when I fought the *oni* the sword was useless," I reminded him. "It broke on his skin."

"The *oni* was a special case," said the tengu. "He was protected by many enchantments. The only weapons which could hurt him were those once wielded by his great enemy, your ancestor."

"Which is exactly my point," I replied. "You are training me to use a sword which, when it comes right down to it, might well be useless. I'd be better with a machine gun."

"Americans," said the tengu with infinite disdain. "You think a *yōkai* which is impervious to the edge of a katana would be vulnerable to a hail of bullets? You know nothing."

"Then tell me," I reposted. "What should be my go-to move if I'm really up against it."

His eyes filled with irritated confusion. *"Go-to move?"* he echoed, baffled. *"Up against* what?"

"I mean what happens if I find myself fighting something like the *oni* and he doesn't happen to be carrying the one weapon that will kill him?"

The tengu nodded solemnly, finally acknowledging the validity of what I had been saying. "Raiko's sword is lost," he said. "His tanto—the knife you used—was entombed with the *oni* when you slew him."

"Okay," I said. "And he didn't have any other magic weapons that you forgot to tell me about?"

The annoyance flashed in his eyes again, but he took a breath, and just as he opened his mouth to deliver another lesson or a reprimand, something caught in his mind and he hesitated.

"What?" I demanded.

"It is probably nothing," said the tengu. "Forget it."

"How can I, you haven't told me what it is yet?"

Saito took another breath, longer this time, and when he breathed it out it was loaded, like a sigh.

"Raiko wielded many weapons," he said at last. "Most he had with him in Japan when he died. Somehow, after his battle which opened the mystical prison in which the *yōkai* were bound, the *oni* came to be in possession of his tanto. I saw that it was missing from his inventory when he was laid to rest in Yamanashi."

Again he hesitated.

"And?" I pressed.

"That inventory included a set of three shuriken. They are..."

"Like throwing stars, right? I saw them in a show about Ninjas."

The tengu winced and he made a "not really" gesture with his hand. "These are not stars," he said. "They are small, flat-bladed throwing knives made of iron."

"And they were missing from his inventory?" I said, feeling my excitement spike.

"Just one of them," said the tengu. "The other two were in their case. The third must have been lost during his fight which ended in the mystical prison."

"Here," I said, "in Portersville."

"Or close to it," he said, "possibly."

As you may recall, Raiko had fought the ogre-like *oni* in an alternate dimension which he had entered from Japan but which emerged here, in the mountains of North Carolina. My grandfather had come here to guard the entrance, but nothing happened for close to a century, and my mother had assumed that it was all fairy tale stuff. Then Em and I were called upon to prevent the ogre's escape a month or so ago, and suddenly it was all very real.

"Hereabouts, but you don't know where exactly," I said.

"I do not. It could have been lodged in the *oni*'s body or in one of his *yōkai* deputies."

"I didn't see it," I said.

"Then it is probably embedded in a tree somewhere in the mountains or left to rust in some creek where it fell during his final battle."

"I get it," I said, "it's lost. It may not exist at all, but if it does, it could be here, one of Raiko's magic..."

"Sacred," the tengu corrected me.

"Okay, one of Raiko's sacred weapons," I mused, feeling the thrill of the possibility. "Imagine what it could do! I'm going to find it."

"Impossible," said the tengu with a dismissive shake of his head. "Even if it exists, it could be anywhere! You could not find it, and trying is a waste of time."

"There has to be a way," I said. "Some form of divination which could lead me to it. If nothing else, I could go out with a metal detector..."

"Learn the sword," said the tengu. "Do not believe that luck and magic weapons..."

"Sacred weapons," I cut in.

"...can replace work and a studied skill," Saito concluded.

I gave him a long look, then shrugged and nodded.

"Okay," I said. "I'll learn the sword."

But in the privacy of my head, I made a decision. If that shuriken was out in the woods somewhere, I was going to find it.

I mulled over how I might start searching for it as I traipsed back home, using a back road that bypassed the town center: I didn't want people asking too many questions about what I was doing every other evening over at the *Hibachi Prince, Asian Steakhouse and Sushi*. One side were the backs of the house on Montrose Street—mostly fences and the rear walls of garages and garden sheds—while on the other was a tree-lined embankment where one of the old railway lines ran. Beyond that was the steep climb into the mountains and forest proper. I never saw anyone back here. It was a good place to spot deer and, if you were very lucky, bobcat. So it was a surprise to feel like I was being watched. I glanced around, slowing slightly, but saw no one. The yard to my left had a chain link fence and I could see the house some hundred yards away, but I caught no sign of anyone in its windows. Lights were on and I thought I saw the shifting glow of a TV, but nothing to suggest anyone was looking in my direction.

Probably just imagining it.

I kept walking, trying to drag my mind back to the question of Kieran West and his plans for a retro-Portersville, but I couldn't shake the feeling that someone—or something—had eyes on me. I scrutinized the tree line, but it was too deep to see more than a couple of yards into the dense, wooded shade. I considered pushing through the trees and walking along the railway line instead, since it ran roughly parallel to the road I was on now, but the prospect of not being able to see the houses spooked me a bit.

So I pressed on. One of the backyards up ahead was surrounded not with chain link or the kind of wooden rails you see round horse paddocks, but with a high wall-like fence of wooden slats between tall posts. One of the posts was different: higher than the others, its top somehow misshapen like something was sitting on it.

Owl, I thought.

That might explain the sense of being watched. I slowed to a stop. About fifty feet away, it was silhouetted against the evening sky. I could see no details. I guessed it was about the size of a watermelon, so maybe a barred owl, maybe a great horned, though I couldn't see the ear tufts. I stood still, not wanting to startle it, and it shifted, revolving slightly. The movement bothered me. It didn't seem owlish at all, and though I knew it had moved, the shape was wrong. But if it wasn't an owl, I couldn't think of what it might be. A possum or raccoon, maybe, carefully balanced on the top of the post with its clawed feet? It was too dark to see.

But I could feel it looking at me, and I didn't like it.

The hairs on the back of my neck were prickling and a sudden chill ran through me. All my instincts said, not owl, not possum, or any other animal.

And as that thought came to me, it slid down behind the fence and out of sight. The movement was strange: not a jump or a clamber. It lowered itself smoothly behind the fence, as if I had seen only a head, though the fence was seven feet high. Someone standing on a step ladder?

Maybe, but then why say nothing? Why be back here in the first place?

I swallowed and started walking again, faster now, eager to be gone, but I forced myself to stop when I got to where the strange, watchful object had been. There I made a standing jump, the kind I couldn't do before becoming Raiko's heir. It took me up to the top edge of the fence which I seized with both hands, locking my elbows and holding myself in place so that I could scan the backyard.

Someone was walking away, hunched over so much that their hands almost touched the ground. Whoever it was had their back to me, and they were wearing an unseasonably long coat, so I wasn't even sure if it was a man or a woman. But I saw no ladder, no steps, no obvious explanation for how they had been watching me over a seven-foot wall.

But yeah. Just a person.

So why are the hairs on my arms sticking up like I am standing in a cold draft?

A good question, but one I couldn't answer, and as the hunched figure vanished into the shade of the houses, I calmed down. After all, what I saw was clearly no giant snake or centipede. This was a human being, probably a regular Portersville resident putting the garbage out or walking a dog. Admittedly, I hadn't seen a dog, but if it wasn't leashed, I suppose it could have been the thing which had been watching me, if there was a way for it to get up the wall. Then it had scampered back inside leaving only its owner to make his or her slow way back inside...

That sounded plausible enough.

And yet...

I couldn't quite convince myself. Something still felt...off. I made for home running a little faster than most regular kids could manage. It was stupid of me, and could have raised awkward questions if anyone saw, but I felt a very real need to be somewhere far from this place.

Late that night, I woke from a dream where the thing I had seen peering at me over the fence was pressed up against my window. I sat up, sweating, and when the prospect of the thing coming back into my dream made me wary of going back to sleep, I got Saito-san's mirror out and considered my face in it hoping for a glimpse of something unusual.

Nothing. Just my own bleary-eyed face reflected back, fuzzy around the rim where the polished tin or whatever coated the bronze surface was tarnished. I wasn't sure what I had hoped to see, but I was disappointed. Somehow it felt like the perfect image of how little I understood. If something was going on in Portersville, I didn't have any clue what it was, and all my ancient abilities were useless. I couldn't fight what I couldn't see, couldn't target enemies I didn't recognize.

At last, too restless for sleep, I snuck downstairs for some juice. Which was when I saw it. Emily's nightgown, fluttering softly from the lowest limb of the dogwood by the back door.

She was out again.

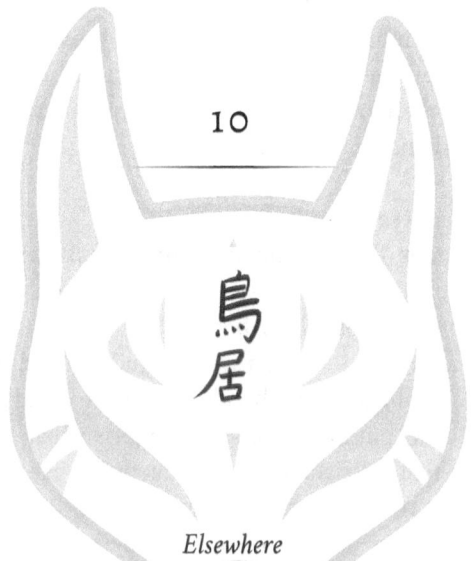

10

鳥
居

Elsewhere

DeMarcus Murphy switched up a gear and pedaled harder, eyes flicking between the digital stopwatch on his handlebars and the dirt trail which wound up through the woods. His record for this route was seventeen minutes twelve seconds, but—though he had started slowly from the railway crossing—he felt sure he could shave thirty seconds or more off that as he got higher.

The problem with the other members of the football team was that they did the same regimen all the time: same laps, same weights, same wind sprints. Cycling gave some of his over worked upper body muscles a rest while burning some serious cardio.

He checked his heart monitor: 145 bpm and climbing.

Faster, he thought. *Push it.*

The music in his headphones cranked louder, lifting his spirits and his energy. It was some Japanese band he had heard Caleb's sister listened to called the Oral Cigarettes, though what other kind there were, he wasn't sure. He didn't understand the words, of course, but the intense, high-octane songs were great to cycle to. Caleb was musically pretty clueless, but since his turn to All Things Japanese, he had learned enough to get him the names of some decent bands. DeMarcus hadn't mentioned any of them to Emily yet, but he would eventually.

Focus, he reminded himself.

He pushed the pedals harder, building a rhythm as his bpm hit 150. There was a tricky bend in the trail, one that concealed a log which had been set lengthways into the path like a step to prevent erosion. The first time he had rounded the turn at speed he had come off, surprised by the sudden drop, and the next time he had ridden this way he had lost valuable time cautiously navigating round it.

Not this time.

This time he was ready for it.

He ducked under the trailing limb of an oak, banked hard as he entered the bend, then lifted himself out of the saddle as the bike shot over the log, both wheels briefly airborne.

He landed perfectly, not losing a second, and grinned to himself.

This was going to be a record-breaking run. He could feel it.

He crouched low, pulling his body in tight so that he was an arrow with virtually no wind resistance, and he kept his eyes on the trail as it wound through the rocks and trees. There was a skittering in the underbrush ahead, and an assortment of bugs rushed out, parting as he rode through.

Gross, he thought, half turning to see what they were up to, then remembering he had a record to break.

Stay on it, he urged. *Eyes front.*

Which is why he didn't see the thing coming out of the underbrush only ten yards behind him, the long, impossible thing with searching antennae and too many legs. It raced after him, winding between the tree trunks, rattling across the carpet of dead leaves and pine straw, loud enough to be heard half a block away.

But DeMarcus had Emily's jangly J-rock blaring in his ears and his eyes were fixed on the clay trail, so he saw and heard nothing of the beast which snaked through the vegetation to his left, matching his speed.

At the pinnacle of the trail, DeMarcus checked the stopwatch. He had caught up to his best time, and—if he could maintain this pace—would beat it on the descent, maybe by a minute or more. There was a gulley in the center of the track, washed deep by snow melt and the recent storms, and his tires hit it like they were entering a chute. His eyes watered as he fought not to blink; he knew there were rocks and roots which would send him sprawling. He was picking up speed as the path began its steep drop toward town. He checked the stopwatch, but it was flashing randomly, spitting up partial figures in a jumble of digital fragments.

He scowled, irritated. If it didn't fix itself soon, he wouldn't know how fast the ride had been.

But he was going to give it all he had regardless.

There was only one more variable now: the traffic on the old Hendersonville Road. If he tore out into the path of a truck, he was toast, but if he had to wait, that was his record up in smoke.

That was the danger he knew of. The other was still coming after him, feelers flicking, black eyes as fixed on DeMarcus as his were fixed on the trail. Its scarlet head was as big as a wolf's now and the segments of its body trailed behind it as long as any alligator, but fast on those sharp, yellow legs. It seemed to roll and weave as it poured through the woods, mouth parts flexing and clicking in anticipation.

DeMarcus hit the base of the trail at a full sprint, lifted himself as the bike skidded through a broad puddle and plowed across the standing storm water which plumed up around him. Then he leaned left as the opening in the trees ahead showed the blacktop of the highway.

Come on, no trucks, he whispered between his teeth. *No trucks!*

He braked, and checked over his left shoulder, seeing the bright, massive front of the eighteen-wheeler hauling its way toward him. Followed by another. And another.

No!

He cursed, braking harder now so that his wheels skidded and sprayed grit as he slid to a brutal, record-stalling halt.

The first trucker saw him and blew his horn in warning.

"Yeah, yeah," DeMarcus replied, turning from the rush of wind as the machine roared past. "I see you."

He still didn't see the beast in the trees, however. It was half coiled round the base of a pine, poised to strike. But it too hesitated, momentarily daunted by the screaming bellow of the truck. The beast didn't know what that thing was and didn't want to get caught under those massive wheels. It clung to the tree, its gaping jaws dripping, but then the truck was thundering away and the boy on the bike was zipping after it.

The thing which had been chasing him found a furrow beside the road and threw itself into the long grass, flattening its glistening body and probing the earth with its forelegs. The hunger burned in it, but it hadn't been fast enough to catch the boy on his wheels. It would be soon, but it needed to eat first. It scraped at the earth, parting the dusty soil, then the solid clods of red clay, still slick and malleable from the rain. It sampled them, then began to dig. In seconds its whole body was a surging, whipping scramble of legs burrowing into the ground and safety. There would be a time when it would be too big, too powerful to fear the exposure of daylight, but it wasn't there yet.

So it dug through the clotted earth and the roots of grass, kudzu, red cypress, and the other trash trees that sprang up along the Carolina highways, and when it was safely out of sight, it tunneled, smelling as it went. The bugs came after it, stirred like fragments of iron by a passing magnet, sweeping unwillingly after it, their primitive insect minds awed and terrified at once. It moved north, then west, then slowed, tasting something in the dirt, something that promised food, specifically meat.

It came up, a thrusting, scrambling push to the surface, the promise of a meal outweighing all concerns about exposure. As it burst from the ground, startling its prey, the beast hissed its terrible delight and set upon them, stabbing, seizing, tearing, feasting on blood and flesh, one after another, and another, until its awful hunger was satisfied.

And as it gorged itself, filling what had been empty, it wondered vaguely what it was, what it was there to do beyond eat. In the moment, it was too drunk on blood and flesh to care, but it would remember eventually, and that, for Portersville, would be very bad indeed.

11

I was on my way home from school the day after my almost encounter with the watcher behind the fence, opting to take the slightly longer way home so I got to walk past the Haversham house —now the West mansion. It was sheer nosiness on my part, but that hardly made me unique. Everyone in Portersville who wasn't gossiping about giant snakes was gossiping about the Wests, their party, and their money. They were just so different from the people I had known all my life, and though it embarrassed me to admit it even to myself, the lure of their glamor was almost irresistible.

My route took me along the fenced pasture of the Sherringhams' cattle ranch, a certified organic farm with the largest dairy in the area. Pat Sherringham had once come to school to talk about his forty years as a rancher, the changes he had seen in how they fed the cows over the winter, their innovations in fencing which kept manure out of the streams, and changes in state law and funding which had helped them to stay afloat in lean times. It had actually been pretty interesting. Useful too, given that there were plenty of students who would probably stay in the area and go into farming.

I often saw Pat and his wife around town and out in the fields, some-times riding tractors. They were getting older now, but the work didn't give them much of a break, and I saw them at all hours, loading bailers, planting pearl millet or spreading manure. They were out in the field now, but they were just standing there, Pat with his hands on his head, Angela with hers clamped to her face like a mask. I got closer, and still they didn't move. It was odd. Like they were frozen.

A five-bar metal gate led from the road to the pasture, closed as usual, but further along, where the fence was made doubly impenetrable by a high hawthorn hedge, a trough had been carved through, as if a huge concrete pipe had been dragged lengthwise by a bulldozer, right through hedge, fence and field. The branches either side were splintered and broken, the grass churned to mud, and the fence rails twisted and snapped. As I reached the opening, I saw what I had not been able to see before: cows lying all over the field.

They were clearly dead, their black and white skins daubed with red. Most were little more than pieces. The air was thick with flies, and the muddy field was crimson, pools of blood thickening in the sun.

I stood there, gripped with horror. Something big had gone through that fence. Not a truck. Something that had attacked the cattle. I hesitated, wanting to say something to the Sherringhams, but I had nothing useful to offer. So I just stood there, one hand over my face because of the smell. At first, they didn't see me. When they did, they gave me a long, blank look and Pat opened his hands in confusion and despair.

"What did this?" I asked.

"Search me," said Pat miserably. He moved to his wife who was crying, her shoulders shaking, and put an arm round her.

"I'm so sorry," I said.

Pat just nodded, all his attention on his wife, though his eyes strayed to the ravaged bodies of his herd. This was going to cost them a whole lot more than money. There was nothing I could say that would bring consolation, but my mind raced with what I should be doing instead. Because in my head, I was sure that this was no normal event. No bear would do that. No bobcat could. Some lunatic with a machete? Possibly, but what had gone through the fence was *big*.

This was *yōkai* stuff. I felt it in my bones. I thought of the thing which had been watching me on the way back from Saito's, and the thing which had attacked the waitress in her bed. The incidents had been radically different and threatened nothing as awful as the Sherringhams' dead cattle, but in my gut, I felt that they were connected. If what had done this had escaped from the mystical prison under the mountain, then this was down to what Raiko had done years ago. And down to me for not containing it.

The lights were out at the inconvenience store, and though the doors were open, there was no sign of anyone inside. That was not so much unusual as unheard of. The register was powered down and the only glow in the store came from the refrigerated cases at the back. They were running off a portable gas generator which was droning steadily.

The power, which had been restored for a while, was out again.

"Hello?" I called out. "Mom? Dad?"

I needed to talk to Bachan and Saito about what I had seen in the field, and if Mom was alone, I might confide in her before I left.

There was a bang and a muffled curse. I moved and spotted my father straightening up in the dry goods aisle holding his head. He had his reciprocating saw in one hand and he looked flushed and a little worried, like a kid caught with his hand in the cookie jar.

"Hey," I said, "what are you...?"

Then I saw and froze. A ragged square hole had been hacked into the sheet rock where the shelf met the back wall. You could see the wooden studs and strands of electrical wire in the dark cavity and something long and shiny that extended from the shelf and through the hole in the wall. I stared, trying to make sense of what I was seeing, and Dad gave me that boyish smile of his that said he had tried to do something he thought would be cool and was now in serious trouble. I stared in disbelief.

"Is that...train track?" I asked.

"Kind of, yeah," he said, his Lancashire accent thickening as it always did when he was caught off guard. "Thought I'd give the bullet train a proper run, you know? Just going up and down on that shelf looked kind of silly so..."

"You cut a hole in the wall?" I said, all thoughts about the carnage at the Sherringhams' ranch driven out of my head. "Mom's gonna kill you."

"Two holes," he replied, glancing to the other side of the store where another chunk had been carved out of the wall. "Got to have somewhere to loop back in, right? It will run along the shelf there, then through the back and round the fridge cases, re-emerging here and running all the way behind the chips and canned goods up to the magazines at the front. It's gonna be great!"

"You are so dead," I observed.

"Nah!" he blustered. "Jennie will love it. Maybe not right away, but eventually..."

"I'm serious, Dad, you should move out for a while. Get a hotel room. Where is Mom now?"

"At the wholesaler. Back in about forty minutes."

"Can you fix it before then?"

"Well, the power went out again right after I cut the holes so…"

"This is bad."

"It will look fine when it's done," he replied, breezy as ever. "She'll barely notice it. I just need a little time to sort it out. What do you say you watch the store for a bit while I get things tidied up?"

"Tidied up? Dad, you cut holes in the walls for your toy train!"

"Model train, Caleb."

"I don't think Mom will see the distinction."

"I think your mother is more flexible than you give her credit for," he replied.

I shook my head emphatically. "Have you *met* Mom?" I asked. "I mean, have you ever spent any time with her at all? They're gonna be finding bits of you all over town."

"You're making a big deal over nothing."

"Is that your defense? Because I don't think it's going to work."

"A few weeks ago, you wouldn't have believed we'd be carrying all these Japanese snacks and candies," he replied. "Now look! Your mother will adjust."

"Those are things from our heritage!" I protested.

"And model trains are from mine!" he shot back, and for the first time in a very long while, he looked more than annoyed. There was something real there, something serious. The moment passed as quickly as it had come, but it made me wary.

"What do you mean?" I asked.

He sighed and looked back at his work, then, avoiding my eyes, said, "I grew up making a model railway with my dad in England, but he's gone now, and I'm not there, so I'm building one here. And it's a Japanese train," he added, his tone softening. "She can't argue with that."

"She let you have the train," I said. "It's the cutting holes in the walls she's not going to like."

"It's going to be great," he said doggedly. "She'll learn to love it."

"Dad, I really don't think…"

"If she can adjust to you being a Japanese superhero and your sister turning into a fox, she can adjust to this."

My mouth fell open and, for a long moment, we just stared at each other.

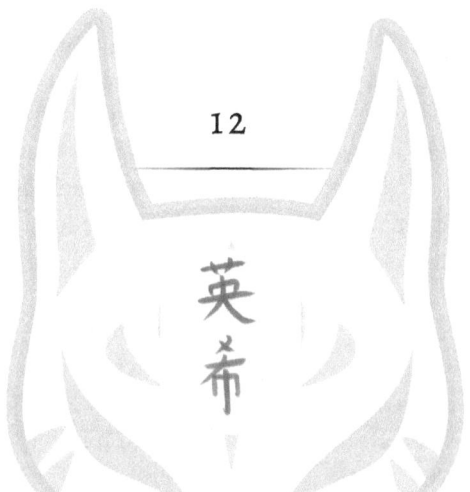

12

"How long have you known?" I asked.

Dad and I were sitting in the backroom of the store. Other than the drone of the generator, the place was silent. He looked dissatisfied, annoyed with himself that he had given the game away.

"A couple of days," he said. "Not, like, since you closed the transdimensional portal on Red Scar Mountain," he added.

"Why didn't you say?" I gasped.

"Why didn't you?" he fired back, and there it was again, that flicker of anger. Or pain.

And now that he asked, I found I didn't have a good answer. I blew out a long sigh. "I guess we thought you wouldn't believe it, or Mom was embarrassed by it, her family's connection to monsters, I mean. I guess it felt like it wasn't your problem, since you're not Japanese…"

"You're not Japanese either, Caleb."

"Mixed," I said, quickly, "I know. But it was that part of my background that had suddenly popped up in my life and…"

"You didn't think I was relevant."

I stared at him, horrified by what he had said and overcome with a sense of wrongness. I shook my head emphatically.

"It wasn't like that," I said. "We didn't *decide* not to tell you. It was just…"

"A given," said Dad. "*Stephen's English. Not really one of us. He won't know*

81

what to think. He won't be able to help. Best not to involve him. But either I'm a part of this family or I'm not. Part of you too, no matter what you call yourself."

He spoke flatly, quietly and without looking at me. The table between us felt as wide as a continent; like we were too far apart to hear each other. Tears filled my eyes, but I couldn't think of anything to say, and when I shook my head again, they broke from my eyes and rolled down my cheeks. He nodded then, smiled sadly, and reached across the continent-sized table and patted my hand. The gesture somehow made us feel even further apart, and he still avoided my eyes.

"Forget it," he said. "I shouldn't have said anything. Just...I don't know. Keep on as you were, and I'll pretend I don't know."

"How can I just keep on?" I said. "I shouldn't have kept it from you. We should have said something."

"It's fine," he said. "Really. Okay." He got to his feet. "Suppose I better fill the holes in those walls."

His exit was interrupted by a shriek of horror and dismay from the store. My mother was back.

"Stephen!" she yelled. "STEPHEN!"

He listened absently, as if the sound was far away and barely audible, rather than the raging bellow of a kaiju in the next room, and then he nodded and picked up a red plastic gas can.

"Tell your mom I've gone to the gas station," he said. "Gonna need to keep that generator topped up."

"How did he find out?" Mom asked.

Em shook her head. "Not from me," she said.

"Or me," I added.

We were sitting in the kitchen while Bachan—who Em had called as soon as she heard—made tea in her methodical, focused way. The room was hushed like a church, the air heavy with something like guilt.

"Maybe Saito told him?" Em wondered aloud. "He was pretty out of it when he was hurt and resting here. Maybe he let something slip."

"He's a tengu," I replied doubtfully. "An ancient spirit of the mountains and forests. He's had centuries to perfect his cover story. And Dad said he'd only known for a couple of days."

"Maybe Stephen saw something," said Mom. "This business at the Sherringham ranch…"

"You think it was a *yōkai* too?" I said, relieved that I wasn't the only one to think so.

"Not relevant," Emily cut in. "The cattle attack was within the last few hours."

"Then how?" Mom tried, desperate for an explanation to make the scale of the thing less. "Maybe he saw something the night we rebound the *oni* cave and only realized later…"

"He was here the whole time," Emily cut in. "If he hadn't been, the town would have torched the store." The truth of that—that he had, in his own quiet way, spent that evening protecting the family—settled on us like shame. "We should have told him ourselves," she added. "I hate it that he found out by himself."

"He'll come round," said my mother. "He always does."

But there was something less like certainty and more like hope, even desperation, in her voice. I wasn't so sure. Now that I looked back on it, I couldn't believe that we had thought it was okay not to tell him. He wasn't prone to freak outs nor was he so wedded to everything being normal that he couldn't have gotten his head round it.

It was Dad! He was the poster boy for the goofy, the unflappably dependable. He would have made dad jokes about foxy ladies and then begged Emily to transform just so he could see it. When he watched me jump or execute one of the cooler sword moves, his eyes would have gotten all big, like when he's looking at his model trains and doesn't think anyone is watching. He would have been so into it. Ancient magic? He would have been more than excited. He would have been thrilled, like a kid whose wishes had come true.

And he would have been proud. Discovering what we could do, what we were, would not have dimmed his love for us for a heartbeat. It would have deepened it.

But we hadn't told him, like he was someone who couldn't handle it all or—worse—couldn't be trusted. We had treated him like a stranger.

The thought cut me as surely as if I had run my hand along the edge of one of Saito's swords, a pain both shrill and numbing at the same time, like the blade was so sharp I severed nerve endings and couldn't feel anything to let me know how much damage I had done.

Bachan poured the tea then sat down, her hands in her lap, and took a thoughtful breath, her eyes almost closing as if she was in prayer.

"I told him," she said.

We stared at her, mouths open.

"*You* told him?" my mother echoed in disbelief. She looked stunned, upset, but the tears in her eyes were complicated by something like outrage.

"There were signs," said Bachan. "I thought we would be called upon to fight once more, as now seems the case, so..."

"You told him!" Mom exclaimed again.

"It was time," said Bachan.

"Says who?" Emily exclaimed. "It wasn't your place, Bachan! Do you know what you have done, what he thinks of us now?"

"He knows the truth, Kazuko," she said. Emily's face flushed with annoyance at the use of her Japanese name but before she could say anything, Bachan added, "You should have told him yourself."

"We would have!" I protested. "It was just that..."

But I couldn't think of how to finish the sentence, and it hung between us like an accusation. At last, my mother got up, her chair scraping unnaturally loudly on the floor.

"You should have spoken to me first, Mom," she said to Bachan.

"Something is coming, Jennie," said Bachan gravely. "I have been warning you, but you didn't listen."

"Wait," said Mom, incredulous. "You told Stephen because we didn't assume the world was ending after you saw a dog chasing its tail?"

"Saito-san agrees with me," Bachan announced. "I said something was coming," she said again. "I was right. It is here."

"The thing that attacked Bernice Sartovski!" I exclaimed with something like triumph. "The roaches in Jason Blakely's car! And now the Sherringhams' cattle!"

But Mom wasn't listening. Instead, she turned to me and Em, her face flushed with fury, a finger of accusation aimed squarely at Bachan.

"You wanted to know why I didn't want her in our lives?" she said, the words bright and hard as iron. "This is why."

She stormed out, leaving Bachan staring directly ahead, saying nothing.

I burst into Saito's largely empty Japanese restaurant.

"*Irashaimasse!*" he called, then saw that it was me and returned to

84

wiping down the counter, scowling. "You are not due for training for an hour."

"Was it your idea for Bachan to tell my dad about...everything?" I demanded.

I had been running, but that wasn't why I was out of breath. These days I could run miles and barely break a sweat.

"Everything?" the tengu echoed blankly.

"My magical abilities!" I exclaimed. "Mine and Emily's. Our family heritage. Was it your idea?"

"Of course not," he said.

"How do I know you are telling the truth?"

He looked up again, and this time his face—in spite of his massive nose—managed to look fiercely indignant. "Because I said so," he declared.

"That's supposed to be proof enough?" I pressed, remembering the time we had first met, and he had thrown a meat cleaver at me to test my reflexes.

"You think I would confide in your *gaijin* father?" he scoffed.

Gaijin meant foreign, non-Japanese. His use of the word annoyed me but immediately proved his point. Saito had barely agreed to work with me and Em in the first place because he thought our blood was tainted by the non-Japanese part of the family. He had gotten used to the idea, sort of, but now that I thought about it, the idea of him pressing Bachan to share our secrets with my Lancashire-born father was preposterous.

"Well, she told him anyway," I said, throwing myself onto a seat at one of the hibachi tables. There were no customers in the restaurant, and though it might pick up around dinner time, this wasn't unusual. For some reason, Portersville residents had an aversion to eating obscure Japanese food resentfully served to them by a glaring lunatic. "So, Mom isn't speaking to her. Worse, Dad thinks we lied to him because we didn't trust him, or don't consider him part of the family."

I said it miserably, but Saito just nodded, as if this sounded like a good assessment of the situation.

"What?" I demanded. "He's wrong!"

"Is he?"

"Of course he is!" I said. "He's our rock. He's the glue that holds the family together. The one we turn to when things get tough, when we turn on each other, when we need stabilizing, calming. The idea that we don't think he's part of our lives is..."

"Apparent."

"What?" I protested. "No! The opposite!"

"Not from what I see."

"Who asked you?"

"Something happened to your family," said the tengu, unflappable. "The most important thing that has ever happened to them. It changed how you thought of yourselves. And you kept it from him. You are right that it does not matter what I think, but I am telling you what I see. You might not see it that way, but I assure you, he does, and he is not wrong."

I stared at him, and I felt the tears spill suddenly from my eyes and run down my face again.

"I love my dad," I muttered.

The tengu frowned. "I don't care about that," he said. "But he probably will."

Elsewhere

While Caleb was talking to Saito-san, his grandmother had made a decision. This was not the time for family squabbles. Too much was at stake. That meant she would have to clear the air and mend fences with her daughter. Again.

Bachan—which was how she thought of herself these days—had assumed the two of them had finally gotten onto the same page after years of mistrust, but telling Jennie's husband about Hideki and Kazuko had opened up a lot of old wounds. She understood why, but it was ironic that they should be fighting about her taking Stephen into her confidence. It was Jennie's marriage to Stephen that had been the root of their dispute years ago. Jennie had been furious with Bachan's lack of support for her marrying someone who wasn't Japanese. Now she was furious that she had treated him as if he was.

Sometimes you couldn't win. Especially with someone as hardheaded as her daughter.

And you know who she gets that from, said a voice Bachan's head.

That too was undeniable, and why they would be able to get through this fight. Unfortunately, Bachan felt in her bones that they didn't have time to wait for her daughter to come around. They would have to swallow their respective prides in order to create a unified front against what was coming.

What that was, whether it was already here, and what it was trying to do, Bachan wasn't entirely sure, but she prepared to set off for the store armed with her ancient oiled umbrella. She could feel another thunderstorm coming. She tied the sash of her ancient olive-green kimono but chose sneakers over the sandals she usually wore. Poison ivy grew along the edge of Almond Road, and she'd seen a young timber rattlesnake sunning itself on the curb only a few days ago.

And the weather has been strange, she thought, *stranger than any TV meteorologist could explain...*

She walked with a slow, but steady shuffling gait along the weedy sidewalk that took her northwest from the shade of the forest and into town. It was still light and uncomfortably warm, reminding her of when she had been a girl in Japan. That was a very long time ago, and her memories were complicated by all which had happened after, particularly with her sister who was now entombed with her *oni* son under the mountains just outside town. How long ago, she wasn't sure. It was many years since she had kept count. Longer than ordinary humans could live, that was for certain, though—unlike her sister—Bachan's magical talents were limited to her instincts and knowledge. She was no shapeshifter, no witch. She was just a very old lady armed with nothing but a furled umbrella.

She moved through the ranch houses on the east side of the town center, turning right in the shade of the Portersville Inn and up along the athletic fields of the high school which were deserted, the flood lights out.

No power again.

If she squinted into the sunset, she could just make out the elegant shape of the Nye barn which the local people had considered old, and whose reconstruction had been masterminded by Saito-san. Strange, she thought, the way Americans thought about history. But then she was older than the barn had been, so her perspective was rather different. Somewhere out there was the Walmart she used to visit, but it closed years ago and Bachan hadn't been north of the convenience store since.

People had lived here or hereabouts for hundreds of years, thousands probably, but there was no trace of that past, nothing to root it or the community. The Cherokee down the road had some sense of their heritage, but they had not been in control of how it was maintained. In Portersville, nothing showed anyone had been here for more than a few decades. It was no wonder, she thought, that people here were always looking for the next shiny new thing, something to grab hold of and wave like a flag. They didn't know who they were.

She rounded the corner onto Bevington East. The street was empty except for a parked Ford pickup with a hand-lettered "For Sale" sign in the window, sitting a couple of feet from the curb beside the manhole grate in the middle of the road. "$5K or best offer," plus a phone number. On the right were four low slung houses set in overgrown yards and surrounded by chain link fence, and on the left was the weedy forecourt of an abandoned gas station, its signs and antique pumps rusted. Bachan considered it vaguely as she walked, rehearsing what she would say to Jennie and, she supposed, to Stephen and the kids. It was important that they all saw eye to eye.

She paused, frowning, as a cockroach scurried toward her from the gas station.

"Shoo," she said.

But then there was another. And another. She took a step backwards. A stream of insects came pouring out of every door and crack of the old building.

The abandoned gas station's office flickered suddenly with blue-white energy. Bachan hesitated. The window glass was fogged and cracked, but the lights inside had flashed on just for a second, revealing the empty shelves hung with cobwebs and furred with dust. The light illumined the scurrying insects which were swarming away.

Curious.

She recommenced her walk, picking her way around the roaches with a shudder, but almost immediately it came again, a flitting and unsteady light as every lamp in the derelict building came on. The museum-piece gas pumps glowed, the needles in their weathered gauges flicking across their dials, and the forecourt was suddenly bathed in an inconstant fluorescent light. With the light came a crackle of staticky radio music over the station's sound system, and behind it, the hum of energy swelling like the urgent drone of cicadas.

Bachan raised the umbrella like a sword. And then she saw it.

Arcing across the inside of the office's window glass was something long and black, something with legs and antennae. Something impossibly big.

Bachan froze in horror as the glass shattered and the massive thing scurried out toward her, a great, shiny black wave of undulating segments and hard, yellow legs. The head was a bright, angry red, and sprouted two long feelers, also red, and twitching independent of the uncannily even movement of the legs. They were searching.

In a terrible instant, Bachan felt sure they were searching for her.

She backed away, but the monstrous centipede kept coming and with it streamed the cockroaches, so many that in places the ground was covered with their hard little bodies. Bachan barely saw them, ignored them as they ran over her feet. All her attention fixed on the centipede.

It was as long as the Ford truck. ("$5K or best offer.")

But even as she thought that, she caught herself. The creature seemed to swell and stretch, lengthening even as it barreled towards her across the gas station forecourt.

It was growing before her eyes! As she stared, horror-struck, new segments popped out along its body until it was almost as long as a bus. The roaches fanned out—hundreds of them—as if compelled to be near the beast but scared of getting too close.

The station lights brightened beyond all possible circuitry, then popped out, showering slivers of glass. The shrill cicada hum died immediately, as did the radio, and there was a sudden and total silence as the terrible beast reached the street and reared up on its many pointed legs, antennae waving. Two black eyes glared down at her, and a pair of sharp, sickle-shaped mouth parts opened, poised to attack.

Bachan shrank back, her umbrella raised in pointless defiance, and the appalling thing arched over, ready to strike. As it swayed, menacingly, Bachan cringed, lost her balance, and crumpled to the blacktop.

The monstrous centipede hissed its triumph, and its awful mouth gaped, saliva and venom dripping from its jaws.

"I know you," Bachan gasped. "*Omukade!*"

13

My family were sitting in tense silence in the kitchen behind the inconvenience store, close enough we'd hear the bell over the door if someone came in, though it was only a half hour until closing. Saito had joined us, but we hadn't been able to reach Bachan which, in the circumstances, was maybe just as well. We needed to patch things up with Dad, and Mom was still too angry at her. Smoothing things over with Bachan would have to wait.

"This is my fault," said the tengu. He executed a deep, formal bow to my father which bent his upper body until it was parallel with the floor and held the position while he rattled off a series of alarmingly loud apologies in Japanese.

My father looked mortified. After all, he barely knew the man. "It's fine," he said. "I understand."

"It's not fine," I said. "We messed up."

"Big time," said Emily.

"I am so sorry," said my mother, taking his hands and giving him a beseeching look.

"I'm okay," he said, smiling. "Really. I was shocked and yeah, you know, a bit hurt, but I just had to get used to the idea. I'm fine now. Honest."

"I love you, Dad," I said.

"We all do," added Em.

"Okay," said my father, getting to his feet as if scalded, flushing with embarrassment. "Yes. Thanks. Me too. Who's for tea? I'll get the kettle on."

The English solution to all problems. Tea. Actually, it worked pretty well for Japanese people too. Saito bowed again, smaller this time, and Mom managed a nod and a wan smile, knowing that this was as much emotional gushing as my father could stomach. We exchanged awkward glances as Dad boiled the water and dropped a couple of tea bags into the iron teapot.

It wiggled.

Dad stared, mouth open, as little black legs sprouted from the sides of the teapot, and it hauled itself up, took a few little steps, then rocked back like a puppy, stretching.

There was a long, leaden silence, then my father looked up, taking in our guilty faces and said in a low, baffled tone, "What?"

"Yeah," I said, shame-faced, "it does that."

There was another loaded silence then Em leapt in, trying to save the situation with a little breezy casualness, as if walking teapots were all perfectly normal.

"Bachan says that when things have been around people for a long time, they can, sort of, come to life."

"Right," said Dad. "Obviously. Okay. Well, maybe we'll give the tea a miss." He hesitated as if his brain had momentarily shut down, then added, "You know, I think that if you don't mind, I'm going to fiddle with my trains for a bit. Assuming they haven't all started driving around by themselves."

He gave a manic, unconvincing grin, then got up, looking slightly dazed, still watching the teapot out of the corner of his eye as it strutted around the table, its lid chittering softly. No one knew what to say.

"Stephen," said Mom, getting to her feet and giving him another imploring look.

"It's fine," he said again. "Just...might take me a minute to get used to... You know. This."

He gestured vaguely, a broad, sweep of his hands which took in not just the animated tea pot and his newly supernatural kids, but the known universe which had turned out to be not what he thought it was.

"I'll come with you!" I blurted.

I never played with Dad's toy trains. I sometimes thought he wished I would. But not this time.

"No," he said, not looking at me, but holding up a hand as if closing the conversation. "It's okay. I just need a minute to myself."

But he didn't get it. Before he could leave the room, the bell over the door into the inconvenience store rang. Actually, it jangled, loud and ragged, as if someone had shouldered the door open and then sprawled drunkenly inside.

Dad frowned and called out, "Be right there!"

As he strode out, the rest of us looked at each other knowing the meeting hadn't gone as we had hoped, but sensing something else, something not quite right. I was the first to go after Dad, but the others came after me. If it was just a customer, they were going to get a very odd welcoming reception.

But it wasn't a customer, drunk or otherwise. It was Bachan, dirty, blood-streaked, and with one hand clasped against her chest as if her wrist was broken. She was assisted by Mrs. Helms who lived out by the disused gas station.

"She was out in the street," said Mrs. Helms. "Knocked over by something. I didn't see what, but I heard a crash and came out to see Jerry's pickup flipped over, the cover off the manhole, and Mrs. Watanabe on the ground, all beat up."

"Thank you," said Dad, taking Bachan's uninjured arm and leading her in. "We'll take it from here."

My mother babbled more thanks and shepherded the neighbor out. Only when she was gone did Bachan speak.

"*Omukade*," she gasped. "I saw it!"

Her eyes were wide with shock and fear, and though I didn't know what the Japanese word meant, I saw it register in Saito-san's face. His great eyebrows arched, and his mouth opened, just for a half second or so, before he got control of himself. My father rushed to support Bachan before she collapsed, followed quickly by Mom and Emily, so I turned on the tengu and gave him a level look.

"*Omukade*," I said. "What is that?"

He bit his lip, and his face locked up as if it was carved in granite, his eyes fixed on Bachan who was being helped into a chair, looking pale and fragile. There was a dark patch above her right eye where it looked like she had hit her head, and a thin trickle of red ran down her cheek. When Mom took her injured wrist to examine it, Bachan winced sharply, and for a second I thought she would faint. Seeing her this way was, frankly, terrifying.

I turned back to Saito. "Well?" I prompted.

"It is bad," he said simply. "I need my books and then I will show you. But yes. It is very bad."

Dad drove Saito-san to his place, clearly glad to be of use and, perhaps, as glad to be out of the way and not talking. He didn't know Saito well, but if there was an Olympic event for sitting in silence, Saito was a shoo-in for gold, and Dad knew it.

After they left, we sat in a silence of our own, Mom busying herself with tending Bachan's cuts and bruises.

"I don't think it's broken," she said, after scrutinizing Bachan's slender wrist. "Just twisted. We can go to the hospital now or..."

"No," said Bachan. "It is fine." She met my mother's eyes, and some stiffness left her posture. "It will be fine."

"Okay," said Mom. "But if it's not..."

"We have real problems to worry about," said Bachan. "Let's not invent imaginary ones." Mom sat back, her lips pursed with annoyance, but Bachan sighed and made a pacifying gesture with her good hand. "Can I just sit for a while?"

"Of course," said Mom. "Em, get your grandmother something to eat."

"I am not hungry..." Bachan began but caught the warning look in my mother's face. "Perhaps I could eat something. Thank you."

So Em made some soup, served with bread from the store which had just reached its sell by date, and she ate in silence while I hovered.

"Why aren't we talking about this *Omukade* thing?" I demanded as soon as I got Mom alone in the kitchen.

"Because your grandmother has been through a traumatic experience," Mom said in a stage whisper, "and I'm not going to pump her with questions for information she will have to repeat when your father gets back with Saito-san, and neither are you."

Those last words were given with a level stare which implied something like *if you want to see the sunrise.*

"Ten minutes ago, you were furious with her," I grumbled.

"Ten minutes ago, I did not know that she nearly died," Mom replied.

Which, I guess, was fair enough.

A few minutes later, Dad returned with Saito-san, laden with a book so big and old it looked like something from *The Lord of the Rings*, a musty tome to be thumbed through by a wizard in an ancient stone tower...

"*Mukade* are a kind of Japanese centipede," said the tengu, flipping through a series of faded wood-block prints whose captions were all in kanji. "They are quite large, and their bites are poisonous. They are common in Japan, especially in warm, rural places, and will often come inside houses, even into beds." He found the page he was looking for and showed me an artist's depiction of a seriously scary looking centipede with a black body, orange pointed legs and a red head and tail, both of which had what looked like feelers, so it was hard to tell which end was which.

"Woah," I said. "These are real?"

"Of course," said the tengu.

"I mean, they are animals? People know about them?"

The tengu gave me that withering look of his which he wore when he thought I was being stupid on purpose.

"The bite of the *mukade* is painful but rarely fatal," he remarked.

"How big are they?" I asked, not sure I wanted to know.

The tengu spread his fingers. "Perhaps eight inches," he said.

I shuddered, then frowned. "But that can't be what Bachan saw. She said it was huge."

"*Mukade* are simply animals," said the tengu. "They are pests, but they are driven only by what drives all animals: the need to feed, to shelter, to reproduce. What your grandmother saw was something different: a *yōkai* which takes the form of a *mukade*. We call this *yōkai*, Omukade."

"So you know all about it," I said. "How to defeat it, and such."

"There are stories from ancient times," said the tengu, turning the pages of his book again, skipping images of beautifully rendered birds and animals. "In the Heian period—about a thousand years ago—one terrorized the dragon palace near Lake Biwa, killing and eating the people of the area, and even the dragons themselves which lived in the water. At last, the great hero Fujiwara no Hidesato, known as Tawara, was summoned to defeat the *yōkai*. He found it above Kyoto, curled around Mikami."

"Who was Mikami?" I asked.

"Mikami was not a person," said the tengu, finding the page he was looking for and laying it flat. It showed a three-panel painting of samurai warriors in battle with a giant monster with bulging eyes, tusk-like teeth, and a body which was so large it didn't fit into the frame. "Mikami is a mountain. The *Omukade* was large enough to encircle it."

I swallowed.

"O...kay..." I said, then a flash of inspiration hit. "Oh, so it's like the thing in *Inuyasha!*"

"What is that?"

"A Japanese TV show," said Em with a roll of her eyes. "Anime. *Hideki* here has been bingeing."

The tengu looked blank.

"In the first episodes there's this giant sexy centipede lady!" I persisted.

Saito scowled, looking annoyed. "The *Omukade* is not sexy," he pronounced severely.

"Okay," I said, "the sexy part probably is not relevant, but in the show Inuyasha killed her with his iron-reaver claws."

The tengu looked at me like he was dealing with an idiot. "Do you have claws?" he inquired.

"No, but in your ancient legend, the hero killed it too, right?" I said, looking for a silver lining.

"He fired many arrows at it," the tengu replied, "but the *Omukade*'s body was too heavily protected. At last, Tawara tried coating an arrow tip with his own saliva, and this proved lethal to the *Omukade*."

I relaxed. "Okay," I said. "Great. So, I lick one of your swords or whatever and we're golden."

The tengu shook his head. "That was a particular *Omukade*," he said. "This one is different. For instance, this one is not so big."

"Not yet," said Bachan.

I had almost forgotten she was there. She looked pale and unsteady, and was still holding her wrist against her chest, but she looked less disheveled and her eyes were brighter.

"What do you mean?" I asked.

"It got bigger in front of me," she said. "I saw it."

"How is that possible?" asked Dad who was standing by the door as if not yet sure whether he was part of the conversation.

"I do not know," said Saito.

"I think I do," said Bachan, frowning at the idea. "When I first saw it, I was immediately struck with fear."

"Understandable," said Em. "It was a massive centipede. Don't be embarrassed."

"I am not," said Bachan simply. "But I think my fear is what it wanted. It could have killed me quickly, but it chose not to. It wanted to feel my terror, to taste it. I think, perhaps, it feeds on fear. Like it is energy. I saw it grow with my own eyes."

"I have not heard of such a thing before," said Saito, "but it seems possible. But the body must also be fed. What I have read about the

Omukade suggests that they are very bloodthirsty, that they need to eat a great deal of meat to stay alive, and that they prefer to eat people. I wonder why it did not eat you."

Bachan hung her head.

"What?" Mom asked.

"I think it recognized me," she said. "Either it confused me with my sister or... I don't know. It was ready to strike, and then I felt it see who I was and decide not to kill me."

"Not good," I said.

Everyone shot me outraged looks and Dad half shouted "Caleb!"

"I mean of course it's good that it didn't kill Bachan," I clarified. "It's great. But remember last time we tangled with *yōkai*? They wanted us alive because we were part of their plan to reopen the mystical prison under the mountain. If this thing chose not to kill Bachan when it had the chance, it had a reason and *that* is not good."

This seemed to pass muster but didn't help the mood.

"Tell them about the saliva thing," I said, still looking for that silver lining.

Saito-san did, but at the end of his tale he cocked his head on one side and made a doubtful face. "But these are magical beings," he said, "And their forms vary. There is no reason to believe that the Portersville *Omukade* will have the same weakness as the one from the legend."

"And you think this okumade..." Dad began.

"*Omukade*," the tengu corrected.

"Right, that," said Dad. "You think this is what attacked Bernice Sartovski and killed the Sherringhams' cows?"

The tengu looked at Bachan, then nodded once. "I fear so," he said. "We must assume that it escaped from the prison below the mountain, probably before Hideki slew the *oni*."

I shot Dad an uncomfortable glance, but he just returned Saito-san's nod.

"So why has it only appeared in the last few days?" he asked.

"An excellent question," said the tengu. "If, as Bachan says, it is growing, perhaps at first it was very small, like a regular *mukade*, and avoided notice until it attacked the waitress."

"No," I cut in. "It was seen before then, in Jason Blakley's car, when all the roaches came out."

"Roaches?" said the tengu.

"*Gokiburi*," Bachan translated. "And yes, I saw them too. Many, many cockroaches."

"Great," said Emily, making a face. She wasn't a fan of bugs.

"Why would these cockroaches associate with the *Omukade?*" the tengu mused. "I have never heard of such a thing."

"They seemed drawn to it," said Bachan. "But also afraid of it."

"Like it was their leader?" Mom asked.

"Their leader," Bachan echoed approvingly, refining the idea further to "Their King."

Saito's eyes narrowed. "We may respect the powerful, without liking them," he said.

"That Jason kid is obsessed with bugs," said Emily. "I don't know if he was before the accident but Sofie Collington says he draws them all the time in his notebooks. Hundreds of them. Over and over."

"How does she know?" I asked, feeling a little guilty that I hadn't been keeping an eye on Jason. "She's not in his class."

Em shrugged and turned back to Bachan, changing the subject. "Where did it go after attacking you?" she asked.

"Into the drain," said Bachan. "There was a truck which it knocked over. Then it used its mouth to pull out the manhole cover, and it went inside. It had to squeeze itself very tight to fit in."

"*Mukade* are experts at crawling through small gaps," said the tengu. "It is amazing how they can make themselves flat."

"Awesome," said Emily. "This is all just awesome."

"One more thing," said Bachan. "It affected the electricity. The lights at the gas station came on and then..." she made a popping noise and opened her hands as if releasing a bird.

"Overloaded the power," said Dad. "Except that that petrol station has been shut for years. It can't still have a live electrical circuit."

"So the power came from the centipede?" I said, "like an electric eel?"

"This is a very unusual *Omukade*," the tengu concluded. "I do not think you should trust your saliva to kill it."

It would have been funny if it didn't fill me with dread and panic.

"No, mate," Dad agreed. "I think you might be right there."

"But there is something else happening," said Saito, his great furry caterpillar eyebrows bunching in dissatisfied thought. "I can feel it."

"Apart from giant centipedes?" I said, not liking the idea.

The tengu nodded gravely. "Something strange," he intoned. "There is power here, a presence that was not here before. I feel it but cannot give it a name."

"You mean, magic?" I said.

Saito made a sour face, but he couldn't think of a better word, and eventually—grudgingly—nodded. "Some form of *kegare*," he said.

"A kind of corruption or defilement," Bachan supplied. "It can happen naturally. But it might also be a kind of curse."

"A curse?" said Emily. "Made by who?"

I frowned at her. I was just trying to get my head around the idea that curses were real, while she had gone straight to who was responsible.

Saito shook his head. "I cannot say," he replied. "There are rituals. They might indicate the source or nature of the power. But I must study them." He looked suddenly far away. "I have not felt anything like this in many, many years."

There wasn't much you could say to that, but Dad nodded as if it all made perfect sense and followed up with what seemed to him the logical equivalent.

"And I think I'm ready to try making that tea again," he said.

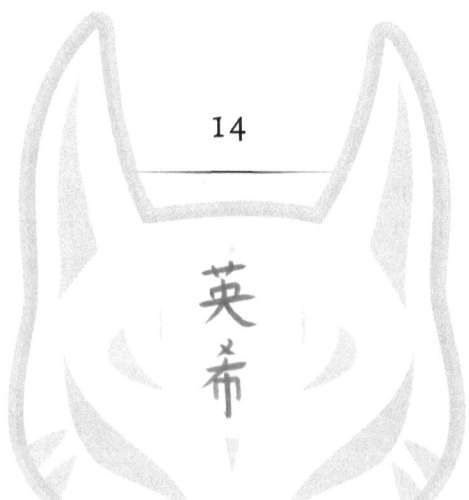

14

I explored the area around the old gas station, trying to look nonchalant, even contriving to study the drain as reflected in the tengu's bronze mirror, but I didn't see or sense anything unusual. Again, I felt useless and stupid.

Some superhero I'm turning out to be. Can't even protect my own grandmother.

The combination of what happened to the Sherringhams' cows with the flipping of a pickup truck next to an open manhole (as reported to the sheriff's office by our neighbor, Mrs. Helms), sent a ripple of panic through town. It led the news on the radio, the TV, and in *The Portersville Chronicle*, and soon the mayor's office and the sheriff's department were making joint statements about investigations already underway, appealing for calm, and touting a sightings hotline, though what people were supposed to be on the lookout for, no one could say.

"Any escaped exotic pets, legal or otherwise, should be reported at once, so as to assist our experts in the hunt," Sheriff Halpern offered, though it looked like the "experts" in question were his baffled, frightened looking deputies.

"What does he think has escaped, a hippo?" said DeMarcus at school the next day.

"Hippos are herbivores," Joey pointed out. "Unlikely to eat cows."

"Have you seen hippos?" DeMarcus fired back. "More than capable of flipping a truck. I think they eat what the hell they like, and I wouldn't advise telling them otherwise."

"Still," said Joey. "My money is on some kind meatosaurus. If not an actual T-Rex, then something that eats a lot of steak, like a tiger."

"But a tiger couldn't flip the truck and open the drain," DeMarcus pointed out.

"Maybe there's four of them working together. One for each wheel. Aww," Joey added. "Animal world cooperation. Kind of sweet."

"A tiger team with opposable thumbs? Highly likely," said DeMarcus with deadpan sarcasm. He turned to me. "Your grandmother really didn't get a look at it?"

I shrugged. "Stressful situation," I said vaguely. "And she hit her head. Nathan West said he thought it could be wolves."

"Why does everyone take everything he says like it's wisdom from on high?" snapped DeMarcus dismissively. "Wolves? That's just dumb."

I shot him a look, baffled by his obvious annoyance.

"Not wolves then," Joey mused. "What about a grizzly?"

"Yes on flipping the truck, no on opening the drain," DeMarcus concluded.

"I think that detail is going to be a problem for most exotic pets," Joey agreed.

"So someone is helping it," DeMarcus went on, "and it's not so much escaped as part of an orchestrated reign of terror."

Joey laughed, then saw that I wasn't. Their face fell. "Okay, Smith," they said. "Spill."

It was no good trying to dodge the issue. I knew Joey of old. "Okay," I said, "here's what I know."

I lowered my voice and told them everything.

"A giant centipede that can open manholes?" said DeMarcus, aghast. "I think I liked the hippo better."

"Way better," Joey agreed. "And this thing is both smart and magical? Not good."

"Definitely not good," said DeMarcus. "But if it's not just an animal, what does it want?"

"How do you mean?" I asked.

"I mean, it sounds like it has a purpose beyond staying alive, right?" he said. "So, what is it trying to do?"

Joey stared at him, their face suddenly pale. "How do you do that?" they demanded.

"What?"

"How do you take the story of a massive, murderous bug-thing and actually make it worse?"

"Is it worse if it has an agenda?" I asked.

"Of course it is!" Joey exclaimed. "If it is deliberately doing something, if it's consciously, intelligently working to some end other than its own survival, then we're looking at something far worse than a feeding frenzy! We're looking at something bigger, and all this brutal destruction is just a step on the way to whatever that other thing is."

"Reopening the prison," said DeMarcus. "Has to be. If this thing escaped from there, it has to be working to free all the other *yōkai* that were trapped inside with it."

"How?" I asked.

"No clue," DeMarcus replied, "but you have to admit that it meets Joey's criteria for something much worse than casual carnage."

And he was right about that.

Portersville's local government offices came up with another solution to the problem of the *Omukade* the following day, one that Dad didn't like at all.

"You hear what that idiot mayor has done?" he announced with withering scorn the moment I walked into the store after school. "He's offered a reward to local hunters for whoever can bag the *exotic pet* which has been wandering around town. Can you believe it? They have no idea what they are dealing with, so they are sending every moron with a rifle on patrol through *our streets!*"

My father has a very British attitude to firearms. "Playing cowboys," he called it. He was arranging a display of Smiths' Smoking Sauce, each jar adorned with a simple but eye-catching label featuring a combination of British, Japanese and American flags. Em must have helped him with that.

"Unbelievable," he concluded scornfully.

"Uh oh," I said. "Not good."

"Uh oh, is right," said Dad. "And since we know what the *exotic pet* actually is, I think we know what this will lead to. Carnage and death. You'd need a bazooka to stop that centipede thing. No hunting rifle will make a dent in it, and that means people are going to die. Yes, Caleb?"

The question felt oddly pointed, but I was forced to agree.

"Yes," I said, sitting at the counter, wary of what was coming next. I was suddenly sure my father had been working on this speech, and he had some specific goal in mind.

"Okay then," he said, as if the first part of his plan had been a success. "I think we have no choice. We have to tell them."

I was genuinely confused.

"Tell who what?" I asked.

"Tell the mayor about the giant centipede," he said flatly.

"Right," I laughed. "They'll have you committed to a mental institution."

"Not if we tell them everything."

"What do you mean?"

"The fracking plant incident, the Japanese folk hero stuff, your abilities…"

"No!" I exclaimed, leaping to me feet. "What are you…? No. Absolutely not!"

"We have to! You said yourself, people are going to die!"

I stared at him aghast. "You can't be serious!" I sputtered. "Dad, you can't mean this!"

"If we explain it properly, they'll see that all this strangeness and magic…it's just a different kind of nature. Like, science. They'll see we are on their side, but they need to act with our guidance."

"It's the mayor, Dad!" I exclaimed, my voice rising in pitch and volume. I couldn't believe what was happening, and to be honest, I was starting to lose it. "Tyler J. Miller the second, and his pals! You think he's going to listen to what we say and then put *us* in charge? The weirdo Japs from the inconvenience store running the town? Listen to yourself!"

"We can't sit on what we know, Caleb!"

"It's Hideki," I fired back, driven by an anger that was two-thirds fear. "Why do you always think everything can be fixed in a reasonable way? You know who these people are, the mayor and his buddies, but here you are, thinking you can explain things and everything will be fine. It's so *English*! You know what talking to them will mean for me and Em? This," I said with sudden, terrible realization. "This is why we didn't tell you."

And I marched out.

This was bad. I'd had fights with Dad before, but this was a different thing entirely. I'd said something I couldn't take back, and I didn't know what he was going to do.

Dad was skeptical about a lot of things, but in his British heart, he believed everyone was basically decent and rational. You just had to find the right way of talking to them. It was, I suppose, a kind of privilege, because it had mostly worked for him. Maybe that's not fair, but I didn't believe it would work for us. At best, we'd be dismissed as credulous outsiders, at worst they'd believe us, and me and Em would be spirited off to a secure lab where government scientists would run tests on us: Homeland Security, the mystical division…

I didn't know what to do. I headed back toward school hoping to catch Em in the pool, but she wasn't there, and the coach said she'd left for the day. I texted her:

"Where ru? Dad wants to tell the town council EVERYTHING. Call me."

I held the phone in my hand, waiting for it to ring, but it didn't. I called Mom, and she picked up. She was at the supermarket. I could hear the squeak of her shopping cart and the echo of store announcements over speakers. I told her what Dad was thinking of doing. I didn't say what I had said to him in response.

"Okay," said Mom, forcing a calm into her voice that she clearly didn't feel. "I'll talk to him. Come home. I need you to man the register for a while."

"Is Dad there?"

"He's about to head to the wholesalers, why?"

I sighed. "I'll be back in an hour," I said.

"Try to make it half an hour. It's the monthly local business owners meeting." And she hung up with an abruptness that told me she was worried.

I went to the woods, my default position when I'm stressed or upset. It gets cooler as you climb up the mountain trails, quieter, and you almost never see anyone. Sometimes I'd find a tree stump to sit on and study the bird song app on my phone in silence for hours, trying to spot the chickadees and bluebirds as they did their bird stuff up in the canopy. Today I just walked, the tension driving me higher and higher up toward the remains of the fracking plant, my mind playing out every possibility that might result from the Portersville bigwigs learning of our family's magical ancestry.

As I walked, I thought about Dad, and about Em. I thought about Raiko's lost shuriken, the one thing that might give me an edge against the *Omukade*. I knew I had no way of finding it, that it could be anywhere and had probably rusted to nothing decades ago, but when you are in a tight corner, you'll believe in any means of escape.

The one place I knew Raiko had been was up in the Redscar mountain caves where we had bound the *oni*, his mother, and their army of *yōkai*. I didn't really decide to go there. My feet just sort of led the way. I walked, my eyes down for the glint of ancient metal, and eventually I found myself at the caves where Southern Shale's fracking site had been.

There were still strands of yellow caution tape snagged on trees, muddy now, and you could just make out where the heavy trucks had carved out the gravel surface of the access road, but it was still and deserted. In places, new weeds were poking through the parking lot and a couple of tiny saplings were pushing up near the tree line. Amazing what a few weeks could do in a place like North Carolina, given enough rain. In a couple of years, the whole area would be lost to the woods again, buried under kudzu and pine trees like it had never been.

Unless the frackers come back.

I thought about how, before Mr. West bought it, Chris Collington had been pressing to turn the Haversham house into office space for Southern Shale. Which meant they weren't done with Portersville. The mayor and his pals were probably working discreetly to clear the way, even if they'd have to build their town offices somewhere else.

It was quiet up there. Peaceful without being silent. Where there had been only the drone of heavy machinery, the birds were back: warblers, a Carolina wren, and the rap of a distant woodpecker. I made my way to the cave mouth and squeezed through the barricades.

It was odd being back. Scary, to be honest. With each echo of my feet in the first cavern, I felt my pulse quicken as the memory of my fight with the *onibaba*, her son, and their servants returned. I winced, suddenly wishing I hadn't come.

But I had, and that meant doing things properly. I snapped my phone flashlight on and looked for both the shuriken and the fissure where the cave narrowed into a passage leading into that terrible, inner space, but it all felt oddly unfamiliar. After a little hunting, I realized why. The fissure wasn't there. I saw fragments of chipboard and saw the holes where anchors had been driven into the rock before I made sense of what I was looking at. Where the narrow fissure had been, there was a solid wall, clearly not made of the granite that surrounded it, but just as solid. It was cement. Southern Shale's solution to the cave collapse they had caused had been to pump concrete into the hollow.

It was good news, I supposed.

Nothing would be getting out of there now.

So why did it not feel like good news? There was an atmosphere to the place that went beyond its dim clamminess. I found myself remembering what had happened the last time I had been up there and—this was somehow more unsettling—not remembering. There were empty spots in my mind. I recalled going into the cave. I remembered the fight with the *onibaba* and her son in vivid, nightmare detail. And I remembered eventually coming to at the shrine with Em. But what happened in between those events was fuzzy.

I was glad to leave and head back down the mountain toward home. I didn't give the lost shuriken another thought.

When I reached the inconvenience store, Mom looked at her watch pointedly before grabbing her jacket and heading out to discuss, no doubt, Mr. West's plans to yank Portersville out of the twenty-first century with other local business owners. I sat myself down at the counter in the shop, and in a half hour I sold three cans of baked beans, two boxes of spaghetti, a couple of newspapers, a six-pack of Diet Coke, and a bunch of bananas. All the thrills of life as a superhero.

My audition for salesperson of the year came to an end with Em's arrival. She looked harried and weary, so I tried to stir up a little interest.

"I went up to the caves," I said.

"Why?" she asked, as if I'd said I had decided to become a professional juggler.

"Thought I'd look for Raiko's lost shuriken," I said.

That will get her attention, I thought, *spark some curiosity, even excitement...*

"Again, why?" she snapped. "It's a wild goose chase. Pointless."

"I know what a wild goose chase is," I replied.

"See, I'm not sure you do, if you think that hunting for a knife dropped by someone centuries ago in a hundred square miles of wooded mountain isn't one."

She didn't even look at me, just helped herself to packets from the inconvenience store's snack aisle.

"How about you just help instead of being smart," I suggested.

"It's a waste of time, Caleb," she said, "and I don't have the time to waste."

"What are you even doing all the time?" I demanded. "You're never here. You quit your job at McDonald's..."

"I still have swim team and, you know, that stuff they give you to do after class: what's it called? Oh, right: *homework*. Remember that? I intend to have a life after graduation even if you plan to stay here forever working in the inconvenience store and saving the world from monsters."

"You weren't at swim team," I snapped back. "I went to the pool."

"So you're checking up on me now, are you?" she fired back.

And with that she stormed out. Again. It was all she ever seemed to do. Usually, she marched up to her room and played BABYMETAL's "Rondo of Nightmares" on repeat until the house shook. Not this time. She headed back outside.

It was annoying. It was also weird, and when I saw Dad's van pull up in front of the store—which meant he and I would be alone together, glaring silently at each other until Mom got home—I followed her.

Dad saw me come out and cocked his head as if to say something but apparently couldn't come up with the words. He did his little head jut acknowledgement and made a tight smile, but he didn't speak and got straight to unloading the van. I put my head down and took off.

I meant to call after Em, vent at her about Dad. Maybe a little shared annoyance would make her less likely to pop off at me every ten minutes. I hurried after her as she made it to the corner but then she hesitated and looked around. It was a deliberate, even furtive movement, like she was checking to see there was no one around, and I responded by shrinking back round the corner of the laundromat. I did it without thinking, and as soon as I had flattened myself against the brick wall, I knew that if she saw me, she'd be livid.

Spying on me?! she'd bellow, full of indignant rage.

Except that I really wasn't; or hadn't been until about a second before. Now, I had to admit, I was curious. What was she doing out here, skulking around like that? The only time I had seen her look so self-conscious was when she was about to shift into her fox form. But why would she want to do that out here in broad daylight? Was it connected to her sneaking out at night?

I hugged the side of the laundromat and leaned round just enough to be able to see her through the corner of the window. She did another quick check then crossed the street heading north.

Which made no sense. School with its pool, library and media center was west. This way there was nothing but woods and—my heart skipped as I thought it—the Sherringham ranch.

She was investigating!

That was good. But why hadn't she taken me with her? Did she have a hunch she didn't want to share? Was she going to approach the house as herself and ask the old couple questions like a reporter, or would she transform, and go sniffing around the pasture looking for clues as to where the *Omukade* might have gone?

But she didn't go to the ranch. She paused again, did another check that no one was around, and headed between the ornamental gate posts of what I still thought of as the Haversham house.

I stared, stunned and confused. This was where she was spending all her time? Why? What could she possibly have to do at the West mansion?

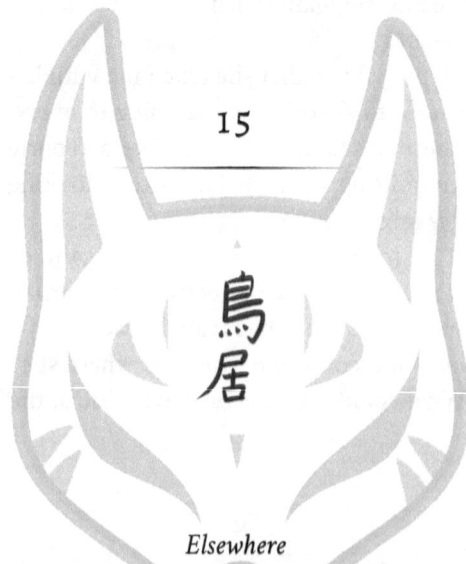

15

鳥
居

Elsewhere

B rian Davenham couldn't believe his luck. Only a couple of days ago he had been sweating about who or what had glimpsed him paying off his son Bobby's math teacher and what they might do with that information, and now a solution had come floating out of the sky like a gift. In fact, it had come from the TV news.

"Mayor of Portersville, Tyler J. Miller II, has today put aside a thousand dollars of public money as a reward for whomever rids the little mountain town of the animal which has preyed on local cattle, causing a wave of panic in a community where most folks leave their doors unlocked…"

Brian had laughed out loud. The reporter had interviewed not just the mayor but a handful of local men, some of whom had showed themselves keen to earn the reward.

"I mean, the money would be nice," said Harold Baumgarten, a local mechanic and "sportsman" who Brian knew couldn't hit a barn door with a sniper rifle, "but I'm doing it to protect the town. Can't have our people and livestock terrorized like this because someone can't control their pet lion or whatever. It ain't right."

Pet lion! It was absurd.

Of course, the truth was even stranger, but no one else knew that.

Brian couldn't decide if the culprit was someone who looked normal most of the time and then changed, or if they always had that twenty-foot neck and the mouthful of shark teeth, but that would only matter after he had gotten his reward. So long as it still looked as weird and monstrous as it had when he glimpsed it at his office window after he'd shot it, things would be fine.

Two birds, as they say, one stone. In this case, the stone would be a .416 Rigby, the same rifle he had used to bag his wildebeest and kudu in Africa.

The advantage he had over his fellow Portersville hunters, including those who might be a better shot than him, was that he knew what he was hunting. They were looking for lions and tigers and bears (oh my!), while he was looking for some mutant freak with a neck like the Loch Ness Monster. Whatever damage those teeth could do—and the Sherringham cows had, by all accounts, been pretty carved up—he figured the creature's greatest advantage was surprise. You were too busy staring in disbelief when that head came flying at you, and it got its first bite in before you got with the program.

Not him. He knew what it was.

He just had to find it first.

Of course, knowing what it looked like didn't really mean he knew what it was, but Brian didn't care about that. It was probably some genetic nightmare caused by chem trails or vaccines or some such thing and had lived out its daylight hours in the sewers, only emerging after dark to spy on regular people like him. Well, that had been a mistake.

The sewer thing had struck him as soon as he heard the story of the old Asian woman who had barely gotten away with her life but had—she said—blacked out before she got a look at whatever had retreated through the manhole and under the town. It was the perfect way for the freak thing to get around unseen. So that was where he would begin his hunt.

He had put on rubber boots and had a couple of those masks Glennis had forced him to wear during the pandemic, to keep out the worst of the sewer filth, but otherwise he was dressed as he had been for his African hunt, rifle in hand and cartridge case at his side. He had notified the town hall that he was officially throwing his hat into the ring, just to cover his bases, and been wished the best of luck by the mayor's secretary. Now he used a half-size crowbar to jimmy the manhole cover clear and shone his flashlight down. There were ladder rungs set into the wall, some of them bent recently, presumably by the thing which had fled this way.

The evidence of the creature's apparent strength had given him pause. He had heard about it flipping a truck on its way into the sewer, but seeing the twisted iron rungs, squeezed almost flat against the walls, made him hesitate.

Could the thing he had seen do that?

He frowned but thought how much strength would be required to control a neck like a Brontosaurus' and decided it made a kind of sense. If he held a pole half that length outstretched, he'd quickly struggle to manipulate it accurately. The muscle power required to keep a head as perfectly poised as he had seen it twenty feet from the body must be enormous. It must be like an anaconda. If it dove into a confined space, all its neck compressed like some great, squirming octopus tentacle, yeah, it could easily bend those rungs.

So he descended, listening hard for something other than the drip of water or the skittering feet of rats in the fetid air. At the bottom, he shone his flashlight in both directions, dismayed to find the sewer was really no more than a concrete pipe about a yard and a half in diameter. He had sort of expected he'd be able to walk along it, maybe on some brick side-walk like he'd seen under the streets of major cities in movies. That, he now realized, had been stupidly unrealistic.

It was, he had to admit, a little scary.

His light penetrated only a couple of dozen feet ahead. If the thing appeared in front of him, he would have nowhere to go, and precious little time to get his shot off before that mouth full of teeth was coming at him.

Maybe this was a bad idea?

No. This needed nipping in the bud. His reputation, and maybe his idiot son's career, depended on it. He checked his weapon and nestled for a moment in the slimy water, breathing shallowly and trying to awake all his senses in the gloom, comforted by the feel of the rifle's wooden stock against his shoulder.

Perhaps he could put the reward money toward his next overseas hunt. He had seen a documentary about rhino poaching for the Asian alternative medicine market, and—in spite of the show's bleeding-heart tone—had come away with an idea to offset the cost of the hunt. He could go out to Africa, legally shoot a rhino as a trophy, get the head home and saw off the horn. He could get a taxidermist to make a realistic replacement for his office display and sell the real horn on the black market. Apparently they were worth their weight in gold in China and Vietnam.

Maybe the family who ran that convenience store across the street from the West mansion could hook him up.

He was thinking about this when the beam of his flashlight caught an odd rippling in the sewer ahead, not just in the thin stream of water, but on the sides, so that for a moment it seemed like the tunnel itself was moving. It took a second to realize that what he was seeing were bugs. Thousands of them, coming toward him. Cockroaches, flashing black-brown in the brilliance of his flashlight, feathery antennae whipping.

He swallowed, sickened, and a memory flashed through his head. Ron Blakely talking about his damn-fool car and bugs coming out of the air vents...

His flashlight sputtered and went out.

Brian recoiled, shrinking away from the sides of the pipe, and hugging the useless rifle as they reached him. He closed his eyes and bent his head as low as he could, glad at least that the mask was covering his nose and mouth, but he felt their feet on the back of his neck, and he roared aloud in horror. The long bellow of revulsion echoed through the drain, filling his ears, so that he didn't hear the thing that came after them until it was already on him.

As his flashlight came on again and grew brighter than seemed possible, he opened his eyes just in time to see something from hell bearing down on him. Not the snake-necked person-thing he had been expecting. Something much, much worse. It resembled a centipede, but it was massive, its bulk filling the sewer pipe, even as it spiraled toward him on a hundred yellow legs. Its eyes found his and its mouth parts gaped, reaching for him like claws.

The rifle went off, and its sound boomed through the drain like a canon, but whether it slowed the creature down for even a fraction, Brian Davenham would never know.

16

I googled Kieran West, hoping to dig up a better sense of the man, what he was doing in town, and what appeal his house had for my surly sister. He had a Wikipedia page, probably a first for anyone in Portersville, detailing his background and employment history, and I recognized a few of the phrases from recent stories in the Chronicle and on Action News. There were references to Silicon Valley investments and management of various software platforms and products, which sounded impressive but didn't mean much to me.

He was apparently CEO of KNI Vision whose emblem was a curly flame. I couldn't figure out whether they made computer chips, configured them, or wrote the software to make them work, but they had "revolutionized high-speed digital processing" whatever that meant. There were photos of West a decade younger, looking hipster cool and breezily confident, more surfer dude than tech nerd, and every image, every sentence told me nothing I could get my head around other than the fact that this guy came from a world I knew nothing about. And, of course, that he was very, very rich, which I already knew.

I pulled up some local news reports, but they said little I hadn't either heard from the man directly or gleaned from the town's gossip mill. What no one explained was exactly why he had left California and come to Portersville. He'd had "a change of heart" about the cyber universe he had helped to usher in, but precisely why was a bit of a mystery. "It was less of a discovery," he told Katie Marsden (the cute reporter at Action News) "and more of a gradual realization, but yes, there was a moment where it all came to a head. When he was in middle school, my son Nathan was given an English assignment in which he had to find a picture of a bird or animal and write a poem about it. A week later he came to see me after dinner, and he was just devastated. Tears in his eyes, barely able to speak. He managed to say it was about the assignment, and I assumed he'd done badly. But he hadn't. He'd gotten an A. 'So what's the problem?' I asked. Turns out, the picture he had used as his inspiration—a bird called a red-headed cuckoo—didn't exist. The image had been some AI fake which had circulated on social media. He was just crushed. He felt stupid and dishonest."

"And that upset you?" prompted the reporter.

"At first, yes," said West. "It broke my heart. But then I got mad, you know? I mean, I'm sure that whoever created that image—or rather the person who generated it with a few prompts and some photoshop tweaks —didn't mean any harm, and certainly had no plans to upset my son, but it was *doing* harm, and these things were just everywhere and getting more prevalent every day, flooding our lives. Suddenly I could see the danger we were in. And I knew I was partly to blame. I had worked on those computer systems. I had worked for the movie industry in special effects, making things up that weren't real. But now we couldn't tell what was real and what wasn't."

The same story appeared in a *Charlotte Observer* article. Otherwise, he had managed to maintain a very low profile for a rich and powerful man. He was listed as "former CEO" on the KNI Vision site, and his name cropped up in several bylines on older stories in passing, including as a "developer of digital content for the biggest names in movies" but it looked like Kieran West had managed to make his money mostly in the shadows.

After a half hour or so of hunting around, I had learned almost nothing new. I had wondered vaguely if his family had deep ties to Portersville which had been forgotten, or to any of the local powerbrokers including Southern Shale. I even tried searching for his name coupled with Japan, but nothing came up. If West was in any way tied to what had emerged from Raiko's prison, I couldn't see it.

I wanted to ask Em directly why she had been sneaking off to the West mansion, but I knew she would have a complete meltdown and figured I should know more before confronting her.

"You ever think it's something ordinary," said Joey, when I raised the matter with them and DeMarcus in the gloomy lunchroom. The power was out again, so the offerings were sandwiches, fruit, candy and canned drinks. "Like, hello, half the school is in love with Nathan West, and the other half wish his dad would adopt them."

"You think something is going on between Nathan and my sister?" I asked. The possibility hadn't occurred to me, and I wasn't sure how I felt about it.

"What?" sputtered DeMarcus, dismissive and indignant. "He's a year younger than her!"

"If it was the other way round—if he was older than her—would you say that?" Joey countered.

DeMarcus hesitated, like he knew he was on dangerous ground. "Well, she doesn't seem to even like him," he said at last.

"Meaning you don't want her to," said Joey wisely.

"What?" I asked.

"What!" DeMarcus exclaimed, his face flushing.

"Whatever," said Joey airily.

DeMarcus gave me a quick look and for a split second we considered each other warily, before grinning and shrugging the matter off, not wanting to discuss it further. There was a roll of thunder overhead. Another storm which the power company would blame for why they couldn't get the lights back on.

"I don't think Nathan is involved with whatever his dad is doing," I decided out loud.

"Meaning you don't want him to be," said Joey.

"Cut it out, Joey," I said. "We aren't our parents. You can't assume a kid is involved in, or even knows about, what his dad is up to."

"But don't you think it's weird," DeMarcus said, "that they arrive in town just as all this weird stuff starts up again?"

"An informed observer might point out," Joey ventured in a low voice, "that the first wave of all that—as you so eloquently put it—*weird stuff* occurred because, you know, *Hideki* was here, and still is here, so…"

"But why would the Wests have anything to do with my grandmother's evil sister and her demon son," I countered. "He's a tech bro from out west."

"You don't think all this anti-internet stuff is…" DeMarcus seemed to hunt for a word other than *weird*. "Odd? The ban on cameras and phones in his house? The war on AI? The plan to disconnect the town from the web? What the TV people are calling his plans to *retroize* Portersville. It's strange, right?"

"Strange yes," Joey agreed. "Pointless, probably, and I speak as someone who hopes to make a living as a coder one day. But being a born-again Luddite doesn't make him in league with Japanese demons."

"A what?" I asked.

"Look it up before Mr. West bans the internet."

"Seriously, Joey, what does it mean?"

"How will you learn if you don't do the work?" Joey replied in a sickly-sweet tone.

DeMarcus pulled out his phone. "Hey, look at that!" he exclaimed. "I have a cell signal."

A Luddite, it turned out, was a member of a nineteenth-century workers group who saw industrialization as threatening their livelihood and culture. They raided factories and smashed up the machines. Ironic, I guess, that we learned that by looking it up online.

"He's trying to create a version of old timey Japan in Portersville!" DeMarcus exclaimed.

"That's kind of a leap, bro," I said doubtfully.

"Agreed," said Joey, shaking off DeMarcus' surly look. "And if he was, he's not gonna succeed. At best, he's gonna get a version of North Carolina modeled on the early nineties. But look on the bright side."

"What's that?"

"Those kids wearing Nirvana Tee shirts might actually hear the music they've been advertising."

DeMarcus shook his head grimly. "Well, I don't trust either of them, father or son," he pronounced.

"Maybe you just don't like cool people," I said. I wasn't sure why I was defending Nathan when I knew there was something weird going on. I just couldn't see him as being linked to whatever his dad was involved in.

"Well, I get along with you," said DeMarcus sharply, "so maybe you're right."

"What's that supposed to mean?" I fired back.

"Figure it out," DeMarcus replied darkly.

"I don't know what you are talking about," I said.

"It means that ever since Nathan West showed up in this school you've been starstruck," DeMarcus said, suddenly agitated. "Ooh, Nathan's so cool! Did you hear what Nathan said in class? I had lunch with Nathan today!"

"I have never said those things."

"Sure you have. You don't even know you're doing it!"

"Just trying to be friendly to someone who's new!" I protested. "Be a little welcoming."

"You already have friends, Caleb."

"Hideki," I corrected.

DeMarcus' face clouded, and he clamped his jaws shut tight looking away. I relented.

"You can call me Caleb," I muttered. "Sorry. I'm just..." But I wasn't sure how to finish the sentence.

"How about we focus our suspicion on Mr. West for now," Joey suggested calmly, "and decide what we think about Nathan later?"

DeMarcus and I scowled at each other.

"Fine," we both said, not liking it.

"Good," said Joey.

"But you're going to look into his dad at least, right," DeMarcus pressed.

"Look into what?" Joey replied. "See if he's listed in catalogs of famous Japanese monsters?"

"You know what I mean," DeMarcus insisted.

"Just do some of your cyber poking around," I added. "See if anything pops."

"*See if anything pops?*" Joey echoed with a grin. "What are we now, the junior wing of *Miami Vice?*"

I shrugged.

"At least it's early nineties," I said with a half-hearted smile, but Joey shook their head.

"Eighty-four to eighty-nine," they said. "The *Vice* never made it into the nineties."

Which was about the most Joey thing that had ever been Joeyed. I shot DeMarcus a grin, but he was looking surly, so I said nothing.

The power was still out and after an hour or two of cell phone signal, that had gone again too, so I had nothing to do but go over DeMarcus' idea that the Wests were somehow invested in ancient Japanese stuff. It made no sense, but I couldn't shake it, so I braved the storm and went to Saito-san's place. If anyone would know what was going on here, it would be the tengu. He would be a calming, logical sounding board and would soothe my swelling anxiety.

He was not. In fact, I have never seen him so wild and distracted as that moment when I poked my head into the empty restaurant and found him crawling rapidly around like a feral dog, his hair unkempt and his eyes flashing around like he expected to be attacked from all sides at once.

"Dude," I said, when he ignored my dripping entrance. "What are you doing?"

"What?" he muttered, returning to his ferreting around. He looked under tables, and pushed chairs aside, staring intently. It was unnerving.

"Have you lost something?"

He sat up at that, staring directly ahead, his bulbous eyes ready to pop out of his head.

"Lost?" he repeated. "No. Nothing has been lost. Things have been *stolen*. I have been robbed!"

"Seriously?" I asked. It had never occurred to me that ancient mountain spirits might have their stuff ripped off while they weren't looking. Being someone who was used to keeping eyes on some of our more questionable customers at the inconvenience store, I found it kind of endearing: humanizing, you might say. "Sorry, man. Are you missing anything valuable? Have you called the cops?"

I scanned the restaurant, but apart from the chaos of his search, nothing was obviously missing. He took in my gaze, my manner, and he scurried over to me and leaned in close, whispering through clenched teeth, "Not from here. From...*the back*."

He rolled his eyes toward the rear door, and I realized he meant the dojo where we trained.

I scowled, feeling something of his panic and anxiety, but then he seized my wrist and was dragging me after him.

"Your swords?" I gasped, as we blundered through the back door and out. "Someone has stolen your weapons?"

"Worse," he gasped, mounting the stone steps and sliding the screen door open.

I wondered what could be worse than losing the ancient swords and spears he had maintained so carefully for generations, as we kicked off our shoes and moved into the main hall, with its broad square of tatami. Saito stepped aside and gestured boldly to the far end of the room, his head bowed, his face dark with perplexity and rage.

The bookshelves, which were generally so ordered, looked like a whirlwind had hit them, and the suit of armor which had stood sentinel over them was on its side, the masked helmet knocked to the floor. There were pages and scrolls tossed all over the place. Ancient volumes lay open on the floor, their dark covers spread like the wings of stricken birds. Papers of carefully hand-lettered Japanese texts lay in torn and tattered fragments. I thought I recognized the book he had used to tell my family about the *Omukade* among them. But it was also clear that the fragments on the ground weren't enough to fill the spaces on the shelves. Some books were just gone.

"Who would take your books?" I said lamely. "Who could even read them?"

He turned his hair-raising glare on me and said simply, "An enemy."

But if he knew who or what that enemy was, he wasn't saying, and when I tried to get him talking about the Wests, he grew even more irritable and dismissive.

"I need to think about what has happened here," he said. "About what to do next."

I expressed my condolences again and left, the wild-eyed spirit too angry and distracted to even say goodbye. The storm—not for the first time—had vanished as quickly as it had come, but I found as I walked home, that I had caught some of the tengu's panic. I told myself it was just a few missing books, but if someone as unflappable as Saito could get this freaked out, there had to be a good reason. I found myself wondering what was in those books that made them so precious.

It got worse.

That evening, just as we were preparing for dinner by candle and lantern light, the power came back on, and with it the breaking news that Bobby Davenham's dad had been killed. His body—or what was left of it—had been found after a dog walker had reported a swarm of bugs coming from a drain not that far from where Bachan had been attacked. A white-faced Sheriff Halpern had made a report on the news warning people to stay indoors. When one of the reporters asked if Brian Davenham had been attacked in the same manner as the Sherringham cattle, the sheriff's face had gone wooden as he chose his words.

"I can't say for sure at this time, pending further investigation, but the attacks are at least superficially similar."

Other reporters tried to follow up, asking if the body had been partially eaten or dismembered, but the sheriff shut the event down at that point, which—of course—everyone took as confirmation of what the reporters had said.

It was shocking, and not just in the scary way. I didn't like Bobby Davenham, mostly because he didn't like me, but I wouldn't wish anything like this on his family, and what had happened to them made me thoughtful. The idea that your father could just be snatched away like that —even if it was partly the result of his own actions—was horrifying. As my family sat down to eat, I tried to think of what to say that would make amends with Dad.

I didn't get a chance.

No sooner had the plates been laid on the table, Dad, who had had been stonily silent, sat back, put his hands together and, without looking at any of us, said, "We should have said something."

There was a heavy silence.

"What do you mean?" Mom asked, though I'm sure she knew.

"I mean that we had information about what was out there," Dad said, spelling it out, "and we said nothing, and now a man is dead."

"What could we have said?" asked Emily. "That a creature from Japanese mythology was loose and it could only be defeated by magic?"

"If necessary," said Dad. "Maybe there would have been a way round it, but yes. If there was no other possible explanation that would have raised the alarm, we should have told the truth."

"They would have said we were crazy," Mom replied.

"Perhaps," Dad agreed. "But it might have made a difference, and we would have done the right thing. I'm going to call the mayor. Maybe it's too late, but so long as that thing is out there…"

"He won't listen," I said.

"Then I'll call the sheriff," said Dad. He thought for a moment as the rest of us stared at him in paralyzed horror. "Now," he concluded, pushing his chair back and standing up. "I'm going to call them now."

"Stephen, please," said Mom. "You know what this will bring to this family?"

"I'm sorry, Jennie," he said. "I'll try to keep you out of it as best I can, but if that *Omukade* thing were to kill again… I just couldn't live with myself."

"How are you going to keep us out of it!?" Em demanded, her face flushed, her eyes suddenly brimming with unshed tears.

"I'll say Bachan remembered what attacked her," he said, thinking it through as he spoke. "I'll say she didn't recall at first because she hit her head, but she remembers now, and that she connected what she saw to the giant centipede stories she was told when she was a child."

"In Japan, hundreds of years ago!" Mom retorted. "You know how they'll respond if they start poking into Bachan's past and figure out how old she is? You can't keep us out of it, Stephen. If you tell them and they believe you, we will all be arrested. Who knows what they will do with us! And then who will stop the *Omukade*?"

"We haven't stopped it so far," said Dad.

I stood up very slowly.

"I'm sorry, Dad," I said. "I really am. We should have told you right from the start..."

"This isn't about that!" he exclaimed.

"Maybe not," I said, my voice low and firm, "but it is about our secret, and we need to keep it. I won't let you do this."

Bewilderment flashed through his face, and then his mouth fell open. "You mean you'd fight me?" he said, aghast.

"I don't want to..." I began, but Mom cut me off.

"Caleb, no!" she said, also standing and extending a hand toward me in a gesture of command. "You will not lay a finger on your father."

And hearing it put like that stopped me cold. Had I really been threatening to hit my dad?

"And you!" she added, turning on my father. "How many times have you ranted about the mayor, about how Tyler J. Miller was just a suit protecting his own interests and those of his buddies?" She enumerated them on the fingers of one hand. "The Blakelys. The Collingtons and their Southern Shale pals. The Davenhams."

"So Brian Davenham was well connected," said Dad. "Doesn't mean his life was worth less."

"No one said it was," Mom replied. "I'm just saying what you have said a hundred times: that this town is run by a handful of wealthy friends who watch each others' backs, and that the sheriff's department is little more than the stick they used to get what they want. Now you talk about them like they are the fount of justice and authority? What would they do if they believed you? Call in more hunters? More armed police? The National Guard? You think armored cars and machine guns will make us safe from ancient magic? Because I don't. I think that will just get more people killed."

Dad said nothing, but I could tell that she had hit a nerve and his certainty was wavering.

"The only people who can stop what is happening here are us," said Mom. "This family. That includes you."

He stood there, his head bowed, his face a mask of weariness, doubt, and anxiety.

Mom reached out to him and touched his arm. "Come on," she said softly. "Eat your dinner and we'll figure out what to do."

At last, he nodded and managed a kind of sad smile which was heartbreaking to look at. He sat down silently. Mom took his hand. Emily and I exchanged anxious looks. Mom had contained the danger for now, but this wasn't over.

We were still sitting in silence, eating our pasta with our eyes on our plates when a distant rattling knock came from the store, sharp and insistent.

"Someone's at the door," I said.

"Store's closed," said Em.

The knock came again, more insistent this time.

"I'll check it out," I said, getting to my feet, glad of an excuse to leave the table even as Emily called after me that if customers couldn't come during operating hours that was their problem.

I flicked a switch as I came through the back, cursed when the lights—of course—didn't come on, and went back for the lantern. I held it up since the only other light in the store was the soft, humming glow of the fridge cases.

Someone's face was pressed against the front door, knuckles rapping. A woman, her face distorted by the way it was squeezed up against the glass.

"We're closed," I called.

But she kept knocking, a slow but sharp, urgent rhythm that was almost robotic.

I threw the latch and cracked the door a little, or meant to, but she was leaning hard against it and practically fell in on me, setting the old-fashioned bell over the door jangling.

I stumbled back, babbling about what time we reopened in the morning but then I heard my mother's voice from the back of the store.

"Maureen," she said coolly. "We are actually closed at the moment. Perhaps you could come back..."

"I know," said Maureen Collington who I don't think had ever set foot in the place before. She looked odd, distracted, and kept running her fingers through her hair. "I'm really sorry. I know we're not supposed to be outside, what with…everything. I just really need… something."

It was a curious remark, curious as the way her eyes flashed around, hungry, but also shame-faced.

"Okay," said Mom while I backed cautiously off and busied myself unpacking a shipment of Japanese rice crackers. As I hung them on a rack in the designated snack aisle, I watched the two women. Mom looked wary, a little stand offish, but had fixed a professional smile on her face. "What can I help you find?"

"You know," said Mrs. Collington, "I'm not sure. I've had the oddest cravings of late, and the Harris Teeter didn't seem to have what I was looking for."

"Okay," Mom said again, cautiously polite. "What did you have in mind?"

"I'm really not sure," Maureen replied with a would-be casual laugh that didn't quite cover her embarrassment. She swayed slightly as she spoke, and I wondered if she–as my father sometimes said–*had drink taken.* "I heard that you stocked a range of…" she hunted for the word and settled on "less common items. Imported, I mean."

"Sure," said Mom, still cagey. "Down there where Hideki is working. Let me know if I can help with anything."

"Thank you," Maureen replied, moving awkwardly toward me. "I really don't know what's come over me."

She moved like she was forcing herself to walk slowly, her eyes flashing hungrily over the surrounding shelves. When she reached me, she forced a smile.

"Hi," she said.

"Hi, Mrs. Collington," I replied.

Her eyes went vague, uncertain, then cleared.

"You know my name?" she said.

"You were at the school trip to the ranger station," I replied by explanation. "And I saw you at the party across the street."

She paused at that, and another dreamy look came into her eyes, as if it took some effort for her mind to reach back that far.

"Yes," she said, vaguely. She looked over the packages I had just unloaded. "What are these like?"

"Senbe," I said. "Rice crackers. Sort of crisp and salty. Really good."

She nodded. "Crunchy?" she asked.

"Yeah," I said with a shrug. "Especially the big ones."

Another nod, and then she took one of the larger packages uncertainly, gave me an awkward smile and snatched two more. She moved off without a word but hesitated in the candy aisle and chose two large bags of vividly colored gummy worms. She moved quickly to the register, hesitated at the sight of my mother, and gave an uncomfortable little laugh.

"Not sure what's got into me," she said again.

"Maybe you're pregnant," said my mother, matching her uncertain smile.

Maureen laughed too loudly at the thin joke, then leaned forward. "I'm not," she said, all her former vagueness suddenly gone, "but you know who is? Kaycee Allen!"

Kaycee was a senior at school. My mother looked even more uncomfortable at the announcement.

"That's nice," she managed.

"Not if you ask her parents," said Maureen, still leaning in close and speaking rapidly in a stage whisper. "Her dad says that if she goes through with having it—which is what she's insisting on—he's going to go over to Topher Ryan's house to have it out with his family. Says he is going to force them to get married. Her mom—Linda—says he's going to do no such thing and that if Kaycee wants to do this alone, it's her decision. And Kaycee says that if her dad goes anywhere near Topher, she's moving to Greenville or Charlotte!"

Maureen waited for a response to these dramatic tidings, and my mother eventually said, "How do you know all this?" whereupon Maureen got that vague look on her face again, as if she couldn't answer the question. For a moment she looked lost, even upset, then she came back to herself and handed the merchandise to Mom to ring up.

"Just these," she said.

Mom, seemingly relieved to be out of the conversation, processed the transaction, and handed Maureen her change.

"I'm sorry about Brian Davenham," said Mom. "I know you were friends. Terrible thing."

"What?" said Maureen, that vacant look in her face again. "Oh, right. Yes. Thank you."

She hunched over a little and turned away, like she was trying to conceal what she was doing, but I saw her tear open one of each packet then reach in, pulling out a fist full of the wiggling gummy worms and two of the large rice crackers, and cram them hungrily into her mouth with both hands. For a moment she looked like a raccoon feasting on garbage, stuffing its face before something came to scare it off. She seemed to have forgotten us entirely.

She hesitated at the door and then stepped out into the wind and rain without another word. When the door closed behind her, my mother gazed after her, then turned as my father came from the back.

"Everything okay?" he asked.

Mom went to him, her face troubled, and laced her hands around his waist, though whether that was about the exchange she had had with Maureen Collington or the previous fight over dinner, I wasn't sure. Both probably.

"That," Mom said, "was very strange."

17

Bobby Davenham didn't show up for school the next day, but his name seemed to be on everyone's lips. The hushed excitement of the whisperings about giant snakes and the West family party had turned into something subdued, stunned even. Tyler looked, for once, dazed, unsure of himself, and when people spoke to him, he just grunted. I considered offering my condolences, but it didn't feel right and probably would have been thrown back in my face. And it wasn't like it was Tyler who had lost his father. When Bobby returned, I'd speak to him: something conventional, unspecific.

Sorry for your loss...

Even in my head it sounded stupid and vaguely dishonest, though the truth was that while I didn't like Bobby and hadn't known his father, I did feel for him. How could you not?

"So this Davenham guy was a local big wig, right?"

It was Nathan West. I was almost as taken aback by his tone as I was by the fact that he was speaking to me.

"I guess," I said. "Made a lot of money in plastics or something."

Nathan nodded thoughtfully, but he smirked slightly. "Maybe my father killed him," he said. "Not a fan of plastics, my dad." It was such an odd remark that I just looked at him. "Just kidding," he concluded, his smile now open.

There was the easy charm again, the TV commercial good looks, but it felt strange to me. Everyone else in the room was subdued, either gloomy or anxious, but Nathan took out a book and flicked through it, whistling softly to himself, like he hadn't noticed the mood.

Or doesn't care.

I was surprised by the thought but found myself rationalizing it. After all, Nathan was new. He didn't know any of the people involved. If I moved to a new town and someone I didn't know died, would I be upset? Probably not.

But would you not pick up on the fact that other people were and act accordingly?

But Nathan wasn't like that. He was more like his father, unconventional, a maverick, unaffected by the way other people behaved. I had assumed that was a good thing, but now...

"What?" asked Nathan. "You're staring."

"Nothing," I said quickly. "I just remembered that I hadn't read the scenes for today. Hope she doesn't call on me."

We were reading *Romeo and Juliet* in Mrs. Springer's English class, but I was behind. It's not easy reading by candlelight. Maybe I should make that point to Nathan before his dad propels us back into the dark (ha!) ages. I watched him as he picked up the book and considered it like it was an alien artifact, his face suddenly a mask of bafflement.

"Why do we have to study stuff like this?" he asked. "Made up stories. I mean, if it was something useful, something you would apply later in life, I would get it. But these people aren't real. The words they say are invented, fake."

I shrugged, not sure what to say. "Language skills, I guess," I tried, conscious that I didn't want to look like an idiot to him, whatever my other misgivings.

"But this isn't even your language," he said. "*Wherefore art thou Romeo?*" he quoted absently. What even is that?" He looked genuinely confused. "Do they want us to speak like this?"

"I doubt it," I said, grinning but with an effort. His perplexity was funny but also unsettling.

He frowned then put his hand in the air. It took a moment for the teacher to spot him, then she smiled.

"Yes, Nathan?" said Mrs. Springer.

"My good lady," said Nathan, his face straight. "How is't with you, this morrow?"

"I'm sorry?" said the teacher.

"I find myself perplexed," he said. The class had gone quiet and were watching, bemused. "Labored, have I, with this book, but fear I see not the merit of the exercise. Hast thou reasons for this study, or do we toil in perpetuity without purpose?"

There was a stunned silence, then everyone began to laugh. Everyone except DeMarcus, at least. He looked surly, irritated.

Jealous, I thought.

Nathan had everyone else in stitches. Even the teacher smiled at what she considered wit. Nathan didn't, he looked around, as if he was as baffled by the laughter as he had been by the assignment, and though everyone else thought he had made a cheeky joke, I wasn't so sure. As he looked around, his eyes narrowed thoughtfully at the laughter and applause, then he nodded to himself, as if making a mental note, smiled as if the joke had been intended all along, and returned his gaze to his book. The rest of the class proceeded as usual, but I found myself checking on him out of the corner of my eye from time to time, though what I was looking for, I couldn't say.

When it was over and we filed out to lunch, I took a seat in the corner of the cafeteria and watched him leave, oblivious to the looks of admiration he was getting from half the kids in the place. Joey joined me and followed my gaze. I looked for DeMarcus, but he had left class the moment the bell went.

"Interesting kid," Joey said.

"Who?"

Joey made a face like I was being stupid on purpose. "Nathan," they said.

"Oh, right. Yeah," I replied, not sure what else to say.

"Seems to like you," Joey added. "Which adds to what makes him interesting: by which I mean, of course, weird."

"Says the weirdest person at Portersville High."

"A badge I wear with pride," said Joey, grinning. "Some weird is good."

"Is this going somewhere?" I asked.

"Funnily enough, yes," said Joey. "I looked into his father as requested."

"And?" I replied. "He's weird too?"

"On the face of it, no," said Joey, head canted on one side and a thoughtful look in their eyes.

"But?"

"It's all new. The most visible stuff, at least."

"How do you mean?"

"The Wikipedia page, the website for KNI Vision, news articles about him," said Joey. "They all went up in the last three weeks."

"That's not possible."

"It could be that the KNI site was simply a massive redesign and the previous version has been wiped from the web, in so far as that's even possible, but it's odd that it would use a new base url. You want your old customers to be able to find you, right? There are mentions of his work going back a couple of decades, and he has a social media presence, but most of their contents are private. Most articles online recycle the same recent pictures of him. I could only find two images of him before 2010 and both looked like they had been altered. And in two cases where I could hack into the code of old news reports, articles which mention him in passing look like they have been edited recently."

"Why would anyone do that?" I asked.

Joey shrugged.

"Creating a past that doesn't exist?" they said. "Got me. But it's not a particularly thorough job. On the surface, it looks fine, but anyone with real skills who started digging into him would find the same things I did pretty easily, so if it's a scam of some kind, it's not intended to last long or go very high up the food chain. If he applied to head up a major corporation or run for Senate, he'd face some sticky questions pretty quickly."

"Is it possible that he's just stayed off the radar until now?"

"I guess," Joey replied. "Seems odd for a tech magnate to have so small a digital footprint, but yes. Maybe he just values his privacy. But if I were a suspicious kind of person, I'd wonder why someone this rich and powerful seems not to have existed a month ago, and why no one seems to care. If we were in California, we could go to the places where he worked and talk to people directly."

"But we aren't," I completed. "We're in Portersville."

"Where all we see is the shine," Joey replied.

"How do you mean?" I asked.

"I'm not sure," they said. "But when you raised the idea that there might be something off about him, I felt...almost annoyed. Like you were being disrespectful in even raising the question. Me! That's weird, right? I didn't *want* to investigate him, and even as I did, I found myself making excuses for why things looked as they did, like I really wanted to believe in him, you know?"

I thought of the man's magnetism, the way everyone gazed at him, basking in the glow coming off him like he was royalty or something. Was that why Emily was going to his house? Was she too just awe-struck by the Wests?

"Weird, right?" said Joey.

I nodded. Seemed like there was a lot of that going around.

"I mean," they added, "it's like you with Nathan."

"What's that supposed to mean?" I snapped.

"DeMarcus is right. You're dazzled. It would be funny if it wasn't also, you know, annoying."

"Why does everyone care so much about who I get along with?" I protested.

"Not everyone, Caleb. Your friends. Remember? The people who stood by you when the world was coming apart?"

"You're still my friends," I said. "Who said you weren't my friends?"

"I'm just saying that from DeMarcus' perspective, you seem to have fastened onto a relative stranger in ways that feel..."

"You're saying DeMarcus is jealous of Nathan?" I said with a scornful laugh.

"Maybe a little," Joey replied. "And maybe you need to show a little loyalty to your friends." I stared with my mouth open, sure my face was red with indignation. "I'm just saying. DeMarcus stood by you when the whole town was against you. Don't forget that."

"I haven't!" I exclaimed.

"Then don't let him think you have."

I was going to argue the point but then just shrugged and looked away, staring at the windows. It had begun to rain again. Joey used my momentary silence to go back to the original point.

"Two more things," they said. "I don't know if you knew this but Chris Collington—the fracking guy—*really* didn't want the Wests to buy that house."

I remembered Dad saying we had dodged a bullet there. "Yeah, I guess he was looking to have it rezoned for Southern Shale's local headquarters," I said. "Right across the street from the inconvenience store. Can you imagine that?"

"Well, there was a lot of legal back and forth," said Joey, "and the mayor's office supported Collington all the way until the West's big-city lawyers steamrolled them. Cost them a mint. The Millers switched sides and hung the Collingtons out to dry. I'm guessing there have been some awkward dinner parties since."

"And the other thing?" I asked.

Joey's momentary glee was replaced with something more somber. "I ran IP address searches on the sites where material on the Wests has recently appeared."

"You can do that?" I asked in spite of myself. I was still annoyed by the accusation that I hadn't been loyal to my friends.

"It's not that hard unless the creator has taken steps to conceal their identity. This one didn't."

"One?"

"Yeah. All the edits to the pages referencing the Wests come from the same IP address. I don't have the tools to nail down specific locations, but they all originated right here in Portersville."

"What?" I gasped. "What does that mean?"

"Well," Joey replied, "I know this makes no sense, but if I had to guess, at least digitally speaking, the Wests didn't exist until they showed up here, when they, or someone who was already here working for them, invented them. They aren't who they say they are, Hideki. And here's the ironic part. Those stories about being misled by AI and fake news? The misinformation which means we need to ditch our phones? The Wests are the walking, talking proof of that very problem. Nothing we know about them is true. What we see of them? None of it is real."

18

Elsewhere

High in the woods of Red Scar mountain, the earth trembled. Birds startled and a rabbit froze mid-step in a clump of ferns, ears alert and eyes wide. Though the topsoil was mostly mulch, the clay deep down was hard, chocked with hunks of granite and knotted with tree roots; so when the crater opened, it did so in a great explosive surge which scattered debris like an erupting volcano. An entire rhododendron bush was uprooted and thrown rolling down the hillside, and a pair of oak saplings shivered and fell. The stillness which followed was like the hole in the ground, a dark, sinister absence from which emerged the *Omukade*.

It came out slowly at first, scarlet head with mouth parts flexing, feelers probing the air, but then, with a great, uniform rush of its many yellow legs, it emerged in a long, unbroken stream which poured down the mountain like poison. It snaked between trees, curled round or over boulders, a great, undulating wave of shiny black nightmare.

The rabbit, unable to contain its fear, bolted, and with it, every creature in the forest which seemed to pause, ears pricking, sensing the centipede's presence, then moving hastily away. All but the bugs. They came after it, drawn by some deep magnetism, pulling them out of burrows and down the trunks of trees, until the forest floor moved in a carpet of ants, crickets, beetles, and cockroaches.

Only one thing in the woods didn't run. An old man was gathering berries and nuts, head bowed, seemingly oblivious to what was coming.

But it was coming. The giant centipede could smell him, and the scent made the beast's mouth drip with terrible anticipation. It adjusted its course a fraction, and flowed down the mountain, quickening as the smell got stronger.

The old man wore loose trousers and a smock shirt, stolen weeks ago from one of Portersville's few washing lines. It was too large and hung about him like a sheet, but he didn't care. On his feet, he wore stained socks and ancient sandals, and on his head, he wore a floppy hat recovered from a dumpster behind the thrift store in one of his few excursions into town. He moved with slow purpose, almost feeling his way along the forest path. There were bears up here, but he had no fear of them. He made appreciative noises as he sampled a late blackberry right off the bush and, satisfied, removed his hat to act as a bag for what he couldn't eat right away.

He had picked a dozen of the plump, shiny berries when he sensed rather than heard the thing moving down the mountain toward him. He stood a little straighter, nodding and smiling to himself, as he took a handful of the fruit and munched thoughtfully.

The *Omukade* slowed as it neared him, flattening itself against the ground so that its final approach was made with serpentine stealth. It approached from behind him, not rising up on its legs until it was in striking distance.

The old man turned at last to meet it, his blind eyes giving his face a curious blankness. He held up one hand, palm raised, like a policeman stopping traffic, and the *Omukade*, as if obeying, became still.

In the center of that raised palm, a single eye blinked.

"So," the old man said, speaking an ancient dialect of Japanese. "You have fed. But your hunger continues to make you forgetful. It seems I must remind you once more of your purpose."

The *Omukade* wavered, as if trying to decide whether to pounce on the old man. It was almost big enough to swallow him whole now.

But it didn't. It smelled something else beneath the tang of blood and meat, something which finally left it daunted and unsure. Memories returned, fragments and patches at first, as when the old woman had called it by its name. At last, it lowered itself to the earth, and its mouth parts grew still.

"Better," snapped the old man. "I will show you what to do. And you will feed again." He beamed then, his mouth wide and his teeth yellow and sharp, and the eye on his visible hand bright with amusement. He picked a blackberry from the hat, raised it in his filthy fingers, and popped it into his mouth.

"A banquet of humans is being laid for you, even as we speak." The purple juice of the berries stained his teeth and ran from the corner of his mouth as he spoke. "Then we will open the world."

19

I set my alarm for two in the morning, ensuring that the volume was so low no one else would hear it, and went to bed. When it woke me, I switched it off in that sleepy confusion where, for a moment, I barely knew where I was, let alone remembered why I had decided to wake myself so early. Even after I remembered, I just lay there, listening.

Maybe Em won't go out tonight.

But she did. Ten minutes after my alarm went off, I heard the muted snap of her bedroom door, and the first creak of the landing floorboards. I was dressed and ready. All I had to do was get my sneakers on, fish one of Saito-san's swords from under my bed and slip his bronze mirror into my pocket. Then I followed her.

I did so carefully, having made a risky decision. I wasn't going to intercept her, call her on her nighttime activities and point out the obvious—that they were destroying her health, to say nothing of her attitude and ability to operate as a functional human being. Instead, I was going to follow her and learn all there was to know about what she was up to. If she caught me, I wouldn't get a second chance.

So I slipped down the stairs once I was sure she was already outside, and by the time I was out in the warm night air, her night gown was already swaying gently on the bough of the dogwood. She—in her fox form—was tripping lightly through the grass toward the back fence.

I went after her, moving a little faster than was humanly possible, and —as soon as we made it to the tree line—vaulting high into the branches. I landed as softly as I could, but the leaves rustled and she stopped for a second, turning, nose twitching. I was, fortunately, downwind, however, and her hesitation was momentary. A noise on the ground might mean a person, but a noise in the trees meant only a raccoon or an owl. She scampered on ahead.

I wasn't surprised when she found the path that wound back round to the street, or when she paused to check for traffic, and trotted across to the woods on the other side. A hundred yards along the roadside she turned into the driveway of the West mansion, passing quickly beneath its imposing gate posts. I wasn't happy about it, but I wasn't surprised.

I considered the stone lions, giving her enough of a lead that she wasn't likely to see me tailing her, then I moved lightly along the long drive through well-trimmed shrubs to the house itself, which sat beside a vast, rolling lawn, perfectly manicured and screened from the road by trees. There was a bright moon that night, and it gave the West mansion an otherworldly silvery caste. I paused in the shade of an ancient elm and watched as my fox sister moved to the forecourt where the select few of our neighbors had parked their cars on the night of the party, and up the steps to the main door.

It was open, and a soft, amber light came from within—so far as I could see, the only light on in the house. As comfortably as if she lived there, Emily trotted in and vanished from view.

I hesitated, unsure of how to proceed, but the door was still open.

Too bad your superpowers don't include invisibility…

I was wearing my sword in a belt at my waist, and though my right hand strayed to it, I didn't draw it. This was a reconnaissance mission, not an attack. I was there to find out what my sister was up to. I'd prefer to do that without her knowing I was even there, and I certainly didn't want awkward questions from Nathan or his father about why I was following a fox and carrying a sword.

Maybe leave it out here? I thought.

I wasn't crazy about the idea, but it was probably the wiser choice, so —reluctantly—I laid the sword on the ground in the shadow of the front steps. Then I went inside.

The hallway was as I remembered it from the last time I was here, grand and marble with an ornate, sweeping staircase. It led into the vast living room which had been the hub of the party, but the light came from one of the side rooms, a library, if I remembered right.

Again, I hesitated, standing on the expensive-looking Persian rug in the soft glow spilling from the doorway, and I listened.

Two people were talking, the voices were quiet, indistinct, but I felt sure that one was Emily who had, apparently, resumed human form. I hoped she had found some clothes before changing back, but then I remembered that—since she came here regularly—she probably had contingency plans on the clothing front.

It was all very strange. What on earth was she doing here and who was she talking to?

I heard more muttering, and an idea occurred to me. Leaning around the door would surely reveal me to whomever was inside, but perhaps if I used Saito's mirror...?

I took it silently from my pocket, reached into the silk pouch and drew it out on its bamboo handle. I stepped cautiously, flattening myself against the wall by the open door and focused on the shiny side of the bronze mirror.

I gasped in shock. Though I hadn't yet positioned the mirror to see into the library, I had seen what it showed, and it wasn't the opulent luxury of a contemporary mansion.

While the hallway had looked to me bright and elegant, the one in the mirror was derelict, the walls stained and half collapsed, the studs exposed and hung with spiderwebs. I clapped my free hand to my open mouth and revolved until the mirror revealed the reality of everything around me. The glorious riches of the West mansion—its marble and gilt, its carpets, tapestries, and elegant fittings—were all gone. What stood in its place was a dank, tumbledown ruin.

The Haversham house!

It hadn't changed at all. All those sudden and inexplicable transformations and remodelings were illusions! And now that my brain knew it, I could smell it: damp and fetid, rank with racoon urine and the subtle stench of decay.

I remembered that now from the party, a strange undercurrent which I had caught on the very edge of my senses and which I had thought was plumbing or standing water somewhere nearby. What I had smelled was the reality beneath the glamor. The thought amazed me. All those people had been here, all astonished by wealth and luxury the likes of which they had never seen before, dazzled by the beauty of a house that didn't exist!

What could do that?

As if reading my thoughts, Emily's voice finally came through loud enough for me to hear.

"I can't do that," she said suddenly. "I can't do more than I already have. It's killing me."

I felt the hair on the back of my neck stand up abruptly, and I suddenly wished I hadn't left my sword outside.

"You will," came the response which I thought was Mr. West, though the voice sounded deeper than I remembered, more resonant. "You have no choice, and you know why. Or do you regret your decision? I could undo what I gave you..."

"No!" said Emily, hot and fast. "Please. No."

"Very well. But you know the price of my favor. I grow weary of hearing you complain about what you agreed to."

There was a long, loaded silence. I angled the mirror around the rotten door jamb but couldn't see who was talking beyond a torn swathe of moldy curtain and a jumble of broken and upturned furniture.

"Okay," Emily said at last, her voice so low I almost missed it. "I'll try."

"Do," he said. There was a smile in the word, but it was a smile with teeth.

There was another pause, and I heard a rustle of clothes. She was coming out, and I needed to be elsewhere.

"Leaving so soon?" purred Mr. West.

"I need to rest," said Emily. She sounded more than weary. She sounded hopeless.

"When we have finished," he replied. "You know what you have to do."

Again, I fought the urge to burst in on them, demand what they were doing, and that my sister be released from whatever debt Mr. West—if that was even his name—was holding over her.

But I felt his power, as I had caught the scent of decay at the party. I picked it up like static, a feeling I couldn't name, but which felt deep and dangerous. In all honesty, it scared me.

So I fled before they found me, leaping fast and light down the hall and out, pausing only to retrieve my sword. With the weapon in my hand, I again considered confronting them, but every instinct said that I couldn't go in blind. I needed to know what I was up against, and that meant I had to talk to my sister alone.

That scared me almost as much as West.

137

I was waiting for Emily when she got back to her room. She came in a half hour later, wearing her nightgown, and looking haggard. She froze when she found me siting on her bed.

"What are you doing in my room?" she demanded, but I could tell she knew. I saw it in her eyes.

"What does he have on you?" I demanded.

"I don't know who you mean or what you are talking about and I'm really tired..."

"Kieran West," I cut in. "Or whatever his real name is. I know you have been working for him. I want to know why."

Her mouth grew thin and her eyes flashed fury, but she said nothing.

"I think you are in trouble," I tried. "I want to help."

"You can't," she snapped. "I already told you that. Just leave it."

"Who is he?" I asked, my voice low but steady.

Emily closed her eyes and shook her head, a rapid, furious movement. When she opened her eyes again, tears ran out, but she wouldn't say anything. Maybe she couldn't.

So I did.

"Here's what I think," I said. "I think he's some kind of... I don't know what the word would be. An old Japanese wizard, maybe? A master of illusion. And I think that he came here and needed someone to invent a past for him, which is where you came in. I think you built a digital trail for him, a fake past. I don't think he's a tech giant or ever was. I think you made that up. I don't know why, but I figure he has a hold over you that I don't understand. It scares me, Em. And I don't know why he is trying to take over this town or move us back fifty years or more, so that scares me too. You know what's going on. Tell me. I can help."

But she just stood there, weeping, hands covering her mouth to stifle the sound of her sobbing, shaking her head from time to time. I've seen some terrible things in the last few months, but I don't think I'd seen anything as frightening as my tough, defiant sister looking so completely broken.

"If you won't talk to me," I said, "talk to Bachan. Talk to Saito!"

Her face flashed with something close to terror then and she shook her head fiercely. "This is my business, Caleb!" she sputtered. "Stay out of it!"

I just stood there, not knowing what to say. At last, she took a step away from the door and gestured toward it, her face turned down, her eyes avoiding me. I gave her a long look, then took the hint and returned to my bedroom, though I couldn't sleep and spent most of the night gazing out through my window, through the trees to the West mansion that wasn't really there.

20

Elsewhere

It was very early in the morning, the sun barely up, and the tengu called Saito was arranging the remains of his ancient books with a sour look on his face. He had tried to make sense of what was missing, trying to determine if this had been a random theft by someone looking to take things they could sell to dealers or collectors, or if there was some more focused and sinister purpose.

He wasn't sure. Most of the *yōkai* bestiaries had been left. So had the history books and the copies of the Buddhist sutras, but the very randomness to what had been taken made him suspicious. Most of it was unimportant: copies of texts he had in other editions, academic treatises he knew virtually by heart, obsolete studies he might not even bother to replace, and a mishmash of modern works of no great value. But Murakami's volume of spells and charms was gone—not something he could easily replace—and his personal transcription of the *Nara Bakemono Zukan*, a book otherwise unknown to history, was a massive loss.

He seriously doubted that any thief would know their value, let alone where to sell them, particularly in this country where people knew so little of his homeland or of history generally. The attack had surely been planned, rather than the opportunistic break-in by what the Smith children would call a "meth head"—whatever that was. So what had been taken was significant to the thief.

Saito sat back on his haunches on the tatami and considered the missing titles again, trying to decide which of the books had been the real target, and which had been taken merely to obscure that purpose. The *Nara Bakemono Zukan*—an encyclopedia of monsters which was almost twelve hundred years old—was valuable primarily as a historical document, though there were certainly observations that had not made it into later accounts. But it was the Murakami volume on magic that seemed most important. It was more than just a catalog of spells and rituals. It was a compendium of magical resources set down in ancient times and revised by Shinto priests, magicians, and mystical warriors. Raiko himself had added his own annotations, modifying directions, potion ingredients, and ceremonial practices according to what he had gleaned from his long years in the field.

The tengu put both hands on the tatami and bowed his head solemnly, his eyes closing as the tip of his long, bulbous nose touched the matting. It was a gesture of deference, of apology. He had lost a tome of wisdom compiled by his magical predecessors, and his side of the eternal struggle against the darkness was weakened as a result.

He should have protected the books better. After the incident in the cave with the *oni* was resolved, he had thought the threat had passed. That had clearly been an error. Worse, it had been a self-deception. He had relaxed his guard because he thought the enemy were trapped, and when he came to know of the *Omukade*, he had thought it merely a beast without a mind.

That had been a gross error of judgment, and it would cost them.

"My fault," he breathed aloud in Japanese. "Spirit of Raiko and all who stood with him against the dark, accept my deepest, humblest apologies. I will rectify my error. If they still exist, I will get the books back before they can be turned against us."

Saito started suddenly at the sound of the sliding door into the dojo opening. It was too early for Hideki's training. He turned as he got to his feet, and his face registered first surprise, then alarm.

"You!" he exclaimed.

But the other said nothing as a strange mist gathered in the empty dojo. It was merely a cloud first, but it became a tighter, darker fog which glided silently toward him like the mouth of an endless tunnel.

No, the tengu thought, as he realized the full scale of his failure. *The children will be helpless. The town will fall!*

He moved toward the rack of swords, but it was too late. The spell had him in its grip. He felt first the pain and then, as he fell to the tatami, the numbing, emptying nothingness.

21

Em avoided me all the next day. She left for school before me, and when I tracked her down at lunch—looking irritable as ever and so weary she looked ready to fall asleep where she sat—she slipped out before I could get to her. She was pale and her hair was messy, and when I asked DeMarcus' sister about her—giving her an apparently welcome escape from Sofie/Sophia Collington's whispering about Kaycee Allen's alleged pregnancy—Ayisha shrugged and made an anxious face.

"Been keeping herself to herself," she said. "Missed swimming twice this week. We kinda thought she was sick. I managed to catch up with her earlier, but she said she was too busy to chat. To be honest, I'm getting worried about her."

This couldn't go on.

Sofie/Sophia Collington was clearly keen to get back to their gossip, so I figured I'd leave them to it, but as I turned from Ayisha, there was Nathan West with a pork barbecue sandwich and a banana on a tray, moving easily through a gaggle of girls whose gazes followed him like he was a rock star. On impulse, I flagged him down.

"Hey Nathan," I called.

He saw me and smiled, seemingly genuinely pleased to see me, so that I blushed inwardly, thinking of what Joey had said.

"Hideki," he said. "What's up?"

"Have you seen my sister?" I asked, forcing the issue.

"Your sister?" he said, looking bemused.

"Emily," I said. "She's in the year above us. She was here a minute ago but..."

He shook his head, perplexed. "I don't think I know her," he said.

"But you've seen her around," I pressed. "Talking to me. Or whatever."

"I guess," he said. "But I've never spoken to her. Why, did you think I knew her?"

I hesitated then managed a shrug. "Guess not," I said, forcing a smile.

"You want to sit?" he replied, pointing his tray at an open table.

I hesitated again then shook my head. "Nah," I said. "Got things to do."

As I left, I caught DeMarcus watching from the counter where he was loading up with fried chicken and biscuits. Our eyes met briefly, but we both looked away without speaking.

What did I think of Nathan's denial that he knew my sister? I wasn't sure. She had been at his house several, perhaps many, times, a house that —as I had to remind myself—wasn't really a house at all, but a dank ruin. Was it possible he didn't know that either, that he was as blinded by his father's illusions as the people of Portersville had been at their open house party? I thought about that evening now, how weird it must have truly been; practically the whole town packed into that rotting, tumble-down wreck of a place in the dark, all standing around and whispering enviously about how beautiful it all was.

That must take some serious magic.

Was it possible that Nathan didn't know the truth, that he was as duped by his father's charms as the rest of us? Could those kinds of secrets exist between a father and son?

As soon as I thought of the question I remembered, with a stab of guilt, that I had kept my magical transformation from my own father. He had found out the truth, thanks to Bachan, but the deception had been there and, for a time, had worked. So, by my own example, it was perfectly possible that Nathan knew nothing about what Mr. West was doing or what he actually was.

It wasn't hard evidence, but for now at least, it would do. I would give Nathan the benefit of the doubt, not because he was cool, but because kids shouldn't be judged by what their parents do. Nathan once suggested we should hang out together after school. Maybe I could go over there, take the tengu's mirror, show him what it revealed...

I was thinking this over when I walked—literally—right into Bobby Davenham. He was back, apparently. He was also alone, which was rare.

"Oh hey, Bobby," I managed, feeling awkward and embarrassed. "Listen, I'm sorry about your dad."

Bobby's face was pale, and his blond curls were messy, uneven. He looked sleep-deprived and jumpy rather than grief-stricken, but what do I know? Someone had said Bobby hadn't gotten along with his father all that well, but that didn't mean anything. Families are complicated. And losing someone must change everything about your relationship with them and how you thought of them. Still, I had no idea how Bobby would respond to me offering sympathy. It felt like putting your hand into a pot of water and not knowing if it was going to be ice cold or boiling hot.

"Don't talk to me," he snarled, his lip curled so it showed his teeth.

I was taken aback, but I didn't argue the point. I put both hands up and took a step back. But he didn't let it go. He reached out suddenly and grabbed the front of my shirt, shoving me into the wall and leaning in close, his voice low as if he didn't want anyone else to hear.

"The sheriff says they think that it was some kind of mutant snake," he huffed, his blue eyes flashing wildly. "The thing that got my dad. Like, one of those pythons and boa constrictors they round up every year in Florida. Not local. *Invasive species.*"

He hissed those two words into my face like they meant something.

"Things what don't belong. Maybe crossbred with a rattlesnake or something. Unnatural."

I was actually scared of him now. I had no idea where he was going with this and his rage was intense, like a hot poker he was waving blindly around, its tip yellow-white and smoking. I didn't know what to do. I could fling him from me, draw on my considerable strength, but we were in school...

"That's terrible," I said. "Like I said, I'm sorry to hear..."

"When did it start?" he demanded suddenly, his eyes burning into me. "That's what I want to know. When did it start? Like, a couple of weeks ago? Or further back, when there was the cave-in at the fracking plant, and Maddie Hayes went missing, and everyone in town—*everyone*—was looking at you."

His face was inches from mine, his grip harder and fiercer than ever but with something in his eyes that might have been a real question.

"Everything all right, boys?"

It was Mr. Grealish, the principal, who rounded the corner just then. I glanced at him, still pinned to the wall like a butterfly in one of those ranger station cases and tried to sound casual.

"Just horsing around," I said.

"Well," said Grealish, either not seeing or choosing to ignore what was really going on, "no wrestling in the hallways, no matter how playful. Off you go." I relaxed a little, but it took Bobby another second to release me, and before he did, he leaned into my right ear and whispered, "Invasive, unnatural."

He lurched off and I just stood there, trying to make sense of what he had said.

"He means you," said Joey unapologetically when I confided in them later. "That's how he thinks of you. Unnatural. Invasive. Because you're mixed race and Japanese. I told you you'd get crap for going by Hideki."

"I don't know." I would have preferred to have this conversation with DeMarcus who would be less quick to give Bobby's remark that kind of significance, but he and I weren't really talking, and it felt weird to go to him with something that seemed that it was all about me. "I think he knows something. Or suspects it."

Joey wasn't convinced. "Things got weird around here a few months ago and, like it or not, you were in the middle of it. That's public knowledge. Now things are weird again, and Bobby—in his own messed up way —is upset and looking for someone to blame. I wouldn't waste any more thought on it."

"Feels wrong," I said, which was absolutely true, even if I couldn't be more precise than that.

"You're not scared of him, right? I mean, if he really attacked you, you could do your demon queller thing and kick his ass, right?"

"I guess," I said, not saying that I had been scared of him, of his strange intensity if not what he could do with his fists. "But that's supposed to stay secret, and besides," I added, feeling the weight of the phrase, "he's not a demon."

I thought about this for the rest of the day, and I realized I needed to talk to someone, and not just about Bobby. I hadn't spoken to Saito-san since his books went missing, something which clearly needed thinking about. But I also needed to talk to him about Emily. Now was the time.

After school, I picked up my bike from home and cycled the mile or so out to the Hibachi Prince west of town. The rain, which had been intense that morning, had stopped, and the sky was almost mysteriously clear, with no sign of the clouds which had dumped so much water on us that the parking lot at the abandoned Walmart looked like an artificial lake.

The strip mall where Saito's restaurant sat was even quieter than usual. The low-end department store where I had once bought clothes for Emily when she had been trapped in her fox form was boarded up now. The few vehicles parked in the lot close by belonged to a dollar store and one of those big box stores which stands empty for much of the year and then opens for a few weeks for some seasonal event. Right now, it was all geared up for Halloween, and the place—temporarily named Scare Mall— was packed with racks of bagged costumes, pumpkin-headed yard decorations and spooky lights. In a matter of weeks, it would be gone. Eventually, when the little furniture store ("Everything must go!") went out of business, the tengu's restaurant would be the last part of the mall still open, the only thing preventing the great concrete expanse from being overwhelmed by the sprawl of the woods. As a spirit of the mountains and forests, Saito-san might actually like that.

So would Mr. West, I thought.

It was an odd pairing, the Japanese *yōkai* and the Luddite with the fake online history, and I wondered again about DeMarcus' suspicions.

"Hello?" I called as I opened the restaurant door. "Saito-san?"

But there was no welcoming call of *Irashaimasse!* In fact, there was no sound at all. The lights were off, though the restaurant should have been open, and the place looked gloomy, almost as abandoned as the department store. I ducked my head into the kitchen, then into the rest rooms, calling Saito's name, but there was no sign of life. I went out back to the dojo, but though it was tidier than when I had been there last, it too was silent and empty.

There were any number of reasons why the tengu might be out. He could be grocery shopping for the restaurant. He could be visiting my Bachan. For all I knew, he had decided to take in a movie or go out for a barbecue sandwich, though these were harder to imagine. He could have been anywhere.

So why does this feel so...wrong?

There was no way round it. The silence felt oppressive, ominous. I stood in the dojo, taking in the faint, grassy aroma of the tatami, and I felt weighted down with dread.

At the entrance where I had hastily removed my shoes—force of habit

—a tight, square staircase ascended to a second floor I had never seen. It was where Saito-san lived. He alone of the people who worked at the strip mall—or who had worked there when it was thriving—lived on site. Despite the countless times I had been here I had never been invited upstairs, and the prospect of going looking for Saito-san up there now only increased my discomfort.

The stairs were old and wooden, climbing in threes with right angle turns at a series of landings so it was impossible to see what was above. The worn treads of the steps made me wonder if the dojo/house building actually pre-dated the strip mall. The carpentry of the handrail was oddly complex, using intricate joints, apparently without nails or screws. It reminded me of the elegantly rebuilt barn on the school grounds, whose construction had been presided over by the tengu. Had he built this place too, years before the parking lot and the sprawl of the department store had been thought of? It seemed at least possible.

The staircase smelled of wax and something fragrant that might have been incense. It was dim, and I felt instinctively for a light switch, but found none, though the power was probably out again anyway. The dojo on the ground floor had no electric light and was lit solely by the soft glow of sunlight on the shoji screens and—rarely—by oil lanterns which hung on iron brackets from the walls. There were no such lanterns on the stairs, and I climbed cautiously, listening for any sound of movement above me.

"Saito-san?" I called softly. "It's me, Caleb. Hideki. You up there?"

No response. I imagined the tengu's fury if he found me invading his personal space like this, but somehow his incandescent rage—terrible though it would be—seemed like the preferable option right now. He wasn't out grocery shopping. He sure as hell wasn't catching a movie. Something was wrong. I felt it in my bones.

I moved warily around the corner of the staircase, leaning slightly so I could see above me, took the next three steps and emerged onto a landing with a narrow corridor leading to three sliding doors, all closed. I knew from the building's external shape that the second story was small and did not extend over the whole dojo. Three tiny rooms was probably all there was. I moved quietly along the hallway and tried the first door.

It slid aside with a gasping sound revealing a room with six inter-locking tatami mats, a low wooden table and an alcove where a scroll covered in brushed Japanese characters hung. On a stone slab below it were two small ceramic vases, one of which contained what looked like incense sticks. A closet with another sliding door held cardboard boxes and a rack of *yukata*. The second door was a bathroom with toilet, sink and a deep, square tub which I assumed was a bath. That meant the final room would be the bedroom. I paused uncertainly. The rooms smelled of wood and tatami and incense. There was barely any sign that someone lived there: no TV, appliances or electronics of any kind, no photographs on the walls, no books beyond what I had seen on the shelves downstairs. Spartan didn't begin to describe it. Saito clearly lived like a monk.

Reluctantly I tapped on the final sliding doors which rattled in its frame.

"Saito-san?" I tried again. "You in there?"

Still no reply. I slipped my fingers into the recessed handle, pulled the door open, and looked inside. A soft glow came from a window which had been covered in translucent paper framed with pale wood, and by its light I made out the prostrate figure of a man lying on the floor.

Saito!

I stepped briskly to him and dropped to a crouch. He was on his back, resting on some kind of futon, and dressed in the black cotton kimono he often wore when we trained. His eyes were closed, but as I stooped toward him, I felt sure I saw his great nostrils flare fractionally.

He's breathing!

"Oh, thank God!" I muttered aloud. He didn't respond. As my previous fears fell away, I found myself wondering how he would react if I woke him from his nap.

Not well.

But this felt weird and there were things we needed to discuss. For a second my eyes lingered on the scabbarded *wakizashi*—short sword— which sat on a standing rack within arm's reach, then I took a deep breath.

"Saito-san," I said again, louder this time. "I'm sorry but I need to talk to you. Saito!" I leaned in a little closer and said his name again.

Still no response.

Gingerly I reached for his right wrist. He was wearing some kind of bracelet with red embroidery on it. I touched his hand. Then prodded it. At last, I took hold of his hand and raised it.

"Hello?" I said. "What the hell, man? What if I was a ninja assassin come to take you out? You call this vigilance?" He said nothing. I let his hand flop down, but no change came over his face. "Dude, seriously. You're starting to freak me out."

I reached across his body and shook him firmly by the shoulder. He continued to lie there, eyes shut, like he wasn't just asleep. It was as if he was in a coma.

And now I really did freak out. I scrambled to my feet and bolted for the corridor, not bothering to close the door behind me. I ran down the stairs, fumbling for my phone, trying to decide who to call first.

Bachan! I decided, pulling up her contact information.

By the time I was outside, the phone was already ringing.

"*Moshi Moshi*," said Bachan, her habitual Japanese greeting on the phone no matter who called.

"Bachan, it's me, Hideki. I'm at the tengu's place. I need you to come. Now."

Mom drove Bachan over. They bustled into Saito's house in anxious silence, and I pointed the way to the bedroom. It was impossibly cramped with three of us in that little room, so after looking around the door, Mom waited in the hall. It felt wrong; the powerful mountain spirit lying there unconscious, shrunken somehow, reduced to just an old man.

I remembered the first time I saw one of my teachers outside school. It was Miss Jolly, the young biology teacher. She was at the Tidy Shack diner with a man I didn't know, dressed all fancy and weird, like she was on a date. It was freaky, like something had gone wrong with the fabric of the universe. I half-expected to go home to find that my parents were different people and we ran not the inconvenience store but a coke bottling plant or a nail salon.

I felt like that now. Saito-san looked so ordinary, so defenseless that for a moment I felt sure I had dreamed my entire relationship with him to this point. He was just a strange old waiter and cook at a restaurant hardly anyone went to, and any memories of skill and magic were insane delusions. I blinked, turning to Bachan as if for confirmation that this really was the man I remembered, that he was still a person of power and wisdom, not the sleeping husk of some average old dude which he seemed to be.

It bothered me so much that I got up to go downstairs, but at that moment Bachan reached for the curious red fabric charm tied to his wrist, turning it over in her hands and peering at the characters written on it. It was rectangular and ornately woven, the writing embroidered in red and gold silk.

She gasped and muttered a few words of Japanese.

"What?" I asked.

"This is a curse," she said. "Or rather, it is what holds the curse in place."

I frowned, then knelt beside the futon.

"Okay," I said with a shrug of relief. "Let's get it off then." I tried to undo the strangely regular knot which held the charm in place, but the scarlet cord wouldn't come free. "Okay," I repeated, refusing to be defeated by a bit of string. I reached for the *wakizashi* on its stand, drawing the short sword from its scabbard. Carefully I set the edge against the red cord and pressed. When the string didn't break, I used a sawing motion. Still no joy. Frowning, I tested the blade against my thumb, snapping my hand quickly away as I felt the metal bite. It was razor sharp. I tried it against the cord once more, muttering with annoyance, but even though the string was no thicker than a few braided threads of cotton or silk, it was tough as wire.

"I need some pliers," I announced. "Or, like, tin snips. Maybe a Dremel with one of those cut-off wheels..."

Bachan shook her head. "The thread is part of the enchantment," she said. "You will not be able to cut it off. The only way is for the one who tied the curse holder to remove it."

"What?" I exclaimed. "That's crazy! There has to be another way!"

"The other way is to defeat the one who placed the curse."

I thought for a moment, taking in the prone, motionless Saito and decided. "Then we'll do that," I said. "But I'm still going to try the Dremel."

The Dremel didn't work. Neither did Dad's modeling knives, boxcutters, and an assortment of saws. When I finally accepted that I was more likely to cut the tengu's hand off than the little red charm, I gave up.

"We need to know who did this," I said. That was obvious, but I felt like I had to say it anyway, like I was promising Saito-san that I would find a way to wake him.

"Someone wanted him out of the picture frame," said Bachan.

It was an odd phrase, but I knew what she meant. The tengu had been deliberately removed from the game board, probably by the same person who had stolen his books. That meant something was about to happen. Something Saito might have disrupted or stopped.

"Should we call the cops?" Mom asked. She didn't sound convinced.

"And tell them that someone put Saito into a magic sleep?" I replied. I thought of Sheriff Halpern grinning at us and asking if we'd considered trying to wake him with a kiss.

"But someone broke in," Mom persisted, "stole his books. Maybe we could present it as a burglary."

"We should not involve the police," said Bachan, who had had more than enough bad experiences with the local sheriff's office.

"What would the police even do?" I asked, genuinely unsure.

"Take fingerprints?" Mom suggested. "Catalog what was missing in case it showed up at pawn shops? Check area CCTV?"

"Yes!" I exclaimed. "There are still some working stores in the mall. If any of them have cameras at the back, they might show the entrance to the dojo. If we could see who went in…"

"I will handle it," said Bachan.

Mom and I exchanged looks.

"You'll do what now?" I asked.

"I do not want the police involved," my grandmother replied with cool finality. "They will make things worse and they cannot be trusted. I will handle the matter of the CCCP."

"CCTV," I said, not very optimistically.

"Exactly," she replied.

Mom stayed with Saito, in case there was a change in his condition, though that seemed unlikely. I went with Bachan to the three mall stores which appeared to have people working there. One was a dollar store which had no access to the back lot and therefore no cameras. The second was a furniture wholesaler which was currently having a half-hearted going-out-of-business sale. It was part of a national chain and the uninterested manager said that they had strict protocols for who could view their CCTV footage though it didn't matter either way: the recent power outages had fried their system, and they weren't recording anything.

The last was Scare Mall, the Halloween supplies store. It was staffed by high school students overseen by a couple of harried-looking adults, one of whom—a big guy in an orange polo shirt spotted with mustard stains—asked us, not very enthusiastically, if he could help us find something. Bachan gave him the same story she had rehearsed in the previous two stores.

"I work at the Japanese restaurant three buildings down," she lied cheerfully, "and we have had some problems with people breaking into our storage facility at the back and stealing some of our teriyaki chicken."

It was a curiously specific fabrication, but it gave the whole thing a blend of seriousness and silliness, suggesting that the matter was worth looking into but not worth involving the police. Mustard shirt grinned.

"Can't have that," he said. "Gotta love that teriyaki chicken."

"I was wondering if you had cameras at the back which might cover that area," she added sweetly.

"Let's have a look," he said. "We aren't here for long, but it always pays to be on good terms with your neighbors. That's what I always say. You never know when you might need a little help, right? Plus, today it's teriyaki chicken, but what will it be tomorrow? Glow in the dark skeletons? Motion activated inflatable cats? Better nip this thing in the butt."

I considered pointing out that the phrase was 'nip it in the bud' but he was being helpful, so I let it slide. He led us to a chaotic office full of half-open filing cabinets and a desk covered with packing slips and burger wrappers.

"Does your CCTV work when the power is out?" I asked.

The manager waggled his hand: kind of.

"There's a backup generator which is supposed to come on automatically, but it can't get power to every circuit. To be honest, I'm not sure what's connected. Let's see what we can see," he mused, plugging a cable into his laptop and pulling up a series of black and white camera feeds. "Camera four is our best shot. Yeah. See? Cameras one and two are out. No power. Camera four...?" He hesitated, clicked his mouse a couple of times and then smiled. "You're in luck. That your storage building there, half in the woods?"

"That's the one," I said, peering at the dojo.

"Can't see much of it and it's pretty far away, but is that the front door?"

"Yeah," I said. "Can you make it bigger?"

He tried but it quickly got grainy and distorted. "Best I can do, I'm afraid," he said. "When did this happen?"

Bachan and I exchanged looks.

"Most recently," Bachan said, "it happened within the last twenty-four hours."

"But," I cut in, thinking of the book theft, "we should probably go back a few days. Make sure it's the same culprit each time."

The Scare mall manager frowned. "I can speed the footage but," he said, "but it could still take a while."

He wound it back, then set it running, clicking to increase the speed when there was clearly nothing going on. You could make out the stairs to the dojo/house and the patch of path leading to the back of the restaurant, but other than a couple of small trees, there wasn't much else to see. On fast forward, the light shifted, the trees waggled, but nothing else changed. As the image got darker and darker, what little detail there was of the grayed structure got even harder to make out.

"There!" said the manager suddenly. He paused the playback and rewound it, but the figure mounting the steps and opening the door was obviously Saito.

"That's my brother," Bachan improvised wildly. "He works there. Sleeps in the loft."

"Is that legal?" said mustard shirt. "This area isn't zoned for residential."

"The restaurant is older than the mall," Bachan said. "We are exempt from those restrictions."

I didn't know if that was right, but she said it with total conviction, and the manager went back to scrolling through the footage. I watched the time indicator flicker the days away, but there was nothing except for Saito coming and going.

"Who's that?" asked the manager, spotting a new figure going inside. It was dark on the screen and the time index read three in the morning. We leaned in as he rewound and slowed the playback.

An ethereal figure in a white dress was visible coming out of the dojo, head bowed, arms laden with something that looked like...

"Books," said Bachan, her voice low and troubled. I didn't need to ask why.

"That's a girl!" exclaimed the manager. "You can't see her face, but it's a girl in a dress with long hair. Bachan and I said nothing. We couldn't even meet each other's eyes. "Let's see if she comes back," he continued, clearly enjoying himself. "Maybe get a better look at her."

I couldn't speak. I could barely look at the screen as the figure reappeared, sharp and unmistakable. I felt paralyzed with horror and misery.

"This is from last night," said the manager, advancing the footage hour by hour as, once more, the bright daylight dropped to nothing. Midnight came. Then one o'clock. Then two in the morning, and there was nothing.

"Wait," said Bachan suddenly. "What was that?"

"I didn't see anything," said the manager, but he wound it back a few frames anyway. We stared at the computer screen, leaning in close as a small gray shape appeared and bounded up the stairs. "Well, I'll be!" the manager exclaimed with a delighted chuckle. "Mystery solved! The great teriyaki chicken thief has been exposed." He turned his chair to face us, beaming like he'd won the lottery. "Now you just have to find out who owns that dog!"

But it wasn't a dog, and neither Bachan nor I returned his grin. The image quality was low and pixelated, but there could be no doubt.

It was a fox.

And that meant...

"Emily!" Bachan said, as we trudged back to where Mom was waiting on the stairs of Saito's house. "I don't understand."

I sighed. "Neither do I," I said. "Not exactly. But there are things I have to tell you."

We argued over who should talk to her. I felt it should be me because I knew the most and didn't want Emily to feel I had spilled all her secrets, which—of course—I had. I had to admit, however, that I had already tried to talk to her about her nocturnal visits to Mr. West and gotten nowhere. Mom said it should be her because she was her mother and that was what mothers and daughters did - talk about tough things. Bachan said it should be her because she had known Saito the longest and knew the most about the paranormal dimension to our lives. Then I suggested it be all three of us, but Mom said Emily would resent what would feel like an intervention, though that was pretty much what it was. No one thought to suggest Dad, or even considered when we would tell him, though I only realized that later, when we had him come over to carry the tengu down and into the car. We figured he would be safer at our place until we could work out how to wake him.

In the end, we all confronted her, not because we had planned it that way, but because she was in the house—looking miserable and exhausted as ever—when we manhandled Saito's body in through the back door.

Her eyes flashed to the charm still lashed to his wrist, and then she took in our faces and saw that we knew. I expected tears, but what she gave us was defiance.

"Emily," said Mom. "I think we should talk."

Em's face froze hard, then she nodded knowingly and made a grim little smile, as if we were just ganging up on her which was exactly what she had expected us to do. She stalked out through the store and slammed the front door so hard that the bell rang for almost a full minute.

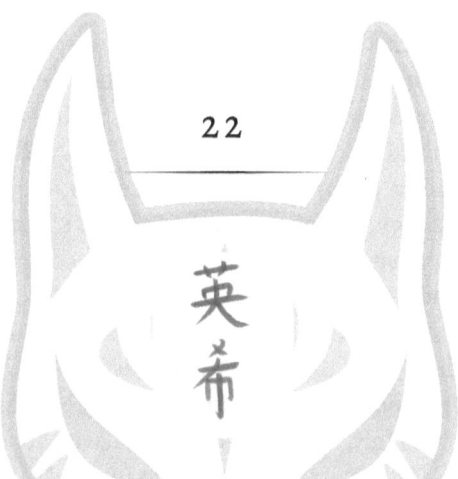

22

After another highly focused storm blew through the area bringing down trees and power lines, the lights were out in school again, and everyone's nerves were frayed. I had looked everywhere for Emily, but so far as I could tell, she hadn't come in at all, and no one at home had seen her since she marched out yesterday.

"This is maddening," Mr. Hardy, our physics teacher, muttered, as he struggled to read from the textbook by the light of a flashlight. He snatched his glasses off and peered at the page. "It's impossible to work in these conditions."

The classroom wasn't dark, exactly, but it was dim, and unpleasantly warm. In another week or so we'd get real fall weather, but even though we were close to the end of October, the Carolina summer wasn't quite done with us. We were missing the air conditioning badly. You could hear what wasn't working, or rather you could hear the silence where the background drone of fluorescent lights, AC, and computers used to be. It was weird, like being out in the woods at night, except there were dozens of kids in the classroom trying to keep going as if everything was fine. Without our phones to glance at for texts, newsflashes, and goofy TikTok videos, we all just sat there, staring at nothing, sweating.

"Why don't we have a generator?" someone asked. "Get some fans in here at least."

"They should let us go home," said Jason looking up from a notebook in which—I couldn't help noticing—he had been furiously doodling sketches of bugs. "I'd get more done there."

I watched him, the furtive way his eyes flicked around the room, the way his fingers twitched involuntarily, and of course the pages and pages of obsessively scribbled insects: roaches, crickets,...centipedes.

"You're not thinking about this in the right way," said Nathan suddenly. It wasn't just a muttered gripe: he was addressing the room. "You keep imagining the world you are used to, the one with power, phone signals and such, so you are frustrated that it's not like that now. If you could accept what now actually is, instead of wishing for what is gone, you would adjust much better."

It was an odd speech delivered oddly, and I stared at him.

"What if we don't want to adjust?" demanded Tyler.

"Then you are going to be frustrated and disappointed for a long time," said Nathan calmly, "and you still won't have phone service."

My focus on him narrowed, but I saw DeMarcus give me an appraising glance. We usually sat together, but lately he had taken a seat in the corner. "What do you mean, 'long time'?" he asked.

Nathan paused for a fraction of a second as if calculating. "The damage is obviously extensive," he said. "We've been mostly without service for over a week. Sometimes it comes back for an hour or two, sometimes just in certain places, but then it goes again. If you could treat the absence of power as the normal state, rather than a temporary aberration, you'd be a lot happier."

I didn't think I'd ever heard a kid my age use the phrase 'temporary aberration' but everyone was used to Nathan being different, so we rolled with it. Maybe everyone in California talks about temporary aberrations.

"I haven't been able to use my Playstation for nine days," Francine Kohl said miserably.

"Maybe if you stopped waiting for it to come on," Nathan observed, smiling, "you'd find something better to do. Read a book. Go outside."

"I don't want to read a book," said Francine, irritation showing through her misery. "I *want* to play *Baldur's Gate 3!*"

"Forget *Baldur's Gate* and focus on what you do have!" Nathan persisted, still smiling benevolently. "This is a beautiful part of the world…"

"I'm not interested in this world," snapped Francine. "I want to go back to Faerûn."

Several people laughed and someone cheered. Nathan's eyes narrowed and again he paused, as if watching, thinking. "What is so great about it?" he asked.

"The landscape is really immersive and cool looking," said Francine, jolted out of her annoyance. "I just like being there, interacting with the other characters..."

"You like that it feels real," said Nathan.

"I guess so."

"But you have real," he replied, gesturing to the classroom. "This is real."

"This sucks!" Bobby inserted.

More laughter and cheers. Bobby was mostly as he had been before his father died: more tired, perhaps, his eyes a little sunken, but there was no trace of the fierce strangeness he had directed at me. Francine grinned at him.

"Well, if I were you," Nathan concluded, something of his smile freezing. "I'd try to get used to life without computers, the internet, cell phones. My father has been meeting with the mayor and the town council, and they are very interested in his proposals."

No one knew what to say to that. Nathan just smiled again and shrugged, like it was no big deal, then glanced at his book and asked Mr. Hardy a question about how light could be both a particle and a wave, as if the previous conversation hadn't happened.

There was a ripple of bemused shock and resentment from the class, and for the first time, I realized that Nathan hadn't carried his audience along with him on a wave of charisma. Quite the contrary in fact, they looked at him as if they had never seen him before, as if taking his father's side had revealed him as *not one of us...*

Now, I've spent much of my life outside the lines of what Portersville considered "us" so you'd think that would have made me sympathetic to his plight, but somehow it didn't. I don't know why. Partly it was that he seemed not to care either way. Partly—stupidly—it was that he hadn't given me a knowing shrug or something that said he wanted me to understand or thought I would. I was just the same as the rest of them.

It's funny how much you can understand from a glance or a nod, or from its absence. We weren't friends, and I had been an idiot to think we were. And of course, there was all that stuff with Emily and his father, the secrecy and lies, and I was suddenly asking myself the obvious questions about how you could actually live in a damp and derelict ruin without knowing it...

As the other kids muttered, I found myself watching the odd kid from California, until I felt DeMarcus' gaze burning into me, and turned to face him. DeMarcus' face was hard, his eyes wide and staring as if to say: "See?" And, because I kind of did, I gave him the smallest of nods before turning my eyes back to the textbook.

At lunch, though, Nathan was proved sort of right. The power came back on just long enough for us to see a hastily compiled report from Action News Twelve on how Portersville town council were seriously considering a "technological regression" proposal submitted by Mr. Kieran West, details to be posted online later today. The council were keen to insist that no decisions had been made, and that the public would have ample time to express their feelings on the matter in the coming days with a nonbinding referendum on November 5th.

"A meeting to discuss the matter—to which the entire town has been invited—will double as a Halloween party at the West mansion on October 31st!" said the anchor, apparently delighted at the whimsy of the thing. "There'll be some ghoulish fun sprinkled into the deliberations."

"To quote Bobby Davenham, for the first and final time in my life," said Joey, "'this sucks.' A free party thrown by the guy who wants everyone's vote a few days later? How transparent is that?"

"A nonbinding vote," I said darkly. "You know what that means."

"That the mayor and his pals will say they took the town's wishes under advisement and then do whatever suits their own interests."

"This is crazy though, right?" I asked. "People won't agree to this, will they? It's voting against their own interests!"

Joey gave a snort of bleak amusement. "Wave the right flags," they said, "and people will vote themselves into poverty and servitude."

"Not me," I said, making my mind up on the spot. "Portersville needs to move forward, not back."

"And you, my friend," said Joey patting my arm, "don't get a vote. None of us do. Over eighteens only. Excluded from voting on our own future!"

I looked over at DeMarcus who was sitting by himself. I wanted to go over there but didn't know how to.

"Sure sounds like Nathan is on board," said Joey.

"Doesn't make him in on the magic and such," I said, not really believing it.

"No," Joey agreed, "But it's sketchy as hell."

That was hard to argue with, and I nodded, unable to keep the disappointment out of my face.

Joey patted my hand and smiled. "Never trust the shining ones," they said.

"Oh yeah," I replied, trying to sound merely amused, "why's that?"

"You know what they say about swans?" Joey replied.

"That they're mean as hell?" I suggested.

"No," Joey said, "that while they're gliding around gracefully along the water their big ugly feet are pumping away like crazy under the surface."

"Not sure I see..." I said.

"Being cool, being popular...takes a lot of work," said DeMarcus, getting there before me. He had walked over from his spot on the corner and now loomed over us, his eyes watchful and apprehensive.

"And when people put that much energy into making you like them," Joey concluded, "there's usually a reason. It might not be anything sinister, and it might just be sad, but it's probably something they don't want you to know."

I nodded and looked at DeMarcus. "You gonna sit down or what?" I asked.

"Is that an invitation?" asked DeMarcus, making me work for it.

"Oh, for crying out loud," said Joey.

"Yes," I said. "It's an invitation. And sorry for, you know. The other stuff."

"Specific and articulate," Joey observed, but DeMarcus just grinned. I grinned back.

"Something I've been thinking," he said, moving on, to Joey's amused disbelief. "The *Omukade* is getting bigger, right?" he said. "So you should fight it as soon as possible before it gets, you know, mountain size."

"Not crazy about that phrase, but go on," I said.

"It's already big, but we only seem to find out where it has been by following the bodies afterwards."

"If this is supposed to be motivational speaking," Joey said, "you need to work on it."

"My point," said DeMarcus, "is that it's hiding out somewhere."

"In the woods," I suggested.

"In the caves in the mountains," Joey countered.

"Both possible," DeMarcus said, "but a long way from what it seems to like eating."

"Cows," said Joey. "People."

"Okay," DeMarcus persisted. "We need a way to track it."

"Even if we could hack into the local CCTV, the power outages would make the process difficult and the data spotty," said Joey.

DeMarcus beamed. "I think the power outages might be our best asset," he said.

"How?" I asked.

"You said the centipede thing discharged energy, right?" he said.

"Yeah," I agreed, remembering what Dad had said when Bachan described her encounter at the gas station. "Even when there was no power it generated some kind of electrical pulse. Like an electric eel."

"What if we could track that?" DeMarcus said. "The power keeps going out all over the area. When it does, the only electrical activity will be generators and this thing. That should make it easier to see."

"How are we going to track electrical activity?" I asked.

"You know when you look at the radar stream from a weather channel online?" DeMarcus began.

"Lightning strikes!" Joey exclaimed. "DeMarcus, you're a genius!"

DeMarcus grinned but I was still fogged. "How about explaining it for those who aren't," I said.

"There is a national monitoring system for detecting lightning," Joey said. "Combination of satellite imagery and ground monitors. They detect radio frequency spikes and use them to map electrical storms to help fight forest fires and such. If the *Omukade* is putting out a lot of electricity at a time when the local grid is dark, it should light up like a Christmas tree on those monitors."

"Can you access the system?" I asked.

"Easy peasy," said Joey. "But I need power and a stable wifi connection to do it."

"Road trip," said DeMarcus. "We only need to go as far as Hendersonville."

"Where they have that general store with all the old-time candy," I said, grinning at him.

"Bonus quest," said DeMarcus, offering me a high five.

Joey grinned. We were back.

———

Of course, it didn't make sense for me to go with them. DeMarcus's sister had recently passed her driving test and needed no convincing to drive them; there wasn't much to do in Portersville at the best of times and even less when the power and cell towers were out.

"Text me if you get an obvious hit on the *Omukade*'s location," I said, "in case we get a signal. Otherwise, come to the store on your way home."

In truth, I would rather have gone with them, and not just for the old-time candy at the Hendersonville general store. I was going to have to do something I had kind of been avoiding.

Emily wasn't at school or at home, but I had a pretty good idea of where to find her.

I crossed the street and walked through the elegant gateposts of the lavish West mansion AKA the ruined Haversham house, the tengu's mirror in the pocket of my jeans. I climbed the stone steps and hesitated at the beautifully carved front door surmounted by a fan light and flanked by columns. This time I didn't stow the sword I had brought with me. I didn't know what I was going to find inside and needed to be ready. I reached for the doorbell, then changed my mind.

I knew that everything I saw was an illusion, and I remembered from years ago what sort of shape the real house was in. I held up the tengu's mirror, then put the flat of my hand against the polished wood and concentrated. Then I pushed.

At once the door seemed to flicker, and in the mirror I saw—as if it was beneath or inside it—another door, stained and split, half hanging off its hinges, which groaned and shuddered as I pressed on it. With a judder and a long, slow creak, it opened, dragging on the threshold. Moments later, I was inside.

To the naked eye, the hallway still looked like fine marble and for a second I felt the pressure of something in my head, something that said I was breaking and entering, that I was merely a criminal violating the domestic space of my wealthy neighbor. The feeling soon passed and I could smell the damp and the sour edge of the septic system. I paused, listening, but there was no conversation coming from the first doorway this time. I used the mirror to scan the hall, if only to remind myself of what was real and what wasn't.

The first room was indeed empty. Its windows were boarded up, and the curtains hung in a great moldy swag that mounded on the floor. There was a cold, dusty fireplace and a series of high-backed armchairs, their stuffing swollen with damp. I moved to the next door: the library, its walls lined with shelves of moldy books. A brass chandelier had fallen at some point and lay on one side in the middle of the room like the beached hulk of a wrecked ship. I pressed on into the main living room which had been the hub of the West's opulent party. When I scanned it with the mirror, it changed before my eyes, one minute a bright and sophisticated testament to the highest taste in contemporary design, the other a derelict ruin of bare, decaying boards, mildew, and sickly blooms of rubbery fungus. There was a grand piano just where I remembered it from the party, but instead of being a pristine, glossy black, this one was missing its leg and was canted on one side. Most of its keys had been torn out and there was what looked like a raccoon nest in its dust-caked innards.

There was still no sound anywhere in the house, but I felt like I wasn't alone. I wandered to the foot of the great spiral staircase, with the mirror angled overhead so I saw a pair of fat brown rats scurrying ahead of me, their bald tails held above the cluttered floor as they ran. I shuddered but kept going. I didn't touch the filthy handrail but drew my sword and began to climb the stairs, the katana held in front of me like a torch.

There was an open landing at the top with a series of rooms which I had not explored during the party. One had a set of double doors which, to my mind, said master bedroom. I held the mirror in one hand and my sword in the other, and, checking the floor for signs of rot, entered.

The room was huge, and like everywhere else in the house, opulent with detailed carving and delicate trim work. Unlike most everywhere else, however, it was real, and when I checked the mirror the two versions of the room aligned almost perfectly. The true version—the Haversham version—was older, aged and dank, but it was essentially the same. It was as if Kieran West had merely put a magical lick of paint over whatever was already there.

A strange pearly light lit the room. It had a blue-green tint as if it was shining up through water, but it seemed to come from an open box no more than a few inches square which sat on a nightstand by the canopy bed in the center of the room, with another high-backed armchair beside it. The first held my sister. The second, Mr. West.

Em looked like she was asleep. She was lying on her back in a way that reminded me of the comatose Saito. West was sitting forward, looming over her, one hand over her head, his fingers splayed as if frozen in the act of trying to grab her face. By the strange light from the box I could see that his eyes were closed, but at the sound of my horrified gasp, they snapped open. Without altering the rest of his body at all, he turned side-ways to face me and smiled. Both the movement and the smile made him look like a puppet, like he was a machine being worked by someone else.

"Hideki," he breathed. His voice was low, satisfied. "I wondered when I would be seeing you here."

"What are you doing to her?" I demanded, the sword raised.

"Nothing she didn't agree to," he replied easily.

"Liar," I said.

"On the contrary," he said, his smile widening. "It is exactly as I say."

"Nothing is what you say it is." I held up Saito's bronze mirror. "I know what this place really is. I know that you invented your own past and that you are none of the things you claim to be." I thought this might enrage him, but he just sat there, smiling that fixed, sinister smile. "So no," I concluded, "I don't believe my sister gave you permission to do…whatever this is."

"Very well," he said, sitting back in his chair and snapping his fingers sharply over Emily's face. "Ask her yourself."

Even as he did it, her eyes opened, and she took a quick, unsteady breath. Her gaze strayed around the ceiling as if she could sense something was wrong, and then she sat up a little and found me. Her mouth opened in a silent cry of despair and her exhausted eyes filled with tears. She looked impossibly tired.

I reached for her hand.

"Come on, Em," I said. "Let's get you out of here."

I watched West in case he tried to stop me, but he just sat there, grinning that wide, knowing grin which felt like sandpaper on my skin. For a moment, I could feel Em move with the tug of my hand, but then she stopped. To my amazement, she tore her hand away and shook her head as fiercely as her minimal strength would let her.

"What have you done to her?" I demanded of West.

"As I said," he remarked affably, "nothing she has not agreed to. You see Hideki—Caleb, or whatever—all this…" he gestured vaguely around the room, "requires a great deal of power to maintain. I could do it myself, but I need to conserve my energy. It is useful to have what you might call a battery."

His eyes flashed briefly to the glowing box, and I gaped at him.

"You're treating her like…a generator!?" I said aghast.

His smile widened. "You do understand!" he said. "Excellent."

"It's killing her," I said.

"No," he said. "I have not risked her life. Just drained it a little."

"I still don't believe you," I snapped back. "Why would she let you do a thing like that?"

"She has no choice!" he barked, the smile gone, his eyes bright as the weird little box. I thought he was standing up, but then I realized he was changing. The clothes became pale fur. The face lengthened until only the eyes looked like Kieran West. Long, bushy tails suddenly filled the huge armchair, fanning out behind him like the hood of a massive cobra. He leaned towards me, jaws parting as the transformation concluded.

He was a fox. A giant fox, taller on his haunches than any man alive, almost white, and with at least six tails.

Not a fox, I corrected myself, staggering back with dread and under-standing. *A kitsune.*

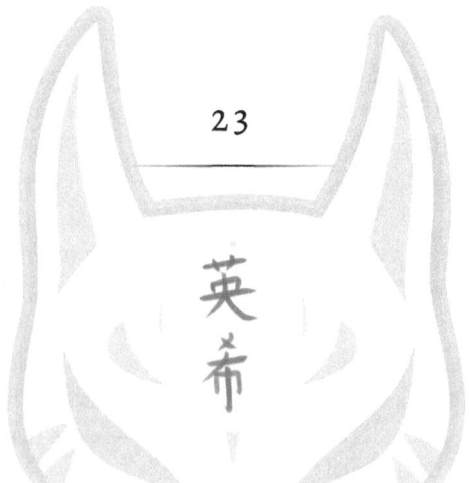

23

英
希

L et her go!" I demanded, flourishing my katana.

The fox creature bristled, though whether that was simply anger or outrage that I would defy it, I couldn't say. It leapt out of the chair and onto the bed, feet splayed, its many tails lashing the air in synchronized pulses. It was immense, seeming to fill the room. It bared its teeth, and a rumble came from deep in its throat which I felt not just in my ears but in my gut.

Its eyes fixed on me, and I felt lightheaded. I looked quickly away and slashed with the sword, but the light from the box had died as soon as he got up and the stroke was largely blind. The fox was as agile as it was strong. It leapt vertically to the ceiling and came down with a swat of its paw that slapped the blade clear. I fell back and it pounced, pushing me down so that I landed on my back.

Then it was on me, one paw on the wrist of my sword hand, its lolling jaws gaping, dripping over my throat. I punched with my mirror hand, amassing all the strength I could muster, and as the fox shrank away, I tore myself free and rolled out from under it. With a deft little hop, I was up on my feet again, pocketing the mirror and turning to face the great white brute, grabbing and raising my sword in one movement. I spread my feet as I had been taught, finding my balancing point, and taking a fighting stance with the katana level and poised to sweep a clean and lethal cut.

The huge fox just glowered at me, and as its eyes sparkled, I felt the weight of the sword increase. It was as if I was holding a barbell by the end. I fought to keep it up, drawing on all my considerable strength, and for a moment I thought I saw a flicker of surprise in the fox's unflinching stare, but then it lowered its head as if intensifying its concentration, and the sword grew heavier and heavier. Sweat broke out across my body, and I groaned as beads of it ran down my face. The fox fixed me with its beady glare, and at last, all my energy spent, the sword clattered to the ground.

I collapsed, exhausted with the effort of trying to hold the weapon up, and when I reached for it again, it wouldn't move at all, like it weighed a thousand pounds. Wearily I slumped down, panting.

"Now do you see?" said the fox that had been Mr. West in a voice that was still his but fuller and sharper, like it contained oceans and boulders and endless wilderness. "You think you know what is real, but you do not. I am real, and the deals I make bind forever."

I was breathless, woozy with how much the brief struggle had taken out of me, but I knew instinctively that I had to buy myself some time.

"What deals?" I managed. "What are you talking about?"

The fox looked momentarily taken aback, and then its black lips rippled with something that might have been amusement and it spoke again.

"Is this a ruse?" it said. "If it is, it's a thin one."

"I swear I have no idea what you are talking about," I replied, exhaustion making me honest.

"You really don't know!" He turned to Emily, who had managed to sit up but was rigid with terror. "Oh Kazuko, you have been strong, haven't you?" There was real surprise and even a hint of admiration mingled with the mockery. "All this time and you never told him."

Emily shook her head again, not in answer to his question, but as in a blanket denial of everything. She was refusing to speak.

"Oh, come now," said the fox. "I think it's time, and I wouldn't want to miss the revelation. Tell your little brother why you are here. Tell him why you have been helping me build my identity and power the illusions necessary to keep your silly friends and neighbors satisfied that I was one of them. Tell him, or I shall."

"You're a liar," I said again. "I don't believe anything you say. You've forced her. You've made her do these things..."

"NO!" he roared, and his bellow rippled through his sleek white flanks and shook the house. "Tell him, Kazuko, or I will kill him where he stands."

I stared at Emily. Tears were flowing down her face and her hair hung in her eyes. Her shoulders shuddered with one final sob and then she looked up and spoke, her voice so low that I almost missed it.

"I had to," she said. "I promised I would."

"What?" I gasped. "Why?"

"He was the only one who could give me something I wanted," she said. "Something I needed. So I said I would help him."

"What could be worth all this?!" I demanded, a note of disbelieving anger coming into my voice.

All the sneaking around? The lying to me and deception of the people who cared most for her? The theft of Saito's books and the magical attack on him, one of our greatest allies? What had she been thinking?

Emily just shook her head silently, and my irritation spiked.

"Em, tell me!" I said, my voice louder than I meant it to be. "What could he possibly give you that was worth becoming his slave, turning you against everyone who loved you?"

Something about that last phrase lit a spark in her and she threw her head back and howled with grief and sorrow. The sound, raw and animal as it was, made my skin crawl, and a ripple of panic ran through me, but before I could say anything, she turned on me and shouted.

"You, Caleb!" she shrieked. "He gave me you!"

I blinked, more than confused.

"What do you mean?" I said. "That's crazy. I was here all the time."

But she was shaking her head, weeping.

"No, Caleb," she said, quieter now. "You weren't. I haven't just been helping Enko-sama," she said, with a nod toward the great fox that was almost a bow. "He is here because of me. I brought him. It was part of the deal: his residence here, for you."

I was still flustered, and a part of me was annoyed that I was somehow being blamed for her actions.

"What does any of this have to do with me?" I demanded.

"You don't remember," she said softly, "that night at the caves, when we defeated the *oni* and closed the mystical prison."

"Of course I do..." I began but she shook her head sadly.

"Some of it, perhaps," she said, "not all."

"We fought the *onibaba* and the *bakeneko*," I insisted. "I killed the *oni* with Raiko's knife..."

169

"And we rescued Maddie," Em whispered, "and then we ran."

"I know!" I said. "What are you talking about?"

The giant fox's eyes had narrowed with satisfaction, as if he was savoring the moment.

"We came out through the cave fissure," she said, speaking wearily, as if reliving it all was taking more from her than she had to spare. "I went first in my fox form."

"I know! I remember."

"And then what, Caleb?"

"What? What do you mean? We got away and…everything was fine."

My voice had gone quiet. I felt suddenly uncertain, anxious. Something was nagging at the edge of my memory. Emily saw it in my eyes and she nodded silently. The pale fox I knew as Kieran West which she had called Enko-sama had become still and silent, but his eyes were locked on me, watching intently.

I shook my head, trying to clear it.

"How did you get out, Caleb?" Emily asked.

"What?" I asked, the worry building. I felt like I was in a tight space that was filling with water. Like I knew it would close over my head eventually, but I couldn't stop it.

"Bachan's sister, the *onibaba*, stabbed you in the fissure as you left the cave. Remember?"

In my head I saw the dimly lit cavern, the narrow passage, the desperate rush to get out, the scrambling of the demon's mother behind me, the silken ring of her knife and then…

Pain.

I remembered the shock of it. Hot and cold at once. But then… There was something missing.

"Yes," said Emily. "You remember the fight. You remember running. But you don't remember dying."

I stared at her, feeling the tears come to my own eyes now.

No, I thought. *No. No. No.*

"You don't remember the cave, where Mom and Bachan and the others were, because you were already gone."

"No," I whispered, aloud this time.

There had been the darkness of the cave and the pain and then… waking up with Em at the shrine in the woods. In between, there was void, black emptiness…

"No…" I said again, but my heart wasn't in it.

"Yes," Emily replied softly, tenderly. "I carried you to the shrine. I begged for your life, but it was too late. And then I was offered...this. An impossible thing that could be done once and once only—bringing you back—a deed which put me in debt forever. I agreed to it on the spot. That's where you woke up. You remember that, right?"

I did, but I couldn't speak. I just nodded.

"I'm sorry Caleb," she said. "It wasn't fair, and I wish there had been another way. I just couldn't let you go."

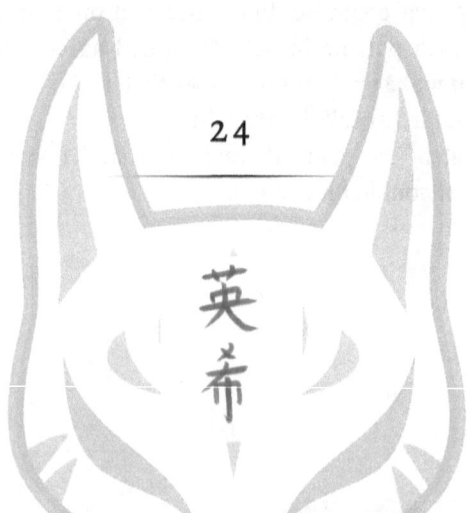

24

The fox the world knew as Kieran West allowed Em to go home with me. For now. She walked unsteadily, using my sheathed sword as a walking stick but stumbling with fatigue as we made our way along the driveway up to the road and the inconvenience store. She filled me in on more of the logistics, but then we barely spoke. What, after all, was there to say, and how could I begin to put anything this massive into words?

Mom and Dad were both in the store and Bachan was in the back sitting with the tengu, who still slept his charmed sleep. When they saw us come in, they rushed to us, all asking versions of the same questions: what happened? How was she? What could they do to help? You know, family stuff. I waved them off and helped Em to her room.

"Rest," I said. "I'll explain to Mom and Dad."

She gave me a quick glance as if ready to argue, then closed her eyes and nodded so small and weak that I hardly saw it. And I did. I told them everything. I had expected bafflement and disbelief but Mom and Bachan remembered a lot more than I did and they just sat in silence.

"I didn't ask," said Bachan, "but I wondered. When Kazuko took you from the cave," she said, giving me a bleak look, "you were beyond anything we could do for you."

"We thought we had lost you," Mom agreed. "And then Em was back, and you were fine, and I guess I didn't really want to know how she had done it."

"You...died?"

It was Dad. He hadn't been at the cave. Hadn't known about any of this until long after. Now he looked more than stunned. He looked hollowed out. He stood there, stiff and tall, trying to hold it all together, but there was a blank horror in his face that I had never seen before.

"And now this thing..." he went on, the words coming out with difficulty, like he was winching them up from a deep well, "is using Em because she saved you?"

"The fox, this Enko-sama, is very old and very powerful," I said.

"And family," said Bachan.

Everyone stared at her.

"He was the father of Raiko's wife, Mayumi," she said.

I hadn't known this, but it made sense.

"So he is like the spirit of Raiko who appeared to us at the shrine?" I asked. "A kind of ancestral guardian from a different part of the family, the kitsune part?"

Bachan tilted her head to one side: her 'not really' face. "Raiko died long ago," she said. "His spirit lives on, but he is gone. Enko is very old, but he did not die. He faded from the human world, became a higher form of *yōkai*. I think perhaps he moved to a different..." she paused hunting for the words and gesturing with her hands, both held flat, one a few inches above the other.

"A higher plane of existence," said Mom.

"Yes," said Bachan. "Perhaps he forgot about this world for a while, and when he wanted to return to it, he could not."

"Why not?" I asked.

Bachan shook her head. "That is all I know," she said. "Saito-san told me long ago."

"So Emily's desire to save me gave him a way back into the human world," I mused aloud.

"I think so," Bachan agreed solemnly. "The spirit of Raiko gave the responsibility to her. She is the kitsune of the family and probably the only one who could have brought Enko back. He used his power—his old and powerful magic—to revive Hideki, and in return..."

"He came here and made her his slave." Dad spoke flatly, with a kind of grim resolve, and when he turned to the door, I instantly knew what he was going to do.

"Stephen?" said Mom. "Where are you going?"

"Speak to this fox thing," he said darkly.

"No!" called Bachan. "You don't know what he is capable of!"

"Dad!" I called, moving quickly to him. "You can't. Seriously."

"I have to do *something!*" Dad hissed through gritted teeth. "This is my family. It is my job to protect them…"

"Dad," I said softly. "Please don't. He's way too strong. He'll kill you."

He saw the earnestness in my face and seemed to wilt before me. Suddenly he looked as weary and sad as Emily had. At last, he nodded once but said nothing, and the sight of him, strong and quiet, full of love and outrage and the need to do something he couldn't deliver broke my heart.

The door to the inconvenience store kicked open, sending the bell jangling, and DeMarcus burst in followed by Joey. What with everything that had been going on here, I had forgotten their mission, and with the power and cell towers still down, I hadn't received any texts saying whether they had found anything. I took one look at their breathless faces now and knew they had.

"It's in the abandoned Walmart!" DeMarcus exclaimed.

"What is?" asked Mom.

"The *Omukade!*" said Joey. "The power signature is off the charts!"

I moved quickly.

"What are you doing?" Dad demanded.

"Getting my sword," I said.

The last time I had used a sword to fight a monster, the blade shattered on its enchanted skin, so the tengu's stories about the legendary *Omukade* having armor that was proof against all weapons was concerning, to say the least. The one in the story had only perished when the victorious warrior had tipped his arrows with human saliva. I spat on the blade of my katana, and when DeMarcus gave me a questioning look, I shrugged.

"Worth a shot," I said.

It wasn't really my sword. It was one of Saito's collection. I didn't have a sword of my own. That suddenly felt like something I should address. *If I get through the next half hour or so,* I thought, *I'll get right on that.*

The Walmart was a few blocks north of the high school, over the road. It backed onto the woods and, having been closed nearly six years, was already showing signs of fading into the rampant undergrowth. The parking lot was pocked and weedy, and the cables which ran to the building over uneven telephone poles were hung with tendrils of kudzu snaking out of the forest and onto the roof. The perimeter fence was rusty and a padlock on one of the gates had been cut off so that the metal frame flapped open. One of the store's sliding doors had been smashed.

That was new. It looked like someone had rammed a truck through it, though the store had been empty for years, so there was nothing inside to steal.

"You think the *Omukade* did that?" asked Joey uneasily.

"Kind of hope not," I admitted as we picked our way to the entrance through the glass fragments. "What you got there?" I asked, nodding at the bulging backpack slung on Joey's shoulder. They tugged it open to show me. "Bug spray?" I said, incredulous.

"It's a centipede," said Joey. "Your dad said I could take it."

"It's a centipede the size of a bus," DeMarcus said.

"That's why I brought several cans," Joey said, grinning hopefully.

To be honest, I wasn't sure why either of them had come at all, and though I knew they had earned the right to be there, and that I wouldn't have found the monster's lair without them, I was suddenly anxious that I would have to devote too much of my attention to looking after them. DeMarcus had a baseball bat and Joey had bug spray...

"Guys," I said, "Maybe I should do this alone."

"No way, man," said DeMarcus. "I want to see it!"

"How about you wait until I've killed it, then come see it?" I suggested.

"You may be the demon fighter," Joey cut in, "but we're a team."

I sighed. "Okay," I said, "but stay behind me. Oh, and Bachan said she thought it fed on her fear. So, you know, try not to be scared."

Joey and DeMarcus gave me a long stare then plastered unconvincing grins on their faces.

"This is going to be awesome!" said Joey with a manic thumbs-up.

I held the sword in front of me and ducked in through the smashed door. It wasn't just the glass that had shattered. The metal frame of the whole portico was buckled as if it had been hit with a wrecking ball.

Not a good sign.

"Do you have a plan?" DeMarcus whispered, taking in the twisted steel. "Like, you know, tactics?"

"Sneak up and stab it?" I suggested.

"Worked for Julius Caesar's pals," Joey muttered.

"Julius Caesar wasn't a bug that ate cows."

"Technically," Joey said, "centipedes aren't bugs, if by that you mean insects. They are arthropods, but while all insects are arthropods, not all arthropods are insects."

"Not sure knowing its biological class is going to help me kill it," I said.

"Phylum, not class," said Joey.

"Joey," I said, giving them a hard stare.

"Sorry," they replied. "The sense of imminent mortal combat is making me hyper."

"You don't have to come in," I said.

"No," Joey said with a look for reassurance at DeMarcus. "I'm going to help."

Joey was always pale. Now they were white as a sheet.

"Just remember..." I began.

"Stay behind you," DeMarcus completed for me.

We stepped into the store's gloomy lobby. Apart from the ruined doorway, the glass was boarded up, and where there were skylights high in the walls, they were thick with dust and a greenish mold. Structurally, the store was a huge concrete box, the vast roof supported on steel pillars with a grid of horizontal trusses and girders on top, where the ventilation system and lights hung. It had long since fallen into disrepair and was now cobwebby and rust-pocked. There were pools of rainwater on the linoleum floor, all thick with algae and weeds that had been there long enough to generate entire ecosystems.

Racks of shelves had been left, many of them still advertising sale prices, and here and there were bins of discarded merchandise—moldy towels and damp-swollen books—but for the most part the store had been picked clean long ago. The air felt pretty much the same as outside, and with good reason. In addition to the wrecked door, a portion of the ceiling had collapsed and kudzu dangled in. One set of shelves labeled "home appliances" was twined with the stuff, so it felt oddly like we were inside and outside at the same time.

There was no sign of the *Omukade*, but that didn't mean it wasn't there. I gestured to the others to wait and moved to where the greeters would once have welcomed us to the store, for reasons I never understood. Somewhere a crow called and a smaller bird—a Carolina wren, I thought—rocketed away cheeping like a crazy thing.

"If I was a giant, supernatural centipede thing," Joey breathed, "where would I be?"

"Meat and produce?" DeMarcus suggested. If there had been any left, that would have been a good call, but there had been nothing like people food in here for years. "Home and garden?" he said. "Dairy? How are killer centipedes with lactose?"

I gave him an exasperated look, and he mouthed "my bad" and made a lip-zipping gesture.

I moved quietly forward, past the islands where the checkout registers had been on the right, and the pharmacy on the left, the latter hung with fading pictures of implausibly happy people collecting their meds. Directly ahead was the area which now would have been cluttered with Halloween stuff but when the store had gone under, had being gearing up for Christmas. A jolly Santa Claus cutout hung lopsided from the ceiling rails and fragments of ravaged fake holly trailed onto the floor like a sickly green snake.

On the far right wall, almost a hundred yards away, were produce signs in white on a green background and, as I looked, a flicker of light pulsed through what I thought were freezer cases. I froze, and the lights above us flashed on, pulsed a couple of times and went out. There was a crackle of sound overhead, as if the intercom system had turned on, played a second or two of static, and gone off again.

DeMarcus gave me an anxious look. Until that moment, I had thought there was a decent chance that the *Omukade* wouldn't be here. Suddenly I wondered if I was ready for this. Then I heard it move and knew I wasn't.

It was immense. The rattle of its legs sounded like machine gun fire, and one of the huge banks of shelves pivoted like it was made of balsa wood and crashed to the ground. I turned wildly to face the sound and saw it coming over the wall of the women's section. It came face first, mandibles the length of my arms flexing. Its antennae—if that's what they were—weren't the whiplike filaments I associated with centipedes, but bright red sectional rods, long as fishing poles. It had glossy black eyes set high in its head, and the mouth parts were hook like claws, yellow as the legs but their sharp points black as the segmented body which snaked after it.

I don't know how it knew we were there, but it was aiming right for us, flowing on nightmare legs. In a couple of seconds, it had halved the distance between us and was still coming.

I ran at it. Actually, I took three long strides, slashed with my sword at its face, and skipped left, vaulting clean over the closest shelves ("Rollback deals on Fall wear!") and landing within striking distance of its armored body. I picked my spot between segments and lunged, but the sword point glanced off the gleaming shell and the follow through left me off balance.

I fell.

So much for spitting on the blade. My attack had done nothing but anger it, and as the *Omukade* whipped round to face me, I was suddenly sure that coming here to face it had been a colossal mistake. I was on my back on the dusty floor. The *Omukade* reared up, its spindly legs splayed and those awful pincer-like mouth parts flexing. Some thick and oily fluid glistened on the tip of each.

Venom.

It plunged down at me. I tried to roll aside but it was just too big, so I lunged upward. The sword clanged on the centipede's gaping maw, and though it still didn't penetrate, it blocked the attack. The creature pulled back and stabbed down headfirst, the claw-like fangs reaching for me. Again, I parried, using both hands to force the beast back. Its segmented antennae curled and brushed at my face, feeling for its target as it prepared another assault.

"Kawabunga!"

It was Joey (who else would say "Kawabunga"?) and DeMarcus, the latter swinging his bat at the creature's head as Joey unloaded streams of insecticide from a can in each hand. The Omukade flinched, more surprised than fearful, and pulled itself up, as if trying to get a better view of this lunacy. It gave me the moment I needed to get back on my feet and leap up, cutting wildly. I managed two clean swings at the apex of my jump. Though neither cut through the monster's carapace, it moved backwards, shimmying along its length as it went up the next set of shelves. It was long enough to easily span whole aisles of shelving, and for a horrible second I found myself looking up at its many legs as it lifted itself into the next bay and vanished from sight into the baby care section.

I wafted the cloud of toxic spray from my face and stared up. The light fixtures were flashing and a recorded voice was booming "Attention Walmart shoppers" fuzzily over the store's sound system. I suspected the *Omukade* was merely confused by this attack on its home, but there was a moment of unexpected calm.

"Are we winning?" Joey asked, their voice dripping with doubt. "I mean, we're still alive, which is awesome, but it doesn't feel like we're winning."

I shook my head slowly, keeping my eyes on the bank of wire shelves marked with prices for strollers and diaper bins.

"We're annoying it," I said. "Not hurting it. If one of those fang-things tags us, we're toast."

"The waitress survived," said DeMarcus trying to sound hopeful.

"When it was about a hundredth of the size it is now," I said. "Trust me. You don't want those fangs near you."

I was about to say more, but DeMarcus held up a finger. He had heard something. It was faint at first, distant, a thousand tiny clicks, a million, but it was getting louder, closer. It sounded like...

"Bugs!" yelled Joey.

Beetles, silverfish, wood lice, ants, millipedes, crickets and roaches. Thousands of them. They flowed out of the baby department toward us like a gray-black wave. They covered the floor and the shelves. They dropped from the ceiling. You could hear their hard little bodies as they fell, righted themselves and ran at us.

"Oh, hell no!" shouted DeMarcus, turning to head out the way we had come.

Joey was swatting at their hair, their clothes, eyes wide and mouth clamped shut. In the confusion, I saw the *Omukade* surge upward over the top of the shelves, but instead of charging us where we stood, paralyzed with terror, it kept going up, a rhythmic, pulsing slither that rippled through its body as it clambered over the joists and girders and up into the ceiling. I stared as it threaded itself through the metal framework which supported the roof, scurrying upside down along the underside of the ceiling, its mouth chittering.

All around me the dusty paleness of the store had grown dark with shiny, swarming bodies. The floor seemed to swim. The shelves rippled.

We ran. It wasn't a tactical decision. It was deeper than that, a cry of revulsion that came from our very flesh and the marrow of our bones. We sprinted back the way we had come in. DeMarcus hurdled an abandoned shopping cart as Joey weaved around jewelry counters whose lights flashed on, illuminating the teeming insects which flooded over the cases.

We ran, but up in the ceiling, coursing along upside down in defiance of gravity on its rattling pointed feet, the *Omukade* ran faster. By the time I realized, I had lost it. I spun around, forcing myself to ignore the moving carpet of bugs, focusing on the door that was fifty yards away on the other side of the abandoned checkout counters.

And then it dropped, unspooling itself gently out of the ceiling, in between us and freedom. It snaked down to the floor, settled and lifted its head, mouth parts opening and closing, those sickle hook fangs dripping with poison. Behind us, the bugs hemmed us in, like they were herding us toward it.

We had done it no damage. None. I still held my sword in front of me, but that was only because it was all I had. I could block with it, maybe hold off an attack or two, but I couldn't cut it. The monster was immune.

I flashed a panicked glance at my friends. They had followed me here, believing I could protect them. Now they were going to die.

It's all your fault, I thought with a pang of despair. *Em. Dad. Saito. Everything.*

The *yōkai* took a couple of steps towards us, all its legs replicating the movement in a sickly ripple that ran along its length to the weird antennae-like things that made its back end look almost the same as its front. Instinctively we moved back, but we were up against the pharmacy wall, one of the few solid structures in the whole store. We had nowhere to go.

It reared up and its mouth parts dripped, though whether that was venom or saliva, I didn't know and couldn't linger to find out. I rushed it, leaping high over its head and landing on the back of its neck. I seized one of those gross, tubular antennae with one hand, and I hacked with my sword at its armored spine.

In the same instant, Joey opened up the insect spray again, spinning in place so a cloud of the stuff filled the air. DeMarcus charged the beast's closest legs, swinging his bat like he was trying to launch one out of the park.

The *Omukade* whipped with rage as it tried to dislodge me. As it spun, it threw DeMarcus clear across the floor and he slumped hard against the pharmacy wall. Its huge body lurched until it was over Joey and then flattened itself to the ground. Joey cried out, pinned. I kept chopping with my sword, but all I was doing was enraging the monster further. The creature's slick, black armored shell showed not so much as a crack from all my cutting and stabbing.

This was futile.

I vaulted down, sprinted under the *Omukade*'s arching body and dragged Joey free, bracing myself for the deadly fangs in the back of my neck.

"DeMarcus!" I yelled.

"I'm okay," he said, rolling first onto his knees then hauling himself upright. He looked and sounded woozy.

"We gotta go," I said.

DeMarcus winced. "Well, when you put it like that..." he said, taking a backwards step toward the front door.

"I was kind of hoping you'd say that," Joey said. "Good plan."

"I don't mean to dampen the mood," said DeMarcus, "but how, exactly?"

He was right. The huge creature was blocking our way to the shattered front door.

"There's a back door, right?" I said. "An emergency exit. Probably too small for that thing to get out of..."

"It's all the way on the other side, by the computer games and restrooms," said Joey. "We'll never make it."

But even as they said it, I noticed something. I could hear the fear in Joey's voice. I could almost taste the waves of it coming off all three of us.

The monster could taste it too, and as I watched, I could see something was happening to it. It tightened, its segments bunching and popping as its body arced.

It's getting bigger!

It was, too. Right in front of me. I could see it stretching and expanding, new segments and legs bursting out along its body. Even as I felt spellbound by the impossibility of the thing, I knew this was our chance.

"Run!" I shouted, bolting back into the store.

Joey's spray had left a hole in the army of pursuing bugs, and I ran into it, cutting left toward DIY and Vehicle Maintenance. DeMarcus, who could give any of the school's wide receivers a run for their money in terms of sheer speed, was right with me. Joey was already lagging behind. I hesitated, looking back, urging them on, and my eyes found the *Omukade*. It was already almost a third bigger than it had been, and still growing.

"Come on!" I yelled at Joey, extending my hand and grabbing hold as soon as they were in range.

"You ever wondered," Joey gasped anxiously, "if they lock the emergency exits after a store closes?"

"No," I said grimly. "Keep running."

Knowing I could catch them, I waited as they passed, looking back. The wave of insects was coming after us now, but they wouldn't get to us, not unless—as Joey feared—we couldn't open the back door. The *Omukade* had clearly decided that its fastest route to us was through the ceiling. It was spiraling up again, twisting through the roof's steel bracers as it barreled after us.

I bounded off, quickly passing Joey and closing on DeMarcus, my eyes flashing around for signs to the door. Electronics. Restrooms. Then, up in the corner, flashing with green light: Emergency Exit. I ducked around a set of shelves and there it was. But there was something between me and it; a man, his back turned toward me.

A janitor or construction inspector?

"Get out!" I yelled. "Something is coming! You have to go..."

But then he turned and something in his stance rang a distant bell, the way he held his hand, palm up like a cop stopping traffic. I realized who he was before I saw the blind face or the eyeball glistening in the center of one hand. In his other, he had a length of chain that he was trying to loop around the door's exit bar.

"You!" I bellowed.

"Who the hell is that?" DeMarcus demanded.

"Don't let him block the door!" I called back.

DeMarcus didn't need telling twice. He lowered his shoulder and charged. The *yōkai* half-skipped away, flicking the chain at him, but DeMarcus leaned round the attack and slammed into him. The little old man went flying and, barely breaking stride, DeMarcus reached the door. He leant on the bar and, with a snap, it opened. He stepped through, holding it open.

I turned. Joey was coming, laboring hard. Their running was ragged, clumsy with panic and exhaustion. I turned to see if the eye-hand-guy was going to be a problem, but a great metallic screech from the heart of the store behind me spun me round.

Now what?

The roof behind Joey was buckling as the *Omukade* scrambled toward us. It was vast now, seeming to fill the giant box store's ceiling. I could hear the groan of metal under stress, then a sudden keening whine. Joey glanced up and cried out, but kept running. I reached for them, urging them on, as part of the structure further back collapsed. I grabbed Joey with one hand, shoved the eye-hand man aside as he tried to block our way, and then DeMarcus was pulling us through the door. Even before we were out, the iron trusses above us buckled and twisted, and then the whole ceiling was coming in, bringing the mammoth centipede down with it.

"Run!" I shouted again as we bolted out into the sunlight.

My only plan...

DeMarcus dragged Joey with him, but I was right on their heels as we cut round the building back to the front across the parking lot. I sheathed my useless sword as I ran, doing all I could to get away from there. Behind me, I heard the rumble and crash of the building caving in as a great cloud of concrete dust rose above the site as if a bomb had gone off.

Let it be crushed in the wreckage, I thought wildly. *Let it be buried forever!*

But I knew it wouldn't be. It was too strong.

It was *way* too strong.

And all we could do was run.

25

I could barely stand by the time I got home, and not just because I was exhausted from all the running. I was weak with a deep sense of powerlessness. I had done what I could, used all the abilities I had—natural and supernatural—and had failed to score any kind of meaningful win over the *Omukade*. And if I saw it again, it would surely be even bigger and more powerful.

We were doomed.

The collapse of the old Walmart supercenter had made the news. I even went along, with a bunch of other local gawkers, when they sent an inspection crew in to investigate, even though I knew there would be nothing I could do if they ran into the giant centipede *yōkai*. Fortunately, they didn't, deciding that what was left of the structure was too dangerous to allow anyone close. The bystanders were shepherded outside the perimeter fence, which was quickly reinforced and protected with new locks, while the investigators explained to the sheriff's office, and eventually to the journalists and TV news crews, that the building's structural integrity have been compromised by a sinkhole opening up near the rear of the store.

"That's how it got out," I said bleakly to my family as we watched the report on Action News Twelve in the backroom of the inconvenience store. "What they are calling a sinkhole was probably a tunnel. The

Omukade's weight brought the building down, part of it at least, but then it must have burrowed out. That's what centipedes do."

"So it went where?" asked Dad.

I shrugged. The work crews had reported no sign of it, and they hadn't said anything about the sinkhole itself. Perhaps if the passage had partially filled up with debris behind the creature as it left, it didn't look like a tunnel at all. Which meant it could be anywhere. I doubted even something as powerful as that could burrow through solid rock, but if it had come up in the woods, the chances of anyone seeing it were slim.

"How are Joey and DeMarcus?" asked Mom.

"Okay," I said. "Mostly. Physically fine but pretty shaken up."

That was an understatement. I knew they still wanted to help, but they had had more than a nasty scare. In my heart, I suspected I would not be able to rely on them in the future.

"They could have been killed," said Bachan. "You shouldn't have taken them with you."

It wasn't so much a scolding as a statement of fact and, knowing it was true, I changed the subject. "That guy was there," I said to Emily. "The one with the eyes in his hands."

She hadn't said much since the revelations about her deal with Mr. West AKA Enko, seeming dreamy and disinterested, but she looked up now.

"So he escaped from the cave," she said musingly.

"*Te no me*," said Bachan.

"Gesundheit," I remarked reflexively.

"A *yōkai* who appears as a blind man but has eyes in his hands? *Te no me*. That is his name."

"Great," I said darkly. "We know his name. Maybe we can send him a Christmas card."

"Caleb," said Dad quietly.

"This *te no me* guy is working with the *Omukade*," I replied quickly "Which means..."

"They are going to try and reopen the prison," said Emily. She sounded almost too weary to speak. "The centipede *yōkai* will burrow through the physical confines, the rock and packed earth that holds it in place and keeps people out..."

"And then this *te no me* guy will perform whatever ritual the *onibaba* used to break through the mystical energy."

"Didn't they need your blood last time?" asked Mom, her face pale with dread and revulsion.

"To release the *oni* specifically," said Em, "not to break open the vault."

"The cat monster and those faceless shapeshifters got out long before they did the blood ritual thing," I confirmed. "We're back to square one. They're going to break the prison open and all the *yōkai* inside are going to get out."

There was a stunned hush, then Em whispered, almost to herself, "So, everything we did was for nothing." It was a statement loaded not just with our previous shared experiences but with all that she had sacrificed to keep me alive.

"No," said Bachan sharply. "There was a threat. A dangerous one. You stopped it. Now there is another, and you must stop that one as well. We go from crisis to crisis. A new problem does not invalidate your previous successes. It is just life. We continue. We fight."

That seemed like a pretty bleak way of looking at the world, but I couldn't fault her logic.

"What are they waiting for?" asked Mom.

I gave her a blank stare.

"If the centipede thing can tunnel through the physical walls of the prison," she replied, "and the eye-hand-guy can do a ritual to break open the mystical energy barriers inside, what are they waiting for?"

A good question, and one none of us had an answer for.

"I wish Saito were awake," I said without thinking. I shot Emily a look. "No offense."

Her face filled with confusion. "What do you mean?"

"Nothing," I replied quickly. "Just that. I don't see how we can fight the *Omukade*, and it would have been good to have his input."

"But why 'no offense'?"

I blushed and looked down.

"Because," said Bachan peering shrewdly at her, "he thinks you attacked Saito-san, but you didn't, did you?"

"What?" Emily exclaimed, leaping to her feet. "Me? Of course not! Thanks a lot, Caleb."

Everyone gaped but Dad raised his hands in a calming gesture. "Now, Em," he said, "don't take on. It was an honest mistake and, to be fair to Caleb, we all thought the same."

"You *what*?" she gasped.

"There was CCTV footage of the dojo," I said. "We saw you take the books. Then we saw a fox go in."

"It was Enko-sama!" said Emily. "I took the books, but I would never hurt Saito-san!"

"Well, I see that now!" I replied.

"But you assumed it was me," she said darkly.

"We didn't know there was another shape-shifting fox in town!" I exclaimed, "which, in the circumstances, was a fair assumption."

Emily was unmoved. "All this time I've been slaving away because I made the choice to keep you alive and you didn't even have enough faith in me to…"

"Em, that's enough," said Dad, standing up. "Caleb didn't know what you had done for him. None of us did. We had no idea of your situation. You could have told me!" He caught himself. "Us. You could have told us." He was upset.

Whether Emily was affected by that or was just too tired to argue, she lowered her eyes and said nothing.

"This household needs to be a whole lot more open and honest with each other," he said, almost to himself. "Enough with the secrets! We are a team. A family. If we can't act like one, then what's the point of anything?"

Mom reached for him and took his hand, smiling sympathetically and holding his eyes until he got self-conscious.

"I'm just saying," he ended lamely.

"We get it," said Mom. "No secrets."

She gave us all a significant look.

"No secrets," said Bachan.

"No secrets," I added.

Em rolled her eyes and sighed.

"Em," Mom prompted.

"Fine," she said. "No secrets."

There was a lengthy pause, and in the silence, everyone sat down and took a breath.

"How's the sauce selling?" I asked, trying to sound upbeat.

"What?" asked Bachan.

"Dad made this really great barbecue sauce, sort of a combination of different flavors connected to… doesn't matter. It's really good. And it's for sale in the store."

Bachan frowned like I had gone crazy right in front of her, so I turned to Dad.

187

"Haven't sold any yet," he admitted miserably. "Maybe I should lower the price or…"

"So now what?" Em asked abruptly.

Dad went quiet.

"The way I see it," said Mom thoughtfully. "There are two separate problems."

"The *Omukade*," I said.

"And Enko," said Bachan, "the fox everyone in town thinks is the billionaire who will lead them to a new and simpler future."

"Which looks a lot like the past," I added.

"Are we sure they are different problems?" asked Dad. "Are we sure they aren't related?"

The question hung in the air for a moment because there was only one person who could answer it, but no one wanted to ask her directly. At last, Emily shook her head.

"Enko-sama wants a foothold in our world," she said. "In this country. I think that's his sole agenda. He knows that technology can expose who he really is and that it gives people power which is beyond his control or understanding. His stranglehold on the world depends on illusion, on tricking people's minds into seeing what he wants them to. You can't do that if people can check their cameras and see what's really there. You can't tell them black is white if they can look it up online and see otherwise. Phones and computers are not just his blind spot; they are his undoing. He thinks that if he can get rid of it, it will make things as they were centuries ago, when he was loved and feared as a figure of great power. My situation…"

"Our situation," I corrected.

She acknowledged that with a tiny sidelong look at me and pressed on. "Our predicament after the fight at the caves gave him an opening. For all his magic, he doesn't know our world or how to live in it. That's what he used me for, to bring him information, and to help power his illusions. He probably knows of the *Omukade*, but I don't think he is allied with it."

"But two Japanese demons in one place!" Dad said. "It can't be coincidence."

"It's not," I said. "But the reason they are here is us and our ancestors."

"And they are not demons," said Bachan thoughtfully. "They are *yōkai*."

"What's the difference?" asked Dad, who was getting impatient.

"Demons in your world are evil," she said. "There are no good demons."

"Are you saying the centipede thing and the fox who enslaved my daughter are good?" Dad asked, his eyes flashing dangerously.

Bachan shook her head emphatically. "Certainly not," she said. "But *yōkai* can be many things, morally..." she hesitated, struggling to find the words in English.

"The way Saito put it," said Mom, coming to her rescue, "*yōkai* are like people. They can be good or bad, or neutral. Some are evil, creatures of hatred and malevolence who will do anything to spread misery, pain, and despair. Others are more self-involved and the trouble they cause is often merely selfishness or playfulness."

"Playfulness!" Dad scoffed.

"The desire to amuse themselves at people's expense," Mom clarified.

"I don't think the okumade..."

"*Omukade*," we all chorused.

"That," Dad continued pointedly, "is not just being playful."

"I agree," I cut in. "It's a monster with a purpose and it's in league with the servants of the *onibaba*."

"Shio," said Bachan grimly. "My imprisoned sister."

"But Enko, the West fox," I said, "sounds different."

"Less evil?" Dad demanded, daring me to say *yes*. As if it was acting by itself, his right hand went to Emily's and grabbed it.

"Not from our perspective," I said carefully. "But its purpose, what makes it tick, seems more like selfishness, and yes, though it doesn't feel like it to us, I think he's kind of playing with us."

"The way a child might play with ants," said Mom, working it out as she spoke. "Kids don't consider ants to be sophisticated creatures with feelings because their own superiority seems so obvious."

Dad was about to argue, turning to Emily as if he felt he needed to defend her, but she nodded.

"Mom's right," she said. "I have never felt anything from him that isn't about his own comfort or amusement. I don't believe he has any interest in aiding the *Omukade* or reopening the *yōkai* prison." Dad gave her a long look, then relaxed slowly. "But he is...pragmatic."

Bachan made a face. "What is...?" she began.

"Pragmatic means, practical, someone who pursues real or simple solutions to problems," said Mom, sounding like a dictionary. "Someone who will put his feelings aside to get what he wants in the long run."

"So he could ignore the whole thing," Emily continued, "or he could make a deal with the *Omukade* if it—or the imprisoned *yōkai* it is allied with—can make him an offer which appeals to him."

That was a worrying thought, and we all went very quiet. At last, Dad broke the silence.

"What if we got him to make a deal with us instead?" he said.

Emily shook her head hard. "No way!" she said, color rushing to her face for the first time in days. "I won't do any more for him than I already have."

"Doesn't have to be you," I said. "I'm the other heir of Raiko, remember?"

It was Bachan's turn to shake her head. "Enko cannot be trusted," she said. "He will use every..." she faltered and tried a few words in Japanese, but none of us knew what she meant. "Like a lawyer," she clarified.

"He'll exploit every loophole," said Emily quietly but with the certainty that comes from direct experience, "every advantage."

"And he is extremely powerful," said Bachan. "Many, many years ago he had five tails."

Dad stared at her, clearly wondering if this too was a translation failure.

"Multiple tails are the marks of age and power in kitsune," said Mom. "The nine-tailed fox has god-like power."

"He has seven now," said Emily flatly.

Bachan stared, mouth open.

"I saw them," I said.

"What can he do?" Dad asked. "I mean, specifically. The kinds of magic or whatever."

"Illusion," said Bachan. "He can change his appearance and can use other kinds of deception."

"He can affect weather," said Emily. "Only in a small area, but quite powerfully."

I stared at her. "The storms that keep knocking out our power?" I said.

"Yes," Emily replied.

"I knew it!" I exclaimed. "I mean, not knew it in the sense that I had actually figured it out, but it felt weird, all this rain and wind." It sounded less impressive when I spelled it out.

"Good job, Caleb," said Dad encouragingly, like he was complimenting the kid in class who has stopped eating crayons.

"And of course he is physically very strong," said Em, ignoring me, "especially in his fox form."

"I can attest to that," I agreed, not happy about it. "And we are on our own," I added, remembering the catastrophe at the Walmart. I couldn't involve my friends in this further.

"Worse than that," said Emily. "I am still bound to Enko-sama. I must continue to do his will, and we should expect him to block us if we do anything which inconveniences him in any way."

"The books!" I exclaimed. "The tengu's books. Where are they?"

"In Enko-sama's study," said Emily.

"Can he read them?" asked Bachan.

"I have never seen him read anything," said Em. "He knows a lot, remembers a lot, and he knows enough to be able to recognize the characters in a book's title, but if he can read, he chooses not to. It's part of why he needed me, and why he wants Portersville to separate itself from technology. The internet, phones, they are things he doesn't know how to use. Human stuff. Maybe he thinks of books like that."

Bachan looked uncertain. "Many *yōkai* are scholars," she said. "The tengu among them. They study ancient wisdom. They read and write."

Em shrugged. "I can only tell you what I've seen," she said. "He treats the books as important things, treasures, but when I brought them to him, he didn't even open them."

"If he doesn't read," I said, "why did he want them?"

"Same reason he finally wanted Saito-san out of the picture entirely," said Emily. "What the tengu knows or can find out, must be some kind of threat to him or his activities."

I thought of Saito lying on the cot in the hallway upstairs, still in the same position he had been when we brought him home, breathing, but motionless. Dad, as if following the same line of thought, stood up.

"I'm going to have another go at untying that charm thing on Saito-san's wrist," he announced. "I'm usually pretty good with knots."

The rest of us looked at each other, knowing both that he was trying to help and that it was futile.

"We need to get hold of those books," I said.

"Even if we could, we couldn't read them," said Mom. "Old Japanese is very…"

"I could read them," said Bachan. "In time. I don't have the tengu's knowledge or his power, but maybe I could find something useful."

"There was only one book he really wanted," said Em. "The Murakami.

He made me memorize the characters so that I would recognize it. That and a jumble of handwritten pages that came with it. The others were just a blind."

"Do you know what the book is about?" I asked.

When Emily shook her head, I looked to Bachan, but she didn't know either.

"Then we'll have to take it and find out," I concluded.

"I can't," said Emily. "I mean, literally can't. If I try to go against his orders, I will be paralyzed like Saito."

"Then it will have to be someone else," I said. "I can get into the house. Maybe I can get Nathan to invite me over."

Emily's face clouded with bafflement.

"What?" I said. "I know he probably knows something of what his father is doing but…"

"Caleb," Emily cut in, as if the crayon-eater was at it again. "There is no Nathan."

"What do you mean? He's in my class and…"

"Are you serious?" asked Emily looking at me like I was the village idiot. "He doesn't exist. *Nathan* is just another of Enko-sama's magical disguises. You hadn't figured that out? That's why they are never in the same place at once."

I stared at her. It was official. As well as being useless as a hero, I was deeply, hopelessly stupid.

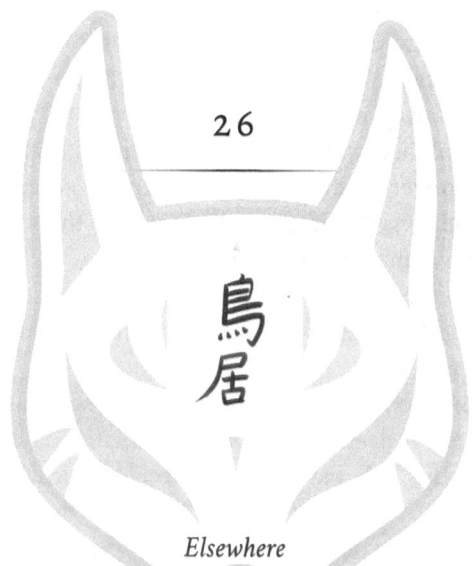

26

Elsewhere

Tony Altzinger, the ranger who presided over school visits to his station, fumbled in his pockets with an unsteady hand.

"Mind if I smoke?" he asked.

The sheriff and Mayor Miller shook their heads. Chris Collington shrugged and looked away. They did mind, he could tell, but they weren't going to object given what they had just shown him. Thad Mortimer, the austere and wire-thin coroner, however, wasn't having it.

"Can't smoke in here," he said.

"Then can we go somewhere else?" Tony asked. The chilly morgue, with its smells of stainless steel, disinfectant and—underneath it all—blood, was getting to him. The room was low ceilinged and dim, because only the backup lights were working. The coroner had made his points about the corpse with a flashlight which made everything horribly bright. Tony knew he was pale, and he felt lightheaded, even a little nauseous.

But who could blame you for that?

Still, he was embarrassed. He didn't have many dealings with the town's bigwigs and this little group comprised pretty much the entire set. In fact, apart from that West guy, the only one of the local movers and shakers who wasn't standing around the gurney, was on it: Brian Davenham, a man Tony had known, albeit not very well. Tony had also never been summoned to an autopsy before, and it hadn't been a pleasant experience. Not that there had been much to look at, as far as the body was concerned. Most of it was gone.

"See how the torso has been sheared off here?" the coroner had said with professional calm, aiming his flashlight. "Other than a few fingers found a few yards away, everything above the waist is just gone. As is the left leg. If he hadn't been carrying his wallet in his back pocket, it would have taken a lot longer to identify him. The force required to do this, and the size of the incisions would generally make me think that he had fallen into a piece of heavy machinery, a baler."

"An accident or done on purpose?" asked the mayor.

"Murdered and then mutilated with a machine to conceal the crime?" the sheriff suggested.

"I don't think so," said the coroner. "These wounds are almost certainly the cause of death. They weren't inflicted on a corpse after the fact. And there's this." He paused and directed their attention to a deep scar on the thigh of the remaining leg. "See how the wound is weeping there? That's an incision point, several inches deep, very slightly curved as if it was made by a large tooth or claw. And it is leaking fluid."

"Blood and such?" asked the sheriff.

"I'm afraid not," said the coroner. "It's a clear, viscous liquid, and it didn't come from Brian Davenham. Preliminary tests suggest it's a kind of toxin containing..." he paused to check a printed sheet of paper, "cysteine-rich, disulfide peptides of a highly unusual structure."

"Meaning?" the mayor cut in.

"I would prefer not to say until we've heard the ranger's report from the scene," said the coroner. He was an elderly man whose bright blue eyes shone over half-moon wire spectacles. Those eyes found Tony now. So did the others.

"Can we do this somewhere else?" said Tony. He hated the way the question made him sound weak, but he couldn't stand another minute in the morgue. "I mean, if there's nothing further to see here..."

He didn't look at the remains.

"My office," said the coroner. "Upstairs."

They left the awful room, and as the door banged shut behind them, Tony breathed a sigh of relief. They ascended concrete steps up from the basement by the thin light of some hastily positioned battery-powered lights. The next floor up, though still dark, felt totally different, with its linoleum tiled floor and green trim paint. There were even a few tasteful pictures on the walls. Tony thought it felt like a doctor's waiting room. As they walked, they discussed the funeral which would be the day after tomorrow.

"Just close friends and family," said Chris Collington. "No viewing, obviously."

Obviously.

Thad Mortimer's office was behind a pale wooden door with glass panels. There was a desk with a lifeless computer and a battery lantern. The walls were full of shelves loaded with binders, and there were only two other chairs. As the coroner took his place behind the desk, the mayor and Chris Collington took the remaining seats without so much as a word. The sheriff hung back by the door like he was on guard, and Tony stood awkwardly by the window.

"Do these open?" he asked. The office was stuffy with all four of them in there, and he felt like he had the air of the morgue in his lungs still. He didn't wait for an answer, fumbling with a catch until one of the windows opened onto the night. Two floors down he could make out the parking lot, but the lights above it were all out. Tony snatched a cigarette from the packet, shoved it between his lips and lit it on the second attempt. Thad Mortimer opened his mouth to object but decided not to bother.

"Your report, Mr. Altzinger," he said instead.

"I'm not sure what to say," said Tony. "There were tracks around the pipe and leading into the woods. They matched the trail in the Sherringham field in form, but these were notably larger."

"A bear?" asked Sheriff Halpern.

"A bear couldn't do what we just saw," inserted the coroner.

"What then?"

Tony swallowed, blew smoke out of the open window, then turned back to face the others.

"There were no paw or conventional footprints," he said. "And though I'm not an expert on such things, no wheel or tire marks either. The ground was quite soft because of the rain so I would expect to see impressions from a tracked vehicle like a bulldozer or..."

"So rather than say what you didn't find," the mayor cut in, "how about you say what you saw."

"Parallel sets of pointed feet," said Tony with a flash of annoyance. He wasn't paid enough for this. It wasn't his job. "One row on each side of a long body."

"How long?" the mayor pressed.

"In the Sherringham field, at least twenty feet," said Tony. "At the site of Mr. Davenham's demise, close to double that."

"So, there's two of them," said the mayor.

Tony ignored the question.

"The first two sets were about six feet apart. The second, by the pipe, more like eleven."

"This has to be a prank, right?" said the sheriff. "Like those crop circles and such. Somebody having fun, trying to confuse the scene, get us chasing our tails…"

"I'm afraid not," said the coroner. "I think we are dealing with a large and previously unknown form of animal."

Collington made a scoffing, dismissive noise, and when the others glared at him, said "Like what?"

"The chemical analysis I mentioned has only one clear known analog," said the coroner gravely. "It's roughly equivalent to the venom produced by certain large and exotic centipedes."

There was a loaded silence, then Collington recovered his previous scorn. "A forty-foot long centipede wandering the streets of Portersville and no one saw it before!?" he snapped. "This is absurd. mayor, I think it's time you found another coroner."

"My suggestion matches Mr. Altzinger's observations of the scenes, and he is our wildlife expert."

"He's a park ranger!" snapped Collington. "No offense," he added disingenuously to Tony.

"There was also the report made by the waitress who was hospitalized a few weeks ago…" the coroner continued. "And those made by the old Japanese woman who encountered something near the convenience store."

"Hysterical nonsense," said Collington.

"You're a businessman, Chris," the coroner fired back, his patience snapping. "When I want your medical opinion, I'll ask for it."

"Chris's concerns aren't without merit," said the mayor, moving easily into full politician mode. "However accurate your various analyses may be, it stretches credibility to suggest that these creatures have been wandering around unseen."

"Maybe they just appeared," said the sheriff.

There was something cautious in his manner, Tony noted, and he wouldn't meet their eyes directly.

"Meaning?" Collington demanded.

"There was a lot of seismic activity in the mountains recently," said the sheriff evasively.

"You mean at Southern Shale," Collington shot back, staring him down.

The mayor looked up quickly, then down again. Tony felt the weight of previous conversations hanging in the air, as if the other three knew things he didn't, things they didn't want to discuss.

"I'm just sayin'," said the sheriff, hands raised. "We have some new critters running around which we've never seen before; maybe that's because they were underground for hundreds or thousands of years and they just got out because half the mountain side collapsed!"

"That's absurd!" said Collington.

Tony shook his head. "It's actually not," he said. "But if there was some unknown arthropod under the mountains, living in the dark, I'd expect it to be much smaller. I don't see how it could find enough food in underground caves to sustain anything of its apparent size."

"Maybe it was eating a bunch of *other* huge unknown creatures living under the mountains," suggested Collington with bitter sarcasm.

"Unless..." Tony began.

He hesitated, but the mayor stared at him. "Go on," he said. "Tony, we brought you here because we want your opinion. I know tempers are running high and Chris takes criticism of Southern Shale somewhat personally, but if you have a theory, we want to hear it."

"What if it wasn't big to start with," said Tony simply. "The waitress's story suggested that what bit her was quite small. A few feet at most. Subsequent reports suggested something bigger."

"Because the so-called witnesses embroidered the story or flat out made it up," Collington argued.

"But the tracks are bigger now too," Tony insisted, feeling the color rise in his cheeks as he got flustered by Collington's attitude. "Much bigger. I don't think you have a lot of different bug-like predators all over the place. I think you have one. It lived in the caves and fissures under Red Scar, but it got out. It was small under the mountains because food was scarce, and it was built to survive on what was available. It can probably go for long periods without eating at all like some snakes do, but its body has evolved to make the most of a glut of nutrients when it finds them. If it runs into a rich food source, it sheds its exoskeleton and expands, perhaps very quickly, and perhaps reaching sizes far greater than it was for most of its life. The natural world is full of insects, arthropods, and snakes which all behave like this, albeit on a less extreme scale."

"You're saying that it's gone from eating bugs in caves to eating cows and people?" the sheriff demanded.

"Yes," said Tony, taking a neutral tone so he didn't sound hysterical, "and—as a result—it's gotten a whole lot bigger."

Collington laughed and rolled his eyes, but it was clear the others weren't with him. "You can't be serious!" he exclaimed.

"I think we have to be," said the mayor.

"And do what?!" Collington spat. "Tell the town that some underground monster is eating the population!"

"I think we have no choice..." Tony began, but the mayor held up a hand.

"Let's not be hasty," he said. "Once we make that announcement, we can't take it back, and we don't want a panic on our hands. We already have a lot of attention on us because of the West proposal. News crews from all over the state on every corner, interviewing people. Gawkers coming from God knows where to see what the town that wants to turn the clock back a century looks like..."

"Maybe that's our out," said the sheriff. "Keep things under wraps, say we have a lot of migrants coming through, suggest that it's unsettling the delicate balance of the town. An out-of-town killer would be easier for the community to get its head round. People don't like all these foreigners around..."

Tony couldn't believe his ears. "Were you not listening?" he said. "We just concluded this was an animal attack."

"And I don't think the town would be calmed by the idea that Brian Davenham was murdered by a drifter," said the mayor. "For now, we stick to the bear story."

"No one will believe it!" said Tony, close to Collington's contempt.

"They will if we all stick to the script," said the sheriff.

Tony stared at him open-mouthed. "But it isn't true!" he exclaimed.

"People don't want truth," said the mayor in a calm, friendly voice. "They think they do, but mostly they want reassurance. We can give them that while we explore other options."

"Such as?" demanded Collington.

"Let me take care of that," said the mayor. "Okay, Tony? Just follow my lead, and everything will be fine."

Tony looked at him, angry and confused, then nodded quickly, though in his heart he didn't believe it. The mayor gave him a one-armed hug and an encouraging smile, but Tony said nothing. It wouldn't be fine. He knew that as surely as he knew the sun would rise in the morning. They could misdirect and lie and insinuate, but it would absolutely not be fine.

He wanted to say so, but what would be the point? The coroner read the doubt in his face, and as the others filed out, he raised a finger.

"Mr. Alzinger," he said. "You have a moment?"

Tony hesitated, not wanting to stay any longer, but nodded warily.

"Have a seat."

Tony glanced to where the sheriff was closing the door behind him and felt sure this little chat had been agreed upon by the rest of the group.

In advance of their meeting or during it somehow, arranged with a series of sidelong glances and nods while he wasn't paying attention?

"You doing okay?" Thad Mortimer asked him, like they were friends. "I know this was a lot to take in."

Tony shrugged, glanced at the still open window, then turned back to the coroner.

"Sure," he said.

"Yeah?" said Thad, obviously skeptical. "Because we need to be able to rely on your discretion here. Need to know you are a man to be trusted."

Tony gave him a mirthless smile. He knew the game they were playing now. He was the low man on the totem pole, and the others would dangle the implication that he was one of them—someone to play golf with or join for dinner at the country club—so that he would play ball.

"I'm fine," he said.

Thad clearly wasn't satisfied. He leaned forward into the lantern light trying to look sympathetic. "I know what you must be feeling right now," he said in a friendly voice, "but..."

He stopped suddenly, his face frozen.

"What?" Tony asked.

"Did you see that?" gasped the coroner. He was looking past Tony to the open window. "Thought I saw a bird or..."

He stopped again, and this time he cried out wildly and pointed.

Tony spun round. There was a face at the window. They were two stories up, but there was no denying it. A human face, but distorted, eyes bulging with madness or rage, jaws open and slavering. It hovered there impossibly, as if it had been simply watching, listening, then it snaked its way inside on a long, sinuous neck...

Tony shrieked and bolted for the door. Thad leapt to his feet, but the

A.J. HARTLEY

thing lunged at him snapping, and he dropped to the floor in horror. Tony flattened himself against the wall as that serpentine neck slid through the air, the head spitting wordlessly as it hovered over the desk. Thad scrambled round the side then got up and dashed for the door. He seemed to have forgotten Tony was even there.

Tony was paralyzed. He had both palms flat to the wall, mouth open in a soundless scream. The head swung round to glare at him, and for the briefest of seconds Tony's terror was jolted aside by something else.

Couldn't be...

But then he was running after the coroner and the head was snaking after him, snapping at his heels with its teeth. He ran blindly, finding the stairs as much by chance as memory, and sprinting down them to the lobby and out into the dark parking lot. He found his truck without looking behind him, locked himself in and turned the engine on, headlights blaring.

As he turned the truck around, his high beams found the head rushing toward him, and now he could see not just the impossible neck, but the body it was attached to, a person, stooped over so her hands reached the ground as if bracing herself.

Her, he thought.

Because in that moment when the head had almost pinned him to the wall of the coroner's office, Tony Altzinger's terror had been momentarily replaced by the shock of recognition. This was no giant centipede. He knew that face. It was twisted with something almost demonic, and the neck made it impossible to believe that it belonged to an ordinary person, but he had looked into its eyes—*her eyes*—and he knew who it was.

27

It's amazing how little you can do without power. Our only generator was used to keep the store's fridge-freezer cases working because they were essential to the business, but we had nothing hooked up to the house. Dad looked into it periodically, but it was too expensive to get anything that would run more than a couple of circuits, so we hadn't done it. Some kids at school—Tyler included—went on about how great it was not be disrupted by the outages because they had multiple "gennies" but most of us weren't so lucky, and having power didn't get you wifi when the cables and cell towers were down.

As I've said, I'm not a tech geek like Joey. Compared to most people at school, my social media presence is minimal, and I don't remember the last time I updated my Instagram feed. But not having electricity is about a lot more that not being able to check out Tik Tok crazes. It means no light, except for candles and flashlights. No TV. No stereo. No air conditioning—a big deal even deep into the autumn in the Carolinas. No electric kettle for tea. No coffee maker. No hot water for showers or in the kitchen sink because our water heater is electric.

No opening the fridge or freezer to conserve what cold there is inside though, as Dad constantly reminds us, they don't make appliances like they used to, and both get close to room temperature within a few hours of losing power. The electric oven is useless so we can only cook on the gas range. We conserve batteries on phones and laptops because each time the power goes out it could be minutes, hours, or days before it comes back. Even during the day, the clouds lower the light so drastically that it's not bright enough to read indoors without a lamp. I can't tell you the number of times I flicked a light switch, before remembering it wouldn't work without power.

You forget how totally accustomed you are to having all the conveniences of the twenty-first century at your fingertips, how little you can do without them. We go to bed early because the darkness is complete and depressing and we've run out of things to do. There's only so many jigsaws you can make by candlelight, so many rounds of *Ticket To Ride* and *Clue* you can play, and that number goes down fast when you're thinking about giant centipedes trying to eat your friends. If Kieran West—or rather Enko-san—thought that people would embrace this by choice he was out of his *yōkai* mind. People romanticize the past, but trust me, most of us wouldn't last an hour back there.

And let's not forget that the power outages were not the only problem. They were caused by intense wind and rain which brought trees and utility poles down. That meant live cables lying in the street. It meant throwing away food you couldn't keep fresh when your fridge turned into a cupboard, food you couldn't afford to waste. It meant damage to houses, offices, and other buildings, some of it little more than an inconvenience —clumps of sticks and leaves in gutters, cracked windows and the like— but some of it extensive and lethal. There were mudslides on the west side of town and the main access roads had washed out in two places, which meant nothing coming in or out. The grocery stores were fast running out of supplies, and there was no milk, bread, or toilet paper to be found.

And that was still on the 'inconvenience' end of things. A creek burst its bank and swept away half a mobile home park, though the folks who lived there were able to get away—some of them in boats—before the devastation hit. A concrete parking lot which backed onto the creek flooded, destroying half a dozen vehicles before subsiding into the kind of sinkhole which the authorities thought had opened up under the Walmart.

There wasn't much rental property in Portersville but there was an apartment building on Albermarle Street which was almost split in half when it was hit by not one but two massive elm trees that fell on it within seconds of each other. The building was evacuated, but it was a miracle no one had been killed. If it had happened at night, rather than in the middle of the afternoon, they would have been. No question. Creeks and streams which had been reliably calm for decades, maybe centuries, burst their banks and washed cars away.

Dad was right. Enko-sama might be *less evil* than the *Omukade*, but I wasn't sure it made much difference, and if he kept up like this, people were going to die.

And he won't care.

Because he was a superior being and we were like ants, right? I thought about those washed-out roads and found myself wondering if that was part of the plan too: isolate the town, cut it off from the rest of the world so it could be turned into his own little Edo period Disneyland. It made me angry. The arrogance of the guy, taking our lives, turning them upside down, putting people in real danger, and then refashioning them to whatever put him in the center of things so that they would know nothing but what he told them was true. It was infuriating.

I wanted the book he had stolen. I wasn't sure how I was going to get it or what it would let us do, but I was going to get it and find out. If West wanted it out of the tengu's hands, it had to be of use.

"How big was it?" I asked.

Em gestured with her hands. Regular book size.

"How thick?"

Maybe two, two and a half inches. I could do that.

"What are you planning?" she asked.

"Steal the book," I said, like it was obvious.

"No chance."

"He doesn't read, right, your fox pal?" I said, ignoring her dismissive tone. "So we take the pages from the book and put something similar sized inside the covers and he won't know the difference."

"He's not my pal," she said.

"No," I said. "Sorry. I'm just..." I thought quickly and opted to be honest. "I'm responsible and didn't even know it. And I've been hanging out with him and didn't know that either."

"Hanging out...?"

"Nathan," I said darkly.

"Oh. Right. I should have warned you, but I'm bound by a magical contract."

"Tell me about that," said Dad.

I hadn't heard him come in, but when I turned, I saw him in the doorway with Mom, standing shoulder to shoulder. They did this when they wanted to present a united front. Em gave him an embarrassed look, then shrugged.

"What do you mean?" she asked.

"Well, he doesn't seem to care much about reading," said Dad, "so I guess it wasn't written down."

"Right," she agreed. "In return for bringing Caleb back, I agreed to help him establish his presence in our world."

"That's it?" Dad pressed.

"That's it."

"But exactly how you were going to do that...?"

"It was never specified," said Em miserably.

"And there was no time frame stated," said Mom. "No point at which your task would be considered complete?"

Em shook her head, but Mom nodded thoughtfully. "We might be able to work with that," she said.

"How?"

"Claim you've done it already," said Dad. "Say you acted in good faith and did what was asked, but that you're done."

"I don't think he'll see it that way," said Em.

"He's only one party," said Mom, who always handled the legal side of the store. "You are the other. As a party to the agreement, he can't also be the one who dictates its terms. We need an arbitrator. A judge or someone else with authority to whom we can appeal. Get a ruling on whether or not you have satisfied the terms of the contract."

"Like who?" asked Em.

Mom and Dad looked at each other and their helpful confidence buckled.

"The spirit of Raiko?" I suggested.

"How?" Em asked. "Last time I summoned the shrine spirit, it appeared because we had completed the task he had set for us. I had some bargaining power."

"We're fighting the *Omukade*," I said. "That's a continuation of the same problem we were entrusted with in the first place, right?"

Em considered this. "Only one way to find out," she decided. She got up and marched out, heading upstairs to her room. I went to follow her, but Dad stopped me in the hall, Mom hovering at his elbow.

"Caleb," he said, "I mean, Hideki."

"Caleb is fine," I said. "At home."

Dad bobbed his head. "You know your mom and me will provide whatever help we can," he pressed on, "whatever advice we can offer. Your grandmother too." He hesitated. "But you two are the only people who can really handle this. And I don't want you in any more danger than is absolutely necessary."

I just patted him on the arm and smiled as convincingly as I could manage, but there really wasn't anything I could say. "Listen," I said, "I'm sorry about what I said before. About why we didn't confide in you."

He waved my apology away. "No problem," he said. "I get it." He hesitated, and for a second it seemed that there was more he wanted to say, but either couldn't find the words or opted not to speak. "Going to work on the train," he said at last, snapping his trademark smile on in that way that made him look like he was about twelve.

I smiled back, watched him go, then took my place at the register in the store while I considered my options. Whether Enko might actually kill one of the heirs of Raiko seemed debatable. He was, Bachan said, bound to our family by blood. As the father of Raiko's wife, Mayumi, he was not just the source of the kitsune spirit in Emily, he was our great, great, grandfather. Or something. There were probably more 'greats' in there but I was fuzzy on the details. Some of our family—my grandmother included—lived a very long time, and it rather confused the family tree.

What I knew for sure was that there were two major strands in our family; one, descended from Raiko, was magical but human. The other, descended from Mayumi, was *yōkai*, specifically kitsune. Though she was implausibly old, Bachan was human, but her sister was the *yōkai onibaba*, and had given birth to a full-fledged *oni*, but whether that was about bloodline, personal choice, or something else entirely, I didn't know.

Bachan had married Raiko's son, so neither her nor her sister descended from either side of our family but brought to those descended from her—including Mom, Em and me, new genetic material or whatever you called the magical equivalent. When we first met Saito-san he had refused to work with us because our blood line was, he said, impure, since Mom had married someone who had no Japanese heritage at all. Bachan had opposed the marriage for the same reason and, though they were reconciled now, Mom had fought with her about it for years.

All of which led to one question; if Enko caught me stealing his stuff and subverting his plots, would he consider me family, descended—albeit in a watered-down sort of way—from his own daughter? Or would he think of me as indistinguishable from all the other Portersville ants whose lives he thought had no value?

I couldn't say. What little I knew about foxes in Japanese folklore suggested that whatever Dad and I might think, they were mischievous rather than truly wicked, and when they did truly bad things to people, those people usually had it coming. Often the humans had persecuted or killed foxes only to find themselves on the receiving end of the kitsune's vengeance.

But there were also less morally clear-cut stories of people possessed by fox spirits, and tales of foxes who disguised themselves as people— often as beautiful women—in order to marry humans, living with them for years, working on their farms, and raising families, before revealing their true natures and vanishing into the woods. Their motivations were harder to guess at. Did they act out of love, curiosity, or some kind of strange, distant humor, amusing themselves until they got bored? At the other end of the spectrum there were the *inari* foxes, white envoys of the god of life and fertility, benevolent beings so powerful that even their representation in stone was considered enough to drive evil away from shrines.

Where Enko-san fell on this range, I couldn't begin to guess, but I knew one thing; power changes people even, I was prepared to bet, when the 'people' were foxes. This was no minor *yōkai*, no local trickster playing jokes on farmers. This was a powerful magical creature with an agenda of its own. I would have to be very careful.

The other thing I knew was that while it was possible that Enko might have a conflicted attitude to me that might—*might*—make him merciful or at least less lethal than he could be, he would have no such feelings to any humans working with me who he did not think of as family. That meant that whatever I was going to do couldn't involve Joey or DeMarcus.

Or Dad, I reminded myself.

I sighed. It was almost a relief—after the nightmare at the Walmart— to have an unassailable reason not to involve my friends, but shutting my father out felt awkward to say the least. The last thing I wanted to do now, just as he was getting over feeling excluded in the past, was to push him out. But it was for his own good. I thought of those buildings split by trees toppled by Enko's winds, the cars carried off in the creeks swollen by Enko's rain, and I knew I could not risk Dad straying into the West-fox's fury.

"If I go into the West house," I asked Em as soon as she came back down, "will he know?"

"When he leaves, he sets charms that alert him when someone has entered," she said. "But it's not like a doorbell camera or something. He wouldn't see you. He'd just know that someone had been in."

"Immediately, or only when he came home?"

"Not sure," she said.

"And he can only be in one place at a time," I said.

"Yes. But he's fast. If he realizes someone is in his house, he'll be back quickly. He never goes far away. The illusion charms on the house, the things that make people see it as a mansion rather than a ruin, are always there, so long as he devotes a small stream of his power—or mine—to maintaining them. They are like...background systems. Once activated the real work is done in the minds of the observer. That's why he can't have cameras around.

"If he were to receive a real shock, those systems might fail, but other-wise, they are always in place. Everything routes through his mind. He might have to focus on it to be conscious of it: like, he might register it as a feeling if the charm was somehow broken, but he'd have to then, sort of, *find it* in his head to know what it meant. I don't know how long that would take, maybe only a few seconds, but I think the entrance warnings work in a similar way."

I considered this, putting it alongside the time I had followed Em in and overheard her conversation with Enko.

"But if he's actually there, present in the house himself, he wouldn't necessarily know if someone sneaked in," I said. "I mean, unless he saw them."

Em made a face. "Creeping around right under his nose?" she said. "That's really risky."

"I've done it before," I said. She gave me a narrow-eyed stare, and I looked down. "Followed you. Sorry." Her face got that chiseled-out-of-marble appearance for a second, then she relented, and nodded. "Did he know?"

"Never said anything to me if he did," she replied.

"So, when he's actually in the house, his guard is down," I mused.

"It's lower," she qualified. "It's less active. It's not down."

"Still might be my best option," I said.

"He has a fine sense of smell," said Em. "Which is to say he's not reliant on magic alone."

"But if he was busy," I said, afraid of what I was going to say next, "pre-occupied. Like, sorry and all, but if he was doing that magical energy draining thing he does to you....?"

She had known that was coming and, after a long stare, just smiled a little sadly and nodded. "Maybe," she said.

I'd take that.

"And what are you going to do?" I asked, mostly for something to say. I was too much in her debt already.

"I'm going to speak to the spirit of Raiko," she said. "Want to come?"

"When?"

"Tomorrow," she said. "After school."

That evening, I was putting the new magazines in the ranks when the bell rang over the door. It was Jason Blakely. He looked, as he often seemed to these days, preoccupied, even furtive, but I pretended not to notice.

"Oh hey," I said, heading over to the counter. "Help you find something?"

"I'm good," said Jason, but instead of walking to get what he wanted, he sort of hovered on the spot, shifting from foot to foot and glancing around.

"Okay," I said, trying to appear busy by taking the last receipt I'd processed and sticking it on the spike behind me. "Something on your mind?"

"You know about the bugs, right?" He spoke in a rush, the words falling out as if he needed to get rid of them. "The big ones, I mean."

"The bugs?" I said, turning slowly to face him. "Like the ones that were in your car?"

"You know what I mean," he said, and his eyes—which had been wary, secretive—suddenly flashed with frustration. "Don't say you don't know what I mean."

"Okay, calm down," I said. "Sure. I guess so."

He pointed at me, a series of odd, stabbing motions, smiling alarm-ingly. He looked... unstable. "See, I knew it," he said, tapping the side of his head. "Figured it out. You knew way back. Like, when we were at the ranger station. You knew. It's a Japanese thing, right? This bug? I looked it up. It's called…"

I held up my hands, gripped by panic as if the name of the thing would summon it.

"A *mukade*," he said.

He pronounced it like it rhymed with 'spade' but I didn't correct him.

"I mean, I've heard of things like it before," I said, trying to sound noncommittal.

"The big ones though, right?" he persisted. "Like things not of our world."

I gaped at him. "Okay," I managed at last. "I think you're getting carried away on this bug thing, Jason."

"No," he said, giving me that knowing smile and the head shake. "You know."

I didn't know what to say. Deny it? Tell him he should speak to the school counselor? I couldn't. But I also couldn't have him discussing what he thought he knew with other people. "It's in hand," I blurted on impulse. "I mean, you know, don't worry about it."

He blinked. "When you say that, do you mean…?"

"Just… Things will be okay," I said, calming.

"You can control it?" he said, his voice low and conspiratorial.

"What? No, I just…"

"Then it's not safe!" he sputtered, his anxiety shooting back up to fever pitch. He looked like someone on a narrow ledge and ready to fall.

"I mean yes," I gasped, desperate to shut him up before someone came in. "Maybe. I think I can control it. Probably. Don't worry about it, okay? And don't tell anyone."

He paused for breath, calming, then nodded several times with that same crazed energy. At last he tapped the side of his nose, gave me a relieved smile and the same little pointing gesture he had done before, and left without a word.

Not good, I thought. *Not good at all.*

———

I didn't tell anyone about my conversation with Jason. The kids at school were giving him a wide berth, including his former friends, but he didn't seem to care, spending his time furtively scribbling insects in his notebook, oblivious to what was going on around him. A couple of times I saw the teachers' gazes linger on him with concern, but if they were trying to reach him, they were doing so outside class time. If he started telling other people about giant bugs, they wouldn't believe him. It felt low and somehow disloyal, though we had never been close, but for now that would have to do.

That afternoon was Brian Davenham's funeral and anyone who wanted to attend was allowed to leave school early.

"It's important the community comes together in solidarity," I heard Tyler Miller say solemnly. Probably something his dad had said.

I doubted I would be especially welcome, but I felt I should show my face, so I left with the others and we traipsed over in awkward silence, uncertain what we were supposed to be feeling. Bobby was part of the cool set: jock, sidekick to Tyler—Portersville's mayor-in-waiting—and his family, by local standards, was rich, but he wasn't especially well-liked, and he didn't have Tyler's blunt object charisma. Few people outside the cool set had known his father personally, of course, so—at least for the kids—the funeral felt less like a shared mourning than a Dramatic Event.

And his death wasn't just tragic and unexpected, it was mysterious and shocking: like something from a movie. He had been murdered, or—depending on which rumor you believed—attacked by a wild animal. So while we filed into the bare church and stood in the hushed, reverential air among its candles and battery lamps—the power was out again—there was an odd ripple of excitement which even the boring church music couldn't quite dampen. It felt weird, and I was glad to slip out the moment it was over.

I saw him in a huddle of well-wishers immediately after the service ended, standing pale and stoic in his black suit, nodding and shaking hands with the adults who ran the town, the Blakelys, Chris and Maureen Collington, the mayor and his wife, the sheriff, and Kieran West, looking suave as if he had stepped out of a magazine. Bobby was basking in the attention beside his mother, holding her hand when he thought no one was watching, and he appeared...oddly content, almost happy.

The days were definitely getting shorter, and it cooled down much faster in the evenings now, even though the leaves hadn't fully changed. By the time the funeral was done, and Em and I could make it out into the woods to hunt for the Raiko shrine, it was almost dark and there was an unexpected chill in the air. The paths I knew by heart were also hard to find because of the runoff from the various streams in the mountains, and in places there were downed trees which we had to clamber over or cut around.

I could hop over considerable distances and land gracefully, but Em thought I was showing off, so I stopped and went at her pace.

"Why don't you change?" I asked. "Your fox form would get through all this underbrush no problem."

"I need to be able to talk to the Raiko spirit," she said. "I can't do that clearly as a fox."

"Clearly?" I asked, rounding a clump of heavy rhododendron.

"I can communicate with my mind," she replied. "But my fox thoughts are broader, like big splashes of color. I can't do words as a fox, and I need them to argue logically. Plus, I don't want to have to keep getting dressed and undressed in the woods near my idiot brother."

Couldn't argue with that.

"Wasn't the first *torii* gate here?" I asked. We had been hunting for an hour but there was no sign of the great horned arch, the stone foxes, or the ancestral shrine.

"Feels different, doesn't it?" Em replied, her face troubled.

"Like it's not here," I said. "Is that possible, that Raiko—or his spirit, or whatever—turned us loose to fight his battles and then just took off? Left us to it?"

Emily frowned. "I haven't been back since...that night," she said.

The night she saved my life, she didn't say. "How did you find it then?" I asked.

"I just came to the place I thought it was—here, pretty much—and it was here. I mean, it was in my head that I had to find it. That the spirits owed me an audience. But yeah, the *torii*, the torches...they just appeared."

I looked around at the familiar woods, willing the shrine to show itself. "Maybe we don't want it badly enough?" I wondered.

"Oh, trust me, I want it plenty," said Em.

For a moment, we stood there in silence, staring fixedly into the trees, but there was nothing unusual.

"Is it possible," I said, thinking aloud, "that Raiko considers our business closed, because we resealed the prison..."

"Or because I brought you back..." Em added anxiously.

"And we've been alone ever since?" I concluded. "Cut off from the ancestral spirits who set us on this path in the first place?"

"If so," Em added miserably, "I have no recourse. No means of appeal. I'm stuck as Enko-sama's slave forever."

"We'll find a way," I said. "I'll fight him if I have to."

Em smiled gratefully but shook her head. We both knew that, much as I wished otherwise, I couldn't fight him and live.

"I wish Saito were with us," she said, as we wound our way back down the mountain through the woods. "I don't know if the book will help us wake him, or if it'll teach us something crucial, but if Enko-sama thought it worth stealing, showing his hand in the process, then it must contain something valuable, and we need to get it."

"On it," I said.

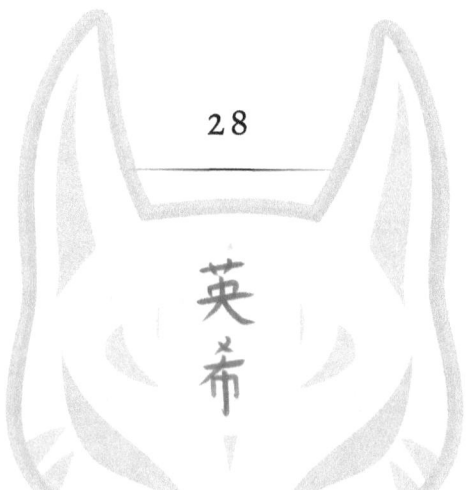

28

I had no way of hiding myself from Enko's magical sensitivity so I did the only thing I could think of. About a quarter mile southwest of the inconvenience store was an abandoned shot gun shack on brick piers with a front porch where a broken Adirondack chair sat, though no one had lived there for at least five years. No people, at least. A family of raccoons had taken up residence under the porch. I used to watch them poking their inquisitive little bandit faces out from between the rotten boards. The place stank to high heaven, because cute though they were, they sprayed their pee absolutely everywhere and it reeked like you wouldn't believe. I found a scummy, greenish puddle and, wrinkling my nose, stepped into it and stood there long enough for my sneakers to absorb some of the stench. See, I could be pretty light on my feet, but if I was to sneak around Enko's house I wanted to offer an explanation for any sounds he might hear. If his fox nose would make him think raccoon before he thought thief, it was worth putting up with the smell.

Em was already there. I checked the time on the watch I had taken to wearing since my phone had become mostly useless, though I carried it out of habit: 9:17. It was fully dark, but some traffic was on the road, and I wasn't supposed to get there until ten. She would be in what the West-fox had called her 'battery' mode by then: barely conscious and locked into something I thought of as a combination of a Vulcan mind meld from *Star*

Trek and that bit from *Dracula* where Lucy Westenra is being drained by the vampire in the churchyard. Not good, in other words.

But she would be holding his attention as he siphoned off her power, and that was as close to an opportunity as I was going to get. If it came to a fight, she wouldn't have the energy even to change shape. But if it came to a fight, we would lose anyway. In the light of my last encounter with the great fox spirit and the Walmart fiasco, I hadn't even bothered bringing my sword.

I picked my way through the grounds of the mansion with nothing but the tengu's bronze mirror to help me find the stolen books. No friends or family for backup. Just a backpack with a boxcutter and the *Percy Jackson* book I had brought with me to replace the magic book's pages.

Not very James Bond, I thought. But then the world's best equipped secret agent would probably attract fewer casino ladies if he went around stinking like a family of incontinent raccoons.

I mounted the steps, marveling at the power it must take to make the dank ruin of the Haversham house look like the grand mansion which seemed to loom over me. I stood under the colonnaded portico and considered the fan light glowing over the beautiful double doors, and I had to remind myself it was all fake. I even checked the tengu's mirror which revealed the cobwebby and woodworm-riddled gray wood and fractured brick, and I inhaled deliberately until I caught the air of damp and decay. Holding onto that scent, I ignored the doorbell as I had last time and pushed my way carefully through the real but ragged door which hung on rusted hinges. Holding the mirror up over my right shoulder so that I could use it to check what was ahead, I pressed through the stained, rat-infested hall with slow, careful steps.

I made, I think, no sound at all. If Enko had some kind of magical alarm system that alerted him to intruders, I was screwed, but if he was reliant on his ears, I thought I was doing pretty well. I listened as I walked but could hear nothing from any of the downstairs rooms. That was to be expected. Em had said he preferred to do his battery-charging routine upstairs in the master bedroom where I had interrupted them last time. Fortunately, his study—where we thought he had stashed the stolen book —was on this floor. I don't mind saying that the prospect of going upstairs was scarier. Not sure why. Maybe it was just that it was further from the exit, but going upstairs felt exponentially creepier.

I slipped gratefully into the library. Unlike the rest of the house, the reality of this room wasn't much different from the illusion: there was less dust, less damage, less mildew, and though the imaginary books were pristine hardcovers with hand-tooled leather bindings and gold trim, instead of the tattered wrecks that were really there, the bones of the thing, and its core purpose hadn't changed. When I had come to the party, I had glimpsed this room and immediately fallen in love with it. Though I now knew what the real state of the place was, I still kind of liked it. It felt more than quiet or private. It felt secluded: a bolt hole from the world.

But I couldn't find Saito's book. I had studied the characters for Murakami, but not a single book in the room was marked by Asian writing, real or fake. I worked my way slowly through every shelf, one hand running over the spines of the books as the other held the mirror so I could see what was really there, but it was all in English: swollen copies of Dickens sprouting stale-smelling fungus, faded volumes of Twain, Faulkner, Hawthorne and other American classics, seemingly mixed at random with mid-twentieth century paperbacks on motorcycle maintenance and guide books to France, Italy, and England. They were kind of fascinating in their obsolescence, and I had to suppress the impulse to flick through them.

Next shelf, I told myself each time I reached the end of one without finding the Murakami book on spells and charms. *Next cabinet.*

But it wasn't there. I searched for almost twenty minutes, being as painstakingly quiet as I could, moving cautiously around the bashed and dented chandelier which lay on the floor, and then I sat on the moldy floor and wondered what to do. Emily wouldn't be up there forever. She usually made an appearance at home around eleven, even if she then sneaked out again during the night, so as not to rouse suspicion. That had become her routine. That meant I had—I checked my watch in the dim light—twenty minutes. Thirty at the outside.

But where should I look? Was it possible that this wasn't what Em meant by Enko's study?

I got up and went back into the hall. I paused again to listen but heard nothing, so I set about a cursory sweep of the other downstairs rooms, holding the mirror like a bizarre flashlight. As I walked, I wondered if I could have missed it in the library, if I should go back and look again, search the places I had already gone through, like you do sometimes when you are so desperate to find something that your brain shuts down and you search based not on logic but on hope alone. It wasn't down here. The longer I searched, the more obvious that became.

I stopped to think, checking my watch. I had blown ten of my twenty minutes.

He could have buried it in the garden or something, but there was no point thinking like that. If he was that careful, I had no chance of simply stumbling on it. But my gut said he wasn't that careful. The legends of foxes in Japan were dotted with moments where the fox made a mistake, revealed a paw or a tail under their kimono, say, and while Enko was obviously brighter and more powerful than those folktale tricksters, he didn't think like a human. That's what Em had said. And he didn't hold humans in high regard.

No, I decided. *He wouldn't have hidden it like a person would. But if he valued it, he would keep it close to him.*

Which meant...

You're going to have to go upstairs.

I had been hiding from the truth of it, but in my heart, I think I had known within seconds of searching the library. There was nothing resembling a study down here.

I moved to the foot of the great slow spiral of the staircase, and braced myself, suddenly wishing I had brought my sword with me, if only for moral support. I strained to hear the sounds of reality beneath the illusion: rats pattering along the wooden floor or the groan and snap of a loose shutter blowing in the wind, but I couldn't find them, even though I knew they were there, so I focused my attention on the bronze mirror and began to climb the stairs. The house felt oppressively silent, and with each step it seemed to close around me, as if I was entering a pressurized space. I felt my senses dull, like I was wrapped in invisible cotton, though whether that was some additional magical protection set up by Enko, or just my own fear, I wasn't sure.

I tested for creaking boards with every step, but I reached the landing without—I think—making any real noise. The double doors of the master bedroom were over on the right. They were open, but I couldn't see in from where I was. I hunched low, trying to make myself as small as I could and moved softly toward them. Once I reached them, I put my back against the wall beside the open door, held the mirror against the jamb and then, adjusting it centimeter by slow centimeter, angled it until a portion of its rim showed me the dim interior of the room.

I had expected a deeper darkness, but that was because I had forgotten the little box by the bedside. It was there again, as I had seen it before, lighting the room with its pearly, submarine glow. By its light, I could see the heavy carved trim, the canopy bed, the winged armchair beside it. And Em, lying on her back like she was in a coma, while Kieran West—Enko—leaned over her face, one hand hovering over her, his eyes closed.

I ducked back behind the wall and thought frantically. I felt my heart racing. The strangeness of seeing them together, as he literally drained her of power like some magical leech made my skin crawl. But I wasn't here for him. I was here for the book, and I had only minutes left to find it.

I still hadn't seen what I would call a study, and I couldn't decide if a house that had a library would also have a study. It wasn't something we had ever considered at the inconvenience store. I imagined Dad speaking in a posh English accent utterly unlike his own saying, "Well, we could add a study below the east wing tower, beside the conservatory…"

Yeah, no.

I was out of my element. And I really didn't want to go into that bedroom unless I absolutely had to. But to get down the hallway and explore the other doors which opened off the landing to see if any of them contained a study meant crossing the open door of the bedroom in full view of the West-fox…

I took a breath and considered my option. Move quickly across the gap and risk making a noise, or move carefully, silently, and be visible for longer? If he kept his eyes shut and got only the stink of racoon off my shoes, I might be okay…

I went for the quick option not for any good tactical reason but because the alternative was terrifying. I settled into a sprinter's stance, my muscles tight as coiled springs, then launched myself across the doorway.

I cleared the gap with several yards to spare and landed neat as one of those Olympic gymnasts in the floor exercise, feet apart, one hand down to spread my weight on the rotten floor. But before I landed, I risked a momentary midair glance into the bedroom, and the two things I had seen brought me to a thorough and sickening halt.

First, I had glimpsed a nightstand by the armchair in which Mr. West sat. On it was a green leather volume with Japanese characters on the spine.

Second, the light from the box went out as Mr. West opened his eyes.

Elsewhere

Emily felt the fox spirit's attention shift. Something had tripped some primal alarm in Enko-sama's head, and he was suddenly more alert, less present in her mind. It came to her like the ripple in a dream, where the story resets, the characters turn into other people and the setting shifts, the narrative of the thing derailing and turning into something else. She was still mostly unconscious, incapable of movement until he released her from her paralytic thrall, but her mind stirred, and in some dark and secret recess a pair of truths bubbled up from her waking memory and said,

Caleb is here. He is in danger.

She immediately pushed the image of her brother down, but she felt a relaxing of the fox spirit's grip on her mind, and in that moment, she thought of Enko's hold on her as being like a chain. It was iron and heavy, wound tight around her like she was one of those magic-show escapologists who would be tied up and lowered into a vat of water but would dazzle the crowd by bursting free. But that was just a trick. There would be a link which unsnapped or something, some way the escapee had of releasing himself.

Her chain had no such convenient flaws.

But it's only in your mind, she reminded herself. *And my mind is mine.*

While her body lay unmoving, she kicked and roiled in her head; she strained at the chain, thrashing, wriggling for that crucial inch of space that might get her free.

"Be still," said Enko's voice in her head, but she fought all the more, rolling from side to side, raising her imaginary legs, rolling her mental shoulders, wrenching at the chain around her mind.

She could hear own voice now, murmurs of protest, moans of discontent, all charged with outrage and frustration but seeming to come from far away. She shouted as she rolled and fought the chain, bellowing her defiance, and even though the sounds were mere muted whispers, she felt the fury of her fox master spiking.

"Stop it!" he demanded. "Be silent. Comply! You swore to serve me. Now do it, or I will unravel all I gave you."

That stopped her. Emily felt the reality of the threat and she hesitated. Instantly, the imaginary chain around her seemed to stiffen, wrenching her until her mind was as quiet and immobile as her body. Enko-sama's grip on her thoughts tightened, and she slid deeper into unconsciousness. But before she did, before the dark waters of sleep closed over her completely, the image of her brother flickered across her mind's eye and a frail hope surfaced briefly.

It had been enough.

Just.

———

The box began to glow again. I dropped to the floor of the landing. It was clear what I needed to do, whether West had seen me or not. I had to enter the bedroom with him sitting there. I had to walk up to his chair, and I had to take the Murakami book which was on the nightstand beside him. I had to do it without alerting him, without breaking his vampire-grip on my sister's mind. It didn't seem possible, but I had no choice.

I lowered myself to the floor, moving on all fours into the bedroom. I couldn't use the mirror to guide my way, but I knew where the book was, and frankly it was easier to accept the lie of the beautiful room with its immaculate carpet than confront the reality of crawling through rat droppings and dead bugs. I hugged the ground, figuring that if his eyes were open, he wouldn't be able to see me from where he was without moving. I listened for that, but I heard only his words, loud and sharp in the quiet.

"Be still!"

I froze, my heart seeming to stop entirely, but then he spoke again, and I knew he wasn't talking to me.

"Stop it!" he snarled. "Be silent. Comply! You swore to serve me. Now do it, or I will unravel all I gave you."

He's talking to Emily.

She must have somehow felt him sensing my presence and had provided a kind of distraction. What he said sent a pulse of anger through me, chased by a sense of powerlessness. She was here because of me. She was suffering because of me. Gritting my teeth, I flattened myself to the illusory carpet and inched my way silently under the bed.

I could hear his breathing now, but how long they would stay locked together like this, their minds networked like computer servers, I couldn't guess. Maybe her resistance would add to the time he would take to drain her power, maybe it would shorten it. Either way, I had to move faster than this infinitesimal crawling. I raised the mirror to my face, keeping my arms tight to my body, and used it to scan the reality of the space under the bed.

The bed frame was high and the only part where the mattress clearly sagged through broken springs was near the foot. I saw no mouse bones that might snap under me as I moved. I took a steadying breath, then straightened and, carefully, rolled myself lengthways toward the armchair. As I reached the edge of the bed, I eased myself out into the open, emerging behind the high-backed chair. Slowly, I stood up.

By the strange greenish light from the box I could see Enko's pale, slim left wrist on the arm of the chair. I shifted slightly and saw the rest of his upper body leaning forward and over Emily on the bed, his right hand over her face, fingers splayed like he was trying to draw something out of her. I couldn't see his face, but his head was bent in concentration. I had to assume his eyes were closed.

I took a step sideways and reached for the book on the nightstand. I almost had it when I touched something else and realized with a shock of horror that I hadn't checked the mirror to see what else was really there. I felt something hard and cold, something that shifted as I made contact.

Using all the speed and instinct of my new abilities, I swept my hand down toward the floor, fingers spread, snatching at air...

They closed around a dusty brass candlestick a half second before it hit the ground.

For a moment, I kept very still. Then, when I was sure the error hadn't alerted Enko, I put the candlestick back, checking the mirror to ensure it went back in the same ring of dust on the nightstand, then I took the Murakami spell book which was bound shut with a faded silk ribbon. It had the curious heft of old books, like it was weighted with more than mere paper.

I wanted to run. To get out of there as fast as possible with my prize, but I knew I couldn't. Enko might not be interested in reading it, but he had kept the leather-bound volume close to hand. He would miss it if it wasn't there when he finished draining my sister. So I nestled on the floor behind his chair and, delicately opened my unzipped backpack and untied the silk. I took out the boxcutter and the *Percy Jackson* paperback and, as quickly and quietly as I could, I sliced the pages of Japanese text from the charms book.

Saito-san will hate this, I thought, as I desecrated the ancient volume. *If he ever gets to see it.*

When I was done, I inserted the novel I had brought in between the covers—a tiny bit thinner than the original, maybe, but close enough—and retied the silk ribbon around the book. Satisfied, and keen to be gone,

I stood up and leaned around the motionless Mr. West to replace the book where I had found it, but in the process I saw that it had been sitting on a sheaf of stained and yellowing papers covered in an illegible scrawl of handwritten Japanese. I remembered Em saying he had told her to bring the tengu's notes with the book. Were they important? What should I do? If I took them with me, he would notice as soon as he woke up, but I didn't have anything superficially similar with which I could replace them, like I had with the book. I stood there, my breath held, then—almost groaning aloud at every extra second it took—I put the book down, carefully gathered the stack of papers and laid them out on the floor behind the chair. Then I took out my mostly useless phone, which had almost no charge left, checked that the sound was off, and took a series of hasty pictures, capturing as much of the writing as I could. They had the underwater tinge from the strange light which came from the box, which—now I was close to it—I could see was shiny and black but adorned with a design of gnarled pine trees in gold. It felt old and distinctly Japanese, and reminded me of the shrine where all this craziness had begun.

The battery, I thought.

This was where he stored Em's energy to power his various illusions. The thought was like a stone in my gut: cold and hard.

I could feel him less than a yard away, like background noise, and knew that he could snap out of his reverie and turn on me at any moment. At last I bundled the papers together again, put them back where I had found them, set *Percy Jackson* with its antique Japanese cover on top of them and considered the fastest way out.

Crawling under the bed again suddenly seemed impossibly slow. I needed to get out of here, to be away from *him*. I moved around the edge of the room, giving the bed as wide a berth as I could, and made it out of the bedroom door without—I thought—making a sound. I didn't look back to see if Enko's eyes were open, if he was watching me this whole time with that knowing smirk on his face. I just kept walking, until I was out and moving down the stairs a little faster than I probably should, though the thought of leaving Emily in there with him tied my stomach in knots.

Twenty-five minutes later I was at Bachan's door. She opened it warily and when she peered round to see who was knocking so late, she looked scared.

"Hey Bachan," I said, thrusting the pages of the book with Saito's notes at her without preamble. "I got it. Now, tell me why he stole it."

29

英希

"omething you should know," said Emily. She still looked gaunt and hollow-eyed, but she had crossed the cafeteria with a purposeful-ness I hadn't seen for ages. We had spoken after my little adven-ture in the West mansion and she confirmed that, thus far at least, she didn't think Enko had detected the theft of his—or rather Saito's—book.

She had returned late that night for another of his loathsome "battery sessions," but when I had spoken to her over a hasty breakfast, she had had nothing to report. The relief I'd felt at that time drained as she walked over now and—for perhaps the first time ever—plopped herself between Joey and DeMarcus. Em valued her coolness, and that was never helped by reminding the world she was related to me and my friends.

"'sup?" said DeMarcus in a noncommittal way that didn't square with the joy which flashed in his eyes the moment he saw her. Ayisha, his cute sister had come over with Emily and now hovered by the table, but DeMarcus had eyes only for Em.

Emily gave him the briefest of baffled looks, then turned to me and leaned forward. She spoke in a hushed, urgent voice. "Sofie Collington has just been holding court in the girl's bathroom," she announced.

"The weekly gossip girl session," Ayisha dropped in. "Tea with Sofe. It's the hottest ticket in school."

"And?" I said, trying to look suave and hoping I didn't have yogurt round my mouth.

"Usually it's who's dating who, who's dad's a drunk, who's been busted for nonpayment of taxes," said Ayisha.

"Today it was what killed Brian Davenham," said Em.

DeMarcus sat up attentively, but I shrugged.

"Everyone has been talking about that since the day it happened," I said.

Em nodded but leaned in closer. "And how many of them have been blaming a giant centipede?"

"What?" I gasped. "How...? Who...?"

"Where did she hear that?" Joey asked.

"Sofie isn't saying," said Ayisha. "'*Good authority,*' she says. A top gossip never reveals her sources. Takes away the mystery."

Jason Blakely? I wondered. It was hard to imagine one of the cool kids —and Sofie was one of the coolest—taking him seriously given the state he was in, but I didn't know where else she could have heard it. And if it was him, what else might he have said? Jason thought I was somehow connected to the *Omukade.* I had practically told him as much in an attempt to calm his nerves. That now seemed like a very bad idea.

"Who has she told?" I asked.

"The inner court," said Em. "Us, a couple of girls on the swim team, a few other ladies-in-waiting."

"And they believe her?"

"They're not saying otherwise. But here's the thing. She says she's going to tell Bobby."

"What?" I exclaimed again.

"Says he has a right to know."

Em got up as quickly as she had sat down and moved away.

"Bye Hideki," said Ayisha, shooting me a big smile. DeMarcus saw that and frowned. Joey grinned at him with manic delight, then turned to me.

"I'm gonna go out on a limb," they said, "and say this is not good."

"How did she find out?" I wondered aloud.

"And what will Bobby do when she tells him?" DeMarcus asked.

"Check it out though," said Joey, managing to find wry amusement even in this. "Kids in the cafeteria gossiping about monsters that might be tunneling right under the school even as we speak. Like we got our very own Hellmouth right here in sleepy old Portersville, NC. It's all so *Buffy!*"

"It's buffy?" asked DeMarcus baffled.

"The vampire slayer," Joey replied with withering disdain. "Man, kids today have no culture."

"You're our age," I pointed out.

"Only chronologically," Joey replied, standing up and shooting us a parting grin.

DeMarcus and I looked at each other and shrugged. We were used to not understanding Joey's pop culture references.

"You think he'll connect it to me?" I asked. I hadn't meant to say it, but the question just fell out.

"Connect what to you?" asked DeMarcus.

"The giant centipede. Supernatural Monsters R Us, remember? Unnatural and invasive species. If he finds out what the *Omukade* is, it's gonna lead him to me. He's going to blame me for his father's death."

"I don't think he got on with his dad very well," said DeMarcus.

"Not while he was alive, perhaps," I said. "But I'm guessing things like that get complicated after someone's gone."

"How so?"

I shrugged. "I don't know. Like he never got a chance to fix the problems between them, so anyone responsible for his dad dying early..."

"You're not responsible!" DeMarcus exclaimed. "Are you serious, man? You're blaming yourself because he went hunting a supernatural monster and got more than he bargained for?"

"A Japanese supernatural monster," I hissed. "One imprisoned by my ancestor which has escaped because I wasn't fast enough at resealing the prison after it was damaged."

DeMarcus shook his head. "That's crazy," he said. "And as one of the few people who has actually seen this thing browsing the outdoor gear in Walmart and lived to see another day, anyone who says you haven't worked hard enough to beat it doesn't know what they are talking about."

I nodded and thanked him—because his support mattered to me more than I had realized—but it weighed on me anyway. I had to do something that might move this all forward to some kind of end. Whatever DeMarcus said, it was all my fault, and I had to find a way to fix it.

I went over to Bachan's house to get a report on the book I had taken from Enko. I knew the moment he realized it was gone, it would be me and Em with our necks on the line, and I doubted we could do anything to keep him at bay. I needed to know what was in those pages before he came after me.

I found her sitting in her tiny kitchen at an ancient table barely big enough for two people, reading by the amber light of an ancient hurricane lantern. Nothing in the house looked like it had been purchased this century. She was studying the Murakami pages in almost total silence, murmuring occasionally in Japanese, and riffling through the thin pages of an ancient Japanese dictionary. When I asked how she was getting on, she waved me into silence, so I sat there, doing nothing, waiting.

For hours.

Sometime around five o'clock I actually fell asleep in the chair, but when I woke at eight to find everything but her little table in almost total darkness, she didn't seem to have moved.

At some point in the last few hours, Em had come over, and she was curled up asleep on a kind of love seat in the corner. She was pale, apparently worn out, her sleep so deep and motionless that I felt the need to keep checking that she was in fact still breathing.

"Leave her be," said Bachan without looking up. "She has been through a lot."

I sat back down, rubbed my eyes, and yawned. I couldn't remember the last time I had fallen asleep in a chair.

"Any news?" I asked.

Bachan pursed her lips, as if I had been bugging her about it nonstop for hours, but eventually said, "This is interesting."

"Okay," I said, waiting for more. She didn't offer anything, so I just sat there, counting twenty, thirty seconds in silence, trying not to scream "Interesting how?" I asked at last. "Kind of on the clock here, Bachan."

She sat back and gazed at the ceiling. In the low angled light, the wrinkles on her face became deep cracks and her eyes were dark hollows with just the smallest glimmer of life.

"Much of it I cannot read," she said finally, "and much of what I can read I cannot fully understand." My heart sank, but she continued. "Saito-san understands far more than I, far more than I realized. But his notes are helpful. The Murakami book is a history of spells and charms. Much of it is…" she hunted for the phrase. "Hearsay. Things the writer has heard but cannot say for sure are true. It does not tell you exactly how to perform the magic it describes. It does not say 'add a cup of this on the third night of the full moon and recite these words.' Rituals, ingredients, ceremonies… You mostly have to infer them from context. It is more a description than a how-to."

I considered that, marveling at my grandmother's remarkably erratic, if halting English. I could study Japanese all my life and never be able to talk about *inferring rituals*...

"Is there anything on the *Omukade?*"

"A little," she replied, "but nothing we have not already heard. Legends about how a great hero used saliva on his arrow tip to bring the monster down, but the writers seem unsure why it worked. Apparently other warriors used the same technique against another *Omukade*, without success."

"Meaning?"

"It ate them and scattered their bones."

"Excellent," I said miserably. "But we kind of already knew the saliva thing didn't work. I spat on my sword at Walmart, but it made no difference." That sentence, I thought, even without directly referencing giant centipedes, might never have been spoken aloud before in the history of the universe.

"In the first instance," Bachan said, "the saliva was somehow significant to that specific *yōkai*. The *Omukade* was vulnerable to the warrior's spit because it meant something to the monster. Or to the warrior."

"So how do we find out what matters to this one?"

Bachan shook her head and frowned. "*Wakaranai*," she said. "I don't know. But Saito's notes on the Nara Bakemono Zukan," she continued, "are very helpful. Much of them concern the detailing of unusual *yōkai* in the manner of a bestiary. But there is some overlap between the two books, and I think it is that connection which interests Enko-san. Something about the description of kitsune and some of what the Murakami says about spells of illusion."

I sat up. "You think there's a way to undo Enko's glamor spell?" I asked.

"I believe so, but I am not sure that all the details are here. I will need to study some more." When I sighed with thinly veiled frustration, she leaned into the light and said "*Nana korobi ya oki*. Fall seven times, get up eight."

"You sound like Saito," I said.

"Thank you," she replied.

I didn't bother saying it hadn't been a compliment. "What about waking him up?" I asked. "Is there anything in the books about that?"

"Not that I can see," she said. "The only way to wake him is what I said before. Either we defeat Enko-san, since he is the one who put the sleep curse on him, or we convince Enko to untie the thread himself."

"So the books are interesting but useless," I snapped. "Great. We are no further forward."

"That is not what I said."

"We need Saito!" I exclaimed. "We are out of our depth, here, Bachan, or hadn't you noticed? I can't fight the *Omukade*. Not even close! Em's out of commission because she's been enslaved by Enko. My friends can't help, and the one person who might be able to offer something useful has been asleep for days. No offense and everything, but I need a bit more than the *books are interesting*, yeah? Because we are beyond screwed!" I yelled the last part. Actually, probably more than just the last part.

Bachan just sat there, watching me, saying nothing, until I relented. "Sorry," I said. "I just feel sort of useless. Not sort of. Totally useless."

She nodded at that. "This is to be expected," she said serenely. "Now, go home. I have some charms to fashion and the process requires concentration."

I got up to leave, then said, "Wait. What charms?"

"I think I can help you find Raiko's shrine."

I stared at her. "Really?" I exclaimed. "That would be great. Why didn't you say so before?"

"You were yelling," she said simply.

"If I'd known you had found a way to summon the shrine, I wouldn't have yelled."

"Perhaps," she said. "But I think you wanted to yell, so you would have found a reason. Now go. I have work to do."

"I can help if…"

"No. You are too full of anger and impatience. It is annoying."

And you couldn't argue with that.

So I went home, slept a bit, tried to focus on my math homework, gave up after half an hour, and watched the rain from my window. I squinted through the driving droplets and wondered if the dark rooftops of the West mansion over the road stayed dry during these freak storms.

A little after ten in the evening, Bachan arrived, the book I had liberated from that very house wrapped in plastic shopping bags.

"I am ready," she announced, shaking the water from her umbrella.

"Ready for what?" Dad asked.

"I think we're going to find the shrine," I said. "Talk to Raiko's spirit about Em's contract with Enko. Right, Bachan?"

She inclined her head in silent agreement.

"We're coming with you," said Dad. "Present a united front."

I gave Em an anxious glance, but she looked unexpectedly relieved.

"That's settled then," said Mom, off her silence.

"Bachan too?" I asked, looking at her doubtfully. The path through the woods was steep and even in daylight it was harder than usual after the storms had brought down trees and washed paths away.

She shook her head. "I will slow you down," she said a little ruefully, "and someone should stay with Saito-san. Besides, I need to say the words."

"Words?" asked Dad.

She raised the bound pages from the Murakami book. "I speak the first part by candlelight in a circle of bamboo ash," she said. "Then I take some of that ash, mix it with sake and draw certain characters on my face and hands before reciting the second part in darkness. I have already burned the bamboo."

Dad opened his mouth to respond but turned to me, his face a cartoon of bewilderment.

"Last time we looked," I explained, "we couldn't find the shrine. Not sure why, but Bachan is performing a kind of ritual to remove anything actively hiding it."

Bachan cocked her head onto one side and made a doubtful face. "Weaken," she said. "Not remove. Make it less strong. Maybe."

Not a ringing endorsement, and I saw Dad's confident smile waver, but I breezed ahead as if it was nothing.

"Okay, then," I said. "We ready?"

We left Bachan in the darkness of the backyard sitting on her haunches beside a box of gray powder containing fragments of charred bamboo, in a pool of candlelight, and surrounded by pages of hand-written sutras. She positioned a mirror on the ground and balanced a broad calligraphy brush across a lacquered wooden bowl of clear liquid. Consulting the mirror, she dipped her brush in the ashy paste and began to paint characters onto her face. It was pretty surreal. Her lips moved silently with concentration, and she barely looked up as we announced our departure.

It was weird, leading my parents into the woods and up the path. Em sensed it too and glanced at me, eyes wide with something between amazement and amusement. I wasn't used to instructing my parents, but I knew the woods best, so they were passengers, and I was driving. Or at least I would be until we got to the shrine. Then Em would take over. Maybe Mom's legal experience would be called upon. And Dad? Dad was there for moral support, I guess.

This is a bad idea, I thought.

I had put my friends at risk already and made a vow to keep them out of further danger, but here I was marching my parents into who knew what. But this was just about talking to the spirit of Raiko. How dangerous could that be?

If we could even find the shrine.

The rain had stopped, but overcast skies blocked out the moon and stars, so we relied on flashlights as we climbed uncertainly into the wooded mountains. All things considered, we reached the same spot Em and I had been to the previous day quickly, but after pressing on up the uneven track for ten minutes, there was still no sign of the *torii* gates or the unearthly lanterns.

"Maybe we should double back," Mom suggested.

"We need to give Bachan more time," Em said.

"You sure this is going to work?" Dad asked. "Magic spells and bamboo ash...?"

His voice trailed off. It wasn't skepticism exactly, not disbelief, but I gave him a level look and spoke with more confidence than I felt.

"I'm not sure, no. But Bachan knows what she's doing."

He thought for a second then nodded and smiled. It might have been a decision, but I felt that his commitment was to me rather than to the strange methods we were using. I couldn't really blame him for that. He wouldn't get it—not really—until he saw the things we had seen.

We pressed on through the forest. The hard, flat light of our flashlights didn't reach very far and made the tree trunks around us look like a wall beyond which the darkness seemed even deeper. Sometimes we could hear rushing water that we couldn't see, even though it was clearly close by. We picked our way along a ridge where a usually thin creek down to our left had turned into a torrent tearing the clay from the roots of several trees so that they had fallen, smashing half the forest canopy in the process. We picked our way through them, but Mom slid on the muddy ground and toppled dangerously close to the edge.

"Mom!" Emily gasped over the roar of the water.

"I'm okay," she said. "Just lost my balance."

"Got to get you some proper hiking boots," said Dad, helping her up.

"Those things have no grip. You want something with ankle support. When I was a kid and we used to go hiking in the Lake District..." He fell suddenly silent.

On the densely wooden rise ahead, a light had appeared.

"Someone is coming," said Em in a low voice.

But it didn't look like a flashlight. It was at once softer and larger, like the source of the light itself was almost man-sized. We stood motionless, and the light shifted as it moved toward us through the trees. It was a brilliant white at its core, but gold as it spread, and it made shafts of amber light flash out through the leaves and branches like lasers. It took what were clearly steps, its whole body not just illuminated, but producing the illumination, and my mind pieced together what logic said it couldn't be. Four slim legs, a sleek body, a graceful neck, and an elegantly elongated face, over which slender horns rose and branched like young trees.

"It's a deer!" Dad exclaimed.

It was. But a deer made of light, beautiful and strange. It stopped walking and became statue-still, standing on the raised ground ten yards ahead of us, its wide eyes seemingly fixed on us.

"Bachan's spell," Em whispered. "She has summoned it."

"Or revealed what was already there," said Mom. "One of the books was from Nara," she added, thinking it through. "Home to the sacred deer which carried Takemikazuchi, god of swords and thunder, to the capital."

Excuse me? When did Mom become an expert on Japanese mythic history?

Even in a moment already loaded with magic and mystery, the rest of us turned to gaze at her with amazement. Her face was lit by the golden glow of the deer so that she looked like she had stepped out of an ancient legend herself. Before I could say anything, the light shifted.

"It's going up the track," said Mom.

"Follow it!" said Em.

We did, though Dad was still stunned, and his eyes lingered on Mom as she walked on ahead. I gave him a reassuring smile, but his mind was playing catch up and he couldn't manage his usual grin.

We climbed to where the deer had been and could see it winding through the trees, turning the blackness of the forest to vivid green and gold. It moved delicately, picking its way slowly, as if making sure we could keep up. When it reached a point where the path had been enlarged by a rivulet of water which had cut a swatch a couple of feet wide and twice as many deep it waited, its ears flicking. As we approached cautiously, basking in its ethereal glow, it turned and bounded easily across the gap, then cantered up the hillside. As it climbed, greenish torches flared on either side of the path, and a horned *torii* arch shimmered into view.

We had reached the approach to the shrine.

Without a word we crossed the cutaway path and went up through the torchlit way, marveling in silence, feeling the energy of the place. As we passed through the *torii* gate, we saw dense columns of bamboo rising skyward on either side of the track. It bent in the breeze and their leaves whispered like distant water. On the ground, ancient moss-covered stone lanterns led the way, and as we reached the crest of the hill, a pair of great stone foxes loomed into view on chest-high pedestals. They stared out into the woods, mouths open, teeth bared.

"This is...*amazing*," Dad whispered to no one in particular. His eyes were alight with wonder and joy.

Now he gets it, I thought.

The air was scented with the rich aromas of incense. There was the belfry I had seen only once before, and beyond it, the shrine proper, its tiled roof sweeping up at the corners. The giant bronze bell, green with age, seemed to invite us, but this time it was Emily who pulled back the wooden beam on its heavy rope and released it.

The deep, resonant bong echoed through the woods. I could feel it in my belly, like it was more than sound alone. And then, just as it sounded like it was fading away, it came swelling back, and with it came a wind which bent the bamboo and kindled a light in the ancient shrine.

The glow within the recesses of the structure swelled, hardening into brilliance along the crack beneath the lid of the bound black box at its heart. It grew with the sound of the wind, and then the cords sprang apart, and the box flew open. I felt my parents shrink back, but Em and I stood firm, as the shadow of a great warrior blossomed in the air before us, a samurai made of swirling smoke. He hovered before us, his winged helmet and oversized panels of armor making him massive and imposing though we could make out no details and could not see his face.

"We are Hideki and Kazuko, heirs of Watanabe Raiko, demon queller!" I announced. "We demand audience."

Em gave me the smallest of glances. We hadn't discussed the tone we would take. In the moment, it seemed that we should meet strength with strength, confidence with confidence, belonging with belonging. That was what I had gone for anyway. When it came out, however, it sounded thin, whiny and annoying.

"*Kare wa dare desu ka?*" the spirit responded. Before the gruff words could reshape themselves into English in my head, I sensed what they would say.

"Who is he?" If the shadow warrior had eyes I couldn't see them, but I knew who they would be glaring at.

"Oh," I said. "Right. That's our dad."

There was a leaden pause, then the spirit drifted toward my father until it hovered over him like a great storm cloud and spoke again, the words now slower, lower and loaded with anger.

"Who. Is. He?"

"Yeah, I kind of answered that already," I began. "He's our father. He came along because..."

"YOU DARE TO BRING SOMEONE FROM OUTSIDE THE FAMILY TO THIS PLACE!?"

"See, he's actually part of the family too," I persisted, feeling Dad's eyes on me but trying not to look at him. "He married my mom, so he's, you know, one of us."

"I SPEAK OF *MY* FAMILY!" boomed the spirit. "IN WHICH HE HAS NO PLACE. YOU VIOLATE THE MEMORY OF YOUR ANCESTORS BY BRINGING AN OUTSIDER TO THIS SACRED SPACE!"

"Well, no," I tried, feeling the moment slipping away from me like the muddy banks of one of those storm-eroded creeks. "He came along to be supportive because he's, you know, on board, helping out, kind of, and he's, like, totally trustworthy and..."

"HE HAS SEEN FORBIDDEN THINGS! HE CANNOT BE ALOWED TO LIVE!"

And the spirit drew its ghostly sword, sweeping it out with that same easy precision which Saito had and raising it above its head in both hands.

"No!" I yelled, stepping toward it. "He meant no harm! He's here for us."

"THE REASON MATTERS NOT. THE OUTSIDER MUST PERISH!"

I glanced around wildly, desperately. I had no idea what to do. Mom snatched for Dad's hand and gripped it tight, but she looked terrified.

The Raiko spirit stretched its arms higher, shifting the angle of the sword so its blade was poised for a diagonal downward slash that would split Dad from shoulder to waist.

"*Chotto sumimasen, Raiko-sama*," said Emily in a small voice. She bowed, and spoke more Japanese, halting words and phrases. I had no idea what she was saying, but I was staggered by the *way* she said it, delivering her words with a kind of gentle sweetness, as if they were discussing the special virtues of the tea they were sharing. I was freaking out. My mother was at her wit's end, and my father was standing, head bowed, waiting with dreadful resignation for death, but she was making what sounded like small talk.

And the spirit's sword stayed up. Whatever she was saying seemed to have frozen him in time, caught him in indecision or surprise. I had no idea which, but she continued to murmur along and the sword which had been poised to slice my father in two, stayed still.

Em had reached the limit of her Japanese, however, and was now speaking English, though her tone was the same—polite, conversational and containing the hint of a smile—and her eyes remained on the ground.

"He is a part of us, and if your part of who we are is not in him, is not his devotion to us—the whole of us—all the more impressive? He came here not because he had to, but by choice, and if that was a mistake, it is ours—Hideki's and mine—not his. We apologize. Deeply. He does not know this place or the power it represents, but he has embraced it because his love for us is complete and unending. He stands before you, as we do, as sworn to serve our ancient obligations, to be a beacon of truth and light in the face of terrible darkness. Is that not worth something?"

There was a long, pregnant silence, and then the spirit lowered the sword slowly, slotting its smoky tip into its scabbard and resheathing it in a single, smooth action.

"You have spoken well," it said. "He will not die. But we swear him to secrecy and command him to leave immediately."

"Now, hold on a minute...!" I inserted, but Em turned on me, her eyes flashing.

"Caleb!" she exclaimed warningly.

"It's fine," said Dad quietly, sadly. "I'll go."

I turned to him, but he just shook his head and managed a wan smile at my mother, then let go of her hand. I wanted to yell my outrage, but Em was glaring at me, and I felt the situation hung in the kind of balance that a wrong word from me could upset with disastrous results.

So, for once, I held my tongue.

We stood very still, staring at the shadow warrior, and I listened to

Dad's receding footsteps in the fallen leaves until I couldn't hear him anymore.

There was a long, wary pause after that, and me, Mom, and Em just stood there as the smoke warrior loomed over us, like a sentinel. At last, it spoke, and again the words began as Japanese but slid into English in my head.

"Why have you come?" he demanded.

"There is a new threat to the mystical prison," said Emily.

Her manner was different now, businesslike rather than demure, one captain addressing another. "A *yōkai* escaped and is trying to reopen the vault."

"It will fail," said the shadow figure.

"You know about it?" I demanded, not quite able to keep the bitterness out of my voice. I wasn't happy about it threatening Dad.

"What we know is beyond your comprehension," said the spirit, its words uncoiling like the smoke of which it was made.

"Possibly," I said, needled, "but let's be specific, shall we. Do you know about this particular threat, the *Omukade?*"

The insubstantial form flickered, and at first, I thought I had offended it again, but then it returned, and its voice faded back in, as if it had been far away.

"The *Omukade?*" it said, and for the first time I heard uncertainty, confusion.

"So you *don't* know!" I snapped. "Great. You know, before you start pronouncing on what is and isn't possible, and before you threaten my family, you might want to actually listen to..."

"Caleb!" Emily fired at me.

I glared at her, then shrugged expansively: a knock-yourself-out gesture.

"An *Omukade* escaped from the prison," she said matter-of-factly, "before we could reseal it last time, we think. It was small then but has grown many times since. It is large and strong enough to break the stone beneath the mountain. And it has an ally. The *te no me* which served the *onibaba* is with it."

The *te no me* was what Bachan called the creepy eye-hand guy I had seen at the Walmart.

"*Omukade...*" said the spirit. He said it slowly, as if he had to find the word in the depths of its memory, and it brought all manner of unpleasant baggage up to the surface with it.

"Yes." Emily gave me a quick look and took a breath.

Here it comes, I thought.

"We cannot fight it," she said. "It is too powerful. And I cannot help because I am trapped by Enko-sama."

The statement hung in the strange light between us, and I held my breath. At last, a rumbling sound came from the smoke warrior which turned into a question. "Trapped?"

"I am bound to him because of our agreement," said Emily. "I have helped to establish his presence in our world, in our time, working in good faith on his behalf. But he drains my spirit to preserve his illusions and makes me work against those who could help us. He has bound the tengu in a magical slumber from which he will not wake, and taken away my freedom to act, so that the *Omukade* has had free rein to grow in power and danger, killing a man from our world as it prepares to break open the prison and release all you once bound under the mountain."

I felt Mom's anxiety coming off her like steam. If the spirit blew us off, I wasn't sure we had any recourse. I'd have to stand alone against the giant centipede thing, and I knew what the result of that would be.

I'd die. Plain and simple.

"Have you not completed the tasks assigned to you by Enko-san?" demanded the warrior spirit.

"She has!" Mom inserted, stepping forward and standing up straight. "And more. But he insists the agreement puts no limit on her service and that she must do his will in perpetuity, a term that was never part of the original oral contract."

The smoke figure rippled, taken off guard both by what was being said and who was saying it. It turned to her consideringly.

"You are Ritsuko," the spirit said. "The mother."

There was a stunned silence. Neither Em nor I even knew Mom had a Japanese name.

"I go by Jennie," she said.

The spirit made a guttural noise, part understanding, part dissatisfaction. He turned back to Emily. "Is what she says the truth?"

"Yes," said Em.

"And you cannot complete your other duties because of your service to him?"

"That's right."

"That is unfortunate," said the warrior spirit. "But Enko-san is an ancient and wise being, and he is your master. Your own pledge made him so. I cannot release you from your debt without you giving up what was returned to you."

"You are not taking my son!" Mom's voice was low, but each syllable was clipped and sharp as knives.

"I did not take him," said the spirit. "He was taken by the *onibaba*. We brought him back in exchange for your daughter's promise of service. If she cannot fulfill her part of the deal..."

"I can!" Em shouted. "I will."

"But you said..."

"Forget it, okay? We'll go."

"Very well," said the smoke figure. "You will have to find a way to serve Enko and fight the *Omukade*. Much depends on your victory."

"No!" Mom declared.

There was another loaded silence as the spirit returned his attention to her.

"What do you mean, no?" it said.

"The terms of the contract were vague, unspecific," she replied. "Enko's age and wisdom are not valid arguments for his position in law. They give him no authority of themselves. So his interpretation of the contract's terms are no more valid than ours. We say she has done what she promised and that the contract should now be terminated as complete."

"You have no right to make this claim," said the spirit, its voice deeper, loaded with something ominous like anger or warning.

"We have the same rights as any plaintiff," said Mom, defiant. "Law is not about power. It is about justice. We are making our case in good faith, and it ought to be heard regardless of the standing of our opponent."

"You dare to question our wisdom in this matter?" said the spirit, its voice moving from rumble to bellow as the surrounding wind increased, scattering leaves and swirling the bamboo. Dust devils popped up all around us and the torches flared and guttered. "You flaunt your world's ideas in our faces! Be gone, and do not summon us again!"

The storm built to a fever pitch, and then the glow of the shrine flashed out like lightning in a sudden slash of dazzling brilliance. We clamped our hands over our eyes, and then came a clap of thunder which bent us double.

Then there was silence and stillness.

We opened our eyes to find the shrine gone. The woods were as they had been before, dark and undisturbed. Somewhere an owl began to hoot.

"So much for that," said Em miserably.

"I'm so sorry," said Mom, taking her hand. Em shook her head.

"You were great, Mom," she said, managing a thin smile. "But they were never going to listen. Come on. Let's go home."

And we did, trudging through the dark forest down into town in virtual silence, weighed down by a sense of failure and, at least in my case, a growing terror of what would come next.

30

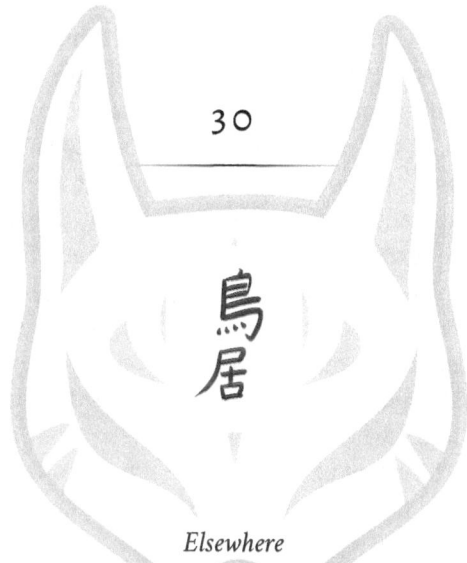

Elsewhere

Stephen Smith did not go straight home. He found the trail, but instead of following it down to where it emerged by the highway rest stop on the northeast edge of town, he began to climb. He hadn't been up here in years but was pretty sure there was a clearing a half mile or so higher, with a rocky outcrop that looked out over the Red Scar and across the Smokies into Tennessee. There might not be much to see in the dark, but there was a big, almost full moon, and now that the uncanny storm had blown away, the sky was cloudless.

It took him ten minutes before he was sure he was on the right path, and another fifteen to reach the open spot where pine straw made a carpet on the smooth granite outcrop of the mountain. He and Jennie used to come up here before the kids were born. Even before they were married. It had been special to them, and it felt strange that he hadn't been up for so long. Wrong, even.

He breathed in the scent of the fir trees, the aroma of resin, almost as heady as the incense in the shrine he had been ordered to leave. The moon was big and brilliant, its own mountains and craters visible as a mottling of the palest blue-gray. The same moon he and Jennie had looked up at from their picnic blanket on those rare occasions when they had come up here at night.

That felt a world away.

Now there was work. Stocking shelves and counting invoices, being polite to customers, and endless runs to the wholesaler. And there were the kids. They were great, mostly, he reminded himself, but a part of him was always on alert for the next thing they needed. Once it had been diaper changes and spoon-fed meals. Then it had been rides to sleepovers and sports tryouts. It was making sure they were fed and rested, that their homework got done, that they were planning their academic futures, and that they were basically happy. He didn't mind it. None of it. In fact, it gave him a sense of deep satisfaction because Stephen Smith needed to be needed. He had his hobbies and his little games, but at the bottom of his sense of self, he wanted to be useful to the family he loved.

But that was getting harder. As the kids grew up, they needed him less and less. A decade ago, Caleb wouldn't go to bed without a story, and there had been times when Stephen—exhausted from the workday and looking forward to curling up with Jennie in front of the idiot's lantern— had almost resented having to do it night after night, the little games and rituals that his son so loved.

Needed.

Not anymore.

"Night," Caleb would say, and before Stephen could grab a hug or a word, the boy would be gone, upstairs, his bedroom door closed. If Stephen went up after him and knocked, Caleb would be lying on his bed, phone or laptop open, ear buds in, giving him that expectant but baffled look as if to say, "Yes? Can I help you with something?" Like Stephen was a customer approaching the counter of Caleb's store...

He had tried to keep Caleb close with talk of sports and music, playing him bits and pieces from the bands he had grown up with, and for a while that had worked. But Caleb had his own tastes in music now, groups Stephen didn't know or understand, and Caleb had never really cared about American football or baseball, sports Stephen had not understood when he first came to the States but had worked hard to like so that he could fit in. Even the model railway had been an attempt to give them a shared hobby, as it had with his own father long ago, but Caleb wasn't interested in stuff like that either. He thought it was lame and a bit weird...

"You must be Mr. Smith."

Stephen spun around. Standing on the path he had just used was Kieran West. He was wearing some kind of quilted dressing gown over a collared shirt and slacks. He wore a silk scarf or cravat at his throat, like he had stepped out of an old movie or a Sherlock Holmes story. Stephen was wary, but he smiled anyway.

"I must," he said, "And you are Kieran West."

"Among other things," said the other. "But you know all about that."

"Some of it," said Stephen, his guard up now. "I know you have been employing my daughter."

"You disapprove?"

"She's exhausted and miserable because of you," said Stephen, still calm but direct. "So yeah, I disapprove."

"These things are negotiable," said Mr. West. "I'm sure we can come to some agreement. Man to man, as it were."

"As it were," echoed Stephen pointedly. "But you need to make your deal with her. And the spirit of Raiko."

He felt uneasy saying it, but he felt the need to suggest he knew more than he did, that it would give him an edge. This man was dangerous, and not just because he wasn't really a man at all.

West smiled knowingly at that and nodded.

"She has appealed to Raiko," he said, fixing Stephen with a penetrating stare. "I thought she would. Just now, I see. But you were... unwelcome."

Stephen almost took a step back in alarm. The *yōkai* was somehow seeing into his head. He raised his hands. "You leave me out of this," he said, flustered.

"As they have done," said West. "Yes, I see that. That must be galling after all you have done for them. Raising them, keeping a roof over their heads and food on the table, to be dismissed because you are English rather than Japanese? Must be maddening."

"It's fine," Stephen managed. "And it wasn't my family who pushed me out."

"Oh," said West with mild surprise, "I was under the impression that they kept secrets from you. That they concealed their true natures from you. Is that not so? I thought that this latest rejection was just another instance of them asserting that their true family didn't really include you. Or maybe I'm mistaken."

Stephen just stood there, teeth clenched. At last, he unfroze enough to say, "I'm very much a part of their family."

"Oh, no doubt," said West, smiling. "No doubt. Hard though, isn't it, to feel like you are on the outside of what matters most to you? Pushed to the side of your own life. Hard to be unnecessary to the people you care most about, to be unable to help. Tough thing for a father."

Stephen glared at him, feeling the prickle of tears in his eyes but fighting them back.

"Is there something you want to say?" he asked, "a point you are trying to make?"

West took a step toward him, then another, until the two men were only a foot apart. He turned his face sideways, taking in the moonlit view, and spoke in a low, amiable voice.

"I can give your children back to you," he said. "Raiko will not release your daughter from her deal with me, not without sacrificing your son, but I can lessen her duties, give her more time for homework, rest, family time."

"In return for what?"

West made a face and shook his head. "Nothing really," he said. "After all, there is not much someone like you can offer me, is there? It's not as if you can sway the town council or loan me ancestral magics. What could you offer me, discounts on Twizzlers and potato chips?"

He smiled unpleasantly, and for a moment, Stephen saw the fox within the man. "What do you want me with, West?" Stephen demanded. He was tired of being belittled.

"When I know," the other replied, "I'll tell you."

Stephen frowned, taken aback. "I don't understand," he said.

"You can have your daughter back. No more energy drain, no more nocturnal visits leaving her dead eyed with exhaustion. Everything goes back to normal. But when I need your help, you give it, no questions asked. Do we have an accord?"

Stephen considered him. He was smiling and his eyes had a twinkle of private amusement.

"Sure," said Stephen. It was a trap of sorts, he knew, but he agreed to it anyway without a glimmer of hesitation. "Just leave my daughter alone."

West held out his hand and, after a fractional pause, Stephen took it and shook it once.

"It will be as if I have never met her," said West, and he flashed that foxy grin again.

Stephen stared at him. "You could help them," he said. "Fight the Okumade."

"The *Omukade*," said West, grinning wider still.

"Right," said Stephen, infuriated with his error. "That."

"And why would I do that, even if I could?"

"Help make sure it doesn't reopen Raiko's prison!"

West cocked his head on one side thoughtfully, and again Stephen could see the animal side of the man.

"Human concerns," he said at last. "Why would I care if this becomes a playground for *yōkai*. They are more my kind than you are."

"But these humans are your family! If the monsters get out, they will kill everyone!"

"Those *monsters* are my family as well," said West, his smile curdling. "And who is to say they will kill everyone? In the past, humans and *yōkai* lived together. Not always harmoniously, and sometimes quite the opposite, but they shared the natural world. Now your kind want it to themselves. And it's not just *yōkai* they want to banish. It's the animals, the trees, the very stones on which you stand. Human arrogance and entitlement will tear this world apart. Perhaps turning the world over to the *yōkai* is not such a bad idea. If nothing else, forcing your people to share it with beings they cannot easily overpower may serve to check their hubris and entitlement. And the resultant struggle is sure to prove entertaining."

He grinned and winked suddenly, like it was all a game, an elaborate joke, and that—as much as everything else—reminded Stephen just how different he was from the thing that looked like a man but wasn't.

"You just want to be able to control people," said Stephen. "To dazzle them. That's why you don't want them to have phones and cameras and electricity. You don't want them to be able to see you for what you are."

West's eyes tightened as if he was annoyed, but his smile slid back into place. "True," he said. "But in my position, you would do the same. Besides, much of what I have said about the stupidity of your digital world is actually true, and you know it."

"Then you have to at least wake Saito," Stephen shot back, determined to salvage something from the conversation.

"Have to?" said West with an arch smile. "Why on earth would I do that? The tengu is old and tired. A nice long rest is just what he needs."

"Then I'll find a way to wake him," Stephen blurted.

The West-fox chuckled at that and shook his head, unflustered and amused so that Stephen felt a rush of impotent anger. The other man saw his frustration and, still smiling, said, "It must pain you that I do so effortlessly what you have never been able to manage."

"Oh," said Stephen, on his guard again, "and what's that?"

"Fit in," said West simply. "Your family are Japanese, or half Japanese,

243

so it makes a kind of sense that the locals don't think of them as the same as them, but you look like they do. It's only when you talk that they can hear you don't belong. Manchester, yes, or thereabouts? England, America. To me the difference is negligible, but to them... Humans, eh? They do love their little groups."

Stephen could think of nothing to say to that, so he just stood there, looking into West's foxy grin before the *yōkai* turned on his heel and walked back into the woods, whistling jauntily. Stephen watched him go, his simmering resentment gradually cooling.

It was probably a mistake, Stephen thought, making the deal with the shapeshifter, but he didn't care. Em would rest easy. She wouldn't know it was because of him, but that didn't matter. One day he would have to pay for what he had just received, but that didn't matter either. Stephen Smith was useful again, and that was worth everything.

31

E mily burst into the store singing the BABYMETAL line about being a *megitsune* and grinning from ear to ear.

"Who are you," I demanded, staring, "and what have you done with my sister?"

"Ha ha," she replied dryly without losing the grin.

"I thought you were with Enko," said Mom.

"Well, that's the thing," she said, snatching a soda from the fridge cases and popping it open. "He sent me home."

"Until when?" I asked.

"Until...never," she replied, toasting me with the soda can and beaming widely.

"What do you mean?" Mom exclaimed.

"He says I'm done," Em replied, sashaying toward her, taking her hands and dancing a little circle. "Finished! My debt paid."

"You're kidding!" I said.

"Nope," said Em, blowing me a kiss over her shoulder. "Apparently, it's convincing people that their eyes are misleading them the first time is what takes the most power. Once your brain has accepted a lie..."

"That the Haversham ruin is the swanky West mansion, say," I completed for her.

"Right," she agreed. "Illusions that have already been established take a lot less power to maintain."

"That's amazing!" I said. "Guess what we said to the spirit of Raiko paid off after all!"

"Guess so," said Em. "I can stay home. Watch Netflix. Play music. Go grab pizza with my friends. Do an hour in the pool. Anything I want!"

"Em, this is wonderful!" Mom gasped, her eyes shining.

"What's going on?" asked Dad coming in from the back, his arms loaded with boxes of chips.

"Mr. West released her from her obligations!" said Mom.

Dad blinked, and for a split second I thought he hadn't heard. "That's great," he said at last beaming.

"No, Stephen, you don't understand," said Mom. "I mean, he has released her forever."

"My debt is paid!" said Em, dancing over to him and throwing her arms around his waist.

"That's fantastic, Em," he said.

"All thanks to Mom's keen legal sense," said Em.

"And Raiko's knowledge that Portersville would be overrun with *yōkai* if it wasn't for us," I added.

"Also true," said Em, breaking from him and waltzing over to the senbe stand and selecting a bag.

"Dream team!" I announced, high fiving her as she passed.

"This is such wonderful news!" Mom agreed. "We were so worried, weren't we, Stephen?"

"That we were," said Dad.

There was a flicker of something in his face, a delay before the smile reached his eyes, presumably as he recalled his previous concern.

"We should celebrate!" said Mom. "Eat out."

We never ate out as a family. Dad's anxiety returned. "The store has been sort of slow, Jennie," he said softly, "since all the power outages and such."

"I don't care," said Mom. "I got my little girl back and we're going to paint the town."

Dad nodded and smiled, but he turned away while the rest of us discussed our dining options. I kind of hoped Em didn't notice. This was no time for penny pinching.

Of course, Portersville didn't have that much town to paint. Drake's Barbecue was top of our wish list, but Mom shot Dad a look as he paused thoughtfully by the rack of sauces and condiments.

"What are you doing?" she demanded.

246

He looked guilty but rallied and held up one of the bottles of Smiths' Smoking Sauce.

"Thought I'd take some along," he said. "Let Harry Drake try it. Who knows, maybe he'll consider it as an option."

"You put that back right now, Stephen Smith," said Mom sternly.

"I just thought it might be a mutually beneficial opportunity for..." Dad countered but Mom gave him a flinty stare and he fell silent.

"We are not taking our own sauce to a restaurant," she scolded as if this was the absolute height of bad manners, "and we are not doing business when we are celebrating getting our daughter back. You hear me?"

"Yes Ma'am." Dad put the bottle back and when he caught my eye gave a rueful shrug and a defeated smile, which turned to confusion as he spotted a large creamy envelope on the counter. He picked it up and considered the elegant cursive script on the front. "What's this?"

"Came with the mail," said Mom. "I was about to open it when Em came home."

Dad pushed a finger under the flap and slid it sideways, tearing the top edge neatly. He withdrew a letter on rich, thick paper.

"To the Smith family," he announced, reading aloud. "The pleasure of your company is requested at a Halloween party at the home of Kieran and Nathan West, 7 p.m., October 31st. Costumes are encouraged, so come as you aren't. Food and drink will be served. No need to bring anything but your remarkable selves."

His voice altered as he read, beginning with curiosity, even excitement, growing wary and subdued as he went, so that he finished looking somber, staring at the letter for a long critical moment after he had read it.

"Leaving it a bit late, aren't they?" said Mom, glancing at the calendar.

"Think I'll pass," I said. "Costume parties aren't really my thing, and I try not to socialize with people who enslave members of my family and lie about who they are."

"I'm with Caleb," said Em. "I'll hang with my friends, do a little ironic trick or treating."

"Everyone will be at the Wests," said Dad reflectively. "This is the event where they were going to talk about his retroizing proposal."

"So?" said Em.

He snapped out of whatever reverie he had been in and brandished his trademark smile. "Trick or treating when there's no one home to give you candy?" he said. "You may as well go to this."

247

"I agree with the kids," said Mom. "We've had enough social excitement for one season, and I don't like that man. Fox. Whatever. I say we give this one a miss."

"Maybe," said Dad noncommittally.

"You want to go?" Mom asked, stunned. "After all, he has..."

"I'm not sure," said Dad. "But you know what they say about keeping your friends close and your enemies closer. I don't like the idea of the town getting together with him but without us. Not days before they have their town hall referendum."

Mom cocked her head with realization. "You think this is an attempt to butter up the Portersville bigwigs before the council rules on his retroizing scheme," she said.

"I think it's not a coincidence."

"And he has more ways of making a good impression than canapes and a live band," said Em.

"Magic, you mean?" I said. "You think he's going to cast some kind of illusion spell, make them believe all his crazy anti-internet stuff? Could he do that?"

"I don't know," said Em, "maybe."

"I had another thought," said Mom. "I didn't want to say it because it's a bit...bleak."

"What?" Dad asked.

"Well, you know we were wondering why the centipede *yōkai* hasn't broken open the physical part of the prison yet?" she said

"Yes," Dad replied. "Go on."

"I was just wondering if it hadn't done so yet because it couldn't," said Mom. "Not yet. It's been getting bigger, right? With each attack it gets larger, stronger..."

"And you think it's waiting until it's powerful enough to break the rock around the prison," Dad said, nodding thoughtfully.

"But we're on the alert for it now," said Mom. "So if it has to attack more people to make the next step, you know—go from something the size of a bus to something more like the thing from the legend that curled round the mountain..."

"And it would be easier if all those people were together," said Em, completing the thought for her. "One big meal to give it the power it needs..."

Dad held up the invitation again, and this time as he read the final sentence, it sounded very different. "Food and drink will be served. No need to bring anything but your remarkable selves."

There was a tense silence.

"So we are the canapes," I said. "Excellent."

"Hold it," said Em, shaking her head. "He can't have it both ways. Either he wants us on board for his retroizing or he's feeding us to the *Omukade*."

"Maybe he's not thinking about the *Omukade* at all," said Dad. "Maybe he has one agenda, and it has another. But if he gathers all those people together, my guess is that a large hunting monster which, presumably, has a pretty sophisticated way of detecting prey is going to figure it out."

"So whether it was invited or not," I said, "it's gonna crash."

"We should warn them," said Dad.

Mom shook her head sadly.

"No one will listen, Stephen," she said.

"We should tell them anyway," he replied. "West. The mayor. The sheriff. Everyone."

"And explain how we know and what is coming?" said Em. Dad frowned but said nothing. "They'll find a way to blame us."

"That doesn't matter," Dad replied. "If it saves lives..."

"West wants the event to happen, and he has the town's most powerful people in his pocket," said Mom. "They love him."

"The Collingtons don't," said Dad. "He messed up their Southern Shale deal, remember?"

"Doesn't matter," said Mom, making a little gesture with her wrist like she was flicking off a fly. "The Millers, the Blakelys, Sheriff Halpern...they all love him and the Collingtons will go along with them."

"So we do nothing?" said Dad.

"No," said Em with a sigh. "Dad's right. We say nothing, but we go to the party: keep an eye on things."

"And do what?" I asked. "If you remember, the last time I saw this thing it nearly killed me. I have no way of beating it now and even less chance if it gets bigger."

"Well, little brother," said Em, with a glance to the calendar which hung over the counter by the receipts spike, "you have five days to figure something out."

Five days. Actually, four and a half. Then I had to fight an insect—sorry, *arthropod*—bigger than a house, which planned to eat the town, though I had no weapon that would so much as scratch its armored carapace. The mighty fox spirit who lived across the street refused to help me, and might truly be working with the giant bug, and the one person who *could* offer real help was entering week two of the world's longest nap. I was, as I'm sure my venerable Japanese ancestors would have said, utterly screwed.

Joey and DeMarcus offered to help. So did Mom and Dad. But what could they do? Useless though I was, this was on me. The best thing they could do to aid my mental health was leave. I hear Hawaii is nice. Most places a long way from the feeding grounds of a giant centipede as long as a freight train must be pretty great. I told them this, but they just looked defiant and slightly hurt.

"We may not be superheroes," said DeMarcus, "but we have to be able to do something."

"And being a superhero isn't going to get it done," Joey added reasonably. "Said so yourself. We need a plan B."

"Some sort of cruise missile?" I suggested bitterly.

"I'm all out," said Joey.

"The Air Force will have some," said DeMarcus. "Maybe it's time to go to the authorities. Tell them what we know."

"You sound like my dad," I said.

"A smart man," said DeMarcus. "I always said so. Model trains notwithstanding."

"He tried to get the charm off Saito's wrist," I said. "It looks like a red silk thread tied in an elaborate knot."

"I know," said DeMarcus. "I saw it."

"But no matter how you try to unpick it, it won't come loose," I said. "We've all tried. Mom used tweezers. Dad tried cutting it with pliers, wire cutters, a hacksaw, even power tools. Nothing made so much as a dent."

"So?" DeMarcus pressed. "What does that have to do with how to kill the *Omukade*?"

"The charm keeping the tengu asleep is magic," I said with a hopeless look. "Physical rules simply don't apply. No matter what conventional means we use, we can't cut it or unfasten it because the string isn't really what's holding it together. That's just... I don't know, a kind of form the magic has taken. I guarantee that the same is true of the *Omukade*. Come in blasting with tanks, or helicopter gunships or cruise missiles and it will just ignore them all, and worse. It's a *yōkai*. Its fundamental nature is, by human standards, not natural. It comes from another realm, a different plane of existence, and it is essentially magical. We can't use human tools and human logic. We have to find the fairy story solution. Conventional weapons will just get more people killed, people like Brian Davenham who thought he could bring it down with a rifle like he was on safari. Go to the authorities with what we know, and they will apply human solutions, human weapons, which will achieve nothing but increase the human body count."

DeMarcus sat back, lost for words. "You thought some more about this anointing arrows with saliva thing?" asked Joey. "That's the fairy story solution, right?"

I shrugged expansively and blew out a long sigh.

"Already tried and failed," I said. "I could try again, but if it didn't work, I'd have about half a second to come up with an alternative before it had me for dinner."

"I think you'd be more of an hors d'oeuvre," said DeMarcus, looking me up and down critically. "It would need about fifty of you for a dinner."

"Thanks for that," I said.

"But if the principle is sound," said Joey, "maybe we just need to find something else to anoint your arrows with."

"I can't shoot a bow," I said. "Tried once at the summer fair. Nearly killed the woman who ran the stall."

"That was before you became a superhero," said DeMarcus.

"True," I said. "Now I'd totally kill her."

"Can we focus for a second?" said Joey. "The key question is: why was that one *Omukade* vulnerable to human spit? It's not like holy water on a vampire: something that is essentially opposed to what they are. This has a logic of its own."

I rolled my eyes. "Bachan said it worked because saliva was somehow significant to that specific *yōkai*," I said. "But this is a different *yōkai* so it won't work."

"But why did it work? What made it significant?"

"No idea. Maybe it was like how the *onibaba* had to use my blood to open the mystical vault. Heritage. Our blood linked us to Raiko who imprisoned her son."

"And this is basically an extension of the same problem," said DeMarcus, "so maybe it will work again. Saliva. Blood. Your family essence."

"It has a kind of anime logic," Joey agreed.

I wasn't convinced.

"Let's call that Plan C," I said.

"And the Cruise missile?" said DeMarcus.

"What comes after Z?" I asked.

I studied the recovered books with Bachan, or rather I hovered over her and paced around her while she read, because I couldn't make anything of them.

Again.

"You are being annoying," said Bachan. "I cannot focus with you watching me."

"I just want to be here if you find anything useful," I said.

"You are not helping. You are making it harder. Go away."

That was Bachan for you.

So I visited Saito's dojo and perused his supplies, still hunting for the missing shuriken, and experimenting with a few weapons I hadn't tried before including a *yari*: a kind of spear-like pole arm. Saito had a few of different lengths and types, one of which was almost twenty feet long. I chose something half that length, the business end of which was a razor-sharp blade like a sword, flat and tapering, with two straight cutting edges, each as long as my arm from elbow to fingertips. I figured the pole would give me some distance from the *Omukade*'s legs and fangs, but it felt clumsy in my inexperienced hands. I scanned a few of the tengu's *sōjutsu* books and found some diagrams, though the text was all in Japanese so they weren't that useful. Eventually, I just stood in the center of the room on the tatami floor, closed my eyes and tried to do what the tengu had told me.

Feel the weapon in your hands. It will show you how it wishes to be used if you let it.

I felt its weight, its balance. I tried a series of steps and lunges. I swung it in a broad arc, first horizontally, then over my head. I stabbed the bladed end at my imaginary opponent, then swept his legs out from under him with the butt, adjusting my hands and stepping evenly into the movement so that I kept my balance. It felt good. I did it again, and again. Then I parried imaginary blows and turned them into attacks. I used the staff of the *yari* as a pole vault so I could leap the length of the room and end with a deadly upwards lunge...

I felt better, though I knew that a few training sessions—especially training without a teacher—wouldn't make me anything like an expert, and I still had no way of making the blade penetrate the centipede's shell. The spear was just a thing, a human tool. It wasn't the fairy story solution. But I took the *yari* with me, using the path through the woods which ran behind the main road all the way to the edge of the West mansion and over the road to the inconvenience store. No one likes seeing teenage boys carrying spears through built-up areas.

32

The next day was Saturday, and I left the house at first light, the *yari* wrapped and stuffed headfirst into a waterproof case for fishing rods. It wasn't big enough to take the whole thing but would do in a pinch. My mission was simple: prevent the *Omukade* from attacking the party by finding where it was hiding beforehand and killing it. I mean, the thing was about fifty feet long so how hard could that be?

Pretty hard. I started at the collapsed remains of Portersville's once-treasured Walmart, sneaking through barriers and vaulting a ten-foot fence as soon as I was sure no one was around. The structure had already been partly bulldozed since nothing standing was remotely safe, and the center of what had been the store's floor looked like a bomb crater. I was immediately struck by the plausibility of the 'sinkhole' theory, though it rather killed my plan for the morning. I had intended to climb down to where the giant centipede had tunneled into the earth and follow the passage to wherever it was now; simple, but effective, right? Except that the tunnel had collapsed in on itself after the *yōkai* had gone through, and whatever hollow portions still remained had subsequently filled with opaque, brown storm water.

No way was I getting through there.

So I went back up through the woods to the old fracking site, looking for signs of the kinds of damage done by a bug the size of an eighteen-wheeler, but there was nothing. Close to the top of Red Scar I ventured into the caves again but found them as before: empty, their poured concrete plugs unbreached and no sign that the *Omukade* had even been there. I'll admit that, in spite of my failure, I was relieved.

That afternoon I resolved to sit down with Mom, Dad, Em and Bachan, and confess my fears. But before I could, Dad raised his hand like a student asking permission to speak.

"What's the matter?" Mom asked.

Dad looked shifty, embarrassed. "I know this is going to sound a bit..." he made a face: odd, crazy. "Only, has anyone else felt like they are being watched lately?"

"Now?" said Em.

"No," Dad replied quickly. "At night. I keep feeling like there's someone peering in on us. I felt it last night, but it's happened several times, and for a split second, I could have sworn there was a face against the window."

"Nosy kid?" I volunteered.

"Peeping Tom?" Em added.

Dad shook his head. "I was upstairs," he said. "I saw a face up against the glass of the bathroom window. As soon as I turned to face it, it pulled back. But it moved sort of smoothly, not like someone climbing down or jumping. More like someone making themselves small. Specifically," he took a breath as if this was the part he hadn't wanted to say, "like they were retracting a very long neck."

Mom and Emily stared at him.

"Yes!" I exclaimed. "I was coming home a couple of weeks ago and I saw what I thought was an owl sitting on a fence. But it wasn't. It was a head. Like, a person, but up way too high, and then it sort of...*withdrew*. I thought the same thing. It wasn't like someone had climbed down. It was like they'd wound their neck in. I saw them walking off, but they were too far away. I put it out of my mind because it made no sense and I figured it had been a trick of the light or something, but yeah, I'm pretty sure I saw the same thing."

"And it wasn't like a big bug?" Mom asked. "Like the centipede thing?"

I shook my head. "It was a human face," I said. "I'm sure of it."

"That is *so* creepy!" Em exclaimed.

"Right?" said Dad. "Gave me goosepimples."

"Me too!" I said. "But I didn't feel in danger, exactly. Just..."

"Spied on," said Dad.

"Exactly."

"You ever heard of anything like that?" Em asked Bachan.

She nodded seriously. "Is your internet working?" she asked.

Em checked her phone and shook her head. "No signal," she said.

"Hold on." Bachan got up with an effort and shuffled out of the kitchen and upstairs.

"Spying on the house?" said Mom with a shudder. "I don't like the sound of that at all. Could it be Enko-san?"

"Spying isn't his style," said Em. "And I haven't seen any kind of servant or helper working for him—human or *yōkai*."

"Might be either," said Bachan, returning with one of Saito's books. "Look."

She set the open volume on the table, and we all recoiled.

The image beside the characters showed a woodblock print of a woman in a kimono sitting on the ground while her head hovered several yards away on the end of a long, snakelike neck.

"Gross!" said Emily.

"*Rokurobi*," said Bachan. "Could be a *yōkai* but could also be a cursed human. The transformation occurs when they are asleep. The creature may not know what it is."

"Oh, this is just great," I remarked. "We should assume it is working with the *Omukade*, bringing the monster information. If it has been watching us, it may know everything about us already. It will know who we are."

"I assumed it already did," said Em.

"Then it knows our plans," I sputtered, my gaze fixed on the unnerving image in the book.

"We have a plan?" asked Dad brightly.

I shook my head. "No," I said. "I fight it, I guess. But I don't know how to," I said, concluding by admitting the feeling I had been carrying around for days now. "It's hopeless."

"That spear thing sounds like a good idea," said Dad encouragingly.

"But it won't penetrate it!" I exclaimed, annoyed that he still didn't get it. "It's like attacking a tank with a stick! I'm fast, and strong, agile, but in the end I'm only as good as the weapon I wield, and I just don't have what it takes."

"Last time you did all right," said Dad.

"Because last time the *oni* was dumb enough to carry around the one weapon that could kill him," I said. "One of Raiko's swords. But that's gone, and there's nothing else."

"You looked at Mr. Saito's place?" asked Mom.

"Yes, Mom," I said, exasperated, "of course I did!"

"Now, Caleb," said Dad soothingly, "don't take on with your mum, she's just trying to help."

"Oh my God!" I yelled, "don't you get it? We are all going to die! I can't save you. Unless you have Raiko's lost shuriken lying around in the knife drawer..."

"His lost what?" asked Dad, ignoring my fury.

"Shuriken," said Em. "Like a throwing star."

"It's not," I corrected her. "It's more like a weighted dagger. Just a pointed piece of metal."

"I don't think we have anything like that in the kitchen," said Mom with maddening calm. "What about in the garage, Stephen?"

Dad shook his head thoughtfully. "I'll have a look but I don't think so," he said. "I could make you one. File down a piece of rebar, maybe or..."

"NO!" I shouted. "You can't *make* me one! What is wrong with you people? The point is that it belonged to Raiko. That's what makes it special. It is..."

"Magic," said Dad. "We get it."

I hated the sound of the word when he said it and felt the need to correct him. "Power," I said. "It has power. Or it might. I don't know. And it doesn't matter, because we don't have it." I took a breath. "You know, maybe you guys should just go. Take a vacation. Go to Charlotte or Atlanta. Charleston! Get out of the mountains."

"And leave you?" said Dad. "No chance."

"You could come with us." Mom sounded shy, like she had been thinking along these lines before but hadn't wanted to say it. "No one said you had to do this."

"And just leave everyone to face the monster alone?" said Em.

There was a momentary silence, then Mom sagged like one of the Halloween inflatables Mrs. Rensky had in front of her house: a black and white cartoon spook that kept coming unplugged.

"No," said Mom quietly. "I guess not."

"I am making a number of mixtures which have been used in traditional charms," said Bachan suddenly. "To dip your blades in. Sake which has been blessed. Ground incense mixed with cherry blossom and shochu. And we can tie *omamori* charms to your weapons, inscribed with the kanji of the lotus sutra..."

Her voice tailed off.

"Okay," said Dad. "Sounds good. Right, Caleb?"

I sighed, then nodded. "Sure. Thanks, Bachan."

But there was no joy in her eyes, no hope, and her return nod was as close to a shrug of resignation as made no difference. She knew as well as I did. We weren't just grasping at straws; we were waving them hopefully as our only weapon against a carnivorous centipede as big as a barn.

On October 30th it seemed that all anyone at school could talk about was the party at the West mansion. At the end of algebra class several of the girls were comparing costume notes.

"I'm going as an influencer," said Nadine Peterson. "I'll have a picture frame around my head with built-in lights."

"That is so cool!" said Sharon Tensing. "I'm going to reprise my Taylor Swift Eras tour assortment. Why mess with perfection?"

"Two hot parties at the swankiest house in town in under a month!" exclaimed Nadine.

"Don't let Sofie Collington hear you say the West house is swankier than hers," Sharon replied with a grin.

"Oh please," said Nadine. "The Collington house is not in the same ballpark."

"I'd take either," said Sharon.

"Oh, me too," said Nadine, clarifying. "I share a bedroom the size of a shoebox with my sister over a kitchen that hasn't been renovated since the nineties. No, thank you. I'll take the marble halls and the butler getting his cardio in as he brings cocktails from the bar in the east wing."

"Manicured lawns with statues," said Sharon dreamily.

"That grand piano!"

I was tempted to tell them that the house was actually a collapsing dank ruin that stank of marsh runoff and racoon pee, but I held my tongue.

"You guys are definitely going?" I asked.

They gave me goggle eyed stares. "Why wouldn't we?" asked Nadine. "Everyone is going."

Which seemed to be all the explanation I was expected to need, though Sharon did a double take. "Are you going?" she asked.

"I think so," I said.

"Oh." Sharon seemed a little let down, like the fact of my attendance made it all that much less glamorous, but Sharon wasn't a mean person, and she rallied. "Great. See you there."

Great indeed, I thought. *Let's hope we don't get eaten...*

"What are you going as?" asked Joey, materializing at my elbow and beaming like a slightly ironic Cheshire cat. "Come as you aren't, right?"

I sighed. "Kind of focusing on how not to die," I said.

"And how's that going?"

"Not well. What are you going as?"

"That information is currently embargoed," said Joey. "But you can rest assured that it will be awesome."

"You'll probably show up as a character from some eighties TV show no one has heard of," said DeMarcus, shrugging into his backpack.

"And you'll show up in a Panthers jersey," said Joey.

"Keep poundin'," said DeMarcus with a shrug.

"You're going to need a costume with a mask," said Joey to me. "Just in case."

I frowned but saw their point. If the evening called on my fighting skills, it would be wise to conceal my identity on the off chance that I survived the evening.

"So, will it be the tasteful Zorro or the full-face Darth Vader?" asked Joey.

DeMarcus shook his head. "Gotta go crime fighter," he said. "Batman! No brainer."

"Because my corpse should look cool," I observed.

"I wouldn't worry about that," said Joey with an encouraging smile. "If you get killed, I don't think there'll be anyone left alive to see what your body looks like."

"Ah, Joey," said DeMarcus, giving them a hearty pat on the shoulder, "you're always there with the silver lining."

Elsewhere.

Bobby Davenham closed his book as the bell set the class into a flurry of activity.

"Homework assignments will be graded by the end of the day," announced Mrs. Springer. "We begin *Lord of the Flies* on Tuesday so be sure to finish reading it by then. All of it, Mr. Miller, and not the Cliffs Notes summary."

Tylor gave Bobby a knowing wink and stooped to mutter, "Haven't read a thing all semester for this class. Not gonna start now."

"How are you doing your papers?" asked Bobby, wondering if Tyler's dad had made the kind of deal with the English teacher that Bobby's had done with Lewisson, the math teacher.

"ChatGPT all the way."

Tyler gave him a pistol-finger farewell and joined the gaggle of students pressing for the door, forcing his way through when they didn't automatically part for him.

Same as usual, in other words, Bobby thought. It was amazing how quickly things had gone back to normal. For a few days there had been the stunned chaos, the expressions of shock and sympathy, the green bean casseroles and pot roasts brought to the door by downcast, silent neighbors. Then there had been the strange formality of the funeral, and the speeches by Tyler's dad, among others, all painting a picture of a man Bobby barely knew.

My father. My dead father.

Bobby found himself saying the words to himself over and over to try and make sense of them. Sometimes he went into his father's office at home and just stood there, considering the trophy heads of the animals he had shot on safari, trying to feel something other than bafflement and rage.

His father was dead. And for what? Because he wanted to show the world what an ace hunter he was? What use was that? There was insurance money, supposedly, but it would take time to come through and Bobby didn't really know how much it would be. Enough to compensate for his father's lost income, not all of which Bobby understood? Probably not. His dad had been a dealmaker and maybe not always a strictly legitimate one. He had been king of the quiet trade, the back hander, the deals he'd celebrate over dinner with a raise of his wine glass and a knowing wink not unlike the one Tyler had just given him over the homework.

"Ask me no questions," his dad would say with a roguish grin, "and enjoy the profits."

But now there was an audit of his affairs as the lawyers figured out where his assets would go: who was owed what and who would inherit what was left. It was making his mother anxious, not because she knew some of their income was shady, but because she didn't know for sure. Brian Davenham had kept such things to himself.

"Never you mind," he had always said, with his trademark wink. "What you don't know can't hurt you."

But it seemed like maybe it could. His mother didn't even know where all the accounts were.

"I'll walk you through it all one day," his father had said to Brian a few months ago, in one of the rare moments when they had actually been hanging out together, watching a Panthers preseason game. "Your mother is a wonderful person, and—of course—a knockout, but she has no head for business. You keep your nose clean, and I'll show you the ropes someday."

But that day had never come, so now there was only the fog of uncertainty, the nagging anxiety that the next ring of the doorbell wouldn't bring casseroles and sympathy but bailiffs or the IRS ready to cart Bobby's life away.

It made him furious.

"It will get better," his mother had said, the day of the funeral, before the weight of the financial stuff had come into focus, and he had believed her when she smiled.

She's free, he had thought with a kind of strange and unexpected delight. *We both are.*

Bobby hadn't liked his father much, mostly because the feeling was mutual. His father had always been at the office or on the golf course, on a business trip or on some ludicrous hunting expedition. As a little kid, that had made Bobby miserable, wanting nothing more than to have his father at home to sit with him, read to him, play with him. But as that never happened, Bobby shed even the wish for it, so that by the time he was in high school, he no longer cared. In fact, far from wanting more attention from his father, he had come to resent the man more when he *was* around.

So his anger now was confusing, because in the pit of his stomach he knew it wasn't just about the money or legal embarrassments to come. It was something else, a finality, a sense that a door which had always been open just a crack, and might one day have been pushed open, had shut for good.

And he had a good idea who was to blame.

The classroom was empty now. Mrs. Springer was packing up her stuff, and the only student left was Jason Blakely, sitting two rows over and one ahead. He was hunched over his desk and scribbling furiously in his notebook, oblivious to anything else in the world. That was what he always did now. Over the summer they had hung out together some, but this term, after that business with his father's car, he had grown secretive, a loner. Bobby had barely spoken to him in weeks. But he knew what was on Jason's mind. Everyone did, because he drew it constantly, obsessively, on every paper, in every class.

Bugs.

Thousands of them. The cockroaches which had flooded out of his dad's Hummer, along with mantises and beetles, stink bugs, spiders and— now to the exclusion of everything else—centipedes.

"Hey Jason," said Bobby quietly. "Whatcha drawing?"

Jason started, raising his head, clearly surprised to find the classroom empty. His eyes were sunken and furtive, and he looked like he hadn't slept in days.

"What? Oh. Hey, Bobby. Nothing. Just...you know. Doodles."

"I do know," said Bobby, sitting on the back of the chair in front of him. He checked over his shoulder. Mrs. Springer was packing up her purse and leaving. Bobby waited for her to go then leaned over Jason.

"I think we should have a little chat," he said.

"Oh?" said Jason, squirrelly now, like he wanted to be somewhere else. "About what?"

"About what killed my dad, and who it's working for."

Jason repeated the second phrase almost soundlessly, his eyes unfocused, then returned to the first. "What killed your father?" he asked.

Bobby leaned over and planted his finger in the center of Jason's frantically scribbled drawing of a long, segmented body with many sharp legs, antennae, and fang-like mouth parts. "That did," said Bobby. "And you saw it."

Jason shook his head fiercely. "The one I saw was small," he said, blinking erratically, his eyes flashing around the room. "Bigger than it should have been, but not nearly big enough to be the thing that killed your dad."

"But it was, and it did," said Bobby with absolute certainty. "The coroner said so. The mayor and the ranger said so. Sofie told me."

For a second Jason just stared, then he licked his lips. "Yes," he said simply. "I thought so."

"And who else knows?" Bobby pressed. "I just found out, but some people have known for weeks and have said nothing."

Jason shook his head. "I don't know."

"Sure you do," said Bobby, unsmiling. "Who did you talk to about this first?"

Jason's face was blank, then he frowned. "Caleb," he said. "I mean, Hideki. The day of the trip to the ranger station."

"When we lost power for the first time," said Bobby, unsurprised.

Jason nodded.

"Figures," said Bobby. "I knew he was involved."

Jason waggled his hands in distracted protest. "No," he said, "Caleb is controlling it. Keeping it in check."

Bobby got still. "He told you that?" he said, his voice little more than a whisper.

"Yes!" said Jason, missing Bobby's tone and rushing on as if he was giving good news. "I went to their store and spoke to him. He told me not to worry about it. That the giant centipede was under control!"

Bobby sat back. "Is that right?" he said, his eyes losing focus and his voice hardening. "Is that right?"

33

Em's costume involved the classic Japanese sailor suit school uniform with a red armband and her hair divided into twin tails.

"Mizyu," she said, when I gave her a questioning look. "From Atarashii Gakko." That was one of the bands she listened to.

"You know no one is going to know who that is?" I said.

"Not doing it for them," she replied with a shrug. "What about you?"

"Samurai lite," I said.

"Meaning?"

"Going to grab some bits of armor from Saito's place, but not so much that it gets in the way."

She gave me a grim little smile. We weren't going to pretend this was just a costume party. "Had any ideas?" she asked.

I shook my head miserably. "You?"

"Not about killing the *Omukade*," she said.

I sensed something in her manner. "Then about what?" I asked.

"I thought maybe that instead of asking how to destroy it, we should ask what it wants," she said.

"It wants to open the prison and let a thousand monsters out," I said.

"Okay," she said, "but it can't do that yet because it isn't big enough, so what it wants right now…"

"Is to feed," I said. "No offense, Em, but I'm not sure how this helps."

"Bachan says it isn't just after meat," she said, reasoning it out as she spoke. "That what makes it big is something specifically human that isn't just about biological nutrition. It feeds on thought, on fear."

"Fear?"

"What it wants isn't the kind of energy we get from food. It's a *yōkai*, a mystical being. What it really wants is mystical energy."

"Okay," I said. "And where are you going to get that?"

"We are mystical beings, Caleb."

I stared at her. "You're suggesting we sacrifice ourselves to save everyone else so that the *Omukade* can then open the prison, flood Portersville with *yōkai*, and *then* kill everyone? Yeah, no."

Em made an exasperated face and held up her hands to shut me up. "But what if there's another way to give it the energy it wants without actually killing ourselves?"

"Like what?" I demanded. "It's not like we can siphon off our magic into a box!"

As soon as the words came out, it hit me. The glowy box with the gold pine tree on it, the thing the West-fox used—quite literally—as a battery! Em watched the realization spread through my face and smiled noncommittally.

"Might be worth a try," she said.

"Em, that's genius!" I exclaimed. "If we can get the *Omukade* to eat that, it might…"

"Fill it up," she concluded for me, "flood it with energy, so that it won't need to eat any people at all."

"But West won't give it up."

"If I can get it from him," she said, "feed it to the centipede somehow…"

"It's brilliant," I said.

"It won't kill it," she said hastily, as if making sure I didn't get too carried away. "The opposite, in fact. It will make it bigger and stronger than ever. But it might mean that it leaves the people alone. For a little while at least. But then it will head straight to the prison under the mountain where you'll have to stop it."

"How?" I asked. The question I had been turning over and over in my head for weeks.

"No idea," she said. "This is all I have."

I nodded with finality and headed for the door.

"Where are you going?"

"To get that armor for my costume," I said. "It will justify me carrying the *yari* and a sword, for what good those will do me."

She gave me another brittle smile. "See you over there," she said. "Try not to get killed."

"Encouragement worthy of Bachan," I observed as I left.

34

Elsewhere

The power was back. It probably wouldn't last, so Jennie Smith was hurriedly loading the dishwasher. She turned it on, ran upstairs, transferred the laundry into the dryer and turned that on too. She returned to the store, switched the TV on, saw that the local news was covering the details of Kieran West's "retroizing" proposal, and switched it off again. There hadn't been many customers today, despite the crowds that would soon be descending on the mansion across the street.

Not a lot of call for Slim Jims and diet soda when the neighborhood billionaire is laying out a spread for the whole town...

She sat behind the counter and decided to sort through the register. Caleb had been working there for part of the day, so stuff was all over the place: cash in the wrong drawers, receipts left on the counter, the place generally looking like one of Kieran West's mini tornadoes had touched down on the store. Stephen was almost as bad, but he was friendly to the customers, talking sports with the guys and turning on the subtle English charm for the ladies, almost but not quite flirting, snapping on that thousand-watt smile of his. She smiled at the thought, even as she rolled her eyes. He had something she did not, a certain ease with people, or the ability to simulate it, which was just as good. She always felt stiff, out of place, and Em once told her—kindly, encouragingly—that people thought her cold.

"Obviously you're totally not," Em had added quickly, "but you could maybe relax a bit, lower your guard. Show a little more of the woman you are with us."

'Us' meant the family. It was good business sense, and Jennie had tried, but when she made the effort, smiling, making small talk like Stephen did, it seemed to freak people out. Once, when Bernice Sartovski, the waitress who had been attacked by the smaller incarnation of the *Omukade*, had been in to buy milk and toilet roll, Jennie's attempts to engage the woman in conversation had led to the waitress stopping what she was doing, giving her a wary look, and saying "Can I help you with something?" like it was her shop and Jennie was the customer.

She hadn't tried so much since then. Let Stephen be the face of the store while she made it work. That wasn't strictly fair, but it made her feel less inadequate. And it was true that Stephen had no head for figures and the organizational talents of a squirrel on meth. He was practical, good with his hands, but given to flights of fancy. She loved him for it, but she didn't trust him planning the budget or balancing the books. And he was untidy. Take his "tradition" of sticking receipts on the spike in the wall. It was a mess, and an unnecessary one. She had said so many times.

"It's cool!" he always insisted. "Take the receipt and whack it on the nail: the satisfaction of a job done well right there in your hands. You know Stephen King used to keep all his rejection letters on a nail over his workstation?"

"You're not a writer, Stephen," she reminded him. "And that was about motivation, wasn't it? It's not a filing system. We have to keep track of these for tax purposes."

"And there they all are," her husband replied with his trademark grin, "all present and in the right order. Can't go wrong with the spike."

Well, not today. Bachan was sitting with the sleeping Saito-san while working—without much hope—on her charms and spells. Stephen was picking up his costume for the party. Caleb and Emily were making their own preparations for what just might be the last night of their lives.

And she was organizing the register. She felt useless, sidelined, and with a flash of irritation she stood up, stepped to the wall behind the till and pulled the receipts off the spike in one decisive movement.

This is about the running of the business, she thought. *That's my department.*

She laid the receipts in a cardboard box. Later they'd go in the filing cabinet labeled by date.

Tidier, she thought. *More efficient.*

She turned back to the spike in the wall and her face fell. Without the receipts to give the thing a sense of purpose, it was ugly and out of place, like part of an incomplete construction project. They had enough of that with Stephen's ridiculous trains. It would have to go.

She hunted for the claw hammer where Stephen had cut a hole through the wall for his railway track but, for once, he must have put it away properly. She sighed, returned to the spike and gave it an experimental tug.

It came away easily, so much so that she gave it a puzzled look to make sure she hadn't broken it. It was unharmed, and when she ran her finger over the tip, she felt it nick her skin. Though brown with age, it was surprisingly sharp. She considered it, turning it over in the light of the battery lamp she kept on hand at all times now because of the power outages.

They had always called it the receipt spike, but now that it was out of the wall and she could see the thing properly, she could see that it was more than just a spike. The tip actually flattened like a knife blade sharpened on both edges and with a point like a needle. The iron shaft was unadorned but in one place the round of the metal had been flattened. Just a half inch or so, and the surface of that part, unlike the rest, felt rough to the touch.

Damaged, she thought, like when she turned on the waste disposal unit in the kitchen sink and it had chewed up one of her favorite spoons, leaving the handle gnarled and irregular. Stephen had taken an angle grinder to it and rendered it smooth again, but it was slightly misshapen and though no one else noticed, it made her sad.

But this wasn't damage. She held it close to the lantern and saw a shape: a diamond inside a circle, cut into the iron. And underneath it, finely etched characters, so small and faint they were almost invisible.

She stared, and suddenly the word 'spike' was clearly wrong, and a new possibility took its place:

Shuriken.

35

O ur end of town was always pretty quiet, but as I walked along Main Street, I saw signs of festivities and decorations in spite of the recent storm damage. People were pushing through, making the best of things and holding onto as much normality as they could. Many of them would go to the West party in that same spirit, not for the novelty of the California glamor or even to hear more about the "retroizing" nonsense before they had to vote, but for a sense of the town coming together to do something fun, something that didn't involve funerals, or bucket lines and distributing emergency rations, or picking through flooded basements. I had gotten used to seeing people walking around with shovels and flashlights, and to the sheriff department's cars almost permanently around with their lights strobing.

The Halloween store in the strip mall was doing its final hours of discounted sales before shutting up shop, but the place looked deserted and as I crossed the parking lot, the manager came out to take down the advertising banners. There were only three cars in the lot and, of course, nothing in front of the Hibachi Prince. I went round the back, let myself in, and removed my shoes.

I chose a sword in a black scabbard with matching cord binding the hilt, testing the weight and cutting edge even though I knew it wouldn't make much difference either way. A bar of iron, or a stick, would be about as effective against the *Omukade*. I would have preferred to carry the armor rather than wear it, but the *yari*—though light—was cumbersome and I needed to keep my hands free, so I chose the pieces I wanted and put them on, eying myself warily in the mirror Saito-san used to practice form and stance. The armor was mostly made up of metal strips laced together with colored silk not unlike the sleep charm on Saito's wrist and was surprisingly light: not restrictive at all. I took the breastplate, shoulder panels, and armor for my forearms and shins. There was a sort of armored skirt divided into overlapping sections which I wasn't sure about, but I put it on for the look of the thing, then tried the helmet. Two brass horns—or maybe wings—stuck out of the top and there were more laced plates at the back to cover my neck. Like the rest of the armor, it was quite light, but the face mask with its bristly mustache felt claustrophobic, and it limited my vision. It was, I have to say, pretty badass, but I figured that if I actually had to fight wearing this stuff, the mask would have to go.

But I felt... what? Stronger? More sure of myself? Something like that. It wasn't magic—or at least I didn't think so—but for the first time in my life I looked like what I was supposed to be, a demon queller, a figure of power from ancient Japanese legends...

Idiot, I thought, bringing the illusion crashing down. *You are Caleb Hideki Smith, and you are a kid from North Carolina who happens to have some skills, strength, and agility. Buy into your own mystical press and you'll get yourself killed. Even if you don't, you're probably going to die tonight, so let's keep things real, shall we?*

Another peptalk worthy of Bachan. With one last glance in the mirror at the fearsome warrior who was and was not me, I headed out and back through town, walking tall, as ready as I was ever likely to be.

I had made it to Brevard Street when I saw a woman on the sidewalk ahead, standing under one of the ineffectual street lamps with her back to me, head bowed, unmoving.

On her phone, I thought, but I felt a prickle of unease as I approached all the same. I could hear a snuffling sound, like an animal rooting for bugs in the dirt.

I was a few yards behind her when she whipped round suddenly to face me.

Or rather, her head did. A hundred and eighty degrees, spinning like an owl. I froze. The light from the overhead lamp threw her face into strange shadows, but I felt her eyes boring into me. Then, with nightmare slowness, her head craned back toward me, snaking out, as her body remained still, her feet planted.

Her face was filthy, especially around her mouth, and I realized that she had been doing exactly what I had thought, grubbing for bugs in the dirt, not with her hands, but with her teeth.

She gasped now, a kind of malevolent hiss that spat whatever she had been eating, then the lolling head cocked on one side and her eyes processed what she was staring at. I dropped the *yari*, and drew my sword as the head rose up above me, suspended in the air on that long fleshy rope of a neck. I took up a defensive stance, and the head weaved back and forth, looking for an opening, its mouth gaping to show long, animal teeth.

"Who is under there?" the head said. I was so taken aback that I just stared through the mask, speechless. "Ah, Caleb Smith. Now calls himself Hideki. Works at his parents' convenience store. His sister's on the swim team. She's popular, but everyone thinks he's weird, and he hangs out with other social outcasts. Father's English, but not from the classy part. Mother is Jennie, born here, but long estranged from her Japanese mother, at least until recently..."

As it said all this, the head angled and hovered, like it was treading water in the air, the strange, intense eyes always fixed on me even as it shifted around.

"Who are you?" I demanded.

"You don't know?" said the head with satisfaction, its jaws slavering. "You know nothing. I, however, am the *rokurobi* and I know everything about this sad little town and its sadder people."

"You are working with the *Omukade*," I said, raising my sword. One cut would do it, if the creature's neck was not magically protected against my blade.

The head angled slightly, and I thought it looked first puzzled, then hungry.

"What is that?" it said. "*Omukade*. Tell me. I need to know."

"The giant centipede creature..." I began, but it cut me off with a sigh of understanding.

"Oh, that," it said. "No. I am not working with that or with anything. I just am. Now, tell me your secrets," it continued, voice and eyes hardening suddenly, "or I will tear them out of you!"

The change in the thing was alarming, but I stood my ground. If it attacked, I would strike, and the sword would either work or it wouldn't.

"I have no secrets for you," I said.

It hissed again, pulling back a foot or two into the air, snakelike, and as it did so the light from the streetlamp caught its face more fully and I saw something I recognized in its features.

No, I thought, *that's not possible...*

The head stooped like a hawk dropping on prey, jaws agape, and—momentarily distracted by what I thought I'd seen—I missed my chance to sweep my blade at it. Instead, I stepped sideways then vaulted past it. I ran a few steps but could feel the head coming after me, the creature's neck extending with each yard, and though I was fast, I suspected I couldn't outrun it.

"Quick!" oozed the *rokurobi* thoughtfully. "And strong. Too strong for Caleb Hideki Smith, convenience store boy. Curious."

I spun round to face it, but it surged right at me, the head butting hard into my chest, its jaws snapping. It couldn't bite through the armor, but the impact knocked me to the sidewalk. I was on my back, sword gripped in one hand as the creature loomed over me, judging its dive for my throat.

For a split second I felt the weight of despair and failure. I wouldn't fight the *Omukade*. I wouldn't stand with my sister to save Portersville. I wouldn't even make it to the West's party...

"Caleb!"

The voice came out of nowhere, but I knew it. I turned quickly to confirm and gasped in horror.

No! She couldn't be here.

"Mom!" I exclaimed. She was standing across the street in her work clothes. "Get out of here!"

The head twisted and spun on its nauseatingly pliable neck to look, eyes narrow and jaws agape.

I stared at my mother, expecting her to scream, to run, but she just stood there.

"Hello, Maureen," she said.

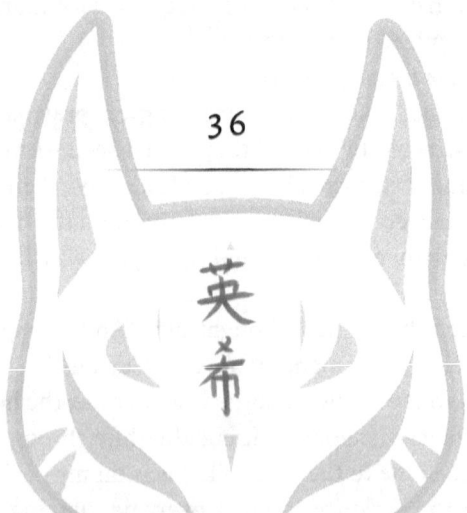

36

R un, Mom!" I bellowed. "It will kill you!"

But it didn't, not right away, and Mom just stayed where she was, as the monster's serpentine neck adjusted to face her.

"What did you call me?" said the head.

"Maureen," said Mom, composed, almost meditative, but with a fire in her eyes I had never seen before. "Maureen Collington."

She was right, of course. I had seen that moments before I had been flung to the ground, though the creature's face was distorted by more than rage.

"I am the *rokurobi*!" warned the head, its jaws dripping with spit as if relishing a sumptuous meal.

Mom held her ground.

"You are Maureen Collington," Mom replied evenly, stepping slowly forward into the street. "And I am Jennie Smith. I am Caleb's mother. He calls himself Hideki now. You will not harm him."

"How dare you…?" spat the head, but the fire in my mother's eyes was like the heart of a furnace.

"I dare because I know you, Maureen," she said, eyes and voice level. "We sat together in middle school for a term, before you went off to private school. You came to my store the other day, for the first time in many years. I was surprised because you don't talk to me much these days. Got fancy. But it seems you also got cursed. But we are still mothers, you and I. We have that in common. So you know I will not let you harm my son."

She kept walking closer and closer, and the head hung in the air above her, cobra-like.

"You cannot stop me," spat the head. "I know you..."

"And I know you, Maureen," Mom replied. "You have forgotten yourself. Your husband is Chris Collington. You have that big, beautiful house on Creekside Overlook. Remember your house, Maureen?"

From my position on the ground, I stared as if paralyzed. The head had also been strangely still, but now it lashed back and forth in furious denial of the name my mother kept repeating.

"I am the *rokurobi*!" it insisted. "How dare you look upon me. *I* am the looker, the watcher, the one who sees all..."

"No, Maureen," Mom replied, continuing to walk slowly but steadily toward us. Her sad smile was touched with pity. "You are just a person, like me. But you *are* the victim of some old and vengeful magic. Your daughter is Sofie. Beautiful girl. Smart, too. Remember Sofie, Maureen?"

The head just hung in the air for a few seconds, the face clouded with uncertainty. The woman's body began to shudder and shake, like a badly tuned tractor which would rattle itself to pieces if not shut off. The trembling spread through it like a seizure, spreading to its arms, so that its fingers fluttered like ineffectual wings.

As I watched, horror-struck, the lolling head suspended in the air on that impossible neck began to shriek, a hair-curling scream of anger and despair. The mouth opened wider than seemed possible, and the eyes tightened into slits as the sound roared out of it. Slowly, as if being reeled in like fishing line, the neck contracted and shortened, drawing the wailing head back to the body.

"Caleb!" called Mom. "Come here!"

I didn't need telling twice. The sound was like grating metal, a terrible, keening howl interspersed with sobs, but as furious as it was distressed. I rolled to my feet, sheathed my sword and grabbed the *yari* where it had fallen, then ran after my mother. She grabbed my hand and together we turned to face the shrieking monster as it dwindled into something more simply and clearly human.

"What did you do?" I exclaimed, mystified.

"I reminded her who she really is."

"And that..." I hesitated, hunting for the right word, "*cured* her?"

Mom shook her head, her face thoughtful. "If you mean did it lift the curse so she won't transform again, no, I don't think so. But it bought us some time."

"More than that," I said inadequately, pulling off the mask and feeling the night air cool my sweating face. "What were you even doing here?"

"Looking for you," Mom replied without looking at me.

The sound had dropped now to a whimper, and the snakelike neck had retracted completely so that the uncanny shape of the thing had shrunk back into a woman, horrified and grief-stricken, weeping on the sidewalk.

Maureen Collington.

"How did you know?" I asked.

"About Maureen? Just put two and two together. Her strange behavior when she came into the store. The way her daughter suddenly had all this gossip. That was always a weakness of Maureen's, the need to know what everyone was doing and whisper about it. Maybe that was what gave the curse its form."

"Cursed by what?" I asked.

"Who did the Collingtons cross?" asked Mom, giving me an expectant look.

"Kieran West," I said. "They wanted the Haversham house land to build on. This was their punishment? Turning her into a monster that spied on people?"

"Taking the worst aspect of her personality and making it literal. I doubt she even really knew what she was doing, but she knew something was wrong. She felt embarrassed. Degraded."

"Why go after her? It was her husband who was West's enemy."

"That's how it goes sometimes," said Mom darkly. "Men go after other men through the women closest to them."

"You might have just saved my life," I said, a bit stunned.

"This is what mothers do," she said, with a half-smile.

I stared in horrified fascination at Mrs. Collington, feeling suddenly, and unexpectedly, a stab of pity. "Will she be all right?" I asked.

She was standing still, her head in her hands. She wasn't coming after us.

"I hope so," said Mom. "Eventually. Come on. We have other things to do tonight."

I turned to say something else, but Mom was walking purposefully away, her eyes fixed unwaveringly ahead. I shot a last look at Mrs. Collington, then jogged to catch up my mother as she reached into her purse, took something out and, still not meeting my eyes, pushed it into my hand.

"What's this?" I said, peering at it in the low light. "Looks like the receipt spike."

"It is," said Mom. "It's also Raiko's lost shuriken."

I stopped mid stride.

"You're kidding?" I said, holding it up and studying it. "You sure?"

"Pretty sure," Mom replied. "It's marked with the family crest and the Watanabe seal."

"Mom, this is amazing!" I gasped. "It was right under our noses all this time?"

"That's also how it goes sometimes," she said. "Come on or we'll be late."

"I can't believe it," I said, picking up the pace.

"So," she added grimly, "ready to party?"

For a moment, I wondered if it should be her wearing the armor to fight the *Omukade*.

"You not dressing up?" I asked. She was dressed for the store: professional blouse and business slacks with low heels.

"Costumes aren't my style," she said, with the beginnings of a smile. "You get the real me, or you get nothing."

"And Dad?"

"Oh, I expect your father will have found something absurd to wear," she said affectionately.

I looked back one more time, but I couldn't make out Maureen in the gathering dark. What the woman must have been going through as she remembered what the curse had made her do, what it had done to her mind and body, I couldn't imagine, but she didn't seem interested in us anymore.

"You'd better put that back on," said Mom, nodding at the mask I had been dangling in one hand.

I nodded and did so, and again, it felt like preparing for battle. I swallowed. My nerves were still jangling after the encounter with the *rokurobi*, but there was worse, much worse, to come. I gave my mother a sideways glance, and I caught a flicker of pain and sadness in her eyes. She knew what was coming as well as I did and knew that she could not help me.

I adjusted the mask of my helmet feeling my sweaty palm slide on the shaft of the *yari*. It was time to stand and fight, for my family, my town, my world.

And I would, because that was all there was, and because no one else could.

It probably wouldn't make any difference, I thought, catching something of my mother's despair, but sometimes, I guess, the fight is all there is, and you do it anyway, whether you think you can win or not. The only real defeat is not fighting.

37

We kept to the main road all the way until we reached the inconvenience store on the other side of the street, by which time we were part of a crowd of energized people, many of them dressed in costume. There were superheroes and zombies, assorted spooks and witches, icons from video games and anime, plus the usual selection of characters from *Star Wars*, *Hunger Games*, and *Harry Potter*. And there was me, Caleb Hideki Smith, demon queller, with Raiko's shuriken tucked into my belt.

"Woah," said Jenny Astor when she saw me through the crowd of party goers heading up the drive to the West mansion. "Who is that? Dude, that looks totally real!" I opened my mouth to speak but changed my mind and merely bowed slightly in acknowledgement. "Cool," she said.

"I'll see you inside," said Mom. "If you're seen with me, I'll blow your cover. And besides, I had better find your father before he makes a spectacle of himself." She gave me a quick eye roll.

"Mom," I said urgently, grabbing her hand. "Thanks. I mean it."

"Of course," she said, like it was nothing. "You'd do the same for me. You are about to."

And then, before we had to acknowledge that flash of doubt and despair in her face, she was pushing past a couple of kids from school who were dressed as pigs, their costumes humming with the battery-powered fans which kept them inflated. For a second I just stood there, watching them all, safe behind my mask, taking in their excitement, their pleasure, and knowing that their safety, their very lives, depended on me.

The house and grounds were decorated for the occasion with massive, carved orange pumpkins and an array of shifting, green and purple lights which played over a thick ground fog flowing from the open front door.

"Check out that dry ice!" Sharon (Taylor Swift) Tensing said gleefully as she hurried past with Nadine (influencer) Peterson, but I wasn't so sure it *was* dry ice. After all, the mansion itself was an illusion: you had to assume all the Halloween décor was too.

The lawn was now an utterly lifelike graveyard packed with lurching head stones and sinister stone angels, all looming ominously from the same eerie mist. Dramatic organ music drifted down from hidden speakers.

No, I reminded myself, thinking it was probably wise not to get sucked into West's fakery. *There aren't any speakers. This is all in our heads. Perhaps this is the last great illusion powered by Em's stolen magical energy...*

Not that it mattered to anyone else. They *oohed* and *ahhed* at the giant moving skeletons welcoming them onto the porch as they had at the marble hallways and grand piano. This was just more from the same sideshow bag of tricks. The adults were as taken in as the kids, though their admiration was less obviously gleeful. They gazed about and exchanged knowing looks, whispering about what this must all have cost with equal parts small-town distrust and awed delight.

More Hollywood glamor...

Bats flitted around jack-o'-lanterns, and the guests exclaimed at how well done they were, speculating whether they were some kind of animatronic or a holographic projection. I wondered if they might actually be the only thing around here that was real.

Inside, the lavish décor continued with a themed buffet of heaped barbecue—brisket, ribs, sausage, pulled pork, chicken, the works—alongside vegetable dishes and salads ranging from local favorites to nameless exotics, all artfully presented with seasonal leaves, a horn of plenty center piece, and the largest Halloween candy banquet you can imagine. It was tempting, but I had a feeling how the evening was going to go so I held off, reminding myself that at the last West party I had eaten endlessly without dampening my appetite, probably because none of the food was real.

There was music playing, and though power was still out all over town, the house positively blazed with light, the vast room in which we were gathered lit by three huge glass chandeliers.

"Must have multiple generators," said a man I recognized as one of the local mail carriers.

The woman with him, who was large and pink and dressed as a flight attendant, nodded and, not resentfully, said, "The things you can do with large amounts of money."

DeMarcus showed up in full Panthers gear, as promised, followed by Joey in white loose-fitting slacks and a matching lightweight jacket with the sleeves pushed up.

"And you are?" I asked.

"Crocket!" exclaimed Joey, as if it was obvious. I looked to DeMarcus.

"The Don Johnson character from Miami Vice," he said wearily. It sounded like he had heard this explanation several times already.

"Cool," I said, which seemed to suffice.

Tyler had come as his father, it seemed, in a suit and wearing his dad's mayoral chain of office. I wasn't sure if that was supposed to be funny or prophetic. Bobby Davenham was in his regular clothes, but Jason Blakely —fittingly enough given his recent obsession with bugs—was Spider-Man. I saw Maddie Hayes, dressed in white satin and with her hair all fancy—some kind of Disney Princess, perhaps—but if she saw me, she didn't recognize me. I spotted Em in her Atarashii Gakko outfit loitering warily by the fireplace.

A moment later, I was nudged in the ribs by an adult dressed in blue overalls with oversized buttons, a red shirt and matching cap with an 'M' on it. A cartoon mustache completed the picture.

"All right, mate?" said Super Mario.

"Dad?"

"Good, eh?"

"It's..." I hunted for the right word, "unmistakable."

"That it is," said Dad, beaming from ear to ear. "I see you are ready for anything."

"Not sure about *anything*," I said, glad that he couldn't see my face behind the armored mask.

"I have faith in you," he said. "You'll be grand."

Sometimes he dipped more heavily into his Lancashire phrases when he got nervous. I just nodded, then said, "Mom's looking for you."

"She's in the other room, with Maureen Collington, if you can believe that."

"She's *what?*" I said.

Dad gave me a quizzical stare. "Seemed like they were having a bit of a heart-to-heart," he said. "Maureen seemed to be a bit on the weepy side, so I kept my distance."

"I should check on her," I said, wondering what Mom would be discussing with the woman who probably still had the *rokurobi's* extendable neck and fearsome jaws.

"On your mom? She's fine. Try some of the prime rib. Melts in the mouth."

"Because it's made of air," I said. Super Mario Dad gave me looks first of puzzlement then of panic and, in spite of everything, I had to laugh. "It's fine," I added. "Illusory, but non-toxic."

"Oh," he said. "Good. Listen, speaking of food, I had an idea..."

But the music died suddenly, and then the fox spirit known locally as Keiran West—dressed as the classier style of vampire—was pushing through the crowd.

"Excuse me, Caleb," he said, his eyes meeting mine knowingly. "Speech time."

Not calling me Hideki was supposed to annoy me, make some kind of point, but I ignored it, shrugging out of his way as he walked, tapping a spoon or something on a crystal whisky tumbler and smiling for silence.

All eyes turned to him and, pulsing with all the charm he could muster, he began to speak.

"Welcome all!" he said. "I can't tell you how much Nathan and I want to thank you for coming. Where is Nathan?" he made a show of glancing around the room, and I had to stop myself from pointing and shouting "there! *You're* Nathan, you lying old fraud!"

When "Nathan" didn't show, Mr. West shrugged expansively and gave a self-deprecating smile. "Kids, eh? Never want to listen to their dads." A knowing chuckle spread through the room, and you could almost hear the magic working, the bond he was creating between himself and the town as they desperately leaned into the idea of being his friend. "You have all made us so welcome that we wanted to throw this little shindig as a thanks. You all—or should that be y'all..." (Another ripple of delighted amusement) "know that I've made some plans for the town which some of you have generously agreed to take on board. We have a vote next week, but if anyone wants to bend my ear on that front tonight, I'm here for you. I will not, however, force you to listen to speeches about the perils of internet misinformation, and our increasingly digital society's many problems. Tonight is a party, one I think we have earned through many recent hardships and sadnesses, and I want you to enjoy it as such. So that's all from me. Eat, drink, and be merry!"

"For tomorrow, we die," whispered Joey into my ear, completing the quotation. "Maybe sooner."

I turned on them quickly. "Wait, what?" I demanded.

"Your dad told us," DeMarcus said. "Imminent centipede attack and all that."

Dad was abashed.

"Why did you tell them?" I demanded.

"Because you didn't," said Joey pointedly. "I thought we were a team."

"I don't want you getting hurt," I said.

"Better to know what's coming than not," said DeMarcus. "We can help clear people out."

"If it happens," said Joey. "Personally, I'm hoping it doesn't. I got a look at that thing once already, and I don't really want to see it again."

The house shook.

"Oh, nice going, Joey," said DeMarcus.

"What did I do?" Joey demanded, but they looked anxious.

The ground was vibrating. Party guests were exchanging worried glances, and some of them had hastily grabbed chair backs or stabilized themselves against the walls. A rumble came from deep below the house, and the floor under the grand piano shuddered and subsided, causing a jangling crash of unmusical notes, and a huge clatter as plates and glasses slipped off it. A great crack buckled the floor, scattering the crowd, and one of the marble pillars near the bay window split with a pop of grit and dust.

And then there were roaches.

They crawled out of the fissure in the floor and spread like spilled oil across the room.

"Everybody out!" bellowed Dad. "Now! Leave your things and go."

But people hesitated, spellbound, and in the next instant the floor exploded as if it had been punched by a giant from beneath. Chunks of stone and wood rocketed upwards, and a plume of dirt and dust erupted like a volcano, filling the room. Only as it began to settle could I see the massive crimson head of the *Omukade* pushing up and through. It unfurled like smoke, but it was all too real. The centipede was so big it filled the huge room, and its lash-like antennae hit the ceiling.

Dad hesitated, staring at it, eyes and mouth wide in disbelief, and then he turned back to Kieran West.

"Take what I owe you!" he shouted. "But save my kids."

I stared at him.

"What you owe him?" I shouted. "What are you talking about?"

But he didn't look at me, all his attention on West who just shook his head, smiling faintly.

"Your fate is sealed," West remarked. "There is nothing you can give me now."

Dad's face fell, then he turned back to the crowd of people and roared at them. "Get out!"

It took a second for the *Omukade* to appraise its surroundings, its shiny eyes blinking, claw-like mouth parts flexing, and then it hissed like a giant cat, and lunged.

I moved a hand to my belt but found...

Nothing!

The shuriken was gone. I glanced frantically around and saw that, despite all the shouting and chaos, Kieran West was still looking smug and amused. In his hands he held the thing which I had thought was a spoon when he had tapped it on the side of his whisky glass. It was Raiko's shuriken. He had filched it from my belt when he pushed into me. He met my eyes with a smirk and a shrug.

"Can't have you always relying on your ancestors, can we?" he said, and though the room was a riot of noise, I heard his words as if he was standing next to me, whispering.

I had no choice. I pointed the head of the *yari* at the *Omukade*'s face and lunged, using the full length of the spear. I caught it squarely below its right eye, but the blade slid off, leaving the shell unmarked. I got the monster's attention, however, and it hauled itself up from the crater in the floor on dozens of yellow legs, each the length of my spear, and spun to attack me. I struck again, then feinted, and stabbed once more, but each strike had the same effect.

None.

I spun and leapt as the centipede snapped at me, but all I could do was dodge and parry. It was still half in the tunnel it had made through the floor, writhing like a segmented snake, pulling itself up until it cracked the ceiling and wrecked the chandeliers. For a moment, it was tangled in their remains, and in that half second, before it shook them off and returned its attention to me, I saw Em, no longer a girl in her costume, but as the amber blur of her fox form which went streaking out of the room and up the stairs.

As everyone else scattered, screaming, Keiran West, stayed where he was, lounging against the edge of the mantelpiece, his eyes switching between the *yōkai* and me, with an interested look which was almost amusement. He resembled a sports fan watching teams he didn't really care about, just wanting to be entertained.

The *Omukade* suffered another couple of hits from the spear and then, as if deciding I was no threat, turned to where the partygoers were streaming out toward the front door, yelling as they fought each other to get out. I sprang into the air, cleared a good twenty feet of fallen masonry, and wheeled to face the creature again, sweeping at its bony, pointed legs with the butt end of the *yari*. The force of the stroke tripped it, and for a moment, it was off balance, clattering into a heap within the ornate chamber. Its tail end whipped round, carving a gash in the wall and scattering vases and statues from whatever tables hadn't yet been destroyed. It glared at me, its eyes full of hate, those giant, venom-dripping fangs opening and closing like monstrous fingers. Its great maw gaped as if trying to suck me inside.

I looked desperately around as Dad and DeMarcus herded people out, and saw that where Keiran West had been, his place—his body—had been replaced by Nathan. He was grinning at me.

"Hey Hideki," he said. "Doing well, considering."

"Help!" I shouted as the *Omukade* surged after the retreating people. "Throw me the shuriken!"

"Sorry Caleb," he said, his smile getting fixed. "No can do. Humans aren't my problem."

He gave me his easy, confident smile, but then his eyes tightened on something behind me, and he frowned with something like confusion. I glanced over my shoulder and there was Maureen Collington in her *rokurobi* form, her long neck arcing and weaving, head turned to face the giant centipede, hissing her fury.

"Leave it!" Nathan ordered, but the *rokurobi* matched the *Omukade* move for move, like a rattlesnake gauging its moment of attack.

The centipede thing seemed confused and hesitant. At each attempt to lunge past the *rokurobi* after the retreating party goers, the head adjusted, keeping itself between the monster and the crowd. It was only a moment, a matter of a few seconds at most, but it made all the difference. Keiran West's Halloween guests were almost all out.

285

And then, scampering toward me, was a red fox, its tail stuck straight out behind it and a black lacquered box clamped in its jaws. As the Emfox bounded up to me, I risked a look back at Nathan, whose doubt had become panic.

"No!" he bellowed, stumbling toward me, hands outstretched, as I snatched the box from the fox's mouth. I pivoted, jumped and dropped between the giant centipede and the partygoers it was chasing. I held the box up, flipped its lid open and, as its pearly green light flooded the room, I tossed it up into the air.

The *Omukade* pounced, snatching the box out of the air like a dog catching a stick. A great ripple flexed its carapace as it swallowed, and then its armor was popping off like steel plates as it got bigger and bigger. In seconds, as Nathan continued to shriek his rage, the monster was simply too big for the room. It swelled until the pillars snapped like toothpicks, shrugging through the ceiling while the floor above split and the walls collapsed.

And only then did I realize that what I was seeing was not the pristine West mansion coming apart, but the ravaged and derelict Haversham house. Enko-san's illusions were disintegrating with the house as the *Omukade* absorbed all the energy from the box-battery.

"No!" shouted Nathan again, but the fox which was my sister stared him down.

The neck of the *rokurobi* snapped back, and the outlandish creature turned back into Maureen Collington, who looked up—her face no longer distorted but still defiant, her eyes fixed on Nathan—as my mother reached to pull her up and out.

And then, without warning, the *Omukade* was diving, smashing the tunnel it had come through wider, scattering rock and dirt and the wet slime of the swampy ground behind it. It knew it had the size and strength it needed to shatter the rock of Red Scar Mountain. It had what it came for and more. It was headed to the prison under the mountain, and I had to go after it.

But first, I took three long strides to where Nathan was looking drained and defeated, and I whacked him hard in the midriff with the butt of the *yari*. He doubled up, gasping, and there was a metallic tinkle as something fell from his hand.

The shuriken.

I stooped, snatched it up, and moved to the buckled and ragged edge of the great hole in the floor which the *Omukade* had left in its wake.

Nathan managed another knowing smirk and a shake of his head. "Won't work," he said. "All you'll manage to do with that is give it a reason to kill you. It's too big. Too powerful. It would take a true, pureblood warrior to defeat a *yōkai* that strong. A half-bred little thing like you? You should run while you can."

"You know I can't do that," I said.

"Then you will die," he replied. "And this time, no one can bring you back."

"Then I'll die," I said. And turning quickly, I stepped over the lip of the crater in the floor and dropped into the dark.

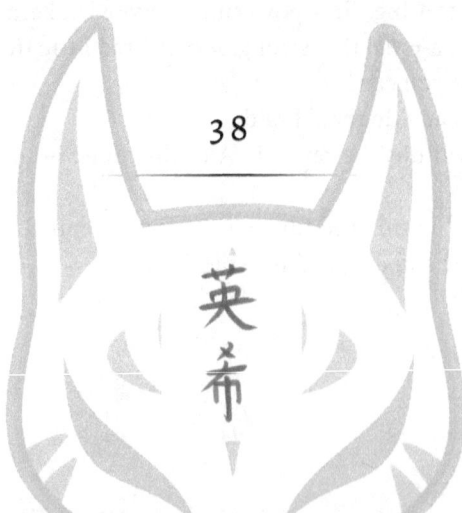

38

I fell maybe twenty feet, then hit the curved side of the tunnel and tumbled another twenty, bouncing and skidding, unable to stop myself, until the tunnel flattened out, coming to an undignified halt in a ragged and filthy heap. For a moment, I just lay there in the blackness, breathing in the close, dank air, gradually testing my arms and legs to see if anything was broken.

I didn't think so. Plenty of scrapes and bruises, but nothing more serious. The armor had definitely helped. I managed a crouch, then stood up cautiously, flinching away as something brushed my shoulder. In the darkness I fumbled for my phone which—by happy chance—I had stowed in my shirt pocket under the breast plate rather than in my unprotected jeans, and turned on the flashlight. The charge was low and I doubted I'd get more than a few minutes out of it, but the passage swam into sudden brilliance.

It was bigger than I had thought it would be, huge in fact, and where it ran straight, it resembled one of the tunnels on the Blue Ridge Parkway, though this was more of a rough tube with no flat ground. The irregular "roof" hung with roots like Spanish Moss and dripped with accumulated ground water. The floor was puddled already, and I suspected that in time the whole place would get wetter and wetter, until it collapsed. I needed to move quickly.

I flashed the light around and saw the *yari* spear half submerged some ten feet to my left. I had released it as I fell—more reflex than strategy—and that had probably saved it from snapping. I checked my pocket for the shuriken and pulled it out. It felt very small, and I couldn't help thinking of Nathan's dismissive remark about it.

No point thinking about that now.

The *yari* seemed undamaged, though the fact that I could carry it easily through the tunnel only reminded me of how big the newly fed *Omukade* had become. Em's plan had worked and had probably saved a lot of lives. Had it also cost me mine?

No, I thought.

The size of the creature was irrelevant at this point. The shuriken would either kill it or it wouldn't. It was fairy story logic. That the centipede *yōkai* was twice the size it had been at the start of the evening didn't make any difference.

So I walked forward, after the monster, beginning to jog, and finally running as I became sure of my footing. I held the phone light high in one hand and carried the *yari* in the other. The saturated clay was gluey under foot, and the tunnel echoed with the sound of my splashing, sucking foot-falls. In places, the tunnel had already begun to collapse in on itself, and great crushing boulders had forced their way into the passage from above. I navigated them as quickly as I dared, and pressed on, knowing that the longer it took me to catch up to the *Omukade*, the more likely it would be that I would arrive to find that it had already breached the prison.

After a few hundred yards, the tunnel turned sharply to the right and began to climb. The damp earth was gradually replaced by split granite which had been fractured and pushed roughly aside, so that the sides were a rolling scree of stone. It was harder work to walk on, requiring more scrabbling over sharp-edged boulders, reminding me again just how powerful the *yōkai* was. If it could smash its way through solid rock, what possible chance did I have against it?

I felt a rush of fresh air from up ahead and was startled to find that, beyond a pile of rock where the ceiling had caved in, I could see stars and treetops. I clambered up and out and found myself in the forest northwest of town, following the trail of devastation made by the *Omukade* close to where the fracking plant had been. Trees had been pushed aside, and the ground was pocked and scraped by the great legs and belly of the monster. Doubtless it was easier to move above ground than below it, and at this point it had nothing to fear from being seen. Still, I was surprised to see that in patches of mud where the *Omukade* had sheared the turf and debris in its passing were a series of human footprints: a single person moving barefoot in the wake of the creature. The prints were about my size: a small man or a woman. I squinted in puzzlement, and then it came to me.

The *te no me* or, as I still thought of him, eye-hand guy.

He would open the mystical prison once the outer rock had been breached.

You may have to kill him, I realized with sudden horror. *If you can't stop the* Omukade, *you may have to kill eye-hand guy to keep the prison sealed.*

I didn't like that treacherous little toe rag but—his weird eyes notwithstanding—he looked kind of like a person. If it came to it, could I actually end his life? Would I?

I hesitated, not liking the idea. It was a lot easier to kill monsters when they didn't look like you.

He's an ally of the onibaba, I reminded myself. *He'll bring her nightmare army out into our world, and they will destroy it. If killing him is the only way to stop that...*

I climbed on, not wanting to think about it, getting higher and higher, feeling the cool air of the autumn night filling my lungs. I hiked on for another ten or twelve minutes, and then the ragged path of destruction plowed across a stream, through a stand of ravaged beech trees, and bore into a cliffside like a drill. The *yōkai* had gone underground again, and what had been a path—albeit a wide and uneven one—was a tunnel once more. I took a steadying breath and went in after it.

I had turned the flashlight off on my phone to save battery while I had been above ground, but I needed it again here, and fifty yards or so into the passage, the light revealed a surprise. The tunnel opened up, becoming a cavern, at the far side of which was a stone doorway. The rock around it had been carved like a *torii*—the great horned gateways which stood in front of Japanese shrines—and on either side of it were statues of foxes, ferocious and stately, hewn from the very rock. The seal of the Watanabe house was carved into the stone lintel in rough but elegant characters. Unlike Raiko's shrine, however, which appeared and disappeared, seeming to be a portal to a different space not entirely of our world, this place felt absolutely real, a physical carving into the Carolina stone, long hidden by the mountain above it.

I paused, sensing the weight of the place around me. The granite foxes glared into my flashlight as if in accusation or challenge. Until the *Omukade* burrowed in, this had been one of the dark places of the world and nothing grew here, so the stone from which the foxes were carved was unblemished by moss or lichen. Their lines were crisp, unweathered, as if they had been carved yesterday, and for a moment, I felt I was caught up in some kind of temporal whirlpool, sucked down into the past, or at least into a place where time was meaningless.

The two columns of the giant *torii* arch were scarred on the inside where the *Omukade* had entered, and beyond the stone gateway I could hear the echo of its chittering and clicking feet. I transferred the *yari* to my left hand and drew the shuriken with my right. Then I followed the sound.

As soon as I crossed the threshold beneath the *torii*, an unearthly light, soft and amber-red as the embers of a dying fire bloomed through the stone walkway. I put my phone away, but walked a little slower, awed by the looming grandeur of the place and the strange power which lit it. Up ahead, I saw a vast round chamber with a heap of rags in the center and a domed roof. Its curved walls were dark and shining like jet, carved into regular panels all connected and several yards high. The ceiling was adorned with more Japanese writing, though these carvings lacked the balance and deliberation of those I had seen outside. They looked random, hasty, their groupings erratic and a little mad, as if they had been scribbled into the stone by someone who was both obsessive and a little crazy.

Ofuda?

These were different, of course, since they were carved, but they resembled the paper charms that had been stuck all over the wall of the fracking cave, part of the seal which bound the demons inside.

I felt a chill run through me. Who knew what terrible things were waiting to get out? I had glimpsed them darkly once before. They had been horrible. And there were a lot of them. Dozens? Hundreds? I didn't know. One of them, an insignificant bug-like thing had scurried out and turned into a monster which could devour the town and crack the mountain open...

Speaking of which...

Though I had followed the monster into what was apparently a cul-de-sac, there was no sign of it.

Weird.

I walked into the center of the room toward the heap of rags where the light was brightest and looked up into the dome. In its center was a circle of crystal in a stone frame, like a porthole in a ship. It was dark, but it swirled and pulsed with strange energy and the shadows of things I couldn't name.

Things trapped inside.

This was the mystical prison, laid bare by the *Omukade* which, its wrecking ball task completed, seemed to have disappeared. As I stood there, overwhelmed by the strangeness of it all, I caught the echoes of a faint whispering. It took me a second to realize that they were coming from the pile of rags, and another second to realize that the rags were moving fractionally. I took a step back, and saw, to my horror, the folds of the heaped, rough fabric part and a thin hand slide out. The fingers flexed, and the hand opened revealing a single bright eye in the center of the palm.

The *te no me*, hooded and shrouded, head bent and feet tucked in so that he appeared to be nothing more than a discarded backpack.

He was whispering his spells or prayers, which would somehow crack the window into the prison. He had to be stopped.

I swung the butt end of the *yari* round, looking to knock him over, but the seeing hand was quick and strong, catching the staff and grasping it firmly. I tugged it free, but in his whispering I caught an extra noise which sounded, alarmingly, like a chuckle. I stared, baffled, and then I understood, because the chittering was back and all around me. The dark, gleaming, sectional walls which I had thought were carved from jet began to move. I hadn't been able to see the *Omukade* in the gloom not because it had gone, but because it had curled all around the chamber, tucking itself into every cranny and presenting only its armored back. Now it unwound itself, its legs spreading out to fill the cavernous room, the long feelers of its head and tail flexing like the steel cables of a suspension bridge. It was all around me, massive, encircling the entire cavern...

Its eyes found me.

I staggered back the way I had come in, the scale of the thing suddenly more than I could take in, and the monster continued to unfurl itself, spreading across the cavern's ceiling. I backed off further, but it matched me step for step, dropping to the stony floor, then rearing up, ready to strike. Its mouth gaped, hissing, and those horn-like forelegs spread their terrible, deadly fangs.

It was ready and eager to finish what it had not been able to do before. For a second I considered running. I was fast and agile. I might get away...

For a little while. If it didn't catch me right away, the consequences of my desertion would catch up to me and everyone I loved all too quickly.

I stopped, jaw set and—for the briefest of moments—closed my eyes.

It has to be me, I thought, as I raised Raiko's shuriken, the last of the great warrior's enchanted weapons, and aimed. *It has to be me. There is no one else. I am alone...*

"I am Caleb Hideki Smith, demon queller..."

I was hit by a thumping tackle which knocked the breath from my body and threw me to the floor. The shuriken skittered away across the stone floor, but I was too stunned to even cry out. Because the attack had not come from in front of me, not from the giant centipede which had been poised to attack or even from the spindly old man with the eyes in his hands who was already snatching up the shuriken.

It had come from behind. It had come from a person.

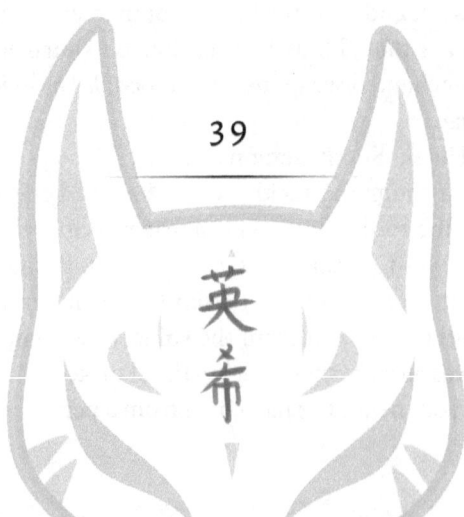

39

I hadn't moved quickly enough. My fear had slowed me down and someone had been able to follow me through the tunnel from the devastated West mansion, all the way here. But who?

I struggled to get free, rolling onto my back, staring up in amazement.

It was Bobby Davenham. He stood over me, his face flushed with rage and pain, his eyes streaming.

"It was you!" he screamed, pointing unsteadily at me. "It was always you! What is this, your pet? Your freakshow monster pal which you've been feeding with our town?"

"What?" I gasped, caught as much off guard by the idea as I had been by his attack. "No. I came to kill it."

"Right," he sneered. "And it's just a coincidence that it's you, here with all this weirdo Japanese stuff!" He gestured wildly around the domed chamber with its scrawled kanji. "You people..." he whispered, his voice full of loathing and fury, "you come to our country, and you bring all *this*." He spat the last word, his eyes flashing up at the monster which watched thoughtfully.

"I was born here," I said, an old fury spiking in spite of the situation, but he wasn't listening.

"You come here and you tear us apart. My father..." he began, but his voice buckled and snapped, and for a second he couldn't speak. Grief doubled him over, and a long, desperate sob slid out, swelling in volume until it became a roar of frustration and loss. His emotion transformed him so that he looked like someone I had never seen before.

I got clumsily to my feet.

"You have to go," I said quietly. "I didn't summon this thing. I came to kill it, but I don't know how to do that. I had a weapon but..." I looked to the shuriken which the *te no me* was now holding, his blind face smiling faintly in a self-satisfied way, his other hand held up, its eye fixed unblinking on us. "So it will probably kill me. If you stay it will kill you too. I'm sorry about your dad, Bobby. I really am. But I wasn't responsible for his death, and I was here to protect you and the rest of the town. You should go."

"You don't tell me what to do!" he shouted. "And don't pretend you care about me! NO ONE cares about me!"

Even under the baleful glare of the *Omukade* I winced as I glimpsed a sliver of his pain, but then the giant centipede, its curiosity exhausted, was moving to strike and all I could do was swing the *yari* up into a fighting stance and step between the *yōkai* and Bobby. I blocked its first attack and those pincer-like mouth parts stabbed into nothing, their poisoned tips gleaming in the strange light of the cavern. Bobby half jumped, half fell backwards, overcome with horror and fear. I swatted and lunged at its underside, but again the blade slid off its armored shell. Again and again I stabbed, adjusted, stabbed again, shouting my mounting despair, and each time the blade glanced away.

The *te no me* had gone back to his prayers, and the light from the port-hole in the dome was shifting, the glassy surface starting to wash back and forth as if whatever solid element was plugging the prison door was dissolving.

The *Omukade* stopped trying to evade my blows, as if instinctively recognizing their uselessness, and gathered itself for a decisive and fatal lunge. Its eyes were fixed on me, so it didn't see the hunk of rock coming at it until it bounced off the side of its head. It flinched, unharmed, of course, but surprised, and turned to see where Bobby Davenham was gathering baseball-sized shards of fractured granite and hurling them with vengeful fury.

The *Omukade* lunged at him and Bobby went flying backwards. I couldn't tell if he had been bitten or even if he was alive, but he fell hard and lay still. The giant centipede stepped toward him, a rippling staccato sound as its hard feet tap danced over the scree towards the fallen boy, and I rushed at it and stabbed again.

The monster flinched, as if it had forgotten I was there, wheeling to face me once more, unafraid but irritated.

Again I struck, and again the point of my spear bounced, sending shock waves through the shaft. I was flagging, fading in strength and what little hope I had come in with. The *Omukade* pushed the tip aside with a lazy nudge of its head, and then it was towering over me, fangs dripping.

I managed one last leap aside, a long spring that cleared half the room even as it sapped my remaining energy. As the *yōkai* turned furiously to pursue me, like a crocodile going after a gnat, I looked back and saw people pulling a stunned Bobby Davenham back and away into the dimmer space beyond the domed room. DeMarcus, I thought. And Joey. I stared in amazement.

I am not alone, I thought vaguely.

The idea acted like adrenaline on my system. And then, as Bobby was dragged clear, two other figures came into view. One—small but fiery in the strange light of the chamber—was a fox, sprinting not to me, but under the *Omukade*'s massive bulk until it was yipping and snapping at the *te no me*.

Em.

Behind her, limping and filthy, was my father. He managed to smile.

"Raiko's lost shuriken was the receipt spike!" he exclaimed, delighted in spite of everything. "You have it?"

I couldn't say that I had lost it, couldn't stand the disappointment in his face when he realized what that meant, so I just shook my head and glanced at eye-hand guy who was brandishing it. The Em-fox bounced and skipped around him, yipping and snarling, but the *te no me* turned with her every movement, one hand open, watching her.

The *Omukade* seemed confused by all these people suddenly appearing, but it was—understandably—undaunted. We could do nothing to stop it. It had fulfilled its mission and could now enjoy the aftermath, which probably included eating us. It arched its serpentine back, watching the fox dancing around the wizened old man with the blank face and the magic knife held over his head, and then it decided to help out. Its mouth gaped and it lunged at her.

"No!" Dad shouted.

But before the centipede's attack could land, it flinched, dodging as something silver and blue flashed by its head. A football helmet.

The *Omukade* twisted round in indignation.

"That's right!" shouted DeMarcus. "You mess with one of us, you mess with all of us…"

There might have been more to the speech, but the monster lunged at him and he leapt backwards, narrowly avoiding its snapping jaws. As the giant centipede readied another strike, DeMarcus was dragged shrieking into the shadows by Joey.

I turned back to where Em was yipping at the *te no me* but the little man had a firm grasp on the shuriken and in a moment of certain horror I saw that she wasn't going to be able to get it. It was way more likely that he would kill her with it. She appeared to realize the same and dropped back, looking defeated. The *te no me* chuckled and muttered words I didn't understand, though his satisfaction was clear. Even the *Omukade* seemed to sense their imminent victory. It had abandoned the idea of chasing my retreating friends and was crawling back toward me. The time, it knew, had come to end this.

"Hideki!" Dad called. I spun round. In the confusion, I had almost forgotten he was there. He shot me a quick version of his trademark smile and held up a bottle which he waggled like it was a trophy. "Brought you something," he added. "Catch!" I stared in horrified confusion as he tossed it to me. Reflexively, I snatched it from the air and stared at it.

Smiths' Smoking Sauce.

I was about to be eaten by a giant centipede and my father had brought condiments.

"The way I figure it," he said, his eyes fixed on the *Omukade*, "spit won't work on that thing. But family might. Bit of Japanese, bit of English, bit of North Carolina, all our favorite ingredients perfectly blended. This is us, in a bottle. What do you say?"

It was insane. I knew that. But what else was there? Bachan had said that saliva had worked on that one *Omukade* in the legend because it was significant either to the monster, or to the warrior who had fought it. I considered the bottle.

This is us…

What we care about. Who we are.

Even as I stood there paralyzed by thought, the *te no me* landed a kick that sent the Em-fox flying, crumpling against the stone wall of the chamber. He gave me a triumphant grin as the Omukade swept toward me.

It was now or never.

I slammed the bottle on the rock floor and it exploded. Pushing the fragments of glass away, I smeared the blade of the *yari* in the sauce, its aroma filling the chamber with tangy sweetness.

The *Omukade* hissed, and pounced, but I stood my ground, and as its awful maw gaped, I guided the tip of the spear in. I did not stab or thrust. I just held it in place and let the force of the monster's attack do the work. I felt it immediately, the moment that the *yari*'s point spitted the *yōkai*'s throat and emerged from the back of its head.

It did not cry out. It merely twisted, whipping briefly, and then went still.

Dead still.

It seemed impossible, but it was true. As I watched, it began to break apart, like I was watching sped up film of it decaying over weeks, months, the particles drifting up as if sucked through the flickering portal in the domed ceiling. My eyes flew to where the *te no me* had gone back to muttering his words. I knew I had to stop him, but my strength was gone, as if it had been bound up with the disintegrating centipede. I slumped to the floor as Dad ran to me.

"I'm okay," I said. "Stop him. Save Em."

He blundered toward the little man with the eyes in his hands but stopped as he reached the *te no me*. He looked so small next to my father, wizened and vulnerable so I knew why Dad hesitated. But it was a mistake. The little man whipped out the shuriken and swept it up to Dad's throat.

I shouted something incoherent, and then two more figures were moving out of the darkness, walking slowly, reciting as they came. It was Bachan and the tengu, woken from his charmed sleep by the breaking of the West-fox's power, and here, his eyes fixed and glaring.

The *te no me* shrieked, one anxious hand glancing up to the shimmering portal which seemed to sputter. The last of the *Omukade*'s fragments were still flowing up like smoke into the port hole, but it was clearly closing under the weight of the counterspells from Bachan, eyes shut, and Saito-san, fierce and determined. They moved forward, chanting their sutras.

The mystical barrier which had been melting, opening, the seal which held the terrible occupants of the prison in place, was solidifying again, locking them back inside.

The *te no me*, still holding onto Dad with one skinny fist, moved quickly into the stream of the dissolving centipede, and suddenly it too was being tugged upward. If it couldn't open the prison, it would join its mistress inside. As I stared, it began breaking into atoms and drifting up to the portal.

And taking Dad with him.

I fought to get up, half crawling toward the center of the room, gaping in horror as the little man with eyes in his hands melted into the portal above him, pulling my father after him.

"Caleb?" Dad managed. "What's happening?" He glanced around him, his confusion making him young-looking, almost boyish, and then his face was full of sorrow. "Sorry," he mouthed, as he faded away, "I was just trying to…"

Help.

Crying, I reached for him, but he had already melted away.

I stared in stunned disbelief as the portal went dark and solid. My father was gone.

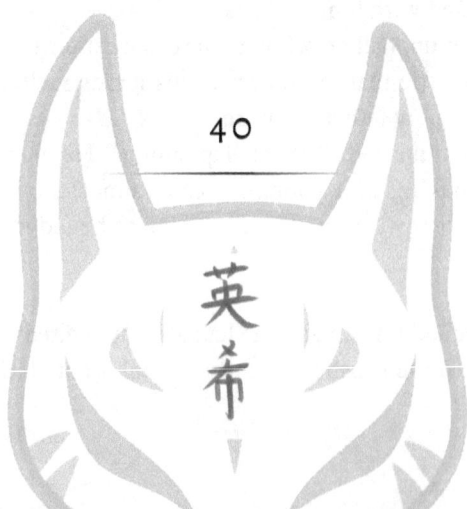

40

This couldn't be. I stared at where Dad had vanished into the swirling chaos of the portal, then turned to Saito-san who was motionless, his eyes on me.

"Get him out!" I shouted.

"We can't," said Saito. "I do not know how to open the prison, and even if I did, we couldn't risk it."

"Couldn't risk it? It's my father!"

"You know what is inside, what is desperate to escape," replied Saito. His eyes flashed to where Bachan was scooping up the stunned Em-fox. "The portal has sealed." As soon as he said it, a great tremor shook the cavern. "The process of closing the cave has begun. We must leave now."

"No!" I roared.

"We must."

There was a crash, and a great boulder rolled across the floor.

"You go," I said. "I'm staying with Dad."

"He is not here," said the tengu, and all of a sudden his ferocity was replaced by an exhausted sadness. "I am sorry, Caleb. He is gone. If we do not leave, we will die too. Come now. Quickly."

Another quake shook the ground, and I heard the rumble of collapsing stone. Somewhere under the mountain the rock shuddered and split. We felt it through our feet, then heard it as the shift set off a chain of subsidence and rock falls all over Red Scar.

"Now, Caleb," said the tengu.

And at last, eyes blinded by tears, I nodded and followed him, as the world fell about our ears. I walked, seeing and hearing nothing, through the collapsing tunnel to the opening in the woods, and then we came down the mountain paths, knowing the tunnel back to the West mansion would soon be gone.

I could not wrap my head around what had happened.

As we walked, I replayed those final moments, not so much wondering what I should have done different—that would come later—as trying to accept that it had really happened. Twice I suggested going back, reopening the portal, but Saito just shook his head and kept walking.

At the tree line, the tengu brought Em back from her fox form and wrapped her in a yukata. She looked worn out.

"Someone should tell her," I began.

"She knows," said Bachan.

"How?" I said. "She was unconscious..."

"She knows," said Bachan with finality, and when I looked into my sister's eyes, I knew she was right.

The edge of town was surprisingly quiet given all that had happened, but the lights were on at the inconvenience store.

"You're back!" cried my mother as we stumbled inside. "The Omukade?"

"Dead," said Bachan. "And the prison sealed."

Mom's momentary joy quavered as she took in our faces. There was one of those silences which last no time at all but seem to take forever.

"Where's your father?" Mom asked. I hung my head, the tears I could not stop since leaving the cave running down my face and falling on the floor. "Caleb?"

I opened my mouth to speak, but the words wouldn't come, so I just shook my head. Mom looked frantically to the others, then sank to her knees, her mouth buckling, her hands coming to her face. A long, sound-less sob slid out of her, and then, without warning, she wailed, a loud, savage sound unlike anything I had ever heard from her before. It hung in the air like pain, and we all winced away from the rawness of it.

We sat down, and as Em hung around her neck, my mother wailed.

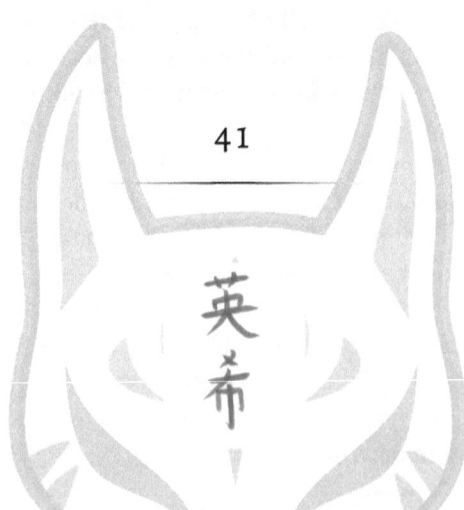

41

T he storms stopped, as did everything that had been tied to Enko-san's power. The moment the *Omukade* had consumed the box Enko-san had been using to power his various spells and illusions, the whole deceptive and manipulative tapestry he had woven unraveled. In that instant Saito-san had woken up, Maureen Collington had become her wholly human self again, and all the glamor around the Wests, their party, their house, their ideas, fell away like the disintegrating body of the dead centipede.

The mansion was just the Haversham house again now, though it was barely recognizable since the structure had given way when the *Omukade* had tunneled out through its foundation. People blamed whatever shoddy workmanship from out of town had been employed by the now disgraced Wests.

"Should have known it was a pile of junk as soon as we figured out that we knew none of the contractors who had refurbished it," said Ron Blakely when he came into the store a few days later.

The precise nature of the Wests' disgrace was less clear, as was what exactly the people of Portersville had seen the night of the Halloween party. Enko's deceptive glamor had still been working right up to the second I tossed the black and gold lacquered box into the centipede's jaws, by which time—thanks to my father and my friends—everyone was out. When the fire chief proclaimed the collapse of the house the result of another sinkhole created by excess storm water in the foundations, no one batted an eye. How much of that was magic, and how much was common sense rationalizing, I couldn't say.

I had seen the *Omukade* come up through the floor. So had my family, and so had DeMarcus and Joey, but they had all known it would come. I had noticed before that knowing the truth of something—like the damp smell of the house—made the West-fox's illusions less convincing, but even so... Perhaps he hadn't bothered trying to deceive those who knew what the *yōkai* was, or perhaps the charm was somehow incomplete, patched together hastily in the moment. I didn't know. All I could say for sure was that in the days that followed, no one outside my family and friends said anything about a monstrous centipede.

The Wests themselves were gone. Embarrassed, some said, though others thought their departure more sinister. The vote about retroizing was already dead, and no one could quite believe they had ever taken the possibility seriously.

"Some kind of long con," said Ron Blakely knowingly. "When they could see it wasn't going to work, they skipped town. Action News are saying they weren't even who they claimed to be, that there was no California IT company, no internet fortune. Just grifters who knew we had seen through them and took off before things got hot." He thought about that and added with a trace of satisfaction, "Probably cost them a fortune."

Chris Collington had been—understandably—the first to turn on his shiny new pal from California, though I knew that had always been more an alliance of convenience than it had friendship. Maureen was saying nothing and when she saw my mother in the street she looked momentarily confused, blind-sided, and then she shook the feeling off and adopted a stare as haughty and self-assured as if none of the *rokurobi* business had happened.

"Probably doesn't remember it," said Bachan. "Not properly."

"It may come to her in dreams," said Saito-san, now fully awake and restored, "but what she did, what she was, probably will not feel real."

After the Collingtons denounced the Wests, calling them interlopers and con artists, the Blakelys and Davenhams had followed suit, with the Millers bringing up the sheepish rear. The rumor—one which didn't come from Maureen Collington this time—was that the final straw came when the mayor realized that Kieran West's "substantial" donation to his reelection fund had vanished without trace, as if it had itself been an illusion created by ones and zeroes on the computers Mr. West so hated.

I doubted Enko was really gone, or at least that we would never see him again—he found us, and the game to keep us running round in circles, too entertaining—but for now, out of sight was out of mind.

And we had enough to think about.

I worked on Dad's train. I had never really done it before, a thought that pained me now that he was gone, but it kept my mind occupied. I connected the track and routed the power and made sure the little engines could handle the curves and the incline as he would like. When I worked quietly on the track, I found that the rest of the family gave me some respectful distance, like I was tending a grave.

Dad's disappearance had been put down to rockslides in the mountains, and since the terrain was considered unstable, it would be some time before any attempt might be made to recover the body. That was the official position anyway. I didn't think they would ever really search for him, and I didn't much care because I knew they wouldn't find him if they did. Still, it rankled, particularly since he had saved all their lives several times over, whether they knew it or not.

Mom went very quiet. Time and time again I would find her...not crying exactly but staring off into nothing, or into memory. Bachan sat with her most days. Em too. I couldn't. I could barely look her in the face. After all, Dad's being taken was my fault. I had been so focused on saving everyone else that I couldn't take care of the man who meant the most to me.

"That's not how he would see it," said Em when I confessed this to her. "He came to help you protect everyone. He knew what he was doing."

"It should never have come to that," I said. "I should have figured out how to defeat the *Omukade* long before."

"I can guarantee you that no book of ancient Japanese law would have suggested homemade barbecue sauce," said Em.

"True," I said. "Only Dad would have come up with something so..." but the words stuck in my throat. "Oh Em," I said. "He looked so surprised, so sad to be going."

I wept again then, and she held me for a time.

"What will you do now?" asked DeMarcus on the first day I went back to school.

"Not sure," I said. "Saito asked when I would resume my training."

"What did you tell him?"

"That I would go back to being a demon queller when he figured out how to go into the prison to get my father out," I said.

DeMarcus glanced at Joey, but neither of them said anything. I knew what they were thinking: that we couldn't reopen the prison without risking the release of countless *yōkai*, that we had no idea if Dad was still alive when he had been pulled inside, and that even if he had been, he would have been subject to all manner of horrors once trapped with the *onibaba* and her minions. I knew all this. But it didn't matter.

"I get that," said Joey.

"Yeah," DeMarcus agreed. "Me too."

I doubted that they did, but I appreciated them not arguing with me.

"And you won," said Joey. "I mean, not without, you know, casualties. But you did. You did what none of us thought could be done."

DeMarcus nodded fervently. "Saved the world, man. For real," he said. "That's got to be worth something."

And it was. Just not everything.

As I left school that day, trudging through the November darkness for home, I saw people standing on the corner of Brevard and fourth. It was Tyler Miller and Bobby Davenham. I braced myself, halting briefly. I wasn't afraid of them anymore, but I was in no mood to be sneered at. I was tired and my guard was down, but I was still strong enough to fight. Too strong for them. I felt a flicker of alarm at my own anger and was momentarily relieved when they began to walk away, but then Bobby hesitated.

"I'll catch you up," he said to Tyler who, in turn nodded, then gave me a searching look before turning and swaggering off.

Bobby waited for me to reach him. I felt my knuckles tightening.

"Hideki," he said.

I paused, surprised.

"Hey Bobby," I said.

He looked around, his eyes strangely vacant, as if he had forgotten whatever he had planned to say or thought better of it.

I moved past him, but he stopped me with one hand. I tensed, ready to swing.

"I'm sorry about your dad," he said.

I blinked, astonished, then nodded.

"Thanks," I said.

"I don't really know what happened," he said, his eyes still vague. "The memories are all...confused. But I think he, and you, and your loser

305

friends…I think you saved my life. It doesn't make much sense, but I think maybe you saved a lot of lives."

I nodded again, not wanting to relive it all.

"Yeah," I said with an empty gesture of one hand. "You're welcome."

"I owe you one," he said, though it seemed the words came hard, and that even he was surprised by them.

"Maybe start by not calling my friends losers," I said, managing a faint smile.

"Right," he said, nodding earnestly. "On that. Okay." He thought again, and then, as if something had been weighing on him, he blurted, "That night I said some stuff about how nobody cared about me. That wasn't true. I was just—you know—*upset.*"

I remembered how he had secretly held his mother's hand at his father's funeral, and nodded, almost as keen as he was not to linger on the conversation.

"Good," I said. "That's good."

He nodded again, slower this time, and then as if not knowing what else to do, turned quickly away and walked after Tyler without looking back.

I watched him go, wondering if that had simply been about the incident under the mountain or if it was something more complicated about fathers and sons. I remembered what he had said about how no one cared about him and knew that our situations were very different. He was grieving for what he hadn't had a chance to fix, while I was grieving for what I had lost. Mine was the simpler emotion, I suspected, and the pain had a keener edge. But then again, maybe not. I barely knew him. I couldn't begin to imagine the world as he experienced it.

I walked home slowly, taking in the settling dusk, the silence of the little town broken only by distant traffic and the occasional sound of blaring televisions as everyone relished having their power supply uninterrupted. I had half-expected gaggles of reporters to be clustered outside the remains of the Haversham house, but after a couple of cursory reports they—perhaps reading the mood of the town—had dropped the subject. Everyone wanted to put the last weeks behind them and move on.

I wasn't sure I could. That night I returned the *yari*, the sword, the armor, even the little bronze mirror to the tengu, thanking Saito for their loan. He greeted me cautiously and eyed what I had brought back with something like concern.

"You can keep them," he said.

I just shook my head and turned for the door.

"You are still the heir of Raiko," he said.

"Not now," I said.

He looked ready to object but saw the set of my face and changed his mind.

"One day?" he replied.

"Perhaps," I said. "After I get my father back."

"And if you can't?"

I thought about that and decided to be honest.

"I really don't know," I said.

I walked home, and I sat with my mother and my sister at the kitchen table, and we talked, really for the first time, about Dad, his hobbies, his odd dialect, his passions, his optimism, his face-splitting little boy grin, and how much he had loved us. We talked and we laughed and we cried and then Mom hugged us and went to bed alone, leaving me and Em to sit in silence.

After perhaps ten minutes of that, Em looked up and said simply,

"We'll find a way."

"To do what?" I asked.

"To get him back," she said, as if we had just been discussing the problem.

"Not sure we can," I said. "Saito says…"

"I don't care about that," said Em. "We've done what was asked of us. The yōkai world threatened ours and we held the line. They tried a different way, and we held the line again, and each time, we lost something precious. Well, not anymore."

"What do you mean?"

"No more sitting back and waiting for them to take the fight to us," said Em grimly. "We know where they are. Now we take the fight to them, and we take back what is ours."

I gaped at her. She seemed older somehow, stronger. I said so.

"I'm different," she said simply.

"Oh yeah? In what way?"

"This way." She made a gesture with her hand like she was snatching something invisible from the air, and in the instant she transformed. Or rather she half transformed. It was still Em, but she sat a little taller, and her face was longer, her ears sharper and behind her sprouted a bushy fox tail.

No, I corrected myself. Two tails!

They rose up behind her, their pale tips pointing.

"Power," she said. "More than they bargained for. And getting stronger every day." She paused to let this sink in and then spelled it out once more. "We take the fight to them."

And you don't argue with a twin-tailed fox.

THE END

ACKNOWLEDGMENTS

Thanks to John and the whole team at Falstaff Books, to my agent, Stacey Glick, and to all who supported the first book in the series and convinced us to write more. Special thanks to our families on both sides of the Atlantic, and our friends on the other side of the Pacific, without whose assistance this book would not have been possible.

ABOUT THE AUTHOR

AJ Hartley is the award winning, *New York Times* bestselling author of 30 novels in a variety of genres. He writes solo and with Tom DeLonge of Blink-182. The *Hideki Smith* series is a collaboration with his Japanese American wife and son. AJ is also the Robinson Professor of Shakespeare at UNC Charlotte (Emeritus) and has a YouTube channel dedicated to writing, model trains, and Japanese rock music. Because why not? Learn more at www.ajhartley.net

ALSO BY A.J. HARTLEY

From Falstaff Books

Hideki Smith, Demon Queller

Impervious

Burning Shakespeare

The Mask of Atreus

On The Fifth Day

What Time Devours

(all three collected in *Past is Prologue*)

Hamlet Prince of Denmark, A Novel (with David Hewson)

Will Hawthorne Series:

Act of Will

Will Power

Darwen Arkwright Series:

Darwen Arkwright and the Peregrine Pact

Darwen Arkwright and the Insidious Bleck

Darwen Arkwright and the School of Shadows

Cathedrals of Glass Series:

A Planet of Blood and Ice

Valkrys Wakes

Steeplejack Series:

Steeplejack

Firebrand

Guardian

Preston Oldcorn Series:

Cold Bath Street

Written Stone Lane

(with Tom DeLonge)
Sekret Machines: Chasing Shadows
Sekret Machines: A Fire Within
Trinity
Time Rider

(with David Hewson)
Macbeth, a Novel

Tears of the Jaguar

As Andrew Hart
Lies that Bind Us
The Woman in Our House

FRIENDS OF FALSTAFF

Thank You to All our Falstaff Books Patrons, who get extra digital content each month! To be featured here and see what other great rewards we offer, go to www.patreon.com/falstaffbooks.

PATRONS

Thank You for Supporting Independent Publishing!

We believe that you should be able
to read your books, your way.
That's why this Falstaff Books
print edition includes a digital copy
at no additional cost!

Just scan the QR code with your device,
follow the directions on Prolific Works,
and enjoy!
You can also join our newsletter when prompted,
and never miss an awesome Falstaff Release!

FALSTAFF

BOOKS

WWW.FALSTAFFBOOKS.COM

www.ingramcontent.com/pod-product-compliance
Lightning Source LLC
Chambersburg PA
CBHW021500110726
47899CB00001BA/232